PRAISE FOR

# The Whole Package

"The friendship between the women is realistic, the characters funny, and the premise well-executed. Readers will giggle and grin from start to finish, and will surely be eager for Ellingsen's next novel."
—*Publishers Weekly*

"A hilarious, laugh-out-loud romp of a novel. A story of sisterhood, and why ups and downs are only minor bumps when your girlfriends come along for the ride, Ellingsen's debut delights."
—Examiner.com

"*The Whole Package* is a delightfully frivolous romp. An excellent beach read, this light but enjoyable fare will have you chuckling (and likely blushing!) throughout. The three main characters have believable relationships with ups and downs, adding a touch of reality."
—*RT Book Reviews*

"A page-turning romance packed with wit and humor. Cancel all social engagements until you've finished this!"
—Louise Bagshawe, bestselling author of *Desire*

"Tender and funny! These best friends really are forever!"
—Wendy Wax, bestselling author of *Ocean Beach*

# Marriage Matters

## Cynthia Ellingsen

BERKLEY BOOKS, NEW YORK

**THE BERKLEY PUBLISHING GROUP**
Published by the Penguin Group
Penguin Group (USA) Inc.
375 Hudson Street, New York, New York 10014, USA

USA / Canada / UK / Ireland / Australia / New Zealand / India / South Africa / China

Penguin Books Ltd., Registered Offices: 80 Strand, London WC2R 0RL, England
For more information about the Penguin Group, visit penguin.com.

This book is an original publication of The Berkley Publishing Group.

Library of Congress Cataloging-in-Publication Data

Ellingsen, Cynthia.
Marriage matters / Cynthia Ellingsen.
p. cm.
ISBN 978-0-425-25800-2
1. Female friendship—Fiction.    2. Brides—Fiction.    3. First loves—Fiction.
4. Married people—Fiction.    5. Weddings—Fiction.    6. Marriage—Fiction.    I. Title.
PS3605.L43785M38 2013
813'.6—dc23
2012029576

PUBLISHING HISTORY
Berkley trade paperback edition / April 2013

PRINTED IN THE UNITED STATES OF AMERICA

10  9  8  7  6  5  4  3  2  1

Cover photograph by Vasaleks / Shutterstock.
Cover design by Rita Frangie.
Text design by Tiffany Estreicher.

*For my mother*

# ACKNOWLEDGMENTS

The most fabulous thing about the release of *The Whole Package*, and now *Marriage Matters*, has been the opportunity to connect with readers, both new friends and old. Thank you so much for your support!

Endless gratitude to the one and only Wendy McCurdy, the best editor ever and the queen of depth, insight and kindness. A huge thank-you to everyone at Berkley: Katherine Pelz, publicity, the sales team, the art department, and everyone who works to make your books amazing.

Daniel Lazar at Writer's House, the greatest day of my writerly life was finding you. Thank you for being consistently awesome.

Jon Cassir at CAA, for the confidence and Cali sunshine.

Lexington, Kentucky, for the incredible support. What a remarkable community. The staff at the Morris Book Shop and Joseph Beth's Bookstore—two of the coolest bookstores in the country—for getting the word out. The Carnegie Center—home to my first reading ever!—for your commitment to the literary arts. To every friend who shared a wedding story.

Bud's Coffee Shop in Interlochen, Michigan—the first draft was composed by your fire. Mr. Delp at Interlochen, for telling me to be a writer.

Traveler's Bookcase in Los Angeles for the travel inspiration. Natalie Compagno, who encouraged me to pick up the pen and Laksa soup so long ago. Love to you.

The members of my writing group: Jennifer Mattox, Frankie Finley and Stephanie Parkin. I cherish our Fridays and your brilliant notes.

Kathy Ellingsen, for a perfect title and for being the best mother-in-law ever. Grandma, for always making me laugh. All of my family and friends, for the humor and support.

And in every way, my husband, Ryan Ellingsen: You are my love story, forever.

When you realize you want to spend the rest of your life with somebody, you want the rest of your life to start as soon as possible.

—*Nora Ephron*

*Marriage Matters*

Part One

# One

Chloe McCallister was just not into getting all dressed up. Give her a nice pair of jeans, a comfy T-shirt and some tennis shoes and she was happy. Her mother and grandmother knew this, so now that she was stuck walking down a rocky beach in a pair of three-inch heels, they seemed to be getting way too much enjoyment out of her misery.

"Just pretend you're on a sandy runway," her grandmother called. "Work it."

Chloe's mother cheered. "You can do it. You're almost there!"

On principle, Chloe came to a complete stop. Almost where? They were standing on the shores of Lake Michigan, with no wedding in sight. The Sleeping Bear Dunes loomed overhead like something from another planet, while herons dove in and out of the water, hunting for prey. She could only hope that fish would remain more appealing than the silver clip holding back her curly hair.

Tugging at her dress, Chloe wished she'd taken the time to pack properly instead of waiting until the last minute, grabbing the first party dress she saw and stuffing it into her suitcase. The dress was a size too small and it bit into the sensitive skin under her arms. Plus, she'd forgotten all about bringing a pair of shoes, which was why she was wearing her grandmother's extra pair of stilettos. At 5'10", Chloe was much too tall to be wearing heels in the first place, not to mention ones made of animal skin that was most certainly illegal in civilized countries.

Chloe sighed. Weddings had really gotten out of control. Wasn't it enough that they'd taken a flight and rental car to get to the destination? Did it have to be out in the middle of nowhere, too?

If anyone ever decided to marry her, Chloe planned to keep her wedding simple. It would be at a small church, with only her closest friends and family. She would wear ballet flats with her dress, marry the man of her dreams and have a wedding cake with frosting that sparkled. For the father-daughter dance, she might even just rock out to "Teach Me How to Dougie."

A fun fantasy, but Chloe knew it wouldn't happen anytime soon. Especially considering the last time she'd even caught a glimpse of the male anatomy was on a biology test for her grad finals.

"Chloe, come on," her mother called, shielding her eyes against the sun. "This wedding's going to happen with or without us. Pick up the pace."

"Not until you tell me exactly where it is that we're going!"

As her mother and grandmother exchanged glances, Chloe felt the first twinge of trepidation. It evolved into full-fledged panic when her grandmother, like an elderly game show hostess, pointed at a group of people in brightly colored dresses and khaki suits, mingling underneath a flowered arch. An arch that just happened to be at the very *top* of a sand dune. Suddenly, Chloe wished the hotel coffee had been spiked with something stronger than cream.

Ripping off the ridiculous stilettos, Chloe picked her way through the rocks until she caught up with her family. "Mom," she gasped, grabbing Kristine's arm. It was warm from the sunshine and spotted with freckles. "I thought we were going to a wedding, not an audition for *Survivor.*"

"What do you mean? This is a lovely hike." Kristine swatted

away a bug roughly the size of her fist. "They have Petoskey stones here. Look." She pointed at a speckled gray rock lying in the water. "The pattern only shows up when it's wet."

"Fascinating." Chloe took note of the camera around her mother's neck and the copy of *Great Hikes of Northern Michigan* tucked under her arm. "In other words, we're the only jackasses not driving to this wedding? Because we thought we'd tack on a nature hike?"

Chloe's grandmother burst out laughing. Outrageous as always, June was wearing a long-sleeved dress made from reflective material, enormous black sunglasses and some sort of a weird, beekeeper-type hat. She took it off and shook it at them. "I say we skip this clambake altogether and go back to the hotel for a mimosa."

"Finally." Chloe lifted her hair away from her sweating neck. "Someone who's not talking crazy." Off her mother's look, she said, "What? The groom's, like, some third cousin I haven't seen since I was ten. Why suffer through another wedding?"

"Chloe! Weddings are fun." Kristine pushed her sunglasses up to reveal a pair of bright blue eyes. "They're magical. They're . . ."

"They're second only to Valentine's Day when it comes to the commercialization of the heart." Chloe waved her naked ring finger. "And a blatant reminder that I'm going to die alone."

June whacked her on the back. "You can't die alone. You have us."

"So, not only do I have to convince a man to fall madly in love with me, I have to convince him to fall in love with you and Mom, too?"

"Absolutely." June nodded. "The three of us, we're a package deal."

"Besides, you'll find someone." Kristine smoothed a strand of hair out of Chloe's eyes. "When you bother to make time for it."

Thanks to her graduate program, internship hours and part-time job, Chloe barely had time to breathe, let alone date. Just getting away for this wedding had taken some serious juggling. "I'd rather make time for you guys," she admitted. "You're a lot more fun."

"That's a fact," June agreed. As though eager to prove it, she pointed at the top of the sand dune. "Race you to the top of that hill," she said, and started to run. In the thick white sand, she moved slowly, kicking up a spray of powder behind her after each step.

Kristine nudged Chloe. "Go! You can beat her."

Chloe adjusted her sunglasses. "I am not about to get even sweatier. Maybe she'll have a heart attack and that'll be the end of it."

June had gone a good distance when she finally turned. Seeing that Chloe hadn't budged, she flapped her arms as though doing the chicken dance at the reception.

"Doubtful," Kristine mused. With one hand, she wound her red hair up into a loose chignon. "And I think she's calling you chicken."

Chloe bit her lip. Even though her feet hurt, her scalp was burning and sand had found its way into places too embarrassing to mention, she was tempted. It had been a while since she'd beaten her grandmother at anything, although Chloe was 99.9 percent certain June had cheated at their last game of gin.

"*Bawk, bawk.*" June turned and waved her hat. "Come on, chicken."

"That's it." Shoving the high heels at her mother, Chloe took off running, determined to beat her grandmother to the top of that damn hill.

By the time Kristine made her way up the sand dune, Chloe and June were hunched over in chairs meant for the reception, breathing heavily. A small jazz quartet played love songs and waiters circulated with trays of ice water.

Kristine surveyed the scene with admiration. "This is gorgeous."

The white sand of the dunes and the view of Lake Michigan stretched into infinity, creating a lush, curving backdrop for the wedding. Along the edge of the bluff, chairs as white as a picket fence were neatly divided by a satin runner that led to a dramatic floral arch woven through with red, pink and purple wildflowers. The flowers danced in the breeze while the lake, in all of its deep blue vibrancy, sparkled against the horizon. Any bride would just love a view like this on her wedding day, assuming she wasn't too nervous to see it. Kristine could remember exactly how it felt to stand at the altar, trembling in her white dress. Her legs were shaking like crazy until Kevin took her hands in his.

"You sure you want to do this?" he teased.

The comfort of his hands calmed her and she felt a rush of love more powerful than anything she'd ever experienced.

*I've found my prince, she'd thought. I'm going to live a fairy tale.*

Kristine flushed at the memory. The sentiment was so childish, so silly. Yes, she and Kevin had been fortunate enough to share many beautiful, passion-filled years, which was more than a lot of people could say. But eventually, like with all things, their marriage had lost its spark.

Nothing specific caused it, not really, just a slow series of life events that chipped away at their foundation. Chloe left for college, Kevin lost his job and Kristine started a business. Money was tight and Kevin finally found a new job, but it required him to travel all the time. Ultimately, it was just a lot of little things that added up to nothing, but something between the two of them had changed.

For example, this weekend marked their twenty-fifth anniversary and they weren't even spending it together. This was nobody's fault, really. Kristine had made plans to go to this wedding, while Kevin booked his typical flight out Sunday afternoon for work. Neither one of them even noticed the anniversary was coming up until last Wednesday. At that point, there was nothing left to do but laugh.

"It's official," Kevin had said. "We're just two old and craggy married people."

Gazing at the flowered arch, Kristine wrapped her arms tightly around herself. It was hard to believe that those sweet, early days when the only thing that mattered was watching the sunset together and cozying up in bed were long gone. It was scary to think that, if they weren't careful, everything they'd built together might just drift away. At the thought, Kristine's eyes pricked with tears.

"Uh-oh." Chloe nudged June. "Mom's getting emotional."

For years, her family had teased Kristine about her tendency to tear up at everything from sentimental moments to sappy commercials. "When I got dropped off at kindergarten," Chloe loved to say, "most parents had to comfort their children. I had to comfort my mother."

"I'm not crying," Kristine said quickly. "I just got a piece of sand in my eye."

She hated to lie but she was not about to admit that something was wrong with her marriage, especially in front of her mother. June wouldn't rest until she'd set up a battle plan for Kristine to resolve the issue. No, thank you. On a day like today, when the sun was shining so brightly and the lake sparkling in the distance, Kristine just wanted to enjoy herself. If that meant pretending everything was just fine when it wasn't, then that's what she'd have to do.

Flashing a bright smile, she said, "Should we find our seats?"

"Not quite yet." June eased to her feet and gestured at a tiny trailer next to the parking lot. "I vote we powder our noses first. These bathrooms actually look just fine for an outdoor wedding."

Kristine turned in the direction her mother was pointing. A squat, compact trailer was perched at the edge of the reception area. June was right; it was an awfully nice setup. Kristine narrowed her eyes, suddenly suspicious. A group of girls in blush-colored dresses were standing just off to the side, chatting with a group of young men in suits and cummerbunds.

"Mother, no. That's the bride's trailer and you know it," Kristine said. "If you'd like to powder your nose, you're going to have to do it over there." She pointed at a row of the expected porta potties. They were set up over by the parking lot, steam practically rising from their surface.

"Unless my memory is failing me," June said with a sniff, "I RSVPed for a wedding, not a camping trip. As a wedding guest, I expect a bathroom with air conditioning and running water."

Chloe elbowed June. "Don't forget you're feeling faint," she whispered.

June's eyes brightened. "And I'm feeling faint." Dramatically, she fanned herself with her hat. "I think I'm suffering from heatstroke."

Kristine sighed. June loved to act like the rules didn't apply to her. Somehow, she always managed to rope Chloe into her schemes.

"I'm sorry," Kristine said. "But I am putting my foot down. You two cannot—"

Before the words were even out of her mouth, Chloe and June were making a beeline for the bride's trailer. With Chloe's long body and June's short and wiry frame, they looked like two mismatched criminals ready to score.

"Unbelievable," Kristine muttered. "We'll be the first family to get kicked out of a wedding."

Then, because she really wasn't given a choice in the matter, Kristine raced to catch up.

As June pushed open the bathroom door, chilly air hit her cheeks and cooled the damp tendrils of her hair. It felt delightful. She'd been just about ready to expire out there in that heat. Peering over her shoulder, June beckoned to Kristine and Chloe. They were hanging back in the doorway, as though there was something to be afraid of. Ridiculous, considering this bathroom was perfectly lovely. It smelled like hairspray and perfume instead of . . . well, all sorts of other unappealing, outdoor-bathroom-type things.

"Come on," June chirped. "This is much bet—" Suddenly, she stopped. Unless she was mistaken, someone in the bride's trailer was sobbing. It was a dreadful sound, full of gasps and sniffles. Taking a few steps forward, June squinted as her eyes adjusted to the indoor light.

A bride stood in the midst of a mess of hairpins, makeup brushes and tissues, holding a bouquet and sobbing as though her heart would break. If you didn't count the tears, the young girl was the picture of bridal perfection. She wore a tasteful A-line gown, with two sheer panels down the front that would most certainly wave in the breeze. A cascade of curly blonde hair was piled on top of her head and accessorized with antique pearl combs clipped into a flouncy veil. Even her eye makeup, which most certainly had to be waterproof, appeared to be flawless.

"*Ooph,*" Chloe grunted, knocking into June from behind. "Grandma! What are you . . . Oh no."

"*Mother.*" June felt a sharp tug at the back of her dress. "We are leaving . . . now."

Even though Kristine was obviously itching to remove her from the premises, June wasn't certain that was the right choice. There had to be a reason that she had stepped into this trailer, at this very moment in time. Perhaps it *was* inappropriate to interfere with a girl on her wedding day, but clearly, this was one bride who needed an intervention.

June bustled forward. There was a box of tissues on the counter next to the mirror. With three quick tugs, she whipped out a handful. "Did the groom get cold feet?" June demanded. She had been to more than one wedding in her life where the mother of the bride clipped down the aisle with a fake smile, making an announcement that "the kids were having second thoughts," the bride wailing in the nave as though her heart would break.

Clearly surprised to see anyone in her trailer, this bride jumped and then her face crumpled. "No, he didn't get cold feet. I . . . I think I did."

June was surprised. It seemed that, for a young lady who had invested so much time and energy into her look, she had failed to give much thought to what it meant to say forever. Without mincing words, June told her just that.

Kristine stepped forward, her freckled face flushed crimson. "I'm so sorry," she said. "My mother is suffering from heatstroke but don't worry, we're leaving. Right now."

Kristine gave her dress another firm yank. June gripped the plastic counter to hold her footing. "Stop," June said as Kristine somehow managed to slide her back a full two feet. "I am simply—"

"She's right," the bride said. After touching a bouquet of pink roses on the counter, the girl sank down onto a white wicker stool. "She's absolutely right."

Slowly, Kristine released her grip. "She is?"

June sniffed, straightening her shoulders. Of course she was right. Whether her daughter wanted to give her credit or not, June often knew what was good for everyone else before they knew it themselves.

"I've dreamed about my wedding day ever since I was a little girl," the bride sniffled. "Now that it's here, it's just . . . not what I thought it would be."

"Weddings *have* gotten a little outrageous . . ." Chloe started to say.

Kristine silenced her with a look.

The bride gave a wistful smile. "I just always thought I was going to marry . . ." She hesitated. "Well . . ."

"A prince," June suggested. "A movie star. Barack Obama."

"A firefighter." The bride's eyes were pained. "I grew up next to a fire station and every night I'd hear the fire trucks head off to rescue someone. I thought I'd marry someone like that. Someone who . . ." Another tear trickled down her cheek. "Someone who could rescue me." Off June's silence, the bride shook her head. "It doesn't even make sense."

"It does," June said. "You want to feel safe." Back when Eugene was alive, June had always felt safe. The hardest part about losing him was the knowledge that the one person who could protect her was gone.

The bride shook her head. "I don't know if I can do it."

The fans of the air-conditioning whirred in the silence. In the mirror, June saw that Chloe was chewing on her lip, as though considering the girl's words, and Kristine was staring down at her wedding ring.

"Every bride goes through this," June said. "Whether it happens six months before the wedding, two days before or even on the day of, there will be tears, regrets and what-ifs. Trust me, I know. I almost backed out of my wedding."

"You did?" Kristine asked.

June smiled. "I asked my mother to send me to a nunnery. But . . . She tapped me on the cheek and said, 'That's a terrible idea. You'll just get kicked out.'"

Chloe laughed. "She was right about that."

"So, I got married instead." June indicated her family. "And it was the best decision I ever made."

The bride studied her engagement ring again. Just beyond the door, the muffled voices of the bridal party talked and giggled. The faint strains of a harp began to play.

"If you're really going to call off this wedding"—June did her best to keep her voice gentle—"you won't want to do it alone. We need to go find your best friend."

Chloe nodded, moving toward the door. "Is it your maid of honor? I'll go get her."

"No." The bride shrugged. "That's the worst part."

June felt a flicker of hope. "Why?"

"Because Robbie's my best friend. I can talk to him about anything, he always makes me laugh and he knows just what to say when I'm feeling . . ." The girl's voice trailed off. "Oh." The sound was barely a whisper.

"You love him, don't you?" June asked.

The bride's eyes widened. "I do." Jumping to her feet, she stared at June as though she were a magician. "I do!"

"Well, save those I dos for the altar," June laughed. "Because there's a wedding out there waiting for you."

"And it's beautiful," Kristine said.

"You should marry him." Chloe nodded. "I mean, if he really is your best friend."

June grabbed another tissue from the counter. Quickly, she dabbed at a tiny smear of mascara just below the girl's eyes then gave her a little push. "Go."

The bride rushed toward the door, her white dress swaying behind her. Suddenly, she stopped and grabbed her throwing bouquet out of the vase by the mirror. "I was going to do this at the reception, but . . ." Raising it up, the bride gave June a mischievous smile. "Catch."

Before June could even register what was happening, the bouquet was flying through the air toward her face. June put up her hands, more as an instinctive block than anything. A hard stem hit her palm and she felt her fingers wrap around it. Kristine's and Chloe's hands folded over the top of hers. Stunned, June looked down at a bouquet of pink and white roses, surrounded by a cheerful spray of baby's breath.

The bride squealed. "You're next! All *three* of you."

Chloe gave a nervous giggle. "Um, do I have a boyfriend I don't know about?"

Kristine shook her head. "I'm . . . I'm married."

June raised her eyebrows. "Wouldn't that be a nice surprise?"

"Thank you." The bride clasped her hands, her eyes bright. "This was . . ." She bowed her head, as though realizing the enormity of what she'd almost done. Looking up, she smiled at June. "Thank you."

The young girl opened the door. Sunshine spilled into the room and Lake Michigan shimmered in the background. The bridesmaids saw her and waved, chattering in excitement.

June extended her arms like an usher. Her daughter and granddaughter grabbed hold, the bouquet in the center. "Come on," June said. "Let's go see what this marriage thing is all about."

# TWO

Chloe eased her eyes open and yawned. They were on the way back home from the wedding, the cab zipping along the Kennedy Expressway. June was fast asleep against Chloe's arm, snoring softly, while Kristine sat by the window on the opposite side of her, reading.

Lowering the cab window, Chloe let the warm breeze whip through her hair as she squinted up at the skyline of Chicago. Sun glinted off the skyscrapers in reflections of blue and gold. She was happy to be back home.

Chloe loved Chicago. The bustle of the River Walk in the summer, the "we'll survive this arctic freeze" camaraderie of the winter and the fact that she could hear live music, find an art fair or even seek out an academic lecture, all on a whim. It was good she'd fallen in love with the city, because June and Kristine would lie down in front of the U-Haul if she ever tried to leave.

At the thought, Chloe glanced at her mother. She was flipping through a travel guide, still trying to learn random facts about Michigan. As she turned a page, her wedding ring flashed in the sunlight.

"*Mom*," Chloe whispered in an effort to not wake up June. "Hey! Happy anniversary."

Kristine placed a finger in the book to hold her spot. "Twenty-five years. Can you believe it?"

"Of course I believe it." Chloe's parents were opposites, but something about them had always worked. "Is Dad taking you out tonight?"

Kristine smoothed down her white polo shirt. It still appeared crisp and fresh, even after the indignity of air travel. "He flew out today. It would be too hard, getting up at four tomorrow to catch a flight."

Chloe's father started working as a regional manager for a solar plant company after the company he'd been with forever laid him off. Chloe thought traveling four days a week would be brutal. Her father just joked it was a great opportunity to eat fried onion rings and drink beer at the airport without a lecture from Kristine.

"Any big plans for you tonight?" her mother asked.

Chloe laughed. "Yes. Working."

"Working" was an understatement. She'd probably be up all night, finishing the two papers due first thing in the morning. With a full course load, internship hours and a part-time job at a kid's gym, pulling all-nighters had become as normal as brushing her teeth. A small sacrifice, considering Chloe was so close to finishing up her art therapy degree. Once she'd accomplished that, her real life could begin.

As the cab screamed to a stop at a traffic light, June stirred. "Ugh," she groaned.

Chloe laughed, patting her knee. "You gonna make it?"

June sat up straight and looked around. She beckoned at a man standing at the side of the road, selling bottles of water. Fumbling in her purse, she gave him a twenty.

"Three waters." Her voice was scratchy. "The rest is for you."

The man's face lit up and he passed three icy bottles of water into the cab. "Ah," June said, taking a grateful sip. "I was wilting."

"That's what you get for being a party animal," Chloe said.

After the wedding, the guests migrated to a bar in downtown Traverse City. Chloe had a vague recollection of June standing on a table, waving that bouquet like a magic wand and screaming, "Who wants to marry my granddaughter?"

The text alert chimed on Chloe's phone. "Ooh, is it a boy?" June peered over her shoulder.

"No, it's not a boy," Chloe said, checking the message. "It's Ben." Turning her phone toward her grandmother, she watched June's lips move as she read: When are you home? I need you. Those same lips pursed.

"I *need* you." June tsked, turning the phone to Kristine. "Can you believe this?"

"Does it . . . mean anything?" Kristine's voice was annoyingly hopeful.

Kristine was always acting like Chloe should fall in love with her best friend from elementary school, but seriously. It was never going to happen. With the exception of a drunken feel-up after their first beer, she and Ben had never crossed that line. Their physical contact was limited to arm punches, high fives and the occasional friendship hug and they were both perfectly happy to keep it that way.

"I don't understand." Kristine pulled a bag of peanuts out of her purse and slit them open. "Why don't you like him?"

June gave a little sniff. "He draws pictures for a living. What type of man does that?"

"He's a graphic artist, Grandma. Those pictures are actually designs."

"And good ones," Kristine said, nodding. "Ben made the sign for the store. And it's beautiful."

When Chloe went to college, Kristine surprised everyone by buying a travel bookstore. She wanted to do something with her time, since Chloe was gone and June had a life of her own. Chloe was proud of her mother, as what had started as a whim had become a passion.

"The sign *is* beautiful," Chloe said, texting him back. "But Grandma's just determined to hate him."

"That's not true." June shook her head. "I simply said I question a man who draws pictures for a living. That's not the type of man you want to marry."

Chloe rolled her eyes. "Well, I don't want to marry Ben. In fact, I don't have time to date until I'm your age, which is pretty ancient, so I think we can all just relax until then."

"Rubbish." June took another swig of water. "Love is going to find you sooner than you think, Chloe. Some lucky man is going to woo you, whether you like it or not."

"Woo-ooo?" Chloe drew out the word with as much disdain as possible. "I don't even know what that is, but I can guarantee you I don't have time for it."

As though to prove it, Chloe yanked her drugstore-bought planner out of her bag. It was as dog-eared as a textbook. Every moment of her life was booked solid.

Kristine shook her head, eyeing the crazy schedule. "I don't know how you do it."

"Caffeine." Chloe dropped the calendar back into her bag. "Lots and lots of caffeine."

"That's not good for you," Kristine recited as though compelled to mother. Instructions to take vitamins, eat vegetables and say no to drugs seemed to show up at the most random times.

"Mom, caffeine's not going to kill me." And according to WebMD, the slight eye twitch Chloe had developed would go away when and if she backed off the diet soda.

"Well, solitude might kill you," June said. "A girl your age should be out there dating. It's a fact of life. One of these days you'll find somebody."

Kristine laughed. "And June will be right there to tell him he's not good enough for you."

Chloe stayed quiet for the rest of the ride. When the cab finally screamed to a halt in front of her apartment, she pasted on a big smile. "It was fun," she said brightly. "I'll see you soon."

After repeated hugs, kisses and promises to call the next day,

Chloe stepped out of the cab and stared up at her apartment building. "Thank goodness," she sighed. Even though she loved hanging out with her family, the way they thought they knew everything about everything got pretty annoying.

Hoisting her bag over her shoulder, Chloe took the steps two at a time. She owed this particular apartment to Ben, as he'd called her the second his neighbor decided to move. Sure, the lobby smelled like onions and the "working elevator" had been on vacation since she'd moved in, but one of the apartment's many bonuses was the fact that she got to live next door to her best friend.

Chloe's keys had barely made a jingle in the lock when his door flew open.

Ben was dressed in a pair of flannel pajama pants and a ratty blue T-shirt. "Hey, neighbor." He had a panicked look on his face. Freshly tanned from the weekend, he'd gotten a little too much sun on his nose. "I've been texting you. Happy birthday!" Desperately, he waved a bottle of champagne and two glasses at her.

"Uh . . ." *Birthday?* It was not her birthday and hadn't been for at least three months.

A skinny arm snaked around Ben from behind, followed by the wispy body of a girl. She was wearing one of his button-up shirts and had a tumbleweed of blonde hair. Gauging by her carefully placed ringlet curls, the girl had an unnatural obsession with Taylor Swift.

"Hello," the girl said, her voice icy.

Ben's eyes widened. "Chloe, this is Sher . . . Shannon. She's being super cool about the fact that I promised to celebrate your birthday with you. Right now." The girl pinched Ben. "Unless . . ." His bright blue eyes looked tortured. "You want to reschedule? I'd really like to spend some more time with her."

As a reward, the girl gripped Ben by the back of the head and pulled him in for a kiss. Ben's hands flailed and the whole production reminded Chloe of a show she'd seen on the Discovery Channel, about the mating habits of the praying mantis. Chloe hoped Ben would make it out alive. He opened one eye and gave Chloe a desperate look.

*Alright, alright. She'd help him. Just like always.*

Dropping her bag with a dramatic thud, Chloe said, "You can't reschedule a birthday. As a . . ." She racked her brain, trying to think of the appropriate astrological sign. ". . . *Leo*, my lion-like personality is not responding well to that."

The girl ended the kiss and glared at Chloe. "I thought that when you get old, you're *supposed* to ignore your birthday."

*Old? Who was old?*

"How old do you think I am?" Chloe demanded.

"I don't know." The girl gave her a disdainful once-over. "Forty?"

Ben burst out laughing but tried to cover it with a hearty cough. "Birthday celebration coming up. Give me one minute."

"It was so nice to meet you," Chloe told the girl. "I'm sure I'll see you a lot." Leaning forward, she whispered, "Ben's shy, so if he doesn't call you, be sure to call him. Until he picks up."

Giving him a triumphant smile, Chloe swept into her apartment. The door clicked shut behind her.

"Forty," she said out loud. "Holy crap." She was only twenty-five! Digging into her purse, she yanked out her mirror. Upon inspection, she saw a tiny line between her eyebrows and, okay, maybe she could afford to wear a little makeup or something, but come on. She certainly didn't look *forty*.

A white streak of fur flew across the room, accompanied by the tiny jingle of a bell. Whiskers, her cat, pressed up against her legs, rubbing that fluffy fur against her like a warm blanket. Scooping her up, Chloe stared absently out the living room window.

The view of the rusty train tracks of the El was so incredibly bad that Chloe had framed it like a painting with dramatic white curtains. They added some romance to the distressed, country-white bookshelves packed with art books, magazines and plants Most Likely Not to Die If Not Watered. In the center of the room sat a turquoise couch and a coffee table that had seen its fair share of paint jobs.

"I might look forty," Chloe told Whiskers, "but at least I've got a cool place to live."

The door banged as Ben raced into her apartment. He slammed it shut, bolting it behind him. For good measure, he pulled the chain lock, too. "She's gone." He slid down to the floor. "Thank God she's gone." Dramatically, he buried his face in his hands.

"She'll be back," Chloe promised. "I told her to call until you pick up."

"That's a whole new level of cruel." Ben's eyes widened. "I'm going to have to change my number." Hopping to his feet, he loped across the room and scooped Whiskers out of Chloe's arms, dropping his face in her white fur. "Hey, Whisk. It's good to see you alive. Somewhat shocking, considering I forgot to feed you."

By the time Chloe moved to slug him, Ben was already in position to block. His long face was scrunched up in a grin. It seemed that, no matter what the situation, Ben was always smiling. Of course, if Chloe got laid as much as he did, she might smile that much, too.

"What did I miss?" She grabbed a Diet Dr Pepper from the fridge. The silver tab on the top wouldn't budge. Ben took the can and popped it open. After taking a hearty sip, he handed it over.

"Not much," he mused. "I hung out with Sally and that whole crew. They miss you terribly and are threatening to file a missing persons report."

Chloe felt a stab of guilt. Sally was her best friend from undergrad. They hadn't seen each other in ages. "I'll call her."

Whiskers scampered over to the treats cupboard and started

to meow. Ben opened the cupboard and fed her a handful of bacon bits. "How was the wedding?" He sniffed the can of cat treats. Giving her a skeptical look, he said, "Do you really think these taste like bacon?"

"No." Chloe sucked soda from the lip of the can. "And please don't eat one just to see." Ben set the container back in the cupboard. "The wedding was fine. Your typical waste of time."

"A waste of time?" Ben feigned shock. "You mean, you didn't do the Macarena? Make out with the bartender? Line up for the bouquet toss?"

"Actually . . ." Chloe hummed "Here Comes the Bride" and dug into her overnight bag. After some grunts and groans, she found the rose and ribbon she'd swiped from the wedding bouquet and held it up. "Ta-dum!"

Ben raised his eyebrow. "You stole a boutonniere?"

"I caught the bouquet! Well, my mom, June and I did. June kept most of it, of course, but I managed to snag a flower."

"Awesome." Ben studied the rose for a moment, then grabbed that silver clip magnet from the fridge. He tied the white ribbon around the stem and, using the clip, hung it upside down to dry. "There." He leaned against the counter. "It might stay in one piece until your post-apocalyptic wedding."

"Thanks." Ben was always creating art in places Chloe never would have even thought to look. "Hey, do you think . . ." She hesitated, taking another sip of soda. "Do you think I really look forty?"

Ben grinned. "No way. We're the same age."

Chloe and Ben had been friends since the first grade, after she stood up for him on the playground. The school bully cornered Ben against the back fence. Lifting his fist, Gerry Sutherland proclaimed Ben a toad-face and a dead man. Ben just removed his glasses and closed his eyes. Unable to witness such an incredible injustice—attacking a boy who wouldn't fight back!—Chloe swooped in and whacked her backpack against Gerry's head.

Later, when they were in the principal's office, Ben admitted there was a reason he didn't fight back. "One playground fight and my father sells the Super Nintendo." As Chloe's mother rushed into the office, a look of thunder on her face, Chloe thought fast. "Then you owe me. I'm coming over this weekend to play Mario Bros." The two had been best friends ever since.

"Besides," Ben added, "getting older is a good thing. It makes us seasoned. Mature. Eligible for the early bird special."

"I don't know." Chloe bit her lip. "Age is different for girls. I don't want to be like a carton of eggs that someone put in the back of the refrigerator and forgot about."

Ben cringed. "It creeps me out when you use words like eggs."

"I'm sorry," she said. "But it's true."

"Well, you're only two in cat years. You've got plenty of time." He studied her. "Why are you thinking about all this?"

Chloe's eyes fell on the drying flower. It was so strange. She hadn't thought about marriage, family or any of it since she'd set foot into grad school. But the wedding had actually gotten to her. The couple had seemed so happy, holding each other on the dance floor.

"I don't know." She set down her can of soda and twisted the tip of her ponytail around her finger. "June was being a pain in the ass about it in the cab, saying I had to start thinking about it all."

Ben laughed. "You know, you don't have to listen to everything she says."

Chloe shrugged. "Everyone listens to what June says."

Shaking his head, Ben popped open the bottle of champagne meant to celebrate her faux birthday. With a flourish that must have come from the days he waited tables on Michigan Avenue, he poured two glasses. "So. What movie are we watching tonight?"

Just the smell of alcohol made Chloe's head ache. "I can't. I have papers due tomorrow."

"Why do you have to write so many papers? You're going into art therapy. You should be drawing pictures instead." Ben held the champagne up to the light and studied it intently. "Unless you're trying to avoid me?"

"Women *stalk* you," she said. "I would be foolish to pass up the opportunity to be in your presence. But, my future calls." Stretching, she felt a crick in her neck, probably from the plane. Or the Macarena.

Ben selected the *Star* magazine from her stack of mail and started flipping through it.

"Ooh, don't wrinkle my magazine." Chloe had been excited about this issue of *Star*. Her latest celebrity crush was on the cover, which definitely meant a juicy story. "I'm going to read it in the tub before I write my paper."

"Sometimes I think I should blackmail you," Ben said. "Does anyone in your grad program know about your passion for trashy gossip?"

"No way," Chloe said, sorting through her mail. "Are you crazy?"

"And unless I'm mistaken, you just said you were going to read this in the tub." Brushing back an unruly strand of hair, he eyed her. "Since when do you take baths?"

"Since always." She looked at him. "Why? Doesn't everybody?"

"I don't know." Ben gave her an impish grin. "I really never pictured that from you."

Setting the mail on the counter, Chloe gave him her full attention. "Why not?"

"You're . . . I've always pictured you more as a shower type of girl."

"I think it's strange that you would picture me in the shower at all."

Ben grinned. "I think of everyone in the shower."

Chloe rolled her eyes. Of *course* he did. "Thank you for taking care of Whiskers." She tucked her phone into the back pocket of her jeans and picked up the can of Diet Dr Pepper. "I owe you one."

"You don't owe me anything," Ben said, going back to the magazine. "It's called being a friend."

Chloe stalked into the bathroom, plugged the drain and turned on the old-fashioned faucet. Since the bathroom got drafty even in the summer, she turned her portable space heater on to seventy and lit a few candles. Then she dumped a few capfuls of lavender bath gel into the water. "Okay," she called, "I'm getting naked so get out. Make sure you lock the door so nobody sneaks in and kills me."

"Don't get naked yet." Ben poked his head around the corner. He stuck out his lower lip and surveyed the setup with interest. "Fascinating. A bath."

Chloe's magazine was tucked neatly under his arm. "*Star*, please." She held out her hand.

"But I'm reading it."

Chloe wiggled her fingers. "Hand it over, Cowboy."

Handing her the magazine, Ben headed for the door. For some reason, he stopped and rested his large hand on the frame. "Thanks, by the way." Turning, he surveyed the scented candles and bubble bath. "You've given me a whole new picture of you." He took a slow drink of champagne, holding her gaze over the rim of the glass. Ben's eyes were bright blue and suddenly, the bathroom felt a little too hot and steamy.

*Huh?* Chloe suddenly felt self-conscious. What was he . . . ?

In the tight space, he took a deliberate step toward her. "I just want you to know I'll be thinking of you." Setting his glass on the sink, he reached for her hand and gently traced the skin of her palm. "Sitting in that water. Your skin all wrinkled and puckered up . . ." He grinned. "Just like the forty-year-old that you are."

Chloe's mouth dropped open. "You jerk!"

Ben erupted into laughter. Racing for the front door, he mimicked, "Call him. Until he picks up."

"You deserve each other," Chloe cried. "See you at your wedding."

Peeling off her clothes, she sunk into the warm bathwater, practically grinning with relief. For a second there, she'd actually thought Ben was hitting on her. Thank goodness she was wrong.

That would have been just too weird.

# Three

Kristine decided she'd eat at her favorite French wine bar before stopping by her store. Even though it was closed, there was always something she could be doing. Besides, Kevin had already flown out for work and she didn't exactly feel like sitting in their house, alone.

Pushing open the heavy door of the restaurant, she smiled at the hostess. "Bonjour, Michel."

"Bonjour, Kristine." As always, the hostess wore bright red lipstick and looked like she'd time-warped from the 1930s. "Just one this evening?"

"Just one." Then, for some unfathomable reason, Kristine said, "I'm celebrating my anniversary."

Michel raised a penciled eyebrow. "Of the store?"

"Oh, no." Kristine felt her cheeks flush. Blushing was one of the many problems that came along with being a redhead. Others included a tendency to get angry, to sunburn quickly and an inability to wear pink. "The anniversary of my marriage. It's my wedding anniversary."

Michel peered behind her, as though the language barrier had gotten in the way. "But where is your . . . ?"

"Traveling." Kristine smiled extra big to show that it was fine, that it didn't matter. "He has to travel for work." At Michel's look of distress, she said, "It's really no big deal. When you've been married as long as we have . . ."

"I will have the server bring you out some special champagne," Michel suggested.

"No, no." Kristine suddenly felt embarrassed. Why had she said anything at all? Maybe June was willing to tell anyone anywhere anything but Kristine was a private person. It wasn't like her to broadcast this type of thing. "Let's just pretend it's a normal night."

"Of course." Michel reached for a menu. "Come with me."

As the hostess led Kristine through the cozy interior with its small tables and hidden nooks, Kristine admired the ambiance of her favorite restaurant. Along the bar, bottles of wine were as colorful as a collection of rare jewels. Everything from the blonde hardwood floors to the tiny crystal chandeliers sparkled as though polished mere moments before.

"Here we are." Michel stopped at a cozy table for two. It was covered with a white cloth and topped with an aged porcelain vase. White geraniums spilled out, bathing the table in their perfume.

"Perfect," Kristine said. "Thank you, Michel."

"Happy anniversary." Michel gave her a sympathetic look before strolling away.

Kristine let out a tiny breath. Plucking her cell phone out of her purse, she called her husband.

Kevin picked up on the first ring. "Hey, Firecracker. Happy anniversary."

Kristine smiled at the nickname. He gave it to her when they first met, thanks to her red hair and quick fuse. Cradling the phone to her ear, she asked, "Where are you?" In the background, she could hear the buzz of traffic. She imagined him standing outside a hotel or an airport, next to a long taxi line.

"Kansas. But don't worry," he said. "The weather's perfect."

"I wish I was there. With you."

"No, you don't." He laughed. "I'm staring at a Dumpster, literally, even as we speak."

Kristine felt a wave of sympathy for her husband. When he lost his job, Kevin had been shocked, hurt and then, angry. Committed to finding something better, he started looking with a vengeance. With over twenty years' experience and a high salary requirement, Kevin lost out time after time to entry-level workers working for entry-level pay. After a year and four months, he was finally offered a position in a new field. It required "up to 90 percent travel," but at that point, there was nothing to do but take it.

A waiter wearing horn-rimmed glasses approached Kristine's table. With one hand, he poured sparkling water into a glass and with the other, set down a basket of freshly baked bread.

"Merci," Kristine murmured.

The waiter nodded and walked away.

"Where are you?" Kevin asked.

"That French restaurant I like." Kristine frowned, realizing that her husband probably had no idea which restaurants she liked anymore, considering they spent so little time together. "It's by the store. I'm going to work a little before heading home."

"Just think," Kevin chuckled. "Twenty-five years ago today, June was insulting us at our own wedding."

"Ah, yes." Selecting a piece of crusty, flour-coated bread, Kristine split it open. Steam rose from its soft center. "The infamous speech." Boy, had June gotten in hot water for that one.

"I wish I was there with you." Kevin's voice was tired. "But don't worry. Our fiftieth is coming up. That's only . . . what? Twenty-five years away? We can celebrate then."

Absently, Kristine reached out and touched one of the velvet petals of the geranium. It fluttered down to the table like a pinwheel. "Yeah," she said, brushing it to the ground. "I'll put it in the books."

Opening the menu, Kristine's eyes scanned the options. What would Kevin order? Probably the skirt steak with rosemary potatoes. "Well," she said. "I love you."

"I love you, too. Have a good night."

. . .

Kristine and Kevin met on the summer travel program at college. The program gave students the opportunity to take classes onboard a ship, while docking in various countries along the way. It was the most exciting thing Kristine had ever been a part of because she finally got to see the world.

As a child, Kristine spent her free time watching television shows about the Yuen Tsuen Ancient Trail in China, the sea turtle rescues off the coast of Turkey and the Harvest festivals in Thailand. She fantasized about being an anthropologist the way other girls dreamed of being lawyers, doctors or movie stars. At the same time, she knew she would never be brave enough to follow her dreams.

Kristine was not a bold person in life; only in her imagination. It had taken some serious guts just to attend an out-of-state college instead of staying in Chicago, as June had wanted her to do. When Kristine signed up for the summer travel program, it only took one phone conversation with her mother to convince Kristine to withdraw her name altogether. Ultimately, it was her father who convinced her to go.

Kristine's father called her when June was out with her gardening group. "Now, you know I love your mother, but you can't let her stop you from living your life. See the world, Kristine. Enjoy yourself."

Kristine tugged at the phone cord. "I'm afraid of traveling so far away. I won't know anybody."

"There's nothing to be afraid of," he said, "as long as you're always prepared."

So, Kristine decided to get prepared. She learned how to say, "I am a student and need your help," in five different languages. She stocked her suitcase with a full medical kit that included Bonine, Dramamine, ginger capsules, ginger candies and Pepto-

Bismol. She even brought along a glass bottle with letters to her parents stuffed into it, just in case the ship went down.

On the day of departure, Kristine's stomach did cartwheels of joy. After a *bon voyage!* that involved confetti throwing and waving at strangers until her wrist was sore, her classmates headed inside. There were group games and snacks to enjoy, but she was perfectly happy on the deck. Staring at the water, the thrill of adventure ran up her arms like shivers. Silently, she thanked her father for helping her make the right decision.

"I don't know about you," a deep voice said, somewhere from the shadows of the dock, "but I'm not too sure about this."

Kristine practically jumped out of her skin. Grabbing the rail, she turned and found herself staring into the fleshy face of a football player who had been in her Political Science class. His cheeks were ruddy and there was a smattering of freckles across his nose. At six foot two and two hundred plus pounds, testosterone wafted off him like cologne.

"Not sure about . . . what?" The ship's foghorn let out a sonorous cry and Kristine pulled the sleeves of her navy sweatshirt closer to her.

"Any of it." He shook his head as though angry. "I don't like water, boats, trips to foreign countries, any of it. I never should have come. No relationship is worth this type of torture." Kristine opened her mouth to speak but he kept going. "You know, I'd give my right nut to be back there." With his massive hands, he pointed at dry land. "On solid ground."

His cheeks were covered with a thin sheen of sweat. Suddenly, Kristine saw a way she could contribute to the conversation. "Are you sick?" Her voice was a little too eager. "I have some motion sickness medicine in my . . ."

The guy's face cracked into a crooked smile. It was one of those face-wrinkling grins full of mischief. Suddenly, Kristine realized he was really attractive and she looked out at the water.

"I'm not sick," he said. "I'm . . ." He gestured out at the ocean. "I just don't like boats."

The ship hit a large wave then and he yelped, grabbing the railing of the boat as if his brute strength was the only thing that could keep him from flying overboard. His upper arm had to be the size of her thigh. In spite of his distress, she giggled.

A wounded look passed over his face. It reminded Kristine of this children's book June used to read, where the big bear is brought down by a tiny thorn in his paw. "It's not funny," he growled. "I don't want to be here. It's like I'm being kidnapped."

Kristine lifted her palms. "Look. I'm not even holding on."

"Then you're stupid." Before Kristine could get offended, he grinned. They stood in silence, the sound of the water churning around them. A seagull gave a cry and laughter drifted out from the game room.

"So . . . Why did you come on this trip?" Kristine asked. "Did your girlfriend make you do it?"

"Yeah." He ducked his head. "She's inside, playing some game. Probably getting drunk. She brought a flask onboard. Rum. If she gets sick I'm not going to hold back her hair. No way."

In spite of his protests, Kristine knew that this guy *would* in fact hold back his girlfriend's hair. He was obviously a big ol' teddy bear, with those sensitive blue eyes and that open, friendly face. She wondered who his girlfriend was. Probably someone in one of the sororities. One of the sororities that Kristine was too shy to pledge, in spite of June's encouragement.

"Well, it sounds to me like you have two choices." He started to interrupt her again but Kristine raised her voice above its normal, soft-spoken pitch. "You can walk around wearing one of those life vests they showed us during the safety presentation—"

The guy nodded, his face earnest. "I was considering that."

"Or . . ." Kristine thought of her father's words. "You could relax and try to have a good time. This is the opportunity of a lifetime. Why waste it being afraid?" The boat was moving faster now and the wind was whipping her hair around. Quickly, she pulled it back into a ponytail.

"The opportunity of a lifetime?" He cocked an eyebrow. "You mean the opportunity to get drunk every single night and blame your hangover on motion sickness? Why not do that on dry land?"

The sun was setting and red streaks stretched across the sky like a painting. Kristine spread her arms wide, as though trying to capture it. "No. The opportunity to see the world!"

The football player cringed. "Oh, boy. You're gonna be the one who gets really into it, right? I bet you already tried to learn foreign languages." At the look on her face, he laughed. "I knew it. You'll take soil samples and try to get in with the natives. I can see it now. You'll even try to bring a goat back onboard because it's indigenous to—"

"I will not!" Kristine couldn't believe he was making fun of her, but she should have known better. In spite of his use of a four-syllable word, this guy was a jock. He had no interest in world events and would spend the trip soaking up as little culture as possible.

"You know what?" Flicking her ponytail back over her shoulder, she glared at him. "You'll be the one who tries to ruin it for everybody. You'll mock the people with accents and you'll make fun of the different cultures. And everyone on land will hate us for bringing someone like you along."

The football player stared at her in surprise. He opened his mouth, but nothing came out. *Good*, Kristine thought. She was done with him.

"See you around." She started to walk away.

Before she knew what was happening, the guy grabbed her sweatshirt. The move was gentle but commanding, and it pulled her right back to him. Kristine gave a little gasp of surprise. She was close enough to feel the warmth of his body and smell his spicy scent.

"You can't hate me already." His blue eyes were locked onto hers. "I don't even know your name."

"Kristine." It came out as a whisper. Once again, she wondered about the girlfriend. Would she be mad if she saw the two of them standing so close together?

"Hello, Kristine," he said, softly. "I'm Kevin."

Kevin stuck out his hand. After a moment, she took it. His hand swallowed hers up like a drop of water in the ocean. Flustered, she took a step back.

"I think I'm going to call you Firecracker." He grinned. "With that fiery temper."

Blushing, she said, "I think I'm going to go back . . . to the . . ."

"Don't go," Kevin pleaded. "I was hoping that, if I keep looking at the water, I'd get used to it. I won't talk anymore." He dropped her hand and crossed his heart. "We can stand here in silence like you were doing before I showed up."

Kristine agreed to stay but of course, the silence didn't last longer than two minutes. They started talking about their families, where they were from and their experience at college. In spite of his humor, he was weighted and serious. She found herself really starting to like him.

The conversation ended when a perky blonde came out of nowhere and leapt into his arms. The girl kissed him and Kristine swallowed hard, embarrassed that she'd developed a crush on a guy like him. Excusing herself, she went back to her cabin.

Two nights later, Kevin came over and sat by her at dinner. His tray was filled with mystery meat, potatoes and two chocolate cupcakes. "Hey, Firecracker." He passed her a cupcake. "I brought you dessert."

Kristine set down her fork in surprise. "Where's the girlfriend?"

Kevin gave her a sidelong look. "I threw her overboard."

From then on, they were inseparable. They sneaked out onto the deck every night and talked until dawn. They shared their first kiss at the edge of the Grand Canal in Venice. Then, one perfect night when the moon was silver and the motion of the boat slow and steady, Kevin took her into his room and shut the door. He removed her clothing piece by piece, before gently guiding her to the bed.

Years later, when celebrating their anniversary with a picnic by the water, Kevin said, "I knew I was going to marry you that first night we talked."

Kristine was surprised. "Why?" Even though she'd liked the cowardly football player, she'd had no idea she'd marry him.

"You offered me motion sickness medicine." He shook his head. "I fell in love."

Kristine laughed. "I had a whole medical kit in my room. It wasn't nearly as romantic as you think."

"Yes, it was." Kevin took her hand, his gaze earnest. "You were the first person I'd ever met who was prepared to face something bigger than what was right in front of us. I loved that about you."

"Well—" Kristine started to say but as usual, Kevin cut her off.

"I also knew that if you fell into the water, I would have jumped in to save you. Life jacket or not."

"Yeah, right," she said, smiling. "You were so scared."

"Doesn't matter. I would have."

Kevin kissed her then; a deep, drowning kiss that left her as breathless as falling into the sea.

Kristine ordered a glass of wine and a roasted hen from the waiter with the horn-rimmed glasses. Then, she pulled out a magazine she'd swiped from the plane. The cover shot was of New Caledonia and she stared at it for a moment, admiring the aquamarine water and vegetation-covered rocks. She'd just started to read the article when a warm hand touched her shoulder.

"Kristine?" a low voice murmured. "May I join you?"

It was Ethan, a part-time employee at her store. In the past, he'd worked as a travel photographer, shooting everything from *National Geographic* to *Redbook*; now he did photography as a hobby.

Since Ethan was still standing by the table, she nodded at the chair across from her. "Have a seat." Hopefully, he was just planning to stay for a moment.

"It's good to see you." Ethan rubbed his eyes, stretching. "I've been in the darkroom all day. It's good to get back to civilization."

"Oh?" Kristine took a sip of sparkling water, deliberately letting her eyes wander the restaurant. She did not want him to invite himself to dinner. "That sounds fun."

"Not fun, exactly," he mused, "but interesting. I lose all sense of time when I work. I'm sure you know how that is."

Yes, she did know. The travel bookstore was an all-encompassing project. Kristine was often surprised to look up from her work, only to discover it was hours later than she'd expected.

"Pouilly-Fume." The waiter set a glass of wine in front of Kristine. Hints of grapefruit and apple drifted up like perfume. "Monsieur, what can I bring you?"

"Ah . . ." Ethan hesitated. "Kristine, do you mind?"

Yes, of course she did. What would Kevin say if she had a drink with another man on their anniversary? Especially a man like Ethan? Unfortunately, she couldn't find a tactful way to say no.

"The same." Ethan nodded at her glass.

Leaning back, Ethan drummed his tanned fingers on the table. Kristine wondered if he was really a travel photographer. Maybe he was actually with the CIA. With his gray stubble and sharp eyes, he certainly fit the profile.

"I love this restaurant." Ethan's gaze swept the room. "It's like stepping into Paris, even for a moment."

"I wouldn't know," Kristine admitted. Her voice was wistful, as it always was when discussing travel. "I've never been."

Ethan's dark eyebrows shot up. A scar cut through the left one, reinforcing her belief that he was a spy or, at the very least, someone dangerous. "You've never been to Paris? You, of all people, should go. It's the perfect time of year. The summer is winding down, the shops are reopening—"

"What do you mean, *you of all people*?" Kristine laughed and pointed at her hair. "Most people assume I'm Irish."

He smiled. "I meant someone with your flair for adventure. For romance."

Kristine hesitated. She had spoken to him what, fifteen times in her life? He had no way of knowing what she had a flair for.

"An interest in travel means you have an interest in adventure," Ethan said, as though reading her mind. "Take it from me."

"Do you have a favorite country?"

It was a rote question, one she asked a hundred times a day in the store.

Ethan's eyes crinkled at the edges. "I don't know. That would be like choosing a favorite child."

"You have children?" For some reason, she didn't picture him cradling a baby with a leaky diaper.

"Ah, no." There was a note of pain behind his dark eyes. "I was smart enough to stay away from the marriage and family thing."

"You stayed away altogether?" she asked. "You've never been married?"

Ethan fiddled with the flower petal that had drifted down to the table. "I think love is the greatest thing in the world." Raising his dark gaze, his eyes met hers. "It can rip your soul apart and change your life in ways you don't want or expect. But everyone makes choices." He reached for his drink as the waiter set it on the table. "I used to be on the road all the time. Travel doesn't exactly lend itself to a solid relationship."

Kristine fidgeted. That was the truth. What would Ethan say, if he knew it was her twenty-fifth wedding anniversary? That her husband was five hundred miles away?

They were silent for a moment. Then his eyes fell on the magazine. "Oh," he said, surprised. "Look at that."

"New Caledonia." Kristine turned the picture toward him. "Have you been?"

Sheepishly, he pointed at the photo credit. "Actually, yes. I shot that."

"What?" Amazed, Kristine studied the pictures. Aquamarine water, billowing white sails, comical fish . . . *Wow*. It was hard to imagine the man sitting across from her capturing all of this with just the lens of a camera. It showed a depth that she hadn't given him credit for.

"Ethan, these are great." She regarded him with a new respect. "Why on earth are you working in my store?"

"It's time to put down some roots. I'm getting old. You know what I mean?"

Kristine shook her head. "Nope. I just turned thirty."

The laugh lines around his mouth twitched. "I would have guessed twenty-one."

"Ah." Kristine touched her glass to his. "Touché."

Ethan ran his hands through his thick black hair. There were a few silver strands around his temples, which she liked. It gave a little imperfection to his perfection. "Getting older is a funny thing. It's made me feel this need to settle somewhere, to become part of a community. And I love the store. You've done a great job, Kristine. It's really given the neighborhood some badly needed texture."

"Thank you," she practically whispered. It was a nice thing to hear. Owning the store was a lot of effort, and sometimes Kristine wondered if it mattered to anyone at all. "You know, I envy you," she said slowly, touching the sleek magazine cover. "When I was younger, I wanted to join the Peace Corps. See the world."

"You didn't do it?"

"No, I got married instead." Immediately, she felt guilty. "I don't mean it like that. I just . . . If I really wanted to join the Peace Corps, I would have done it."

"There's still time." Ethan lifted his glass. "There's always time."

The waiter arrived then with a perfectly browned, roasted hen. Garlic, rosemary and delicious goodness wafted up from the plate. Waving her knife and fork at Ethan, Kristine surprised herself by saying, "You should order something. Otherwise, I'll feel bad for taking down this whole thing in front of you."

"I'll have the mussels and truffle fries," Ethan told the waiter, without looking at a menu. "You have to try a fry," he said, giving her a quick wink. "It might make up for the fact that you've never been to Paris."

"I've had them." Kristine surveyed the familiar restaurant. "This is my favorite place."

"Mine, too," he said.

They smiled at each other.

Just then, a jazz band took the stage. The snare drum set the rhythm and a woman sang a song in French, her voice low and earthy. Kristine and Ethan turned their attention to the stage.

As a sultry breeze blew through the windows, Kristine felt happy for the first time all day. Life was so funny. She'd started out the evening upset about her anniversary and in the process, surprised herself by finding a friend.

# Four

Glancing at the Enfield clock on the mantel, June was pleased to see that it was only nine o'clock in the morning. She'd slept later than usual, because she'd stayed up reading a mystery story. She'd solved the mystery by page thirty-six but had to keep reading to see if she was right.

Sunshine peeked through her heavy curtains. It brightened the Oriental throw rugs and antique furniture, beckoning her outside. June planned to spend the day in her garden because, after a wonderful weekend with her family, the house would feel much too big.

Crossing through the parlor and into the kitchen, June pushed open the heavy screen and stepped outside. Her first thought was whether or not she should see if the tomatoes were overripe on the vine. Her second thought was, *"Aaack!"*

A piercing light was shining in her eyes like a laser beam from outer space. June blinked, covering her eyes and splaying her fingers. Just over the stone fence separating her yard from Charley Montgomery's sat a gazebo with a bright copper roof. It shimmered like a newly minted penny.

"I cannot believe that man," June said.

Turning on one heel, she stomped back inside and dug out the thick wraparound sunglasses she'd worn at the wedding. Then, with as much of a bang as she could muster, June slammed the screen door shut. She strode past the trickle of her fountain, the busy buzz of bees and the hanging blossoms of the Peking lilac tree and stood at the edge of her neighbor's fence.

"Charley Montgomery," she bellowed. "You get over here right this instant!"

Like a silver-haired jack-in-the-box, Charley's head popped up over the fence. "Why, hello there, June." He wiped dirt on the front of his shorts and gave her an infuriating smile. "Did you want to borrow a cup of sugar?"

June pressed her lips together and frowned. Charley looked back, his light blue eyes twinkling. June found it absolutely outrageous that the women in her gardening group found this man attractive. The first time she heard this remark, June said, "Only if you like weasels." Because that's exactly what Charley Montgomery was. A weasel.

When he and his wife moved into the brownstone ten years ago, June had been fooled into thinking he was a nice man. It was not uncommon to see him and his wife bundled up in cardigan sweaters, walking around the neighborhood and holding hands. Charley rarely wasted his time with yard work. He'd rake the leaves or prune the trees, offering the occasional compliment about June's rhododendrons but he pretty much kept to himself. After his wife died, however . . .

Well.

Roughly a year after her death, June had been tugging away at some ivy when she heard a shovel striking the dirt. Turning, June saw Charley digging as though en route to China. June stopped what she was doing and stared, impressed at how quickly he worked. Especially for someone in her age category.

When he turned and caught her looking, June flushed. She certainly didn't want him to think she was one of those nosy neighbors, so she gave a quick wave and headed inside. There, she drank an ice-cold glass of tea and wondered what on earth he was up to.

Only when June was sure he had forgotten all about her, she spied on him from the kitchen window with a pair of binoculars. Charley Montgomery worked that barren piece of land until the mosquitoes came out. June went to bed chuckling over the idea that the poor man had worn himself out.

The next day, Charley was back in his garden before she'd even made her morning coffee. He was sweating and grunting, laying mulch like a hired hand. June didn't know what to make of it. She kept an eye on his progress and narrated the adventures of Charley Montgomery on her evening phone calls with Kristine.

"He bought a crazy mixture of flowers," June reported, peering through her binoculars to get a good look. "He must have picked them up at the local hardware store. Imagine."

"Leave him alone, Mother," Kristine warned. "He's trying to deal with his grief. Just like you did."

"Fine, fine. But this is not going to end well." Not only were the flowers Charley bought completely unorganized, they were incompatible. The roots on those flowers would fight and eventually kill one another, trying to share the space.

June managed to hold her tongue about his lack of skill until that moment Charley watered his plants in the middle of the day. *Of all things!* June could practically hear the water sizzle and burn on the leaves. At that point, she decided to perform an intervention. Smoothing her wavy hair, June walked over to the fence and rapped on it with her knuckles.

"I have something I would like to say." This was more than June had ever said to Charley at one time. Normally, her greetings were, "Good morning," or, "It's hot today," or, on rare occasions, "Hello, Charley." Building relationships with neighbors could be tricky, and June erred on the side of caution.

At the sound of her voice, Charley looked up from his pruning. Surprise flashed in his faded blue eyes. "Yes?"

June took a deep breath. "I noticed you've been gardening. And . . ." She proceeded to instruct him on what type of mulch he *should* have bought, what time of day he *should* be watering his plants and the difference between natural and chemical pesticides. She suggested he read some books, visit a nursery and get an education before trying to take on such a serious task.

Charley listened, wiping sweat out of his eyes, but he didn't say all that much. In fact, the poor man seemed so impressed with her knowledge that he avoided eye contact altogether.

It didn't happen overnight but eventually, Charley's plants grew bigger and stronger. He started to say, "Good morning, June," and look her in the eye. Then one day, when a particular type of violets that were very difficult to grow came in perfectly, Charley walked over to the edge of the fence. As the sun shone down and the birds sang their summer song, he said, "You know, June, you might want to consider clipping back your roses. You're not making room for the new buds."

June almost dropped her spade. "I beg your pardon?" She sneaked a peek at her roses. To her absolute and utter horror, Charley was right.

"I just thought I'd let you know." He gave her a slight wink.

June was stunned. Pressing her lips together, she went back to digging in the dirt. She did not clip her roses back until it was pitch black outside and she was certain that Charley had gone to bed. With every snip, she thought, *Tell me how to garden, indeed.*

Infuriated, June shared the confrontation with Kristine over the phone.

"Mother," Kristine groaned, "he was just trying to reciprocate. I think it's sweet." Then she laughed in that way she had when she thought she'd gotten to the bottom of something. "Don't worry. He'll never have a better garden than yours."

"What? Of course not!" June peered out the kitchen window. Even though the motion lights were the only thing keeping the area lit, Charley was still working away. He was wearing a pair of khaki shorts, black socks with sneakers and a flannel shirt almost exactly like June's. His shirtsleeves were rolled up and his forearms were strong and tanned from the sun. "But mark my words," June said, letting the curtain drop, "he's certainly trying."

June's suspicions were confirmed when she held her annual party for the garden club. She had spent weeks making sure everything was impeccable and even hired a caterer to put out covered tables and serve a high tea. The garden looked radiant and so did June, in a bold-patterned sundress.

Well.

When the members of the garden society arrived, they dared to look right past June, her garden and the high tea. Their eyes went straight over the fence, to Charley and the Japanese blossoms he had planted just the day before. "Lovely," the women said loudly, tossing their blue hair.

It instantly became clear that it wasn't the flowers that were the attraction, but Charley Montgomery himself. He sat in his garden like a prized plant, wearing a crisp white shirt and reading the paper.

June's mouth dropped open. She swept over to the fence and said, "Excuse me. This is a private party."

Charley looked at her, surprised. "Yes?"

"Well." June fidgeted with her dress. Whispering, so that the other women in the garden club couldn't hear, she said, "I wish you would go inside."

"I won't bother your party." Charley lifted the paper back up. "I'll just sit out here and enjoy the beautiful day." June could swear he was hiding a tiny smile.

June had been so infuriated by this that, after giving it some thought, she decided to get revenge. The next weekend, she marched into the local pet shop and marched right back out with a cage full of white long-eared rabbits. Sneaking them into the house had been a task, but she'd accomplished it with the assistance of Chloe and a heavy horsehair blanket. Together, they waited at the front window for Charley to leave.

"This is going to be one of those things I can't tell Mom about, isn't it?" Chloe petted the soft ear of a rabbit through the cage.

June nodded. "One hundred percent."

Just as Chloe decided the sickly smell of rabbit pee was too much to bear and got tired of it all and went home, Charley headed out his front door and down the block. He wore his trusty cap and carried a newspaper, a sure sign that he was off to the local coffee shop to grab a bite to eat. June darted outside with a rabbit tucked under her arm like a weapon.

"Be brave," she said, holding it over the edge of Charley's fence. The downy little body quivered, those powerful back legs dangling precariously over the edge. "You can do it."

The rabbit dropped to the ground with barely a thud. He seemed a little shocked, which was understandable. After being cooped up in that cage, he was suddenly marooned in green grass and brightly colored flowers. The rabbit's nose wiggled and he took two tiny hops. Then he spotted Charley's rhododendron bush. The rabbit raced over and took its first bite.

"Yes," June cheered, wishing Chloe had stuck around for the fun. "Eat!"

It didn't take long for June to deposit all three rabbits into Charley's yard. By the time the afternoon passed, his rhododendrons and trilliums were missing entirely. When Charley came home, June heard some surprised shouts but did not dare go out to see what all of the commotion was about.

Charley did not say a word about the incident, but he eventually got her back. In the fall, June planted an array of tulip bulbs in her garden. They were neatly laid out in an arrangement of red, purple and orange. Whenever anyone complimented her garden, she would say, "Just wait. When my tulips come up, it will be more beautiful than you can imagine."

Well, when June's tulips sprouted, they were not beautiful. They were black. As though an evil witch had waved a magic wand over her garden. June couldn't figure out what on earth had happened, so she called over a horticulture specialist. Were the flowers sick?

"Ma'am," he said, shaking his head. "See the roots down here? These were cross-pollinated specifically to create black tulips. You bought some hybrids."

"I most certainly did not," June said. "I have been gardening for longer than you've been alive. I know exactly what kind of bulbs I picked."

The horticulturist shrugged. "Well, I don't know what to tell you, ma'am. These bulbs are exactly what you put into the ground."

June heard the pages of a newspaper rattle and then a soft chuckle. Charley snapped his paper shut. "It's a shame about your flowers, June," he'd said, walking to the edge of the fence. "Tulips always look so good at Easter. Guess the Easter Bunny won't be coming to visit you anytime soon."

June flushed to her very core. "You didn't."

Charley smiled. A perfect white smile. She could swear the man already had a full set of dentures.

The garden war had officially begun. June sprayed dandelion seeds across his yard, dumped weed killer onto his rosebushes and even, during a particularly hot and dry summer, had stolen his hose. Charley had been up to his share of tricks as well, but a gazebo with a copper ceiling lighting up her backyard like a laser show . . . Well, this was something new. And it had most certainly crossed the line.

"This gazebo is unacceptable." June rested a hand against the stone fence.

"What seems to be the problem?"

"The reflection is blinding. You need to have it removed. Right away."

"Now, June," Charley said. "Why would I do something like that? I just put it up."

Charley seemed so pleased with himself, standing there in his light blue plaid shirt. The idea of competing with this man for another minute suddenly seemed exhausting. Gardening was where June found her peace. Her solitude. She couldn't imagine what the rest of the summer would be like with a copper beacon shining sunlight into her yard. "If you do not take that thing down," she said, trying to keep the tremor out of her voice, "I will have it spray-painted black."

"Then I'll have you arrested for vandalism." Charley shrugged. "I can't imagine they'll let you do a lot of gardening in jail."

Frustrated beyond words, June glared at the roof of the gazebo. Even with the thick black sunglasses covering half of her face, it was impossible not to squint against the bright reflection. He would have to take it down. He would have to!

"I have lived here for my whole life." June shook her finger at him. "I raised my daughter in this home. Then you came along and ruined everything."

"Tell me, June." Charley leaned forward and rested an arm on the fence. "What could I have possibly done to bother you so much?"

June shook her head, unable to find the words to explain exactly what it was about Charley that bothered her so much. "Please." Her voice was uncharacteristically soft. "I have worked hard to make my garden special. Please . . ." Maybe because of the sun or maybe because the situation seemed so incredibly impossible, June felt her eyes smart. Afraid her voice would crack if she tried to say another word, she turned away.

Through her tears, June stumbled across the careful paths she had spent so much time arranging. The fragrant air filled her nostrils with sweet nectar as the bees darted about, buzzing away. Her garden had been her sanctuary and this horrible, horrible man had ruined it.

"June," she heard him call, but she didn't stop. Unwilling to let Charley Montgomery see her cry, June ducked into the house and locked the door behind her.

# Five

Chloe stood in the hallway, staring at the nameplate on the door. *Dr. Geoff Gable, IV* stared back in cool, nondescript prose. She could not believe the renowned psychologist was willing to take the time to meet with her.

Earlier that year, Dr. Gable had made a speech at a fundraising event for her school. The man had such a commanding presence that Chloe listened, riveted, as he discussed the complex relationship between the field of psychology and art therapy. It was pretty impressive. (She couldn't help but notice that his green eyes were pretty impressive, too.)

"Ultimately," Dr. Gable lectured, "you should find a mentor in your field. Someone to coach you." For a brief, breath-catching moment, his green eyes seemed to look right at her. "Email me. I'm happy to advise you in any way I can."

It took all summer, but Chloe finally worked up the nerve to get in touch. She requested a letter of recommendation for a grant she was interested in applying to, pressed Send and expected to never hear from him again. To her surprise, Dr. Gable responded with a time and date to meet. Chloe read the email seven times, certain that he'd made a mistake.

Now that the big day had finally come, Chloe was giddy with excitement. Brushing her fingers over the nameplate for luck, she took a deep breath and opened the door. Inside the office, she stopped.

On her ride up in the elevator, Chloe had imagined that the waiting room would be bright and bustling, with a tight-lipped secretary who would ask her to take a seat. Then, after Chloe had waited a decent amount of time, flipping through worn copies of *AAA* and *Better Homes and Gardens*, the secretary would nod. "The doctor will see you now." But to Chloe's surprise, the white chairs lining the walls were vacant, the lights were turned down low and the tight-lipped secretary was nowhere to be found. If it weren't for a light shining behind the frosted-glass partition by the desk, Chloe would wonder if anyone was in the office at all.

"Hello?" she called. "Dr. Gable?"

No answer.

Nervously, she glanced at her watch. Noon. Being on time was definitely overrated.

Taking a few tentative steps, Chloe peeked behind the glass partition. A long hallway led to an open door. Smoothing her hair, she headed for his office. Her sandals seemed to sink into the thick rug and the strands of carpet brushed against her toes. She'd only made it halfway, when the strains of Louis Armstrong's "I Ain't Got Nobody" blasted out from his office.

*Crap.* Dr. Gable must have forgotten about their appointment altogether. Feeling a flash of disappointment, she decided to leave. She'd send another email asking to reschedule, even though it totally sucked that he'd forgotten all about her.

Just as she made it back to the glass partition, Dr. Gable started singing along with the music. Chloe stopped in surprise. *Geez*, he had a terrible voice. It was surprising, really, especially considering he was so good-looking. But it was like the worst karaoke ever.

As he hit a particularly high note, Chloe had to clap her hand over her mouth to keep from laughing out loud. Unfortunately, Dr. Gable chose that exact moment to barrel out into the hallway. He was bare-chested, dripping with sweat and wearing only a pair of green sweatpants.

Dr. Gable froze, the high note dying on his lips. After a long, horrifying moment, he said, "Can I help you with something?" as though trying to figure out who she was and why, exactly, she was spying on him.

Chloe's hand dropped from her mouth. "Uh . . . hi," she stammered. "I . . . I had an appointment with you. At noon?"

With one swift look, Dr. Gable seemed to take in everything, from her thin-framed, tortoiseshell glasses to her industrial navy wrap dress. "I never make appointments with pharmaceutical reps. I'm a psychologist, not a psychiatrist."

"No, no. I—" Chloe made the mistake of looking at his tanned, heaving chest. Her eyes dipped even lower, falling on a trail of black hair that led from his defined abs to the very top of his pants. Blushing furiously, she forced herself to stare at the carpet. "I'm a student," she mumbled. "I emailed you?"

Dr. Gable turned his sculpted, sweaty back on her and headed into his office. Cautiously, she followed, waiting as he tossed a series of weights over to the side of the room. Apparently, she'd caught him in the middle of his workout. Although, honestly, Chloe could recommend some peppier music.

"If you'd like, I could come back . . ."

"You may as well stay," he grunted. "You've already interrupted my day."

Okay. Maybe he hadn't appreciated the fact that she caught him singing. And half dressed.

Dr. Gable seized a wad of clothing from the back of his desk chair. Stepping into a tiny bathroom, he shut the door. The latch didn't catch and Chloe could hear him changing. When his belt buckle clicked closed, she blushed furiously, trying not to think of those green sweatpants.

Chloe glanced around the office. It was comfortably decorated, with a stately wooden desk, typical green plant and a big, comfy blue couch. An impressive bookshelf lined the walls. If the situation had been different, she might have made a list of titles to look up later.

"What is your name?" he called.

"Chloe McCallister."

Dr. Gable gave a little grunt. For some reason, she pictured him pulling on a pair of black socks.

"I wrote to you about that grant," she said, just in case he still couldn't place her. "I had an appointment with you for noon—"

"Tomorrow." Dr. Gable strode back into the room. He was now fully dressed and sported a tweed jacket, plaid shirt and a yellow ascot.

"Um, no." Chloe stared at the ascot. What the heck was that all about? "Our appointment was for today."

"I think I would know," he scoffed. "I scheduled it."

Chloe snapped open her appointment book, thumbing through the pages. "No. I'm sure it was . . ."

*Shit.* The appointment was for noon tomorrow.

"I'm sorry." Chloe felt like a total idiot. "You're so right. This is all my fault."

"Of course it is." Dr. Gable folded his cuffs. "I don't make scheduling errors. Would you like to have a seat?"

Chloe glanced at the door. It was not too late to make a run for it. Instead, she settled into the pale blue suede cushions of the couch as Dr. Gable walked over to the window and snapped open the shade. Sunshine streamed into the room and she squinted in the sudden brightness.

"So." Dr. Gable turned to face her, his green eyes intent. "You sent me a letter asking for an endorsement for a particularly formidable grant. Is there a reason you're interested in competing so far out of your league?"

Chloe sat up straight. "I don't think it's out of my league."

Dr. Gable assessed her with his eyes. "Historically, it's been awarded to older men with Ivy League connections. That's not you. Is it?"

"That shouldn't be an issue." Chloe ran her sweating palms over the starched fabric of her dress. "It's for a local project. It seems to me, that if someone was going to delve into the psychological implications for the children of our city, it should be someone in our city."

Dr. Gable looked vaguely amused. "Someone like you."

"Yes," she said. "Someone like me."

Chloe met his gaze, remembering what June always said about the importance of eye contact. *It makes you seem strong*, she always said. *Even if you really don't feel that way.*

"Chloe . . ." Walking over to his desk, Dr. Gable rifled through a few papers. "I am always interested in helping students. However." He plucked a paper off the top of the stack. "I did speak with your development professor. He forwarded me a copy of your most recent paper. Given this and your, ah, untimely arrival . . . I do have some concerns."

Striding across the room, Dr. Gable settled in next to her on the couch. Their fingers brushed as he handed the paper to her. Chloe was quick to move her hand away.

*Addicted to Art* was on the viability of using art therapy as a recovery tool for abuse. The paper had been great, even though she'd rushed to get it done right before leaving for the wedding. She wondered why he had "concerns."

Flipping open the first page, Chloe was surprised to see that it was covered in red marks. "Wait . . ." She peered at it more closely. "Oh, my gosh." Mortified, she slammed the paper shut like a diary. "This isn't my paper. This is . . . This is . . . entertainment news."

"Unless you were analyzing the lifestyle of a child star, I found it a bit difficult to see how the supporting information was relevant." Plucking the paper from her lap, Dr. Gable read, "'Duress in the home environment can be demonstrated in several forms. Reports suggest that Madonna was spotted at the Coffee Bean, discussing a new vibe for the national anthem.'"

Looking at her, Dr. Gable raised an eyebrow. "Madonna?"

"No, no, I—" Chloe snatched the paper back. Splashes of

entertainment news were neatly situated within her academic argument, like hot pink fishnets spicing up a graduation gown. Her professor had circled Madonna's name in red ink. "The mother figure???" he'd written in the margin.

Thinking back to Wednesday night, Chloe realized exactly how this had happened. She'd just finished a shift at her part-time job, jammed clothes into a suitcase for the wedding and sat down at the computer to bang out her paper. There was a ton of research to compile and to stay awake, she'd flipped back and forth between the research and entertainment news.

"I was exhausted when I wrote this," she said. "I must have cut and pasted a wrong source or two." Her ears burned. "Obviously."

"Obviously." They sat in silence for a moment. "You didn't cite the source, either."

"I cited the wrong source," Chloe said. "The quotes are all cited."

"Either way." Dr. Gable gave her a patronizing smile. "Not your best hour."

"Not my best *work*," she clarified. "You know, I can't believe my professor would send this to you." Out of all the well-done pieces she'd turned in to her development professor, *this* was what he decided to use to demonstrate her work? How humiliating.

"Don't blame him," Dr. Gable told her. "I asked him to send your weakest performance. I find that the assignments with the least effort invested in them are the most revealing, wouldn't you agree?"

Chloe's eyes flickered to the tissue on the coffee table. No, she was not going to cry. It would give this man too much satisfaction. Suddenly, she was glad she'd caught him singing. At least she wasn't the only one who looked like a jerk.

"May I ask," Dr. Gable continued, "why this . . . nonsense . . . was on your computer at all?"

"Only if I can ask why you listen to shitty music from the 1930s," she shot back.

Dr. Gable laughed. "Chloe." He put what was probably meant to be a comforting hand on her shoulder. "I think your ambition is to be admired. Rumor has it, your work is typically much stronger."

Standing up, Dr. Gable walked back over to his desk. He sat in his chair in a way that could only be described as smug. "However, according to your professors, you seem to have a hard time managing everything. You rush into class at the last minute, take on too many internship hours . . ."

*Show up for appointments a day early* hung in the air, unspoken.

"Slow down." He spread out his hands. "Enjoy your life."

"I don't have *time* to enjoy my life. I have serious goals that I plan to meet by the time I turn thirty. I want to own my own practice, just like you. And with this grant, I could finally—"

"Forget the grant," he said. "It's not going to happen this year. Maybe you can find someone else to endorse you, but I'm here to tell you that you're moving at a pace that is much too fast. You're going to burn out. And I'd hate to see that happen to such a promising little flame."

Chloe's mouth dropped open. "A promising little flame?"

Dr. Gable watched her with dancing eyes. "Isn't that what you are?" He picked up her paper. With a smirk, he read, "The celebrity wedding was witnessed by friends, family and paparazzi, circling like vultures over . . ."

"Asshole," Chloe said, then slammed his office door.

# Six

Kristine sat in bumper-to-bumper traffic, trying to work up some sort of enthusiasm for her latest audio book. It would be at least forty minutes until she could pull into the parking spot next to her store. For the hundredth time, she wondered how to convince Kevin to move back into the city.

After college, living in town was something they both wanted. Their first apartment was a cute walk-up with an old-fashioned stove, a fire escape and ceilings almost too short for Kevin's enormous frame. They'd moved to the suburbs when things like safe neighborhoods and good schools suddenly mattered, but they'd always planned to move back to the city.

It was only recently that Kevin changed his mind. There were a couple of factors, including the recession and what it had done to the value of their home, but Kristine also suspected that losing his job had made her husband emotionally attached to their house. In that year where he couldn't find a job, Kevin put his frustration into remodeling. He redid the floors, reshingled the roof, rebuilt the deck . . . The assistance of his toolbox and the local hardware store helped him to feel like he had a purpose, even if it wasn't at the office.

During this time, Kevin had talked about his upbringing more than he ever had before. Kristine listened to the painful stories: The summer his mother served SpaghettiOs for dinner for three months straight, the time the power got turned off in the winter because she didn't have money to pay the bills, the day the teacher sent a note home with Kevin complaining that he and his brother smelled. Hearing these stories helped her to understand why it frightened her husband so much to lose his job.

"It's going to be fine," she'd say. "You'll find something. We'll be okay."

Kevin had just gone back to retiling the bathroom or laying new linoleum, while waiting for the recruiter to get back to him with interviews.

When he finally found another job, the house looked better than it had in years. Kristine could understand his reluctance to leave, but on mornings like this, when traffic was heavy and her shoulders ached with tension by eight in the morning, her appreciation wavered. It would be nice to have the option of an easier commute, not to mention the perk of living closer to June and Chloe.

Kristine wouldn't push it, though. If Kevin needed to stay in their house, she'd support him in that. Besides, after her behavior the night before, she didn't have the right to ask for much of anything. She'd stayed out at that French restaurant with Ethan for three hours. *Three hours!*

"Kevin would kill me," she said out loud, shutting off the audio book. "I would kill *him*."

Clicking on the blinker, she waited for the lady in the black SUV to let her switch lanes. The woman ignored her, staring straight ahead. Kristine sighed. Drumming her hands on the steering wheel, she tried to determine just how bad her behavior had been the night before.

At first, everything had been perfectly innocent. They'd finished up dinner and were just about to pay their checks, when Ethan mentioned the Dogons tribe in Mali. "I did a study on the Dogons," she said, surprised. "In college." Ethan had actually spent time in Mali and could give her a real-life report.

From there, they just kept talking. They covered everything

from decolonization to global health care to German cheese torts. When she finally noticed the time and panicked, he insisted on walking her the five blocks to her travel bookstore.

Kristine cringed thinking about the walk. The white flowers on the trees had practically glowed silver and she felt a profound sense of stillness. Of course, that stillness was shattered when Ethan reached over and linked his arm in hers.

Kristine was taken completely off guard. Didn't he know she was married? She tried to come up with a clever exit strategy that wouldn't embarrass them but couldn't think of anything.

As they walked arm in arm, Ethan pointed out stained-glass transoms above different doors. They strolled past a house with windows etched with red, green and purple flowers, and he stopped. "Every time I walk on this street," he said, "I feel like I'm walking through cathedrals."

At the memory, Kristine gripped the steering wheel. It had been nice to see the world through the eyes of a photographer, but why hadn't she pulled away? It would have been awkward, especially considering Ethan probably meant nothing by it, but the fact that she hadn't done anything made her feel so . . . guilty.

Back home, she'd felt even worse because Kevin had left an anniversary card on her pillow. It was a silhouette of a sailboat against the setting sun and the caption read: *Looking forward to our golden years.* She could practically picture him buying it at some airport gift shop.

Setting the card on the bedside table, a piece of paper fluttered out. Was it a love letter? Eagerly, she'd snatched it up. *IOU*, it said. *For whatever you want, within reason. Love, Kevin.*

Kristine had been annoyed with herself for feeling disappointed. After all, it wasn't like she'd gotten Kevin anything spectacular for their anniversary—just a silver pen engraved with the words *Patient and mine*—but at least that had meaning. Kevin used to think the words were, "Love is patient, love is mine" instead of "Love is patient, love is kind." Silly stuff, but they'd laughed about it.

Either way, there was no point in being upset. Kevin was busy and they'd been together for so long. Did it really matter what he got her? Besides . . .

Glancing at her reflection in the rearview mirror, Kristine gave herself another guilty look. Her bright red hair was pulled up in a sloppy bun and her eyes looked tired, as though she'd stayed out much too late. She was hardly the perfect wife— she'd spent their anniversary drinking wine with another man. If Kevin knew about *that*, he probably wouldn't give her anything but the silent treatment.

When the sign for the store finally loomed into sight, Kristine felt her spirits lift. The brightly colored wooden cutouts depicted a variety of skylines across the globe and were made up of different shapes and sizes. *The Places You'll Go* zoomed across in fluffy white skywriting.

Walking in, Kristine was delighted to see the store was busy. A young couple flipped through a guide on Hawaii, a student explored the section on travel memoirs and an older couple browsed through books on Ireland. Annie, Kristine's dear friend and associate, was ringing up a customer.

Kristine loved Annie. At forty, the woman still dressed like a child of the eighties and sported an ever-changing array of Kool-Aid streaks in her hair. Considering Kristine was too timid to get her long red hair cut into an interesting style or paint her nails a funky color, she admired Annie's adventurous spirit.

"Hey, stranger." Annie rushed over. As always, she smelled like Electric Youth perfume, which she'd once ordered from eBay as a joke. "I'm happy you're back. And . . ." Her hazel eyes danced behind thick black-framed glasses. "I have something to tell you that will just smack you across the face."

Kristine laughed. "That sounds awful."

"Oh, it'll smack you in a good way," Annie promised. After nodding at Sara, one of their college helpers, she said, "Have some coffee with me."

Intrigued, Kristine followed Annie to the sunken area of the store with the purple velvet couch and coffee display. Slipping off her sandals, Kristine tucked her legs underneath her. The soft velvet of the couch was cozy as a blanket and she yawned.

"Wild night?" Annie joked, pouring them both a cup of coffee.

"You know me." Kristine kept her voice light. "As wild as they come."

"Give yourself more credit." Annie passed over a full mug. "You could be wild if you wanted to." After adding sugar to her coffee, she eyed the display table. "Should we have some cake?"

"Yes," Kristine said automatically. "Without a doubt."

Each day, The Places You'll Go set out complimentary coffee cake from the bakery next door. They spent a good part of each day debating whether or not to eat it or skip it. Considering the selection today was a crumbly pastry covered in powdered sugar, Kristine was not going to let today be a skip-day.

"Decadent *and* messy." Kristine laughed as crumbs spilled down her turquoise button-up shirt. "Okay, so tell me." Brushing the crumbs into her hand, she made a neat little pile on a napkin. "What's this big news?"

"Well . . ." Annie raised a pierced eyebrow. "One of our fabulous employees entered The Places You'll Go in the Valiant Travel essay competition. And . . ." She paused dramatically. "We *won*."

Kristine gasped. "You're kidding!"

Valiant Travel was a well-known online travel site. People from all over the world visited to voice compliments or complaints about hotels, airlines and tour companies. Kristine always encouraged her customers to post their travel clips. It was rewarding, somehow, to watch people she knew climb pyramids or cross a desert while carrying guidebooks from her store.

"That'll be some good publicity," Kristine said excitedly.

"Not just publicity." Annie spoke into her coffee cup like it was a microphone. "The winning essay has won the owner of the store and the essay writer a weeklong, all-expenses-paid trip to . . ."

"A trip?" Kristine's heart started to pound. "Oh, my gosh. Really? Where?"

*"Rome."* Annie bounced up and down. "Kristine, you finally get to go to Rome!"

Kristine set her coffee cup on the table in surprise. *Rome?* She had wanted to go to Rome for years! But just like most of the fabulous foreign cities she ached to travel to, she had been saving it for the future, when she and Kevin could go together.

"You'll have to speak at some luncheon or something that Valiant is throwing." Annie gripped her hands. "But the rest of the time is yours. We just got the message this morning. You'll have to listen to it. I'm so excited for you."

"Wow," Kristine said softly. She imagined what it would be like to see the Colosseum, to explore the ancient ruins. To drink Italian wine with . . . "Oh, wait. Who wrote the essay?"

Annie raised a pierced eyebrow. "Ethan."

"Ethan?" Kristine was horrified. "No, no, *no.*"

Flushing, Kristine remembered the moment when he'd linked his arm in hers. Traveling to the other side of the world with him was *not* a good idea.

"What do you mean, no?" Annie squealed. "It's yes! Just think, you can make him stand next to the statue of David and tell us all which one is better looking."

"David's in Florence. And I always pictured him as a blond."

"Either way," Annie said, taking a big bite of cake.

Kristine shook her head. "I can't do it."

"Do what? Rome?" Annie stared at her like she was the most disappointing human being on the planet. "You're kidding."

Kristine slid the elastic band off her ponytail and wound her hair up into a tight bun. "Annie, love it or hate it, I'm married. I can't travel the world with someone who's not my husband."

"So, tell Kevin to come along." Annie licked powdered sugar off her fingers. "Problem solved."

Kevin spent too much time already traveling in and out of O'Hare. He wouldn't want to go back to the airport on his time off. Kristine opened her mouth to explain, but Annie held up her hand.

"I don't want to hear it. You need to get out there and see the world. With or without him."

"Yes, but—"

"No buts," Annie insisted. "Kristine, you have to stop waiting for Kevin to live your life. He can make a choice. Come with you or kiss you good-bye at the airport. It's that easy." She said this with the confidence of someone who'd never been forced to compromise. Considering Annie had never been married, she'd never really had to.

"You're right." Kristine sighed. "Kevin *should* go to Rome with me. But I'd have to have a pretty convincing . . ." Suddenly, she stopped. "You know what?" The silhouette of a boat flitted through her mind. "I *do* have a convincing argument. Kevin gave me an IOU."

Annie looked puzzled. "An IOU?"

"For our anniversary."

Annie squinted through her glasses. "Seriously?"

"I'm sure he thought it was a great gift."

"It was a great gift." Laughing, Annie got to her feet. "That IOU just bought him a trip to Rome."

# Seven

Thanks to June's horrid neighbor, she spent three perfectly good gardening days indoors. This was all thanks to the glare from the copper roof of the gazebo, which Charley Montgomery hadn't bothered to tear down. June spent the time at her bedroom window, watching him like a sniper.

When Wednesday night rolled around, she had no choice but to step away from the window and make herself presentable for her weekly mahjong group. Her goal was to put together a look so outlandish that no one would notice her eyes were red and puffy from crying. That way, she could keep the ladies of the Chicago Mahjong Club out of her personal business.

The Chicago Mahjong Club was started during Prohibition, in an effort to provide the ladies of society another opportunity to live above the law. June's mother-in-law had been an original member. June was grateful for the group, as its members had become her very best friends. But because they were best friends, June knew better than to share her distress over Charley Montgomery. If she did, the topic could become a point of focus for months.

So, that night, June strutted into her mahjong group wearing a vintage Chanel dress, at least ten strands of pearls and a pair of black lace gloves. The three-inch heel on her knee-high crocodile boots gave her a commanding presence, which she worked to her advantage as she walked.

"Hello, June." The collective murmur was impressed. "Looking good."

June blew a benevolent round of air kisses, then beelined to her typical table. Sliding into her seat, she eyed her best friend, Bernice Bernard. The old dear was as regal as always, with her perfectly dyed jet-black hair and bright red lipstick. Unfortunately, Bernice was watching June with concern.

"Why, you've been crying," she barked.

"Bernice," June scolded. "You certainly do not have to announce it."

It was a pointless statement, as Bernice announced everything. She'd always been the loudest talker in the room. Everyone said the best way to get a good dish of Chicago gossip was to stand within twenty yards of Bernice.

"I don't *need* to announce it." Bernice tucked a strand of her perfect pageboy behind one ear and examined June. "Anyone can see that, behind that black netting, your eyes are bright red."

"I'm sure my eyes look just fine." As though to prove the point, June pulled her compact out of her purse and flipped it open. The rims of her eyes were lined in pink, and the tiny bags under her eyes were shining. "Well." June snapped her compact shut. "Perhaps my eyes are not red from crying. Perhaps they are red because I've been smoking marijuana."

Bernice's brown eyes lit up. "Really? That might be a nice way to pass the time."

"Hello, darlings. How are we this evening?" Rose Weston swooped over in a crunch of taffeta, passing air kisses like an infectious disease. Rose had worn taffeta in some form or another ever since June had known her. Today, the selection was an emerald green shirt with a ruffle along the bustline.

"Why, June." Rose's catlike eyes gazed at her in surprise. "Have you been smoking marijuana?"

June was starting to get annoyed. "No. But apparently, Bernice would like to."

"Bernice, you should," Rose cried. "Perhaps it would help you to loosen up."

"Loosen up?" Bernice glared. "The last time *I* looked in the mirror, I was perfectly capable of moving my forehead and blinking my eyes. You're the one who needs to loosen up."

Rose was a victim of Botox, so much so that it was sometimes difficult to read her expression. June liked to joke that Rose should quit mahjong and take up poker instead. She'd be quite good.

"Honey . . ." Rose patted Bernice on the shoulder. "Don't knock it until you've tried it. And judging by those crow's-feet, you really should."

"I will be getting some aperitifs." Bernice stood up from the table and stalked away. Her full hips swayed with every step.

The tension between Rose and Bernice had started fifty years ago, when they had gone head-to-head for a man. Rose tried every dirty trick in the book, even going so far as to tell him that Bernice was carrying another man's child. It was a particularly low blow at the time and typically very effective. In the end, Rose had lost interest in the man and Bernice married him. But the battle between the two had never stopped.

Rose took a seat at their table. "Darling, *do* tell me before Bernice gets back. Why on earth have you been crying?"

Even though June knew better than to confide in her taffeta-clad friend, crying often took a toll on good judgment. "I've been having trouble with my neighbor," June blurted out.

"Oh, dear," Rose said, delighted. Tapping the tips of her manicure, her nails made a sound that could easily be mistaken for a torture technique. "What sort of trouble and how can I help?"

June considered. Turning rabbits loose in Charley's garden was one thing. Adding Rose to the equation would be like injecting them with rabies.

"Don't worry about me." June sat up straight. "I have the situation with him under control."

"Aha." Rose gave a slow smile. "This mysterious neighbor is a *he*." At the pronoun, at least three women glanced their way. "Now . . ." She fluffed her dyed red hair. "This wouldn't happen to be the delicious man who was sitting outside during our Garden Club, was it?"

June forced her expression to remain blank. "Hmm. I don't quite remember."

"Don't remember what?" Bernice returned to the table with a plate full of spongy macaroons. She pulled out her chair, deliberately whacking it against Rose's leg. "Sorry," she sang, moving to sit.

Rose was quick. Her designer pumps shot out and shifted that seat like something out of musical chairs. Bernice had to grab the table to keep from tumbling to the ground.

June chuckled. Watching their war play out never ceased to be entertaining. However, there were days that she suspected the two women wished they could get past it all and just be friends.

"Rose is speaking of my horrid neighbor. And he certainly is *not* handsome—"

"Scrumptious," Rose insisted, reaching for one of Bernice's macaroons. Her red lipstick smeared across the cookie before she set it back onto the plate. "Bernice, darling, this neighbor was on display throughout the entirety of our Garden Club party."

A flash of recognition crossed Bernice's face. "June, you've been crying over sweet, little old Charley?"

June scoffed. Where were her friends finding these ridiculous adjectives for this man? Charley Montgomery was not sweet. He wasn't little, either. The man was tall, with strong arms. If he was ever inside June's parlor, she imagined he would be knocking into her antique trinkets left and right. Not that there ever would be a reason for him to be inside her parlor, but still. It was something to consider.

"Rose, this poor man lost his wife just over two years ago."

Bernice took a sip of her tea and smiled. "June has been flouncing around her garden, tormenting him ever since."

"I do not flounce," June cried.

"Of course you do," Bernice and Rose chorused. They eyed each other with irritation.

"I vote that you stop torturing the poor man." Bernice's voice boomed across the wood-paneled study. "Invite him over for tea."

"I will not be inviting him anywhere." June took off her hat and tugged at her black lace gloves. "The only thing that gives me any hope of surviving the situation is that it will be winter soon. We will be unable to garden and I will not see him until spring."

"Well, based on what I saw of him . . ." Rose licked her lips and reached for the painted macaroon. "That would be your loss." She chewed for a moment. "Which house does he live in again? The one on the right or the left, if I'm facing your home?"

"The left." June narrowed her eyes. "Why?"

"Sorry I'm late." Dorothy Chambers rushed up and slid into her chair. Slipping on her glasses, she said, "What did I miss?"

"We're talking about June's neighbor." Bernice shook her head. "He's very lonely."

Dorothy adjusted her silver-framed glasses and peered at June. "Widow?"

"Oh, for heaven's sake." June wished she'd done a better job of keeping this conversation at bay. "What is wrong with you people?"

"Nothing is wrong with us," Rose said. "If your neighbor is a lonely widow, with only gardening as a companion, it's our duty as women of society to bring him a casserole. Or two."

June felt as though Rose had slapped her in the face. "I beg your pardon?"

"Rose," Bernice hissed. "Don't you dare."

Rose patted her red hair like a film star. "June doesn't like the man. What would it hurt?"

"Considering she doesn't like him, we should stay away from him altogether." Bernice folded her hands. "Right, June?"

Even though the very thought of Charley made her want to grab the mahjong tiles and throw them across the room, June certainly did not want Rose to make friends with him. The thought did not sit well with her. Not at all.

A bell rang at the front of the room, as though at the start of a boxing match. Rue Gable, with her perfectly coiffed hair and St. John's pantsuit, held up an envelope full of money. "I think it's time to get started, ladies," she said. "Tonight, we are playing for quite a prize."

"We certainly are," Bernice mumbled.

"Good luck," Rose said sweetly, then dealt out the tiles.

# Eight

"Chloe," Ben called, followed by some insistent knocking. "Chloe, answer the door!"

"Go away." Chloe pushed her face down deeper into the starch of the bed pillows.

Chloe had been in bed for two days, with only the warm purr of Whiskers keeping her company. The scene with Dr. Gable repeated itself in her head, over and over. She felt like a total idiot for telling him off. Yes, maybe he'd deserved it with his smug little smirk and ridiculous ascot. Still, that didn't make it right. How could she ever be a good therapist if she couldn't control her own behavior?

"Chloe, I'm going to use my key," Ben threatened.

Chloe let out a grunt and sat up. She walked to the door wearing only a T-shirt and underwear. Flipping the lock, she stumbled straight back to bed.

"What on earth is wrong with you?" Ben followed her.

Chloe drew the comforter up to her chin and stared at the ceiling, not speaking. "Hey." Ben reached under the blanket and pinched her leg. "What's wrong? You haven't answered your phone in two days."

"I've been busy." She pressed her fists into her eyes. "Ruining my life."

"That doesn't sound good." His voice was unnaturally gentle. "Tell me what happened."

Chloe groaned. Whenever she was in particularly bad shape, Ben used this weird, overly caring tone. She had dubbed it the Voice of Compassion and vowed she would never, *ever* use it in art therapy sessions. It reminded her of the moments in her life where she was completely and utterly pathetic.

The first time Ben whipped out the Voice of Compassion was in junior high. This was right after he returned from three months of summer camp, totally transformed. Gone was the geeky guy who wore glasses and collected bugs. In his place was a tall, tanned god with a quick smile for the ladies and a smart-ass remark for the guys. The kids who had ignored Ben for years swarmed around him like bees.

Chloe was stung. For the first time in her life, she had to share her best friend. She suffered in silence for a few weeks, until Ben skipped their usual lunch to hang out with the head cheerleader. At that point, Chloe had no choice but to break up with him as a friend. He showed up at her house with Clue and Sorry!, the games they'd played as kids.

As they sat on her bed, sipping soda and snacking on chips, Ben used the Voice of Compassion to explain that Chloe was his best friend and always would be. "Breaking up with me won't do you any good," he said, calmly moving his Sorry! pawn forward. "I want to hang out with you. Not those stupid girls. With them, I'm just having a little fun."

Chloe blushed furiously. Part of the reason she was mad at him, she realized, was that she, too, had a crush on this new version of Ben. He was so tall, so tan, so kind. But it was pretty obvious that she could keep her preferred status as best friend or become just another girl for him to have fun with.

"Fine," she'd said, rolling the dice and sending one of his pieces back home. "Just as long as you understand that to me, you're the same dork you've always been."

"Good." He dropped the Voice of Compassion. "That's exactly how I want it to be."

At the memory, Chloe smiled.

"Okay, you're smiling." Ben nodded. "That's a good sign. So, what happened?"

Grabbing Whiskers, Chloe pulled the cat to her chest and ran Ben through the story. He laughed at the part where she caught Dr. Gable singing, glowered at her mention of his six-pack and jumped up in anger at the "promising little flame."

"He said *what*?" Ben roared. "Where's the office? I'm going to go have a talk with this guy."

"Don't." Chloe buried her face in Whiskers' fur. "A fight with Dr. Gable and his stupid little ascot would not be fair. He'd be no match for you and your metrosexual protein shakes." Although, based on the sight of Dr. Gable with his shirt off, a battle between him and Ben might actually be a good one. "Look, I took care of it in a very mature fashion." Chloe stroked Whiskers' paw. "I called him an asshole and slammed his office door. Which is why I have been hiding in my bedroom for two days."

Ben shook his head. "You did the right thing. You have no reason to hide."

"Yes, I do." She puffed out her cheeks, then slowly exhaled. "I just got a message from the department head. He wants to meet with me on Friday. I bet they're kicking me out of school."

"You're being ridiculous," Ben said. "The good doctor doesn't even work there. Good thing, or I'd get his ass fired. A promising little flame? What a dick."

"He knows the professors," she said. "I'm sure he told them."

"Good." He nodded. "Then this meeting is probably to applaud you."

Ben paced around the room for a minute, tossing her dirty clothes into the hamper, opening the shade on her window and arranging the collection of picture frames on her dresser. There were photographs of Chloe's parents; Kristine and June; Chloe, Kristine and June; and even one with June and Whiskers.

"Where's the picture of me?" Ben's hand hesitated over the photographs. For her birthday, he had given Chloe a framed photo of the two of them riding bikes down by the water.

"In the living room. I didn't like the way you were looking at me every time I got dressed."

Ben laughed, taking a seat again on the bed. "Look, I think this is a good thing."

"How, exactly? This is going to ruin my career."

"No, it's not," he insisted. "It's a good thing because you finally took a break."

That was true. This was the first time in a long time that Chloe had laid in bed in . . . Well, who knew how long? Even though she'd spent most of the time moping, she finally felt rested.

"Now, since you appear to still be in bed, we are going to make it an official bed-in." Ben's eyes sparkled. "We're going to order some Thai food, drink some wine and watch reality television. You can mope as much as you want. Then tomorrow, you'll forget about it and go back to your real life."

"I don't know . . . Maybe I should get back to work. Catch up on what I missed."

Ben shook his head so hard his golden curls bounced. "You're staying right here. And if you're good, I'll draw pictures of my deepest, darkest feelings. You can look at them and analyze me."

"Really?" She'd been trying to get him to do that for years.

"Really." Ben gave her a smile that could make a lesser girl melt. "You in?"

Chloe thought for a moment. Really, what would she accomplish if she got up now? It was four o'clock and she'd already missed all of her classes. There weren't any papers due until the end of the week. Looking at him, she shrugged. "I'm in."

Before she could change her mind, Ben crawled across the bed, picked up her cell and placed an order for chicken pad Thai and drunken noodles. He turned on the television, leaned against the headboard and crossed his muscular arms behind his head. After a minute, he let out a hearty sigh. "Man," he said. "I thought I was going to have to call your mother."

Sitting up on one elbow, Chloe snuggled against her best friend. "To be honest, you wouldn't have had to call anybody. You had me at reality TV."

# Nine

Kristine stood up eagerly when she heard her husband's key in the door. It was Wednesday night, which meant Kevin was back from the first part of his week. He'd fly out again tomorrow afternoon.

There would only be a short period of time to repack a new suitcase for him, sort through the dirty clothes and put in fresh shirts, razors and toiletries. Chloe teased her about doing this, but it was Kristine's way of staying connected to her husband while he was out on the road. Besides, he wouldn't know how to fold a shirt if his life depended on it.

"Hey, Firecracker!" Kevin strode across the room, his arms open. Kristine fell into the hug. She'd always loved the way he smelled, like lemongrass and musk. "Did you miss me?" He kissed her on top of her head. "I missed you. Cried myself to sleep every night. Like a baby."

"I'm sorry I didn't get to see that." She tilted her head back to look at him.

When their eyes met, his face split into a grin. Even though Kevin's sandy brown hair had some gray in it and there were a few wrinkles around his eyes, he looked just like he did when they'd first met.

"I'm starving." He looked past her toward the kitchen. "Did you make Philly cheesesteaks? Fried onions?"

"Try a grilled chicken salad." Considering Kevin ate at airports and chain restaurants for the majority of the week, Kristine did her best to pump him full of vitamins at home.

"Sounds healthy," Kevin sang, giving her a light smack on the bottom. After grabbing his favorite water glass out of the cupboard, there was the familiar *clink-clink-clink* of the ice machine then a whoosh of water. Such a silly thing, but just hearing the sound made her happy to have him home.

Kevin grabbed the salads and headed down to the den. Kristine gathered up silverware and followed him. He was already watching the sports station on their sixty-inch flat screen. She would have preferred for the TV to stay off, but she'd given up hope on that years ago.

"Kris, this looks great." The plate was piled high with fresh spinach, portobello mushrooms, cherry tomatoes, red peppers, goat cheese and grilled chicken. Popping a tomato in his mouth, Kevin said, "How was your weekend with the girls?"

"Fun." She settled into a brown leather chair and flipped up the footrest. "Chloe is doing way too much, as always. And June was as socially inappropriate as possible, whenever she got the chance."

Kevin grinned, taking a bite of chicken. "Figures."

The relationship between Kevin and June had been rocky from the start. He thought June was a "pretentious busybody," while she thought Kevin was an "overeager ex-jock."

"What else?" Kevin said. "You went to that French restaurant for our anniversary, right?"

Kristine flushed, staring down at her salad. "Yeah . . . How was your week?" Immediately, she felt guilty. Why couldn't she just say she'd had dinner with a coworker and they'd talked travel?

Glancing at her athletic husband, Kristine knew why. If she told him, she'd probably do or say something to clue him in on the fact that Ethan had linked his arm with hers. Then Kevin would show up at the store and tell Ethan exactly what would happen to his arm if he tried anything like that again.

It was definitely not a topic worth bringing up. The trip to Rome on the other hand . . . that was something worth telling.

"So, I do have big news." She set her salad on the coffee table. "Something exciting."

Kevin's mouth rounded into an O. "You got me an eighty-inch flat screen for our anniversary."

She shook her head. "Nice try."

"You're a secret lottery winner and finally decided to tell me?"

"I wish."

Kevin's eyes danced. "June annoyed the air marshal and they threw her out of the airplane?"

Kristine laughed. "*No.* Give up?"

Digging back into his salad, Kevin took a few enthusiastic bites. "Tell me."

"I won a trip to Rome," she said. "At the end of next month."

Kevin set down his salad, clearly surprised. "Rome, Italy? Or Rome, Georgia?"

"Italy, you goof." Kristine still couldn't believe she was going to Italy.

"That's so great, Kris," he said. "How'd you pull that off?"

"Oh, I didn't." Kristine felt another flash of guilt. "Someone in the store entered an essay contest. But since I own the place, I'll get to go for a week and speak at this big-deal conference."

"Well, that's really cool." Reaching for his salad, Kevin added, "Maybe the Pope will show up to your speech. Or that guy from *Gladiator.*" He hit Pause and the TV blared back on.

"Wait." Kristine took the remote out of his hand and hit Pause. "There's something else. I . . ." Her stomach flipped with nerves. "I . . . I want you to come with me."

Kevin's forehead scrunched up. "Honey, I can't just take off with barely any notice. We'll do it another time."

"I knew you'd say that. So . . ." Kristine pulled out a crumpled piece of paper and dropped it on the coffee table. "I want to cash this in."

Kevin read the note. "The IOU?" He laughed. "Kris, no. This is for a pair of diamond earrings or a spa day or something. Not to guilt me into doing something I can't do."

Kristine's heart sank. The last thing she'd buy would be a pair of diamond earrings or a trip to the spa. Didn't he know her at all? But the real issue wasn't even that. It was the fact that he wasn't going to go. It was the opportunity of a lifetime and he wasn't even going to *consider* it. Sitting back in her chair, Kristine felt her eyes smart.

"Kevin, we need this," she said, her voice low. "Our marriage needs this."

"Our marriage?" Kevin looked at her like she had three heads. "What do you—"

Maybe it was time to tell him the truth.

"The other night," she said, "I spent our anniversary sitting in a wine bar, wishing I was having a conversation with you about things that matter to me."

*Okay, fine. Maybe an abridged version of the truth.*

"You're mad that I wasn't here for our anniversary." Kevin turned to her, giving her his full attention. "I know. I was upset, too."

"Not *mad*. I just . . ." Kristine picked up a crouton and rubbed it between her fingers until it crumbled. "I miss you," she said, reaching for his hand. "I miss spending time with you. Please just think about it, okay?"

The Pause button must have expired, because the television snapped back on and football highlights roared through the den. Kevin held her hand, staring at the television with a troubled look on his face. "Absolutely. If that's what you want."

There were many things she wanted. She wanted her husband to look at her the way he had when they'd first met. She wanted to spend the weekends with him, trying new restaurants or going on getaways, instead of just recovering from a hard week of work. But most of all, she wanted him to want these things, too.

"I really want you to come with me to Rome."

Kevin's eyes were still trained on the football field. "Let me just think about it, okay?" Briefly, he squeezed her hand then let it go.

Kristine let out a breath and reached for her salad. Clearly, the conversation was over.

# Ten

The summer sun beat down on June as she stood outside, sweeping the sidewalk. More than one neighbor had peeked out in the past hour to see what she was up to. Probably because sweeping was something June simply did not do.

Well, let them stare. She was not about to miss the arrival of Rose, who, according to Bernice, was planning to pay a visit to Charley. With a casserole. Wearing that bloodred lipstick.

*The tramp.*

It was perfectly fine with June if Rose wanted to establish a reputation. She was welcome to go after every widowed—*or married*—man in town, but when it came to June's neighbor, such behavior was wildly inappropriate. What if Charley actually fell for her tricks? If that happened, Rose would eventually take over Charley's garden and spend every waking minute trying to outdo June. Charley might even start saying things like, "Why, your blooms are the best in town, Rose."

*Oooh!*

June swept furiously. Within seconds, sweat was pouring down her face. Apparently, the sun did not stop shining simply because she decided to spend a little time working on her front sidewalk, which was a shame. She leaned against the broom to catch her breath. While doing so, she noticed for the hundredth time that her legs were covered in inky varicose veins. So many of her friends had gotten that surgery to make them go away, but June was wary of anything that had to do with needles.

"Grandma, what are you doing?" a familiar voice demanded.

June practically jumped out of her skin. Turning, she came face-to-face with her granddaughter. Chloe was dressed in a T-shirt and jeans with that ratty-looking book bag thrown over one shoulder. Her curly brown hair was pulled up in a ponytail.

"Hello, darling." June kissed her cheeks as though they were at a cocktail party. Her granddaughter smelled like pink bubble-gum, even though she did not appear to be chewing any. "How are you?"

Chloe eyed her. "It's a thousand degrees out here. Have you finally lost your mind?"

June blinked. "I'm just keeping the sidewalk nice."

"I can see that," Chloe said. "But A, you don't sweep. B, this sidewalk is perfectly clean. Which leads me to C. You are up to something."

June sighed. She hated the way these schools taught deductive reasoning. "The sidewalk is clean because I've *been* sweeping. You should have seen it before I started. It was a mess."

"Hmmph." Chloe watched her closely.

June leaned against the broom and decided to change the subject. "You are a lovely distraction. To what do I owe the pleasure?"

"Just got out of class." Her granddaughter yawned. "On my way to work. The usual."

June nodded. The kid's gym where Chloe worked was only five blocks from June's home. Not that she would ever set foot inside it. If children weren't related to her, June wasn't interested, thank you very much.

Chloe glanced at her watch. "Can we go inside? I've only got twenty minutes to grab a snack. I need some fuel or those kids will tear me apart."

"Oh." June gave a desperate look around. "Um . . . You go ahead. I just want to . . ."

"Grandma!" Chloe said. "Seriously. Are you feeling okay?"

"Yes, of course. I am simply concerned about a rumor I heard." Leaning in close, June whispered, "If you must know, my neighborhood is in great danger."

"That's it." Chloe whipped out her cell phone. "I'm calling Mom."

"No," June cried. What did the girl want? A full report right here in the middle of the sidewalk? "Chloe, I feel fine. I—"

Just then, June spotted Rose. She was strutting down the sidewalk, decked out in a pair of white shorts, a white polo shirt and tiny pink scarf around her neck. The wind blew just slightly and the scarf flitted in the wind. The whole spectacle reminded June of those music videos Kristine used to watch when she was in high school.

"Toodle-loo," Rose called, waggling her fingers. "Isn't this a beautiful morning?"

Swooping in, Rose kissed June hard on each cheek. June practically choked on the overpowering scent of lavender perfume.

"Hi, Rose." Chloe squinted in the sun. "You look nice."

"She does not," June barked, taking in Rose's outfit. There was no trademark taffeta to be seen. In fact, Rose's shirt was . . . "That's a golf shirt!" This was deeply disturbing, as Rose did not play golf. But Charley did.

"Why, yes." Rose smoothed down the front of the shirt, her augmented breasts shifting with the motion. "I thought I'd take it up again. I've always played a little," she said, "over at the club."

June eyed her, suspicious. "I don't remember you ever mentioning that."

"Well." Rose appeared to check her lipstick in the foil cover of the casserole. "Perhaps you're losing your memory." Looking up, she blinked her cat eyes. "Getting old can be a bitch."

"You can say that again," June muttered.

"It's been lovely chatting with you, but I am actually here to pay a visit to your neighbor. I believe he lives . . ." Rose made a big deal out of scanning the magnificent brownstones, before pointing at the one right next to June's. "There." She gave a happy sigh. "What a lovely home."

With that, Rose swept away in a cloud of perfume. As she pranced up Charley's steps, her legs perfectly tanned and varicose free, June leaned against her broom like Cinderella.

June watched as Charley answered the door. Silver hair shining, he listened closely to Rose. Throwing one last sly look at June, Rose slipped through Charley's front door.

June's heart sunk. "It is truly unbelievable," she said, picking up the broom, "that someone over seventy could be such a complete and total hussy."

Chloe studied June. "Interesting. Very, *very* interesting."

"What?" June did not like the way her granddaughter was looking at her. "What are you saying?"

"Nothing." Chloe shrugged. "I'm not saying anything at all."

# Eleven

"I hate you!" Mary Beth Gable screamed.

Chloe closed her eyes and counted to ten. Even though she loved her job at Tiny Tumblers, the kid's gym, there were days when she just wanted to rip out her hair. Today was one of those days.

"Mary Beth," she sighed, getting down on one knee. "I know you didn't mean to hurt Asher. But when you hurt someone, you don't laugh. You apologize. So, please say you're sorry."

Asher, pale and nervous by nature, let out a sniffle. Chloe put her hand on his back. The poor thing would be traumatized for life, all thanks to Mary Beth. The four-year-old hellion had decided it would be a great idea to leap off the monkey bars and use Asher as a landing pad.

Chloe was across the room when it happened, sanitizing the mats. The moment was awful, like watching a cheetah taking down a gazelle. Poor Asher had screamed in fear and promptly wet his pants. After tracking down dry clothes for Asher and giving him an ice-cream bar, Chloe was doing her best to get Mary Beth to apologize, but the little girl refused.

"Mary Beth." Chloe kept her voice low and calm. "Please say you're sorry."

Mary Beth put her hands on her hips, debating. She was dressed in purple leggings and a pink and purple T-shirt that read, *My dad can beat up your dad*. Chloe doubted that the little girl would indeed be so confident if she actually did meet Chloe's father.

"No." Mary Beth stomped her feet. With each stomp, her tennis shoes lit up. "No, no, no, no, no, no, *no*." Then the little girl made a move to kick Chloe in the shins.

"Hey!" Chloe jumped back just in time.

Shaking her head, she wondered at the textbook aggression. Mary Beth was obviously from a broken home. Chloe would love to get a look at her father, just to see who was raising such a monster. Of course, he was never there. Mary Beth was dropped off at Tiny Tumblers by nannies and rarely the same one.

Since this particular approach to getting an apology wasn't working, Chloe decided to switch tactics. "Asher." She turned to the little boy. "Do you want an apology for what happened?"

Asher squinted through his tears. Mary Beth narrowed her eyes.

He shook his head. "No."

Chloe looked at him in surprise. "Asher, you can't let women walk all over you." The sentiment reminded her of a similar speech she'd made, back when Ben was in the fifth grade. "You need to stand up for yourself. Say, *Mary Beth, I want you to apolo—*"

"What the hell is going on here?"

Chloe leapt to her feet. To her absolute horror, Dr. Gable was standing on the red, blue and yellow mats, his hands on his hips. He wore yet another tweed jacket, as well as a light blue shirt. This time, his stupid ascot was pink and patterned with light blue diamonds.

"What are *you* doing here?" Chloe demanded.

Hopefully, he was not here to tell her off. First of all, that would be a little creepy, considering Tiny Tumblers was her place of employment. Second of all . . . that would actually be *really* creepy, since he was at her place of employment. How on earth did he know where she worked anyway?

Chloe felt a jolt of fear. Mary Beth and Asher were always the last kids to get picked up. Sneaking a peek at the glass door that led out to the busy street, she hoped their parents or a nanny would show up soon.

"Look." Chloe kept her voice steady, so as not to frighten the children. "I'm sorry I called you a name and slammed your office door. But you can't be here. This isn't the time or the place—"

Dr. Gable looked at Chloe as though she were nuts. "I'm here to pick up my daughter." He placed a hand on Mary Beth's shoulder. "And I'm not pleased that she seems to be so upset."

Chloe's jaw dropped. "*You're* Mary Beth's father?" Looking back and forth between the two, she suddenly saw the resemblance. The two shared the same high forehead, curly hair and olive complexion. Not to mention the same air of entitlement and stinky disposition.

"In that case, I'm glad you're here." Chloe's tone was indignant. "Your daughter was bullying this child. She's upset because I was asking her to apolo—"

At this, Mary Beth let out an ear-piercing scream.

"It's okay, honey." Dr. Gable patted her shoulder. "Settle down. Let's go get some ice cream."

Even Asher seemed offended by this.

"Uh, I'm sorry," Chloe said. "But you are a psychologist."

"So?"

"So, you . . ." She squeezed her hands together, trying to remain calm. "More than anyone else in this city, should know that it is completely inappropriate for a four-year-old to bully another child and receive a reward for her behavior."

Dr. Gable opened his mouth as though to argue.

Chloe pointed at Asher. "Your daughter *attacked* this child."

Asher gave a dramatic sniffle.

"This is the third time this month I've seen that type of behavior from her. It's completely unacceptable and . . . and highly dysfunctional. If it happens again, I will have to ask you to with-draw her from Tiny Tumblers."

Mary Beth's eyes went wide. She shoved her thumb in her mouth.

Dr. Gable was outraged. "All over some ice cream? If I want to get my daughter some ice cream, that's up to me."

Chloe considered the wrinkles around his eyes. Dr. Gable had to be about ten years older than her but he had no right to act so superior. He obviously had no idea how to raise a child.

"It's not about the ice cream." Stepping forward, she lowered her voice so that only he could hear. "But if you want to raise a little serial killer, that's up to you."

Dr. Gable turned a bright purple, which clashed horribly with his pink ascot.

Chloe got back down on one knee and regarded Mary Beth. "I really want you to come back and play with us. So, from now on, I am going to trust that you're going to be a big girl and stop hurting other people, okay?"

Mary Beth considered this. Finally, she nodded.

"Mary Beth." Dr. Gable's tone was sharp. "Go get your bag."

Chloe kept her voice deliberately gentle. "Take Asher with you," she said. "Hold his hand."

Chloe watched the two figures stomp across the room toward the colored cubbyholes. Getting to her feet, she regarded Dr. Gable with disdain. The air felt thick between them.

"A little serial killer?" he said, indignant. "I can't believe you said that. And you plan to have a career working with children?"

"An ice cream?" she shot back. "I can't believe you said *that.* And you actually have a career where you give other people advice?"

Dr. Gable studied her for a long moment. Finally, he shook his head. "Look, you're right. I'm sorry." He let out a hearty sigh and shoved his hands into the pockets of his jacket. "About this and . . . that day in my office."

Chloe blinked. "Oh." There was a lengthy pause. "Really?"

Dr. Gable adjusted his ascot. "Yes. We got off on the wrong foot. Initially, I had invited you to my office to discuss a long-term plan for your grant application. But I didn't expect you to be a day early. And I really didn't expect you to catch me singing. I was . . . embarrassed. I'm sorry."

Chloe was stunned. "Is this some sort of reverse psychology?"

"No. It's an apology." Dr. Gable seemed to shift in his shoes. "That day, you surprised me. Not just by being early but with your confidence. I didn't expect that from a student."

"Grad student," Chloe clarified.

He smiled. "There you go again. Grad student."

Chloe smiled back.

"Look, I'd like to make it up to you. Would you let me take you to dinner?" The furrow between his eyebrows deepened. "Let me clarify that I will not write you a letter of recommendation for that grant. In my professional opinion, you lack the time or experience to do it justice. Perhaps it's something to revisit in a couple of years, but not now. Either way, the invitation to dinner still stands."

Wait. He was asking her out on a *date*? Yes, he'd been a total jerk in his office but . . . She blushed, remembering the close fit of those green sweatpants.

"What about Saturday night at eight?" Dr. Gable asked. "Does that work for you?"

Was this actually happening? She thought back to watching him up on the stage, speaking to her school. Was that same man *really* asking her out?

"Uh . . . " Chloe swallowed hard. "Okay."

"Great. I can pick you up . . ."

"Here," Chloe blurted out. She certainly didn't want this man to witness her crappy Wicker Park apartment. Or go through the third degree with Ben.

"Daddy!" Mary Beth sprinted across the room, Asher closely

behind. Obviously, all was forgiven. "Come on. Let's go to the park."

Dr. Gable got down on one knee. "Daddy has to go back to work." He kissed her on the head. "But maybe we can get away with it for a few minutes before I drop you off at Miss Marshall's."

Chloe hoped that Miss Marshall was ninety and had warts all over her face.

Getting to his feet, Dr. Gable studied Chloe for a long moment. Something passed between them. A spark, an understanding, a challenge . . . She didn't know what it was. But she was suddenly very interested to find out.

Chloe felt her cheeks flush. "It was good to see you, Dr. Gable."

"Geoff," he said, smiling. Taking Mary Beth's hand, he headed for the door. "See you Saturday."

Once he left, Chloe realized that her legs were trembling. Literally shaking with nerves. She really needed to stop drinking so much caffeine.

"Miss Chloe?" Asher's pale, serious face stared up at her. "Are you okay?"

"Yes, doll." Chloe put a hand on his tiny shoulder. "Just fine."

"You don't seem fine." Asher let out a world-weary sigh. "But I guess it's just one of those things I'll understand when I'm older."

Chloe laughed. "I don't know about that, kiddo." Through the front window, she watched Mary Beth and *Geoff* disappear in the stream of people walking over the bridge. "I hate to tell ya this, but even when you get older, there are still a lot of things in life that are not easy to understand."

# Twelve

"Hello, hello," June chirped, throwing open the door. "So happy you both could make it!"

Kristine exchanged an amused glance with Chloe. June said this every Thursday, as if spending the evening together was optional. June had started the tradition when Chloe started college and the three had spent Thursdays together ever since.

Typically, they did something tame but on occasion, June liked to shake things up. She'd signed them up for bungee jumping, belly dancing and stand-up comedy. Once, they'd even stalked Oprah's penthouse. Kristine wouldn't be surprised if she said, "Come on, girls! We're getting matching tattoos."

Tonight looked like an art night, as the table in the dining room was piled high with scrapbook pages, family photos and stickers. Chloe rushed past it and toward the antique hutch stocked with snacks. Shoving a handful of chocolate-covered peanuts into her mouth, she said, "The best part about Thursdays is the snacks. I should probably go on a date with a dentist, not a psychologist."

June's eyes widened. "Date? Did you say date?"

Chloe popped a piece of sea salt caramel in her mouth. Then she pointed at her lips as though to indicate they were too busy chewing to say another word.

Kristine laughed. "She loves to torture us. Don't worry, Mom. You'll get it out of her."

June slid on a pair of reading glasses with pink frames, exactly like the ones Kristine had picked up at Walgreens two days ago. Great. She was turning into her mother. *That* should help her relationship with Kevin.

"Hundreds of years ago," June read from the notebook where she stored her research for their Thursday nights, "Englanders invented Commonbooks to record their memories. They'd decorate a page with letters, pictures or whatever to call to mind a particular moment in time. Tonight, we will create a page to represent our lives, using these . . . thingamajigs to do it." She waved her hand at the table. "Who knows?" June shut her notebook and beamed. "Maybe, with time, we'll keep adding to our book and our story."

Kristine sifted through some of the pictures June had set out. There were a couple of cute ones, especially of Chloe when she was little. And a few with Kevin, that just made her feel sad.

"So." June reached for a pink scrapbook page. "Chloe, tell me about my future grandson-in-law."

"It's just a date, Grandma." Chloe groaned. "There's nothing to tell. Besides, it's not going to work out." She crumpled a napkin and grinned. "I called him an asshole when we first met."

"And he still asked you out?" June eyed her from over the frames of her glasses. "It sounds like . . . what's his name?"

"Geoff," Chloe said. "With a G."

"Geoff with a G is *clearly* in love with you already." June applied glue to a pink felt flower and pressed it onto her page. "I predict marriage and children by the end of the year. You did catch that bouquet."

"So did you," Chloe pointed out. "And Mom."

Kristine shook her head. She didn't like to think about the bouquet. Even though June had insisted that she save a handful of baby's breath and keep it for good luck, the whole thing made her uncomfortable. If another marriage was supposed to be on the horizon, what did that say about her and Kevin?

When Kristine didn't say anything, Chloe turned her attention to the window. "Grandma, your neighbor's outside. Working away."

"La di dah." June made a face. "I've been thinking I should call the police and report him."

"Why would you report him?" Chloe asked. "Are his sunflowers back?"

Kristine laughed. "I forgot about that."

Last summer, Charley's sunflowers had grown in so strong and so tall that they shaded a twenty-five percent area of June's garden. Yes, June was certain of this figure. She measured it.

"Laugh all you want." June sprinkled some pink glitter across her page. "But I think it's important for you to know that if anything happens to me, it's because I've finally confronted that terrible man."

"You told him off?" Chloe asked, taking a seat at the table. "Maybe he'll ask you out."

June's hand froze midair. "I simply cannot think of anything worse."

"Midterms," Chloe said as Kristine blurted out, "Inventory audits."

June thought for a moment. "Menopause."

The three of them reflected on this.

"Oh!" Chloe pointed at Kristine. "Mom. When were you going to tell us *your* big news?"

Kristine fidgeted. "Big news?"

"Uh, *Rome*?" Turning to June, Chloe said, "She won a trip. Can you believe I had to learn this from Dad?"

Kristine gave a nervous laugh and explained about the essay contest. She focused on her art project as she talked, placing travel stickers in a neat pattern on her page, wondering how long it would take for—

"I assume Kevin will be joining you?" June asked.

*Ten seconds. Not bad.*

"Um . . ." Kristine reached for an outdated copy of *National Geographic* and started flipping through the pages. "He's thinking about it."

June blinked. "You're going alone?"

"With an employee." Kristine tried to keep her voice casual, already knowing that her mother would not approve. "Ethan wrote the winning essay, so . . ."

June peered at Kristine. "You're traveling with a man?"

Getting up from the table, Kristine walked over to the snack table. Reaching for a brownie, she said, "I'd like Kevin to come. He might. He's thinking about it."

"Dad hates to travel," Chloe said. "Almost as much as Grandma."

"I do not *hate* to travel," June said. "I just prefer to stay in Chicago. Everything I need is at my front door."

There was a loud crash outside and everyone jumped. Charley was standing next to the fence, dumping yard waste into a trash bin. Seeing an opportunity to change the subject, Kristine said, "You didn't tell us why you want to report Charley to the police."

After a long moment, June turned her attention to the window. "I don't know. I just don't trust him," she said. "If I end up missing, he's buried my body in the garden."

"Well," Chloe said, "you always say he doesn't know how to buy a decent fertilizer."

Kristine laughed. "I wish you liked him. He seems like such a nice man."

"Exactly," June said. "They always seem nice. Until."

"Maybe you just need to be a better neighbor," Chloe said. "Then, you wouldn't have to worry about it."

June bristled. "I am a lovely neighbor. I raise the value of our neighborhood just by . . . just by staying alive."

"You're a lovely neighbor?" Kristine said. "Oh, okay. Have you . . . shoveled his snow?"

"Raked his leaves?" Chloe asked. "Baked him some cookies?"

The two of them cracked up. Chloe laughed so hard she pounded the table. The colorful little decorations June had so carefully collected jumped like jumping beans.

June pressed her lips together tightly. "I hope that one of these days," she said, "I'll have a family that takes me seriously."

Chloe squeezed her hand. "If I were you, Grandma, I wouldn't hold my breath."

# Thirteen

Ben rushed into the bar. From his rumpled T-shirt, jeans and baseball cap, Chloe could tell he'd just gotten out of bed. She felt bad for waking him but the things June had said about her date with Geoff had freaked her out. If this date really was a big deal, Chloe needed Ben's input . . . bad.

Peeling herself out of their typical booth, Chloe pushed her way through a small crowd of people. She stumbled into Ben and pulled him into a tight bear hug. "Oooph." Her face smashed into the soft material of his T-shirt. He smelled spicy, like someone who'd just woken up.

Chloe gazed up at him with adoration. "You're a lifesaver."

Ben raised his eyebrows. "Um . . . are you drunk?"

After leaving June's, Chloe had raced to the bar and downed an entire vodka soda. "I'm not drunk . . . I'm just not as alcohol tolerant as I used to be."

Taking his large hand in hers, Chloe led him back to their booth. There was a Sam Adams waiting for him and a fresh vodka soda waiting for her. Moisture had beaded up on the glasses of both drinks, and Chloe reached for hers, taking a hearty sip.

"I don't remember you ever being alcohol tolerant." Ben slid into the wooden booth. "The first time we ever got drunk together, you punched me in the face."

Chloe laughed. "You totally deserved it."

The first time Chloe and Ben had ever tried alcohol was in the eighth grade. She was supposed to be at basketball practice but when it got cancelled, she called Ben. He swiped three bottles of Woodchuck Cider from his parents' fridge and sneaked them over in his blue backpack. After drawing the shades on the window and locking her bedroom door, they took a seat on the bed. Ceremoniously, Ben passed Chloe a bottle. They'd clinked the necks, then took their first nervous sip. Ben raised his eyebrows, as though he liked it, but Chloe thought it tasted like rotten apple juice. Not wanting to seem like a wimp, she drank it anyway.

The alcohol made her sleepy, so instead of sharing the third bottle of cider like they'd planned, she snuggled up next to Ben and dozed off as they watched a movie. She awoke to the sensation of his hand under her shirt, feeling her right breast.

Chloe remembered this moment of her life in vivid detail. She could still see the pattern of the leaves on the ceiling, from the big tree just outside her window. She could smell the cider on her own breath and the powder of her deodorant as it burst into action. And she could remember everything about the way Ben's warm, rough hand felt as he slowly explored her body.

Even though this moment wasn't the first time she'd been touched by a boy—Jake Rogers had felt her up at a movie, brushing his thumb over the fabric of her lacy bra—this was the first time it had happened on bare skin. It was also the first time Chloe actually felt something. At Ben's touch, strange sensations coursed through her body, particularly a longing between her legs.

When Chloe finally turned to look at Ben, the mattress shifting under her weight, she wondered if he was going to kiss her. She was surprised to find him staring at her with an intensity that went far beyond anything that her thirteen-year-old, hormone-tortured mind could handle. So, Chloe did the only thing she could—she drew back her fist and punched him in the face.

Ben yelped like a golden retriever, yanked his hand out of her shirt and bolted, totally forgetting his backpack. Chloe refused to give it back until he swore to never do anything like that again. True to his word, he hadn't.

Studying him now, Chloe grinned. "Did I really wake you up?"

Ben looked at his watch. "It's one thirty in the morning. Take a wild guess."

"You should turn off your phone." She had learned that lesson years ago, when June went through her insomnia phase. Because Chloe was in college, June assumed it was more than acceptable to call her at any hour of the night, letting the phone ring and ring until she picked up.

"I'm not going to turn off my ringer," Ben said. "What if you'd been in trouble or something?" Taking off his baseball cap, he ran his hand through his blond curls and gave a loud yawn. His teeth were big and white, even in the back of his mouth. Ben had never had a cavity, which was incredibly annoying. Chloe seemed to have one every time she went to the dentist.

"Actually, I thought you *were* in trouble." Ben put his hat on his head and leaned back in the booth. "Why else would you call me in the middle of the night?"

"I *am* in trouble." Chloe gave an awkward laugh. "Today, in a *Twilight Zone* turn of events, that mean psychologist guy asked me out on a date. And . . ." For some reason, she felt nervous, like Ben was going to scold her. Like she'd done something wrong. "I said yes."

Ben raised an eyebrow. "You did what?"

She cringed. "Yeah."

"Right . . ." He scratched his head. "This is the same guy that you called an asshole?"

"Yup."

"The same one that you moped about for two days?"

"The very same."

Ben put his head in his hands. "Chloe."

"I know, I know . . ." And she did know. Dr. Gable had been horrible when they'd first met. "I like him." She plucked the lime out of her drink and dropped it onto her napkin. It made a wet spot that slowly expanded out and across the paper. "I've had a crush on him since he spoke at our school."

"Yeah, but come on." Ben grabbed the napkin and wadded it up. "Since when are you into guys who are mean to you?"

"It was a misunderstanding. He was nervous, I was nervous . . ."

Ben took a drink of beer, not saying anything. He pulled his baseball cap low over his eyes.

"Look . . ." Chloe touched his hand. "The man wears ascots. He can't be that bad."

"I'm sorry. Did you just say . . . ?"

"Ascots."

"Huh." Ben sat back in the booth with a thud. "Ass-cots," he said, drawing the word out. "This guy sounds like a douche. I can guarantee he's not good enough for you."

Considering the fact that Dr. Gable was thirty-six, owned his own practice and knew how to rock a pair of green sweatpants, Chloe couldn't help but disagree. Still, she'd called Ben here for a reason.

"I knew you'd say that." She took a deep breath. "But I need your help. I haven't gone on a date in forever. I need you to coach me."

Ben snorted. "Give me a break. You don't need any coaching."

There was a wooden bowl full of wasabi-covered peanuts sitting on the table. Ben scooped up a few and popped them into his mouth. His eyes scanned the bar, as though trying to figure out exactly how he'd been conned out of his cozy bed.

"Ben, I'm serious." Chloe's cheeks colored slightly. "I haven't gone on a date since undergrad."

He stopped chewing. "Come on." Thinking, he rubbed his

hand against the blond stubble lining his jaw. "No. That's not true. You were seeing—"

"I've hung *out* with people." Ben had met more than a few of the guys who had traipsed in and out of her life. "I just haven't gone on an official date. I need you to give me a crash course."

Instead of laughing in her face, Ben's bright blue eyes searched hers. "Huh. I think you're being serious." Plucking the straw from her drink, he twirled it between his fingers as though deep in thought. Finally, he popped it between his lips like a toothpick. "Okay." Adjusting the rim of his baseball cap, he gave her a sly look. "I'll do it."

"Oh, thank you," she cried. "Thank you so much." Embarrassing herself on the date with Dr. Gable would not be nearly as likely with Ben's help. Eagerly, she pulled out a notepad from her purse. Pen poised, she said, "Go for it. I'm ready."

Ben burst out laughing. "What are you doing? You're gonna take *notes*?" He reached out and touched her pen as though to convince himself it were real.

"I'm a student." Chloe snatched the pen away. "Of course I'm going to take notes."

Ben pulled his baseball cap low over his eyes. "Darlin'," he said. "You don't need to take notes. I'm not going to tell you how to go on a date. I'm going to show you."

"Show me?" she said, surprised.

"You're going on a date. With me."

Well, that was a whole different ball game. Chloe considered the idea. It was very Eliza Doolittle. She imagined Ben teaching her how to walk across the room, pronounce certain words and, at the end of the night, engage in a proper kiss. At that thought, she blushed furiously.

It was rare that Chloe allowed herself to think of Ben as a guy but considering they were sitting in a low-lit bar, sitting so close together, it was hard not to. He looked good, as always. In fact, she had to admit, he looked downright sexy.

"No," Chloe said, crossing her arms. "I don't think that's a good idea."

Ben leaned forward. His arms flexed slightly as he reached for another peanut and popped it in his mouth. "You scared? Afraid I might try to"—his eyes grazed over hers—"kiss you at the door?"

Chloe felt an involuntary flutter in her stomach. "Don't be stupid." She shifted in her seat. "I'd—"

"Punch me in the face." Ben finished the sentence for her, laughing. "I know. Alright," he said. "There's nothing to be scared of. We'll do it tomorrow." Catching her horrified expression, he clarified, "Do it, as in, we'll go on a date tomorrow."

Just as Chloe was about to insist that it was a stupid idea, that she never should have suggested it, an image of the good doctor strolled through her mind. Calm, self-assured . . . and for some reason, wearing an ascot covered with grinning alligators. It would be much smarter to make a fool out of herself in front of Ben instead of Dr. Gable.

"Alright," Chloe agreed. "I'm in." Reaching for her drink, she clinked it with Ben's. "Proof as to just how desperate I am."

"Ah," Ben said, looking like a wounded playboy. "Here's your first dating tip: Never tell a guy that you're only going out with him because you're desperate."

Chloe grinned. They sat there in silence, watching the people around them. There was a couple over by the bar making out like they were the only ones in the room. Taking a long sip of her drink, she wondered how long they'd known each other.

# Fourteen

Kristine sat on the floor behind the cash register, sorting receipts. This was one of her favorite tasks. Something about numbers soothed her. When Sudoku became a national craze, she and Kevin competed with each other to solve the puzzles. Competitive to the end, Kevin was always in it to win.

June, on the other hand, was baffled by the game. "Honestly," she'd said, flipping through a book and casting it aside. "I can't think of anything more dull than doing math for fun." Eventually, Kristine found that very same book shoved into a kitchen drawer, each puzzle perfectly solved.

Kevin wasn't surprised. "Your mother might act like a dingbat most of the time, but nine times out of ten, she's the smartest person in the room."

Because June was an intelligent woman, Kristine respected her opinion. However, it was not always welcome. Just that morning, Kristine had found a note waiting at the store.

In pinched handwriting, it read:

*Dearest Kristine, I didn't want to discuss this issue in front of Chloe last night, but please, reconsider Italy. I know that you would never do anything to jeopardize your marriage, but traveling to another country with a man who is not your husband is not a wise thing to do. Circumstance can, on occasion, make us question the choices we've made.*

Thinking of the note, Kristine wadded up a receipt. What did her mother think? That she was going to fall all over Ethan just because he was there? The whole thing reminded her of the summer travel program days, when June's well-placed doubt almost kept Kristine from boarding that boat.

The bell on the door jingled, breaking her train of thought. Getting to her feet, she was startled to see Ethan walk in. His hair was damp, as though he'd just stepped out of the shower.

"Hey." Kristine smiled. "What are you doing here?" Annie was on the schedule that day, not Ethan. In a way, she wished Annie had warned her they'd switched. That way, she'd at least have something intelligent prepared to say about Italy.

Ethan admired her light blue sundress and sandals. "You look nice."

"Oh." Kristine's hair was pulled back in its typical sloppy bun. She hadn't gotten around to putting on makeup yet, either, so she imagined her freckles were in full bloom. "I was sprawled out on the floor before you got here." Brushing some imaginary dirt off her legs, she straightened her dress. "It's a good thing you weren't a customer."

"I don't know that it would have been all that bad for business. I think it would create a very relaxed, no-pressure approach."

All week, Kristine had felt guilty about the time she'd spent with Ethan on her anniversary. She'd felt equally guilty at the prospect of traveling with him to Rome. But now, that all seemed completely ridiculous. Sure, the man was attractive, but he was also easy to talk to. There was nothing odd about wanting to develop a friendship with someone like that, nothing lascivious like June had implied.

"I'm so excited about Rome, Ethan. Thank you so much." She shook her head, still amazed. "Customs should put us on a watch list. They're going to have a hard time getting me to leave."

Ethan's dark eyes danced. "I can think of worse things than

spending the rest of my life in Italy, eating carpaccio and drinking wine."

Looking around her store, Kristine considered what she'd have to leave behind to become an expatriate. Books, travel gizmos, cultural posters . . . and Kevin, of course. He would never sacrifice his beloved Chicago microbreweries for a life of red wine. Cheese, maybe. But not the wine.

Ethan headed to the bookshelves. "Come here," he called. "Have you seen this yet?" Ethan pulled down a photography book.

She walked over to join him. "Of course. I love that book."

The black-and-white photos captured what she imagined as the very essence of Rome. Opening the book, Ethan flipped through the pages. He did this deliberately, as though willing his eye to capture each and every detail on the page.

"In my work," Ethan mused, "I try to convey passion, true emotion. It's such a challenge, but Klein makes it look easy."

"I thought there was a lot of emotion in your work." The comical fish from New Caledonia jumped to mind. "That fish photo was . . ." She smiled. "I don't know. It struck me as funny, in some way."

Turning the page, he smiled. "Ah. This woman reminds me of you."

As she leaned over his shoulder, the earthy scent of his cologne settled over her. There was something sharp behind the sandalwood, almost exotic.

"What do you think?" Ethan asked.

Kristine studied the photograph. It was a picture of a sexy woman in a cream-colored dress walking down an alley and admiring a painting, while a man in the alley admired her. *Did Ethan really think this woman was anything like Kristine?* That was impossible. The woman in the photograph was brazen and beautiful, nothing like her. Still, she felt her cheeks turning bright red at the thought.

"It's her essence," Ethan said. His dark eyes glanced up at her. "She has an elegance about her. A curiosity."

"I think you're giving me too much credit." Kristine was anything but elegant. After all, her life had been spent chasing after a child. Cooking, cleaning, doing laundry. Wasting time learning about places she would probably never see. She had lived a life that was typical, yes. Elegant? No.

Ethan closed the book and cradled it against his chest like a lover. "I don't think you give yourself enough credit," he said, turning to her.

The energy in the room shifted to something soft, intimate. It was like those pauses in between the conversation they'd shared earlier that week, when she got the distinct feeling that, if her husband were there watching, he wouldn't be pleased.

"You know, I have to admit something," Ethan said. "Even though I was happy to win the contest, I felt guilty. I thought maybe I should have asked for your permission to enter first. Considering you were part of the equation."

"Why? I'm thrilled." Kristine hugged her arms against her chest. "You didn't have to ask."

A rowdy group of children chose that moment to rush through the front door. They were followed by their mother, who looked ready to leave them with the first person willing to take them. The kids raced toward the children's section, and the mother made a beeline for the coffee.

"It looks like we're under attack," Ethan said. "I'll take care of it." Carefully, he reached up and re-shelved the book. The muscles in his back flexed just slightly. "Keep me posted on what you need today." He touched her arm as he walked past. "I'm here, so use me for whatever."

# Fifteen

Chloe's eyes blurred as she stared into the mirror. In preparation for her date with Ben, she'd found a makeup application chart online. It had a section on how to create smoky eyes, which she was following like a paint-by-number.

Considering she rarely wore makeup, it wasn't going well. So far, Chloe did not look like Angelina Jolie as the website had promised. She looked like a girl with a black eye. Frustrated, she pep-talked her reflection. "Why are you even trying so hard? It's not like this is a *real* date. It's just Ben."

Still, the date mattered. It was so rare that she took the time to get all dressed up that Chloe wanted to make it count. Maybe to show Ben or even herself that there actually was a girl somewhere in there. Even though the date was just practice, she'd spent the past two hours getting ready.

After a lavender-scented bath, Chloe combed gel through her curly brown hair and let it air-dry as she hunted for an outfit. She dug through her closet until she found a gray pencil skirt and a short-sleeved black sweater that actually made her look like she had curves. Finally, she spritzed on some vanilla and pomegranate perfume.

Chloe was pleased with the results until she'd started in on the whole makeup chart thing. It was so frustrating that she was half tempted to wash her face, take off the fancy outfit and slip back into her normal clothes. But then she thought about Geoff and the fact that she would be seeing him tomorrow. She had to make this work.

Biting her lip, she picked up the makeup brush. "Just keep your hand steady," she whispered. "Like a surgeon."

*Bang, bang, bang!*

Chloe jumped, smearing the liquid eyeliner down to her cheekbone.

"Shit."

Frantically, she scrubbed at the black smudge. It wouldn't budge. Grabbing the concealer, she did her best to cover it up as Ben banged away at the door. Whiskers raced down the hall, her tiny paws thundering against the wooden floors.

"Ben, just key in," she cried. "You're scaring the cat."

"Answer the door," he shouted back. "It's a date."

Letting out a huge sigh, Chloe dropped the makeup brush and stomped into the living room. She threw back her shoulders and opened the door.

"Holy shit," Ben said.

Chloe's heart skipped a beat. "Holy shit, yourself. You look great."

Ben, who was normally dressed in a ratty T-shirt and a pair of jeans, looked hot. He was wearing a pair of fitted charcoal slacks and a short-sleeve button-up shirt. His skin was brighter than usual, as though he'd taken a washcloth to his face and scrubbed hard. His typically unruly curls were neatly gelled into place and there was one persistent straggler hanging over his forehead, giving him that slightly rumpled "I care but I don't" look.

"Uh . . ." Ben studied her with concern. "I kind of meant, holy shit, what happened to your face?"

Chloe's heart sunk. "Makeup. I was going for smoky eyes."

Immediately, he said, "Oh, I see. Yeah, looks good."

That was one thing she loved about Ben. He might tease her or give her a hard time, but the moment he saw she was serious about something, he was quick to be kind. "Thank you," she said. "But no, it doesn't."

Marching into the bathroom, Chloe snatched up the makeup application guide and brought it back out to him. "Look at this thing. It's like a blueprint to launch a spaceship or something."

Ben studied the chart and shook his head. "You followed a diagram. Who does that?"

"A girl who has no clue what she's doing," she said. "Here and now, I would like to apologize for calling the girls that you date dumb. Considering the amount of makeup they manage to slather on, I'd have to say that most of them are actually pretty bright."

Ben nodded. "Rocket scientists. For sure."

"It tried to be helpful. Look. In addition to smoky eyes, it showed me how to define my cheekbones and my lips. I think I did okay."

Ben considered the chart, then her. "Yup. Very precise." He squinted. "In fact, you're kinda like a work of art therapy. We could probably analyze you. That blush definitely represents a fear of clowns."

Chloe raced over to the mirror hanging over the white brick mantel and peered at her reflection. "Totally." She started to laugh. "See the sharp point of the eyeliner? An intense desire to succeed."

"And that horrific pink lip gloss . . ." Ben was laughing now, too. "That obviously represents a deep-rooted hatred for Barbie."

"Oh, my gosh," she said, wiping her eyes. A streak of black smeared against her hand like an oil slick. "This is why I love you."

"You love me?" Ben's face split into a grin. "A little forward for a first date, but I'll take it." He held out a tiny flower. "On that note . . . Chloe, would you accept this rose?"

Oh, how perfect. They'd spent so many nights together watching *The Bachelor*, trying to guess who would get picked during the rose ceremony. Chloe was terrible at guessing who would walk away with the rose. Ben was right almost every time.

"Yes," she said. "I would." Reaching for the flower, she stopped. It was not a red rose, but a dried pink one with a white ribbon attached. It seemed awfully familiar. Chloe studied it for a moment and turned to her refrigerator.

The flower from the bouquet was suspiciously absent.

"You stole my rose! When did you do that?"

"Yesterday. When I pretended I was out of milk." Ben flopped down on the couch, clearly proud of himself. "I was going to get you some real flowers but this one felt much more appropriate."

Chloe was confused. "In what way?"

"Oh . . ." Ben fidgeted for a moment. "It's from that wedding bouquet, right? So, I just thought that . . ." His voice trailed off. Clearing his throat, he reached for a magazine.

Chloe still didn't get it. "Thought that . . . what?"

Ben put the magazine back down and reached for the remote control. Then, he set that down, too. Finally, he looked back up at her, his blue eyes bright. "You know."

"No. What?"

He tapped his fingers against the edge of the table but didn't say anything. She hated it when he was cagey. He wasn't going to tell her what he meant, no matter how long she stood there.

"Okay." Chloe shook her head, looking down at the rose. "Let me go wash this gunk off my face, then we can go."

"Yup." He pulled out his cell phone and started to play a game at full volume.

After hanging the flower back in its rightful spot on the fridge, Chloe headed toward the hallway. For some reason, she glanced back at Ben. His eyes were following her every movement. Immediately, he went back to his game.

Chloe put her hand on the wall, baffled. "Were you just checking me out?"

He gave a slight smile. "Oh, just go get ready." Chloe lowered her hand from the wall. Straightening her skirt, she started to walk back to the bathroom. "But I don't know why you had to dress so hot," he mumbled.

Delighted, Chloe turned back to him. "Really? You think I look hot?" She did a quick twirl, pleased to note that his eyes followed her every movement. "That kinda makes up for the 'holy shit, what happened to your face' remark."

Ben's eyes were intent. "Dating tip number two: If a guy likes you, he's going to play hard to get. It's just safer that way."

Chloe chewed on her upper lip. If her first two meetings with Geoff were any indication, that was the truth. Until he'd asked her out, she had no idea he was interested in her. None at all.

But when Chloe was in the bathroom, scrubbing her face with a wet washcloth, it suddenly hit her. When Ben said that thing about playing hard to get, he was talking about something *he'd* said to her. Did that mean . . . ?

She looked at herself in the mirror, her gray eyes wide. No. It was impossible. Ben couldn't possibly . . .

"Chloe, come on," he bellowed. "We've got reservations!"

Ruefully, Chloe hung up the washcloth and towel-dried her face.

*Nope.*

Clearly, Ben didn't think of her that way at all.

Friday evening, June was curled up in an armchair drinking a cup of hot cocoa and wrapped in a red afghan. The air-conditioning was on full blast, so the room had a nice chill. Sometimes there were benefits to being the only person rattling around this big old house.

Back when Eugene was alive, they had massive fights over the thermostat. June liked it to be cold as she slept, while Eugene wanted it warm. At night, she would pretend to need a glass of water, then sneak off and lower the temperature. He would pretend to want a snack, then go down and turn it up. So it went, until the two finally had no choice but to come to a "happy compromise."

That's what Eugene had always called it.

June smiled at the memory of her husband. It brought her joy to finally be able to think of him without getting depressed. Losing him had been so hard. His heart attack was completely unexpected. One morning he was there, the next . . . gone.

It was a terrible time. June needed medication to sleep, to wake, to do anything. There were times where she'd lie in bed, trying to make a deal with God to take her instead, as though that were still an option. Some nights, she even tricked her mind into thinking Eugene was still alive. She'd listen for the sound of his key in the door.

*Anytime now,* June would think, listening hard. *Anytime . . .*

Once she'd finally accepted the fact that he was gone, June forced herself to get back on her feet. She got out of bed and tackled the basic problems associated with losing a loved one. Should she throw away Eugene's clothing, donate it or store it? *(Donate.)* Read through his personal papers or respect his privacy as she'd done when he was alive? *(Read them.)* Contact the old friends who had not yet heard of his death or allow the Christmas cards to come addressed to Mr. and Mrs. Eugene Thornill one last time? *(She waited. What could one brief season of pretending hurt?)*

Time worked like a salve. Each new day, it became that much easier to wake up in an empty bed. Each new moment, the tears that were so close to spilling over started to dry up. It was a shock to June when her friends decided it was time for her to move on.

About eighteen months after Eugene's death, June's friends

ambushed her with a setup. This had happened at the house of Marigold Mattox, and June was still working to forgive the woman. It was too soon and completely unexpected.

The night of the party, June arrived dressed in a simple black dress and a strand of pearls. It was the fall and the house had smelled like freshly baked pumpkin pie and roasted turkey.

"You look lovely." Marigold beamed, smoothing down a few stray strands of hair. "Follow me."

A slight hush fell over the well-dressed crowd when June entered the room. This was not unusual, as this type of hush had followed her like a ghost since Eugene had passed. Nonetheless, June straightened her shoulders and gave a bright smile.

The smile fell away rather quickly when she realized the group dinner consisted solely of couples. June was seated next to Johnson Bueller, a wealthy but bloated widower. He pulled out the chair next to him and patted it with enthusiasm.

"It looks like it's you and me." Mr. Bueller's cheeks were flush with drink.

Dinner began. Mr. Bueller leaned in close and probed her with questions, everything from if she liked to dance (not at this moment in time) and if she was still in the market for more children, which she did not dignify with a response. The entire situation left June aching for the familiarity of her husband. Why, oh why, did he have to leave her like this?

When Marigold picked up a crystal flute and tapped it with a small fork, June felt great relief to look somewhere other than Mr. Bueller's beady brown eyes.

"Tonight, we celebrate the magic of friendship, love and . . ." Marigold gave June a meaningful look. "New beginnings."

Since everyone was staring, June raised her glass and gave a tight smile.

The moment the guests put their attention somewhere else, June told Mr. Bueller exactly how it was. That she was unaware that this evening was a setup or she would not have come. That she did not intend to date or remarry anyone, ever. And, since the man seemed so incredibly put-out, that he was more than welcome to the rest of her wine.

June gave a little sigh at the memory and pulled the cashmere afghan closer to her. Living without companionship for all of these years had been lonely, but it had turned out just fine. Besides, June liked her life exactly the way it was. If being alone meant spending her evenings reading mystery novels, then that was fine by her.

Turning the page of her book, June focused on the story, trying to piece together the clues. Typically, she spotted the killer by page fifty but this book still had her in suspense. Rodney, an electrician with a fascination for taxidermy, was a suspect but she didn't have enough evidence to hang him.

He and a close group of friends were stranded at a cottage in the woods. A lightning storm had taken out the power. There was a loud *thunk* and . . . yes, a scream! June turned the page, eager to see who had been killed.

It was Rodney.

Well, who on earth was the killer, then?

Taking a deep breath, June kept reading, her physical grip on the book getting tighter with each deliciously frightening word. The heroine fumbled through the dark for a kitchen knife, then started to run. She rounded the corner, the sound of her heart in her ears and . . .

*Knock knock knock.*

"*Ack!*" June shrieked, dropping the book.

Heart pounding, she stared in the direction of the front door. From where she was sitting, she could only see the very edge of the wood and the doorknob. Was it her imagination or had the doorknob started to turn?

June held perfectly still, waiting. Then . . .

*Knock knock knock.*

For heaven's sake, it was as though someone intended to break down the door! Leaping to her feet, she darted into the hallway. With two hands, she grabbed a heavy candlestick off the entryway table. Creeping toward the door, she pulled back the door of the peephole.

It was Charley Montgomery.

His white hair was neatly combed and he was wearing a yellow button-up polo shirt with a white sweater vest. And he was holding a bouquet of yellow roses, which must have been picked fresh from his garden.

Flushing in confusion, June gripped the candlestick even tighter. The man wasn't . . . He wasn't bringing her flowers, was he? *Impossible!*

He squinted at the door as though trying to get a glimpse of the Great Oz.

*Drat.* He must have heard the scrape of the peephole.

"You can stand there all night," June called. "But I am not opening up this door." Even though she was not truly afraid of her neighbor, one could never be too careful.

"June?" he called again. "Is that you?"

June eyed the door in confusion. "Whose house did you think you just walked up to?"

Maybe Charley Montgomery was a bit more senile than she had given him credit for. Then, realizing that perhaps he *had* gone to the wrong house and those roses were *not* intended for her, June threw open the door and practically snatched them out of his hand.

"I assume these are your apology flowers." June gave them a dainty sniff. They smelled as fresh as the outdoors, their perfume as sweet as the nectar of a peach. If the gift had been from anyone else, June would have said thank you. Since they were from Charley Montgomery, she did not.

Charley's cheeks colored, and suddenly June realized she was only wearing a dressing gown. Well, so what? If she wanted to wear her pajamas on a Friday night, that was her business.

June pulled the white cotton tightly around her thin frame. "Was there something you wanted?"

"I haven't seen you in the garden," he said. "I was concerned you were ill."

Dusk was settling and the lights had slowly started to come on in the houses up and down the block. It was a nice night, which meant it had been a nice day. It was truly a shame that, thanks to this man, June had been trapped inside. She crossed her arms, holding the roses tightly against her chest. "The copper on the top of your gazebo is blinding," she said. "As I already told you, if that gazebo is there, you will not see me out in my garden again."

Charley looked disappointed. "June, I'm not taking that gazebo down. To be frank, it's awfully nice to have a place to sit in the shade."

"Wonderful! Sit in the shade. Have a drink with a tiny umbrella in it. As long as *you're* comfortable." June gripped the edge of the door. "I suppose it doesn't matter to you in the slightest that I will be forced to stay inside or go blind in my very own backyard?"

"I know, June. It's a tough one." Charley's eyes twinkled, which was rather infuriating. After rubbing a hand over a full head of silver hair, he said, "Well, I came over here to tell you that I've decided to get the roof oxidized. That will turn the copper green. I thought that might be a happy compromise."

"A what?" June whispered. "What did you just say?"

Charley's face seemed to soften. "I said I know how to compromise."

"Yes, but . . ." She stared at the collar of his shirt. It was sticking up, just slightly, and she had the oddest urge to smooth it back down. "Won't that ruin the copper?"

"I have to do something. You've made that perfectly clear." Charley's forehead wrinkled. "I don't want you to sneak over there and paint it."

A smile tugged at the corner of June's mouth. "Well, that's a shame, as I am actually quite handy with a brush." Then, because there was nothing else to say, she said, "Have a nice night."

He gave a slight nod. "You, too."

June watched as Charley walked down the steps. The man was in good shape, which June couldn't help but envy. Maybe she should talk to her son-in-law about a few strength-building exercises. It couldn't hurt.

At the bottom step, Charley turned. "I have plans this evening," he said, squinting up at her through the sunlight, "with one of your friends."

"Whoever would that be?" June asked, as if she couldn't take a wild guess.

"Rose. Rose Weston," he said. "She's planning to bring dessert. A strudel."

June sighed. She did not have the slightest interest in Rose's strudel.

"Now that you and I are putting this silly war behind us . . ." Charley watched her closely. "Perhaps you'd like to join us."

*Join* them?

"No, thank you. I would rather . . ." June waited for inspiration. "I would rather eat bugs."

A cloud passed over Charley's face. "I see." He regarded her for a long moment.

June fiddled with the lace on her sleeve, suddenly uncomfortable. Why was he looking at her like that? Did he . . . *want* her to come over?

"Then, I just have one request," he said. "I would appreciate it if she doesn't add anything funny to that dessert."

June blinked in surprise. "Like what?"

"Like poison."

"Poison?" June was baffled. "Rose's cooking is just awful but . . ."

"Let me be clear." Charley narrowed his eyes. "Now that we've made our peace, tell your friend that you've called off the hit."

The conversation suddenly clicked. "Charley Montgomery," June said, shocked. "Do you mean to tell me that you did not bring me flowers to apologize, but because you think I'm sending my friend over to kill you? With a strudel? That is the craziest thing I've ever heard."

"I read a lot of mysteries, June." He shook his head. "I hate to say it, but on occasion, you do remind me of some of the more . . . memorable lead characters."

June flushed. "Whatever do you mean by that?"

The smile that Charley gave her might, in any other circumstance, be considered charming. "I don't know that I'd put anything past you."

For once in her life, June did not know what to say.

He gave her a neighborly wave. "I'll tell Rose you said hi. I'm not particularly interested in sharing a strudel with her, but she wouldn't take no for an answer. I have a feeling your friend is quite persistent."

June blinked. "Yes. Quite persistent indeed."

# Sixteen

Chloe dipped her fork into her pasta and swirled it around. "Thank you again for bringing me here," she told Ben.

They were at her favorite Italian restaurant, the one that June and Kristine took her to on birthdays and special occasions. It was small and intimate, with red leather booths and wood paneling. The din of clinking silverware, murmured conversation and Italian music created a pleasant soundtrack for the night and Chloe felt happier than she had in ages.

"Of course I brought you here," Ben said. "It's your favorite." He dipped a piece of bread into olive oil and pointed it at her. "If a guy likes you, he'll pay attention to the little things. You should expect him to."

Chloe thought for a minute. What type of things could Geoff have possibly picked up on? The fact that she liked pop culture? It was hard to imagine him whisking her off to a Britney Spears concert, so she decided to keep her expectations in check.

"Do you want more wine?" Ben asked. Before she could answer, he topped off her Pinot Noir.

"Thanks." Chloe reached for the glass. Holding the stem, she hesitated. "But should I even . . . ?"

"It's okay to drink on a date," he said. "Just don't get hammered. Obviously."

Chloe wondered if Geoff even drank. Based on those ascots, he didn't really seem like the type.

"And be sure to eat," Ben said. "Men like women to eat. It's sexy."

Chloe laughed. She poked her finger into a stray piece of garlic and popped it into her mouth. "If that's the case, I'm the sexiest thing on the planet."

"Yeah." He eyed her with appreciation. "You're doing alright."

Chloe hesitated. It was strange. Ben had been dropping compliments here and there, all night. The one in the apartment about her skirt, something he'd said in the cab on the way over about the color of her eyes and now this. On one hand, Chloe knew he was trying to build up her confidence for the date. On the other, it seemed a little unusual. It was almost like he was attracted to her. For real.

Just like any good study, Chloe decided to test her theory. Stabbing her fork into her spaghetti, she wound the noodles around the tongs and brought them up to her mouth. Feeling totally ridiculous, she placed the fork between her lips and slowly drew it out. Sure enough, Ben seemed mesmerized at her efforts.

Gazing at her lips, he said, "What exactly are you trying to do to me?"

"You said I should eat," she said, embarrassed. "So I'm just . . . eating."

"That's not exactly what I meant." His gaze locked onto hers. "But trust me, it works." He flashed his most winsome grin—all teeth and sparkle—typically reserved for the Brazilian model-types.

Completely confused, Chloe studied the red-and-white pattern of the tablecloth. Back when they were kids, she and Ben used to play checkers all the time. They'd have tournaments that could last the whole weekend, which he typically won. Suddenly, it struck her that if he *was* actually flirting, it was probably just part of a game. A game where he let her imagine exactly what it felt to be on a date with someone who was interested in her.

Chloe looked up and gave him a rueful smile.

Ben had been about to take a bite of his risotto, but he set the fork back down on the edge of the white porcelain bowl. "What's that look for?"

"Nothing." Chloe took another sip of wine. "I just figured something out. It's actually very comforting."

"Do tell."

Chloe hesitated. What was she supposed to say? *Hey, Ben. I just figured out that after twenty years of friendship, you only think of me as a friend?* Well, duh. That wouldn't exactly be a news flash. In fact, it would probably make the rest of their fake date just a little too awkward.

"Nah." She waved her fork at him. "But since we're on a date and I am letting you coach me—thank you again—I do have to know. What exactly are your qualifications for all this? Why aren't *you* in a relationship by now?" Once again, she dug into her pasta, wrapping the long linguini noodles around her fork. But this time, the bite she took was completely, totally and utterly platonic.

"You know why," he said. "I'm having too much fun."

"No." She wiped her mouth with the red cloth napkin. "I don't buy that. You're always pulling the rip cord on the girls who come over. That doesn't sound like fun to me. Why aren't you looking for a relationship? Something serious?"

Ben laughed. "Okay, dating tip number three: Don't ask your date why he's not in a relationship. It's a red alert that you're just dying to get married and have babies. He will run out of the room so fast that people will think he's a streaker."

"So, you don't want to get married or have kids?" she pressed.

Ben paused. "Of course I do. If I end up with the right girl."

"But it doesn't seem like you're in the market for all that. Or that you ever will be."

Ben ran his fingers through his hair and she caught a sudden whiff of his cologne. It was the perfect blend of spice and musk, mixed in with something that was just . . . very Ben. "Do you really think that?" he asked. "About me?"

Actually, Chloe hadn't given it a lot of thought. Ben had always dated this girl or that but he rarely got serious. There was one stretch where he dated a local artist for something like two years but eventually, he broke it off.

"Yes." Chloe laughed at the shocked look on his face. "Ben, come on. You're a playboy. There's nothing wrong with that. But any girl who tries to take you seriously in the love department is kidding herself. I mean, I never would."

Ben took a drink of sparkling water and let his eyes scan the restaurant. For some reason, he seemed a little angry.

Chloe was surprised. "Why does that make you mad?"

Setting his glass of water on the table with a *thwunk*, he leaned in close. "Chloe, we've known each other for years." His voice was earnest. "I'm a good guy."

Chloe was totally confused. Of course Ben was a good guy. "I didn't say that you weren't."

"Yeah, you did." He shook his head. "You just said—"

"I *said* that I don't think of you like that," she said. "I know better."

"Do you seriously mean to tell me . . ." He leaned across the table. "That in all this time you've never once thought of you and me, trying to be more than friends?"

Chloe blushed. Of course she had.

Right after the incident with the cider, she had entered into a massive Ben-crush. Even though she was furious with him for reasons she didn't quite understand, a secret part of her kept hoping that he'd try the same thing again. But this time, she wanted him to profess his love or, at the very least, ask her to go with him.

Instead, after he'd apologized, Ben started dating Lindsey Walker. A perky blonde cheerleader, Lindsey was all of the things that Chloe could never be. Yes, the whole thing had broken her heart a little but she'd never said a word. What was the point? It was silly junior high stuff.

"You've never thought of me like that," Ben said. "Not once. That just seems so—"

"Okay, fine," Chloe blurted out. "Yes, I did." As soon as the words were out of her mouth, she didn't know why she'd said them.

Ben brightened. "Really?" He put his elbows on the table and leaned forward. "When?"

"Once," she mumbled. "For a little while. In junior high."

Ben let out a huge breath. "Thank God," he said, giving his gorgeous grin. "You had me seriously worried there for a second."

"Sorry. That must have really set you back."

"Take this as dating lesson number four," Ben said, once again cheerful. "Never, *ever* tell the guy you're on a date with that you've never thought of him as a romantic prospect. It's just bad business." He took another bite of his porcini mushroom risotto. "So. Let's talk about it. Why did you have a crush on me?"

"I'm not telling you that," Chloe groaned, already regretting the confession. "I'm not going to build up your gigantic ego even more than it already is."

Once again, Ben looked hurt. "I don't have a gigantic ego."

"Come on," she scoffed. "Women parade in and out of your apartment like a women's health clinic. Do you seriously expect me to believe you don't get off on that?"

"Oh, give me a break," Ben said. "I was picked on as a kid. That stays with you, you know."

Chloe nodded. "Textbook psychology. You're salving your bruised ego by getting all the girls."

"I don't get *all* the girls." Ben's blue eyes were bright in the light from the votive candle. "I never got you."

The restaurant seemed to go quiet around them.

"What . . . What do you mean?" Chloe asked, her heart pounding in her ears.

"What do you mean, what do I mean?" Ben demanded. "I had a crush on you for years. You never noticed."

Chloe's heart started to beat faster. *He did?*

"Yeah, right." She forced her voice to sound natural. "I was as skinny as a string bean, wore the same pair of jeans every day and spent all my time at the library. If you liked anything, it was the fact that I did your trig homework for you."

The mood at the table was too tense. Desperate to bring it back to normal, Chloe reached her fork across the table and stabbed one of the mushrooms in his risotto. She wanted to show him that the conversation was not affecting her, and that they were good friends who could talk about all this without getting weird.

"Hey!" Laughing, Ben seized her hand and guided the fork to his mouth. He ate the mushroom.

"You are such a bully," she said, sitting back in her chair.

"Oh, you wanted some of this?" Ben scooped up another forkful and waved it in her direction.

Chloe crossed her arms. "I will not fall into a false trap."

"You know you want it." Ben danced the bite toward her mouth, pressing it up against her lips. Finally, she opened her mouth and let him slide it inside. The risotto was sharp and delicious on her tongue.

"Yum." Chloe reached for her fork. As their hands brushed, she felt a strong jolt of attraction for her best friend. Ben must have felt it, too, because he was suddenly looking at her with a serious expression on his face.

"Chloe," he said.

The waiter swooped in just then, grabbing for the bottle of wine. Efficiently, he topped off both of their glasses and tucked the empty bottle under his arm. "How is everything over here?"

"Great," Ben said brightly.

"Good," Chloe said.

The waiter nodded and rushed off. From somewhere across

the room, she heard the pop of a champagne bottle. A couple laughed and another group sang "Happy Birthday." Absently, Chloe watched a woman in a red dress following the host to a table. It was strange to be reminded that they were in a restaurant full of people.

"Well," Ben said, leaning back in his chair. "We killed that bottle. This was fun." From his tone, it sounded like the date was just about over. She didn't know whether to be relieved or disappointed.

"It was." Chloe's voice was bright, in spite of the fact that she couldn't manage to look Ben in the eye. "You got me away from all the work I should be doing, fed me wine, pasta and hopefully dessert. Thank you." As she said it, she flicked a stray bread crumb off the tablecloth. It landed on the clean floor and instantly she felt guilty. "Should I pick that up?"

"I think they've got it." He pushed his plate aside. "Chloe, listen. I have to ask you something. Do you really like this guy? Geoff with a G?"

"Yes." She thought about how sexy Geoff had looked, standing up on that stage, speaking to her class. And, of course, in the hallway of his office, wearing just those green sweatpants. "Why?"

"I just . . ." Ben looked down at the table, then back up at her. He made a goofy face, raising his eyebrows and widening his eyes. "I don't want it to get too serious."

Chloe was surprised. "You sound like June. Why does everyone think this is going to get serious?"

"I don't know." Ben's forehead wrinkled in concern. "You did catch the bouquet at that wedding. The power of suggestion. Maybe you're walking around right now thinking, *I'm about to get married. I need to get married.*"

Chloe laughed, swatting at him. "Don't be stupid. We haven't even been on a first date yet."

Ben caught her hand. "I'd just hate for you to get swept up in something before I even had my chance."

"Your chance to . . . what?"

The waiter swept back up to the table, formal in his black shirt and black pants. He held out dessert menus, and Ben let go of her hand.

"Can I interest you in coffee?" the waiter asked. "Dessert?"

"Tiramisu," Chloe said slowly. "And espresso."

"Two," Ben said.

When the waiter left, Ben opened his mouth to speak again but the busboy started clearing off their dishes. He took his time scraping the crumbs off the tablecloth. Then he set the candle right in the middle of the table like a flammable chaperone. By the time the busboy was finished, the waiter had returned with two thick espressos. A lemon rind decorated the tiny coffee plates. Automatically, Chloe passed her lemon to Ben, who was already running his over the rim of the cup.

Even though the momentary mood seemed to have been swept away with the dirty dishes, Chloe gave Ben a questioning look. "You were saying?"

Ben shrugged. "I was saying that it would be a shame if you ended up married before I even got to go after you. Graphic designers don't make that much money. To be honest, I'm not going to want to buy you a bunch of gifts."

"I'll keep that in mind," Chloe said, her voice dry. "Look, if you want to go for me, just do it." She spread out her hands, as though laying cards down on the table. "Save some money on gifts."

"Okay." Ben's aquamarine eyes locked onto hers. "You look beautiful tonight."

The light from the candle seemed to flicker and dance between them. Chloe thought about all the years they'd known each other, all of the moments they'd shared. She loved Ben probably more than anyone on the planet, but she also knew him better than anyone on the planet. Tonight, he'd wanted to show her what it was like to go on a real date, to make her feel special.

That was it. Falling for his many charms would be a waste of time. She'd been down that road before.

Shaking her head, Chloe gave him a slow smile. "I know what you're doing."

"Yeah?" He took a slow sip of his espresso, holding her gaze. "And what's that?"

"You . . ." She leaned across the table until she could smell the spice of his cologne. "You are trying to get out of paying the check."

Ben grinned. "Ah, Chloe," he said. "You know me so well."

# Seventeen

That night, The Places You'll Go hosted an event for an Indian cookbook.

Pakshi, the author, was a tiny woman who served up a whole lot of laughter. Walking from this side of the makeshift stage to that, she gave a brief lecture seasoned with jokes about the pronunciation of cumin, her first attempt at cooking laddoos and the trials of loving a man allergic to curry. She not only entertained the crowd, but sold a ton of cookbooks as well.

At the end of the night, Kristine stood at the door, saying good-byes and thank-yous to the regulars and a whole crop of new customers. Most of them were carrying shopping bags stocked with a freshly bought cookbook, travel guides or other trinkets.

When the last person left, Kristine surveyed the mess from the event. It really wasn't bad, just a few dirty wineglasses lying around and trays of appetizers that needed to be stored or tossed in the trash. Annie, who had come in to help out, was assisting Ethan with picking up the trash.

Checking the time on her watch, Kristine was grateful that she'd make it home before Kevin. That would give her plenty of time to think of exactly what she needed to say to get him to agree to come to Italy. She'd left him a message earlier about it but he hadn't called her back, which was not a good sign.

"Okay," Annie said as Ethan tied up the trash bag. She tugged at her dress, an adorable eighties-style striped sweater she'd part-nered with a pair of bright red leggings. "I have to hit the road. It's movie date night."

Kristine hesitated. "Annie, just five more minutes? And we'll all be out of here?"

"Sorry." Annie pulled a sad face. "Roger freaks out if he misses a preview. You know how it is."

Actually, Kristine didn't know. She and Kevin hadn't gone to the movies in years. Would he care if they missed the previews? It was anybody's guess.

"Okay." She tried to keep the grumble out of her voice. Annie didn't *have* to come in to help out at all. She'd done it to be nice, since she wasn't certain Ethan knew how to run an event. But, of course, he'd done just fine. "Have fun. Eat some popcorn for me."

"Absolutely," Annie said. "Piled high with Milk Duds." Blow-ing kisses, she darted out the front door.

Ethan laughed, watching her go. "She's got spirit. I like her."

Kristine picked up a stack of signed cookbooks and moved them to a display. The books smelled sharp and petroleum-like, as though they'd just been printed. Then she turned to see what else needed to be done.

"Ethan, I can finish everything up," she said. "Thanks for all your help today."

"I really don't mind—" he started to say as Kristine's cell phone rang in her pocket.

It was Kevin. Either his flight was delayed or he landed earlier than usual. "Excuse me," she told Ethan. "I have to get this." Rushing back to her office, she said, "Kevin? Hello?"

"Hey, Firecracker." His voice sounded tired like it always did when he traveled. She could hear an automated announcement in the background and a blur of voices pass by. "Listen, I'm not going to make it home tonight. We had some . . . mechanical trouble."

*"What?"* Kristine grabbed the edge of her desk and held on tight. "What do you mean?"

"Oh, it was just one engine. No big deal. When it's two, well . . ." Kevin gave a little laugh.

Kristine's eyes drank in the many photos of her family that decorated her desk, landing on one of her favorites. It was a picture of her and Kevin at the Chicago Zoo. A llama stood next to them, grinning as though mugging for the camera.

"I'm in St. Louis," Kevin said. "I'm going to sit in my hotel room, drink a beer and watch a movie. I'll come home tomorrow morning. Okay?"

Kristine closed her eyes. "I'm glad you're alright." Even though she did her best not to worry, things like this made it hard. After a long moment, she blew out a breath. "Well," she said. "Hopefully that won't happen when we fly over the ocean."

Kevin was quiet for a long moment. "Kris, I can't do it. I can't go."

Kristine's heart sunk. "Why?" she practically whispered. "Kevin, it's—"

"It's a lot of unnecessary stress," he said. "Look, if I'm going to take a vacation, I want to do something relaxing. Something that's fun for me, too. Like my trip to Canada with the guys."

Kristine's eyes widened. Even though she knew his annual hunting trip was important to him, she'd never once dreamed that it was more important than her. But he'd said that. Her husband had just said exactly that.

"Wow." She sank into her desk chair. "I . . . Wow." The pictures, so neatly displayed in their frames, suddenly looked blurry.

"Firecracker, going to Rome would put unnecessary attention on me at work, it would . . ."

Ethan peeked through the glass window on the door. He held up a bag of trash and mouthed, "Don't lock me out."

Numbly, Kristine nodded. What would Ethan say if he

knew how little interest her husband had in her? It was so humiliating.

As Kevin continued his litany of reasons, Kristine stared at a photograph of the two of them watching the sun set over Lake Michigan. She could still remember the cool air on her cheeks, the warmth of his arm and the scent of the bonfire they'd built. She'd been so in love, so happy, so *smug*, she realized now, imagining that they could stay that close forever.

"I'm sorry," Kevin was saying. "I really am. In a few years, when I retire—"

"Oh, just stop it," Kristine cried, surprising herself. "To be honest, I expected it. Everyone, including our own daughter, knew that I would be going to Rome alone. And today, I thought I wouldn't go at all, if you wouldn't come with me. But . . ." She tightened her grip on the phone. *It wasn't right!* Why *should* she miss out on the opportunity of a lifetime just because her husband would rather go hunting with the guys? "I'm going." Her voice was defiant. "With or without you."

As she said the words, the heavy weight that had settled around her heart seemed to float away. Why shouldn't she? It was about time she stopped waiting on Kevin to start living her life.

"I never said that you shouldn't," he said, sounding surprised. "It's a free trip. Take it."

"June doesn't think I should go without you. She doesn't think it's appropriate."

"Kristine, you're a grown woman. You don't have to do everything your mother says."

It wasn't fair for him to say that. Not at all.

"Honey," Kevin said, his voice wary. "I'm sorry. My phone's going to die—"

"I'm glad you're safe." Kristine's voice was short. "I'll see you tomorrow, okay?"

Heartsick with disappointment, she hung up. It was hard to

believe that, after so many years of marriage, it was possible to feel so completely and utterly alone.

There was a sharp rap at the office door. Taking a deep breath, Kristine called, "Come in." She forced her voice to sound cheerful.

The door scraped against the floor as Ethan stepped into the office. "Everything's all set." He paused, studying her. "Are you . . . okay?"

Kristine twisted her hair up into a knot and got to her feet. "Fine. Can I help with anything else?"

"No, no. Everything's set." Ethan crossed his arms. "Kristine, do you need to talk?"

Kristine bit back a hysterical laugh. Seriously? A man who actually asked that question? No, she didn't need to talk, especially not to someone like Ethan. But still . . . it was awfully nice to be asked.

"I'll be okay." She nodded. "Thank you. For your help tonight."

Ethan nodded.

"I should go." Kristine's tone was abrupt. Quickly, she scanned her desk. She liked to start each day with a clean surface, everything neat and in order. There was a coffee ring on the wood and licking her finger, she quickly rubbed it off.

"There's some leftover wine from tonight," Ethan said slowly. "Let's have a glass. Talk Rome."

Kristine's hand hesitated, resting on the surface of the desk. She couldn't do that, could she? Not twice in one week. Not with a man who wasn't her husband.

At her hesitation, he added, "We can order some food from that Japanese place down the block. Have sushi? You look like you have some things on your mind."

Kristine was torn. The last thing she felt like doing was going home, where the only thing waiting for her was a book on Roman history. Besides, the conversation she'd shared with Ethan on Sunday had been so interesting. What would it hurt to spend just a little bit more time with him? They'd talk about Rome, make some plans . . . It would be perfectly innocent.

Kristine's eyes flicked up to Ethan's. He was watching her closely, as if her decision actually meant something to him. Kevin hadn't looked at her like that in years.

*Don't do it,* the voice in her head practically screamed. *Why would you do this?*

What was the big deal? They were about to travel across the world together. She may as well get to know him now so there were no surprises then. There was no point in making it so hard, but something held her back.

"It's been a long day," she said. "I really should get home."

# Eighteen

Chloe and Ben were still talking and laughing when the busboys began stacking chairs on the tables around them. The room had cleared out. Instead of murmurs of conversations, there was just a rhythmic *swish-swish* as the host ran a cordless vacuum over the faded red rug.

"Uh-oh," Chloe said, looking around. Ben had paid their check a long time ago but they'd stayed talking long after the rest of the patrons had left. Their waiter was slouching next to the host stand, doing something on his phone. "I think that's our cue."

Ben also seemed surprised that the place was so empty. Shooting an apologetic look at their waiter, he mumbled, "That guy's gonna kill us. He'll probably jump us out front." Getting to his feet, he tossed an extra twenty dollars on the table. "Sorry, man. Annoyance fee."

Chloe linked her arm with his on the way out. "You are such a nice guy."

"Nice?" Ben was horrified. "No way. I am passionate, dark and mysterious. In other words, incredibly sexy."

"You must be." Chloe checked the time on her phone. 12:45. "I haven't stayed out on a date this late since undergrad."

"Me, neither." Ben nodded. "By this time, I've already got her in bed."

Chloe laughed, punching him in the arm. Outside, the wind

had turned chilly and she shivered. Ben looped an arm around her shoulder and pulled her in tight. With the scent of espresso wafting off their clothes and mixing with the gentle spice of the cologne he was wearing, she felt just heady enough to feel that spark of attraction for her friend.

As Ben raised his arm to hail a cab, she pulled it back down. "Let's walk home."

"You okay in those shoes?" He pointed at her ballet flats. "They're not your typical tennies."

Chloe looked up at the inky sky. She saw the faintest pinpoints of light shining through the haze of the city. "It's so nice out," she said. "It'll be too cold to do this soon."

"Alright." Ben pulled her in closer, his arms firm and strong. "Let's do it."

As they moved toward the Lakeshore, Chloe felt the cool breeze whip against her cheek. They chatted about the restaurant and the meal, wrapping up tidbits of conversation and unfinished jokes. Then, as they passed by the various high-rise apartments stretching up into the night, they fell silent. Every once in a while, he made a comment about something in someone's window but otherwise, they just enjoyed the walk. She tried not to think about the fact that they touched the whole way.

By the time they got to Wicker Park, her legs were heavy but her heart was light. "Well," she said as they approached their four-story brick building. "This might totally be bad form for a first date but yes, I would absolutely love for you to come up."

"Hot." Ben laughed.

When they got to their floor, Chloe leaned against the door of her apartment, sad that the night was over. It was the best date she'd ever had, even if it was just practice. "That was so fun. Thank you." Reaching into her purse, she pulled out her keys. "You've made me feel confident that I will not scare the good doctor away."

"That's it?" Ben's cheeks were flushed a bright red and his hair rumpled from the wind. "You wouldn't ask your date in?"

"Oh," Chloe said, confused. "Did you want to come in?"

Ben shoved his hand into the pockets of his gray slacks and cocked his head. He raised an eyebrow, giving her a look as though to say, *Really? You fell for that?*

Chloe hit her palm against her forehead. "Oh." She felt totally, utterly stupid. "Got it. So, don't invite him in. And if he suggests that he wants to, I'm supposed to play hard to get."

Ben grinned. "Something like that."

"Okay." She smoothed down her skirt. "Let me try that again." Taking a step forward, she put a hand on his chest. It felt firm beneath the thin material of his shirt. "Ben, I apologize. I am going to have to call it a night. But I had a really good time and I hope we can do it again sometime." Looking up at him, she gave a prim smile. "How was that?"

"Good," Ben said. He moved a step closer, his eyes locked onto hers in a way that made her mouth go dry. Suddenly, Chloe noticed that her hand was still on his chest. She could feel the steady rhythm of his heart. Unless she was imagining things, it was beating rather quickly.

"But if he tries to kiss you goodnight," Ben said in a low voice, putting his hand over hers, "you should definitely let him."

She swallowed hard. "Got it—" she started to say, but before the words were out of her mouth, Ben had pulled her into his arms and was kissing her.

Chloe was so startled she squeaked. Maybe it was the wine, maybe it was that incredible spicy scent that had been wafting off him all night, but somehow she managed to forget that he was her best friend and she kissed him back. Gently at first, then as his tongue parted her lips and melded into hers, she felt herself turn to liquid.

She gave up all pretense of not wanting him and pressed her

body up against his. She pushed her hands up and under the fabric of his shirt, until she could feel the taut muscles of his back. Ben let out a low growl, shoving her up against her door. Chloe heard somebody's hand smack against the wood, but all she could feel was the sharp lightning passing between them.

A door creaked open down the hallway and Chloe snapped to her senses. This was *Ben*. Her best friend. Her *neighbor*. What the hell were they doing?

Chloe pulled away, her face probably as flushed and panicked as his. "Well," she tried to say. It was a valiant effort to make some sort of a joke, to tell Ben she understood that the kiss was just another step in the practice date, but words failed her.

Like that day on the bed in junior high, Ben's gaze was locked onto hers. Chloe felt an incredible need to wrap her arms around him and kiss him again, but she knew that if she did not walk away in that moment, they would cross a line they could never come back from.

"Okay," Chloe forced herself to say. Her voice was trembling. "Have a good night." Without ceremony, she ducked into her apartment and locked the door behind her.

# Nineteen

When Chloe woke up the next morning, snuggled deep in her comforter, her hand was on her breast. It wasn't an unpleasant sensation. She'd actually been in the middle of a dream, kissing the man of her dreams. She sighed, trying to figure out who it was. He seemed familiar. In fact, he seemed a lot like . . .

*Aaaack!*

Bolting awake, Chloe sat straight up and the comforter fell off her shoulders. The kiss she was dreaming about was the one that started at the door of her apartment. With Ben.

"No, no, no, no, no." She hit her hand against the down comforter. It made a tiny puffing sound, like a deflated wedding dress. Whiskers, who was curled up in a warm little mound at Chloe's feet, shifted in her sleep.

"Whiskers, wake up," Chloe whispered. The whispering was necessary, on the off chance that Ben could hear her through the wall. "This is a serious crisis. Wake up."

Whiskers lifted her head. Those pretty yellow cat eyes stared as though to say, *You're waking me up? I thought we had an understanding about that.*

"I'm sorry," Chloe said, "but how stupid can I be?" Scooping up her cat, she pulled the furry little body close to her chest. "Whiskers, I kissed Ben. *Ben.*"

Whiskers let out a strangled meow, squirming.

"Don't meow at me." Chloe closed her eyes tight, remembering the way his arms had felt around her. "I kissed Ben. And Ben kisses *every*body."

This was not good. Their friendship had relied on the fact that Chloe *wasn't* everybody. She wouldn't bang on his door at three in the morning, begging him to open up. She wouldn't sit by the phone, praying he'd call. And she certainly wouldn't fall in love with him, expecting to be the one who would finally make him change.

"I'm blaming it on the alcohol," Chloe told her cat. "I had too much wine, we both did and . . ." She flushed, thinking of the way Ben pushed her up against that door. The way he'd smelled, like rosemary and garlic and the seventh grade. Her heart pounded at the memory.

Just then, there was a thump on the other side of the wall. Chloe froze, realizing that the only thing separating her from the man who had turned her body to water was a thin piece of plaster. She drew the comforter back up to her chin and pulled Whiskers in tight.

"How could I have been so stupid?" Chloe buried her face in Whiskers' fur. The cat squirmed wildly, then escaped. She stood at the end of the bed, looking highly offended, her fluffy white hair askew.

"Great," Chloe said, tossing up her hands. "Thanks a lot. But at least you've prepared me. Because that is exactly how Ben's going to react."


As the sun shined down through the trees, June sat on her haunches, tugging at an especially hard-to-extract weed. The oxidation crew had toned down the glare on the gazebo and she was overjoyed to spend the day in her garden once again.

"Oh, you think you're so strong," June told the weed. "Just

you wait. I am going to tear you out of this ground faster than you can say—"

"Giving it a talking to, June?" a voice asked.

June was so startled that she let go of the weed and fell back on her bottom. "Oooph." The grass was slightly damp and the moisture seeped through the thin fabric of her gardening shorts. *Drat.* She would have to go back inside and change. Assuming she could get back up. Her body had landed in a very precarious position indeed.

Charley eyed her with concern. "Are you alright?"

"I am perfectly fine." The truth was, June had landed on a tree root in a way that could require a trip to the emergency room, but she was not about to admit that in front of this man.

"Are you sure?" Charley put up a hand, shielding his eyes from the sun. "You look like you're stuck. Do you need a hand?"

June let out an enormous sigh. She was not stuck, but getting out of this position was going to require some grunting and groaning that she would prefer he not witness. "I am perfectly fine," she said. "The gazebo looks good. Thank you so much. What can I help you with now?"

Charley leaned against the fence, as though settling in for a long chat. "That friend of yours, she's quite a character. She didn't believe me when I said I enjoyed her strudel, so she's insisted on bringing me another one."

June peeled off her gardening gloves. Flexing her fingers, she said, "Oh?"

"Yes." Charley looked puzzled for a moment, as though remembering the details of that night. Then he smiled. "Since Rose is your friend, I thought you could tell me what she prefers to drink? I didn't think to offer her anything, last time."

"I haven't the slightest idea," June said. Of course, everyone who was anyone knew that Rose Weston drank Manhattans, with two maraschino cherries. "I believe she's a teetotaler."

"A teetotaler?" Charley looked genuinely alarmed. "Oh, boy. I probably would have served her a drink and she would have slapped my face. She seems like a feisty one." As he said this, his blue eyes danced in a way that she did not appreciate. "Thank you, June." He turned away from the fence, his form slightly stooped in the summer sun. Whistling, he headed back toward the house.

Gingerly, June placed her hands on the grass and gave a slight shove. Her legs splayed open like a crab just as he turned to say, "You sure you're okay?"

June lowered herself back to the ground. "Just wonderful."

When the man finally decided to go inside, June slid her cell phone out of her pocket and flipped it open. It was strictly for emergencies—she did not want to cook her brain with radio waves on a regular basis, thank you very much—and she was relieved to see that it was in fact charged. Her daughter answered on the third ring.

"Hey, Mom. What's going on?"

June stretched out her legs. The sharp, shooting pain in her bottom was gone, so that was a good sign. Nonetheless, she whispered into the phone, "Don't worry, but I might have to go to the emergency room."

Instantly, Kristine's voice was worried. "Oh, no. What happened?"

June could hear people chatting in the background, as though the store was busy. Even so, it dawned on her that when Kristine picked up, she'd sounded upset.

"Is everything alright?" June asked.

"Mother. You just called me to tell me you might have to go to the hospital. What do you mean, is everything alright?"

A cardinal dropped down into June's birdbath. It splashed around, flashing its bright wings and chirping happily. "Oh, I'll be fine. Stop dillydallying and tell me what happened."

"Nothing. Just . . ." Kristine sighed. "Kevin's not going to

Rome. He would rather save his vacation time for a hunting trip. So, I'm going alone."

The bird rose up in the water, waving its wings. Droplets of water shimmered in the sunlight.

"*What?*" June barked. "That is absolute foolishness. Didn't you get my note?"

Charley came back outside. Since she was still sprawled out on the ground, June leaned her head back as though trying to catch some rays. He went back to fertilizing his shrubs but she could tell he was still keeping an eye on her, which was very annoying.

"I mean it, Kristine," June whispered. "Did you tell your husband about what I said? About the young man in your store?"

After Chloe's remarks about how good-looking this man was, June decided to perform a little reconnaissance. She dialed up The Places You'll Go, asking for Ethan. An oily voice on the other end of the line had said, "This is he." June dropped the receiver in its cradle as though it were a snake and took a cab to Lincoln Park.

With the meter running, she darted up to the window and peered inside. She received a couple of funny looks from the patrons, considering she was decked out in an enormous hat and sunglasses, but the disguise was important. Kristine would kill her if anyone mentioned the fact that her mother was skulking around.

The moment June spotted Ethan, she felt a twinge of fear. The man was much too attractive for his own good. Plus, he moved around the place like a panther. If Kevin wanted to hunt, he might want to set his sights on a new target.

"I don't like this, Kristine." June shook her head. "Not in the least."

"Mother," she groaned. "I am not going to talk about this with you at work. Now, do you want me to call you an ambulance or not? I have to go."

Giving a tiny grunt, June used every ounce of strength she had to push herself up to her knees. The movement startled the bird in the birdbath. With a flash of scarlet feathers, it darted up to the tree and chattered angrily.

"Oh, I'm fine." June got to her feet. She patted her hair, just to let Charley know that she was having no trouble at all. "It's you who I'm worried about."

"Don't worry about me," Kristine said, her voice wry. "I've got everything under control."

# Twenty

Although June was certain that, on some level, Kristine did have the situation with Kevin under control, June still took a cab out to the suburbs later that afternoon. She wanted to have a little chat with her son-in-law.

Kevin certainly would not be open to this, unless he was a captive audience. Considering he did not have any dental appointments on the book, she decided to corner him at the juice bar next door to his gym. Kristine always said he finished off his workout with a protein smoothie, so June was hedging her bets.

She was perched on a red stool at the juice bar, sipping her second apple and carrot juice concoction, when he finally walked in. He was dressed in a sweaty T-shirt, a pair of navy blue jogging shorts and ridiculously large white tennis shoes. As she swiveled on her stool to face him, Kevin's face fell.

"*This* is my son-in-law," June told the barista. Before he arrived, the tattooed girl behind the juice bar made the mistake of asking June how her day was going. Boy, had she gotten an earful.

Kevin gave the barista a cheerful wave. "How ya doing, Myra. Can I get a protein smoothie? With banana and some of that world-famous chocolate?"

Myra shrugged. It was obvious that she, too, didn't understand why he would send his wife off to Italy with another man. "I'll have to go into the back to get bananas."

Kevin clapped his hands together. "Perfect. Can't wait."

The barista sauntered into the back room.

Kevin chuckled, leaning against the bar. "June, you really are something else. Only you could think it's acceptable to stalk me at a juice bar. So. Let's get this over with. What did I do now? And if it's horrific enough to warrant a trek to the suburbs, why hasn't Kristine talked to me about it herself?"

June hesitated, thinking back to the first time she'd met Kevin. It had happened over the summer break, during Kristine's third year at college. Eugene had been delighted to meet him.

June had not.

One of June's fears in allowing her daughter to attend an out-of-state college was the risk that she would meet someone and fall in love without giving June a say in the matter. And like it or not, June's say *did* matter.

That first time Kevin walked through her front door, June was shocked to see that he was a big brute of a boy. He smelled like the outdoors and wore ill-fitting khakis and a faded sweater. It was obvious that he lacked the means to support her daughter, if the situation came to that.

Since Kristine poked a finger into her back like a pistol, June extended her hand and smiled. "It's a pleasure to meet you." The words came out stiff, probably because they were a blatant lie.

A huge smile split across Kevin's face. To June's horror, he tackled her and lifted her up off the ground. "It's awesome to meet you," he said. "Kris talks about you all the time."

"Put me down this instant." The words came out as a hiss. "And don't you *ever* put your hands on me again."

Kevin froze. Face flushed, he dropped her back to the floor. Then he squared his shoulders and looped an arm around Kristine.

*Fine*, his face seemed to say. *Then I'll put my hands on your daughter instead.*

Eventually, June and Kevin came to an understanding. This

happened around the time she realized that, even if he wasn't the man she would have chosen for her daughter, Kevin loved Kristine and would do anything for her. It troubled June that somewhere along the way, his attitude seemed to have changed.

Draining her apple and carrot juice, June set it on the counter. "I simply want to know why you are sending my daughter to Italy. Alone."

Kevin grabbed a straw from the container on the counter and began to fiddle with it. The man was always doing something with those hands. If they weren't pawing at her daughter, they were rumpling Chloe's hair, flipping through the sports section or playing with a nearby item. June wished that for the purpose of conversation, the man would just hold still.

"Things are complicated right now." Kevin wadded up the wrapper and shot it at the trash can, as though it were a basketball. "I can't go. I have too many responsibilities."

June sighed. "Kevin, you have a responsibility to your family."

"I'm well aware of that." His face flushed. "Chloe's in grad school. I'm responsible for that. Kristine has her store. I'm responsible for that. We have a mortgage, I'm responsible—"

"Okay, okay," she said, irritated with his theatrics. "Have you seen the man she's planning to travel with? He has a hungry look about him, Kevin. I don't like it. I don't think it's appropriate for my daughter to travel with someone like him, alone."

"Kristine's a big girl." He reached for another straw wrapper. "She can take care of herself."

"Kevin." June gripped his muscular arm. "She might not need your protection, but she needs your attention. She needs *you*. You're her husband. Step up."

After a tense moment, he said, "Let me look at some things and I'll . . . I'll see what I can do."

"You will?" June's heart leapt. If Kevin decided to go to Italy, it would make her daughter so happy. "Thank you. Thank you so much!"

"I'm not making any promises, June." His eyes seemed tired. "I just said I'd see what I could do."

"As long as you make an effort," she told him. "That's what counts."

The barista must have been listening at the door because she chose that moment to walk back in, carrying a creamy smoothie in a to-go cup. Handing it to Kevin, she said, "Fourteen seventy-four." Off his confusion, she nodded at June's juice. "She said you were buying."

Kevin shook his head, pulling his wallet out of his mesh shorts. "Of course she did."

"Thank you, Kevin." June hopped down from the tiny stool. "I mean that."

Kevin's face broke into that goofy grin. He reached for a napkin from the counter. After spitting on it with a loud, horrible sound, he leaned forward and wiped the wet, warm thing across June's upper lip.

"*Aack!*" Furious, she wiped at her mouth. "What are you doing?"

"You had a carrot juice mustache," he said. "And I hate to tell you this, June, but orange just isn't your color."

# Twenty-one

On Saturday, Chloe made a point of avoiding Ben. This wasn't difficult, considering he seemed to be avoiding her, too. Typically, they texted nonstop but she didn't hear from him all day. Not even once.

This irritated her in a major way.

In her opinion, Ben should be the one to be a little more mature. After all, *he* was the one who kissed her, not the other way around. Besides, he had plenty of experience dealing with the opposite sex. But . . . Chloe glared down at her phone. Maybe this was exactly how he dealt with them.

At two o'clock, her text alert finally chimed. This earned her the evil eye from the serious-looking girl sitting at the library table across from hers. "Sorry," Chloe mouthed, but she really didn't care. She was just relieved that Ben had finally, *finally* gotten in touch.

To her surprise, the text message wasn't from Ben. It was from Geoff, confirming their date for that night. Chloe stared at the message, torn between disappointment and excitement. Finally, she chose excitement and texted him back.

Turning off her ringer, Chloe tossed the phone into her backpack. Whatever. If Ben wanted to be a jerk, let him. She didn't have time for it. Besides, it wasn't like she was interested in him like that, anyway.

Chloe got to work and lost track of time. By the time she

checked her phone, it was seven, leaving her just an hour to get home, get changed and meet Geoff downtown. She raced home and quickly tried on a few outfits. Nothing looked right, so she decided to wear the same thing she'd worn on her date with Ben. It wasn't like anyone would know and besides, he'd said the skirt was sexy.

Since there was no time to take a bath, Chloe spritzed her hair with vanilla and pomegranate perfume and swiped on some brown mascara. Then, after a critical once-over in the mirror, Chloe dug through her closet until she found a black lacquered purse June had given her. She never wore it because it was slippery on her shoulder, but she hoped the designer label would make her look more mature.

With little time to spare, Chloe raced out the door. There, she screeched to a halt. Ben was keying into his apartment. He was wearing a light blue T-shirt and a pair of well-worn jeans, his hair as tousled and sun-streaked as ever. She wondered how it was possible that he managed to look even better than he had on their date last night. The injustice made her want to punch him in the face.

She crossed her arms over her chest. "Hi."

"Hey." Ben fidgeted with his key chain. It was an anime doll with wild blond hair, wearing an orange tracksuit. She wondered who had given it to him. "Going on your date?" His gaze swept over her outfit.

Chloe blushed, wondering if he knew she was wearing the exact same thing. "Yeah." As always, the lacquered purse started to slip off her shoulder. She tugged it back up, saying, "Wish me—" Then, maybe because she'd moved it the wrong way or because the purse was perpetually annoying, it slid off her shoulder and dropped to the ground, spilling pens, lip gloss and papers across the hallway.

At the same time, Chloe and Ben both bent to pick everything up and they cracked heads.

"*Ow!*" she cried, grabbing her hair.

"Come on," he groaned, rubbing his forehead.

Straightening up, they eyed each other warily. Neither took a step backwards.

Chloe's eyes wandered down to Ben's lips. They were slightly parted and just a little bit chapped. She found it hard to believe that, less than twenty-four hours ago, those lips had been pressed against hers. They'd been so soft, while the slight scruff on his face was rough against her cheek.

As though reading her mind, Ben ran the back of his hand across the fuzz on his face. Taking a step even closer, his bright blue eyes held her gaze. Chloe felt her lips start to part and she panicked.

Diving down to her hands and knees, she reached for the items scattered across the floor. The short skirt crept up dangerously over her thighs and she tugged at it, clambering back to her feet. "I've gotta go," she mumbled. "I'm so late." She could feel her cheeks flush.

Ben looked slightly panicked. "Have fun." He put his keys in the lock. "I've gotta send an email for my boss now so—"

"Totally," she said, her voice thick with sarcasm. "Who *doesn't* have to send out an email for their boss at eight o'clock on a Saturday night?"

Ben paused. "Chloe . . ." He eyed her through a lock of his unkempt blond hair.

"It's cool." She gave a half wave. "See you."

Walking toward the stairs, Chloe immediately felt bad. She hated that things were weird with her best friend, especially about something that really, truly, didn't matter. At the top of the stairs, she rested her hand on the railing and turned to face him.

"Ben?" she said, her voice apologetic. "This is really stupid. You were just teaching me how to go on a date. I know the . . ." She swallowed hard. "I know that it didn't mean anything."

Ben didn't respond and instead shoved his hands into the pocket of his jeans.

Damn. Why did he have to do that? Chloe was looking at his jeans now, noticing the snug way they fit his thighs. She remembered exactly what his thighs had felt like, all muscle and sinew, pressed against hers.

"So." Chloe forced her eyes back up to his. "We don't have to make a big deal out of it. It really didn't matter."

Ben cocked his head. For some odd reason, Chloe caught a whiff of his cologne. He was all the way across the hallway, so how . . . ? Dipping her chin, she smelled her sweater.

*Shit*. It totally smelled like Ben!

Shaking her head, Chloe couldn't help but think that dating tip five thousand most certainly had to be: Don't smell like another man when you go on a date. Hopefully, Geoff wouldn't get too close. That could make things a bit awkward.

"Anyway." Chloe tugged at her skirt and gave him a brave smile. "Wish me luck."

"Yeah." Ben ran a hand through his hair. It stood up on one end, just like Whiskers' fur had this morning. She had the distinct feeling that Ben, like Whiskers, just wanted to get away. "Good luck."

"See ya."

"Hey," Ben called.

"Yeah?" Chloe hesitated, feeling oddly hopeful.

"If it doesn't go late, come over." He shrugged. "Maybe we could watch some reality TV."

Chloe drummed her fingers against the railing. Yeah, like that was going to happen. The days of lying in bed together were long gone. "Sure." It was the easiest thing to say. "Have a good night."

Clambering down the stairs, Chloe pushed open the heavy wood door and stood on the stoop, heart pounding. The street bustled with people her age, out enjoying their Saturday night.

It was so strange to think that for once, she was going to join them.

"Alright. Time to go on a date." She waited for the familiar flash of nerves but felt nothing. After last night, it all seemed pretty simple. Maybe Ben had done his job after all.

Fumbling in the purse for her phone, she cued up his name, ready to text the silly thought. Then she stopped. Even though she already missed her best friend, Chloe slid the phone back into her purse.

It would be better to just leave him alone.

# Twenty-two

Kristine was sitting on the sofa, reading her Roman history book and sipping sparkling water, when Kevin slammed the front door. "Kris! Where are you?" Bursting into the living room, he glared at her. "You sent your *mother* to talk to me? How old are you?"

*What on earth?*

Kristine set her book next to her on the couch. "Considering we haven't seen each other in days," she said, "I think a hello would be nice. After that you can yell at me about whatever June did now."

"You really don't know?" Pacing back and forth in his sweaty T-shirt and gym shorts, Kevin told her about June's visit to the juice bar. "*Then* she made me drive her home! As if I didn't have anything better to do with the few minutes I have each weekend."

Kristine was surprised to see Kevin so worked up. His cheeks were flushed and he paced the room, moving back and forth past the glass coffee table and white brick fireplace. She wanted to tell him to take off his shoes but thought better of it.

"I can't go to Italy right now, Kris." His blue eyes were stormy. "I already told you that. No way."

"I know." She tried to keep the bitterness out of her voice. "You made it perfectly clear that you're not interested."

Kevin came to a dead stop. "Honey, I am interested," he said. "I just can't do it right now. Okay?"

They'd already had this conversation over the phone. Kristine didn't want to get into it again.

"Yup," she said, running her hand over the Roman history book.

Kevin slipped out of his T-shirt and draped it over his neck. He stood in the middle of the living room, lost in thought. She took the opportunity to study her husband's upper body. It was as cut as it had been in college, but she didn't feel even a flicker of attraction, which surprised her, considering they hadn't had sex in ages.

On the other hand, why should she feel attracted to him? The only thing she felt was hurt. Hurt that he wasn't coming with her to Rome, hurt that he'd yelled at her and hurt that he couldn't just say he was sorry.

"Are you hungry?" Kevin tugged at his T-shirt.

Looking down at her hands, in particular her wedding ring, she shook her head. "No."

"I'm starving." Some of the familiar humor came back into his face. "After talking to June, I went back to the gym and worked out so hard that I'm practically digesting myself."

Clomping across the hardwood floors and into the kitchen in his gym shoes, Kristine heard him grab a glass out of the cupboard. *Clink clink clink*, went the ice, then *whoosh*. Water rushed into his glass. Tonight, the familiar sounds didn't make Kristine happy. It just gave her a headache.

Kevin poked his head around the corner. "I'm gonna get a pizza. Unless you're going to kill me for ordering Italian."

Kristine refused to smile. "Go for it."

Drumming his hand against the wall, he said, "What do you want to do tonight? Anything?"

Kristine bit her lip. She wanted to plan a trip to Rome with her husband. To watch documentaries, plot out what they were going to see, talk to friends who had already been. But obviously, that wasn't going to happen.

"I don't know," she said. "What do you want to do?"

Kevin yawned. "I'm pretty beat. The flight was so early this morning."

"That's okay." She twisted the strings on a throw pillow. "Let's just rent a movie or something."

Kevin's face brightened. "Maybe we can find a video on how to divorce a mother-in-law."

"That's enough!" Kristine leapt to her feet, tossing aside the pillow. "I have listened to you complain about my mother non-stop for the past half hour. June does what she thinks is best, because she loves us. Maybe if you were coming with me, she wouldn't have anything to worry about."

Kevin stared at her in surprise. "Kris, I was just kidding."

"No, you weren't." Kristine gripped her hands together until her knuckles turned white. "My mother is a remarkable woman." Pictures of June lined the mantel above the fireplace and she pointed at them, as though to remind him they were talking about a real person. "Please show some respect."

"I do respect your mother." Kevin shook his head. "Kris, you should have seen her today, gathering the troops at the juice bar. It was pretty funny." When she didn't respond, he groaned. "Firecracker, come on. I love June." He walked over to her, setting the glass of water on the end table and opening up his arms. "And I love you."

Kristine hesitated. Then, taking a small step forward, she leaned in. His skin was warm against her cheek, his muscles taut. He smelled like clean sweat and faded lemongrass.

"I'm sorry I'm not going to Italy with you." Kevin's voice was gruff. "We'll do it one of these days. I promise you that."

Kristine closed her eyes. She wanted to believe it, but at this point, she had to accept that he wasn't going to change. That in some things, she was just going to have to be on her own.

Kevin's T-shirt still dangled over his shoulders and it brushed against her cheeks. Reaching up, Kristine gripped the bottom of his shirt like an anchor. She held on tight, as though the slightest movement could wash them away.

# Twenty-three

"There you are!" Sally raced toward Chloe in a blur of wild, curly blonde hair. "I can't believe it." Tackling her in a huge hug, Sally bounced up and down. Chloe bounced along, delighted to finally see her good friend.

Sally had been Chloe's roommate at undergrad. They went on to share a crappy apartment in the "real world," until Sally met her future husband and moved in with him. Ben liked to joke that the two friends were polar opposites, thanks to Sally's distinct loathing for academia and, without exception, children.

"Let's go outside and catch up, then," Sally chirped in her adorable British accent. "It's going to get much too loud in here, isn't it?"

Chloe surveyed the club. The small stage was set with microphones, guitars and a drum set. Their friend from college, Michael, had gotten a small deal with a record company and was setting off on a cross-country tour. Even though she hadn't seen Michael in years, Ben kept her up on his latest activities. Supposedly, Ben was coming to the show, not that he'd bothered to text Chloe. Four days had passed since she'd seen or heard from him. Four days! Of course, he'd probably just act like everything was normal when he showed up and pump her with questions about her date with Geoff.

"Do you want to get a drink?" Sally thrust her glass toward

Chloe. "This is pretty good. Some sort of flavored-vodka thing. Peach? Pineapple? I don't know, really."

"No drinks for me." Dramatically, Chloe stuck out her lower lip. "I have to study after this."

"Aww," Sally groaned. "Hurry up and open that practice because I've got a million problems to talk to you about."

In her pink corduroy jacket and with her bright, rosy cheeks, Sally looked like a girl whose biggest problem was finding her favorite marshmallow in a box of Lucky Charms cereal. That was one of the things that Chloe loved most about her. After all of the crazy, heart-wrenching stories she had to deal with day to day, she appreciated being around someone as light as cotton candy.

Outside, it was a little chilly, so they congregated around a fire pit in the center of the concrete porch. Apartments towered over them from above, their lights bright in the dark night. The pungent odor of weed drifted over from a group of teenagers standing in the corner. Chloe grinned, happy to be part of the real world instead of stuck at her desk, slaving away at yet another paper.

"So, my date with Geoff was fun," Chloe told Sally. "I met him next to Tiny Tumblers and he'd set up a whole picnic in that little garden, you know, the one next door?"

Sally's eyes widened. "That's so romantic. I love it."

"It was the sweetest thing anyone's ever done for me." Geoff had set up a blue blanket on the ground with plates, wineglasses and even two long, tapered candles. "He was afraid we'd get busted by the fire marshal, but it was so fun. Then, he took me to that little piano bar for coffee and Irish cream."

"Get to the good stuff." Sally's eyes were wide. "Did he kiss you?"

"Outside the piano bar." Geoff's kiss had been warm and secure. It didn't end with him slamming her up against the door or anything, but who wanted that anyway?

"You kissed him?" a familiar voice growled. "And how was that?"

Chloe turned to find herself face-to-face with Ben. Dressed in a ratty blue baseball cap and a U2 *Joshua Tree* T-shirt, he was more attractive than ever. Crossing her arms, she glared at him.

"The kiss was great," she said. "Believe it or not, he even called me the very next day."

"Ben!" Sally bounced up and down. "Hel*lo*, gorgeous." Rushing forward, she leapt into his arms.

As Sally wrapped her white jeans-clad legs around him, Chloe felt a pang of jealousy for her cute blonde friend. Now that there was some weird boundary between Chloe and Ben, it would be a while before she could hug him at all.

"Ben, can you *believe* Chloe has a boyfriend?" Sally screeched, sliding back to the ground. She boxed Chloe's arm in excitement. "Maybe Norman will stop telling me we got married too young, if we can finally have some decent couples to go out with."

Ben looked at Chloe in surprise. "He's your *boy*friend? That was fast."

Technically, Sally was just being dramatic. But if that's what Ben wanted to believe, then let him.

"Ben, don't be jealous," Sally scolded. "You are just going to have to accept the fact that you officially missed out on your chance with our Chloe."

There was a tense silence, except for the crackle of the log in the fire and the muted sounds of the band warming up indoors. After a long moment, Ben took a step forward and clapped Chloe on the back. The heat of his hand seemed to burn through her shirt.

"Sally, I think it's great," he said. "I thought she was just going to ignore every man on the planet until she opened her practice."

Chloe looked at him, surprised. "I've never said anything like that."

Ben tugged at the rim of his baseball cap. "It's not what you said," he mumbled. "It's how you act."

In some ways, he was right. Her schedule had been so packed for the past few years that she hadn't had time to give to anybody. But if there had been a guy really worth it, someone that she could really be herself around, she would have made the time. Other than Ben, no one fit the criteria.

"You're hardly a person qualified to decide whether or not I'm open to love," she told him. "You don't even know the definition of the word."

Ben ripped off his baseball cap. His blond curls shot out in nine different directions. "What's that supposed to mean?"

"Oh, goody." Sally jumped up and down. "Fight. *Fight!* The band hasn't even started playing yet and it's getting real out on the patio."

Chloe clapped him hard on the back, just like he'd done to her. His muscles were taut beneath his soft T-shirt. "I've seen the way you fall in love."

Ben scowled. "And how's that?"

Chloe gave Sally a knowing smile. "Ben is all whispers and innuendos. But at the end of the day, he goes out of his way— even enlists my help—to send girls far, far away. Do you think that sounds like an expert on love?"

Sally laughed, clapping her hands. "Poor Ben. We'll help you find somebody, one of these days." The muffled sound of electric guitars shot out from the club. "Ooh, they're starting. Shall we?"

As they walked into the club, Chloe could feel Ben glaring at her over the top of Sally's blonde curls. She turned to glare back, then stopped in surprise. The look he was giving her wasn't angry at all. It was . . . hurt.

"I'm sorry." He leaned in close, so that only she could hear. His voice was low, his breath warm against her ear. "I should have called."

Her heart clutched. Yes, of course he should have. Ben was her *best friend*. It was so ridiculous that they'd stopped talking because of one stupid kiss.

After a moment, she shrugged. "It's fine. Next time, right?"

He pulled his cap low over his eyes. "Yeah." He leaned against the back wall and settled in to watch the band. "Next time."

# Twenty-four

Taking a deep breath, Kristine let herself into June's house. It was Thursday night and she was late. Even worse, she'd skipped two Thursdays in a row. June got the hint, though, and finally left an apology message for ambushing Kevin.

Straightening her shoulders, Kristine followed the sound of laughter to the kitchen. "Hi, everybody." Dropping her purse on the table, she hugged them. "I've missed you guys."

June was stiff in her arms. "How nice of you to join us." She plucked Kristine's purse off the table and stomped off. Hopefully, she was going to place the purse in the basket in the living room instead of throwing it out into the street, as she'd probably prefer to do.

Chloe giggled. "It's a good thing you're here. Grandma would have had a conniption if you skipped again. Here, pick an apron."

There were several options on the table. Yellow stripes, navy and white flowers, green polka dots . . . Kristine settled on one with embroidered bluebirds and pulled it over her head.

"What are we doing tonight?" An array of cooking utensils were set on the counter, along with a bag of flour, a carton of eggs and a variety of herbs and spices. Maybe June had hired a pastry chef.

Chloe grinned. "Making homemade pasta, in honor of your trip to Italy." Whispering, she added, "Grandma's trying to prove that she's happy for you. She thinks *you* think she's mad that you're going. Have you been avoiding her or something?"

Kristine fidgeted with a string on her apron. "It's been busy at the store."

Yes, she had been avoiding June. Kristine was mad at her mother for stalking Kevin at the juice bar, but she was also feeling guilty about the fact that maybe her mother was right.

Rather than risk June's interference, she'd been avoiding her mother instead.

"It'll be fun to make pasta," Kristine said, her voice bright. "I—"

"Oh!" Chloe's eyes focused on something behind Kristine. "I have to warn you," she murmured. "The chef tonight is a little . . ."

"Hahl-lo," a raspy voice cried.

Kristine practically jumped out of her shoes. Turning around, she was surprised to see a tiny man with a large nose and crooked teeth standing just inches away from her. He was dressed all in white, other than a bright blue apron filled with a variety of cooking utensils. When he moved, the spoons jingled together, making a sound like that bell Chloe's cat always wore.

"I am Hannigan!" The rotund man stood on his tiptoes to kiss her cheek. "Oh, you are delicious." He sniffed the air around her like a bloodhound. "You smell like coconuts."

"Hello." Kristine took a step backwards, trying to move him out of her personal space. To her surprise, Hannigan followed. She took another step back. He followed again, as though they were performing some odd number on *Dancing with the Stars*.

Kristine looked at her daughter in confusion, not quite sure how to get out of this.

Chloe grinned. "Hannigan is going to teach us about making pasta. Grandma met him through a mutual friend. Although he has asked her on a date, once or twice—"

"Three times, yes." Hannigan nodded, vigorously.

"Hannigan has resigned himself to teaching us about cooking instead."

"Yes, yes." He abruptly abandoned Kristine's personal space and invaded Chloe's instead. Running his stubby hands through her ponytail, he proclaimed, "This one is already my sous chef."

June bustled back into the room. Smoothing down her red polka-dot apron with white ruffles, she said, "Shall we get started?"

"Yes." Hannigan bebopped over to June. "Let's start the party."

June gave a hearty sigh and pushed him away. Reaching for her Thursday night notebook, she cleared her throat and placed a pair of purple-rimmed reading glasses onto her nose. Two days ago, Kristine had picked up the exact pair to replace the pink ones. It was time to get a real pair of glasses.

June cleared her throat. "Harriet Van Horne said, 'Cooking is like love. It should be entered into with abandon or not at all.' The Italians create their meals with love, creating dishes with few ingredients and enjoyed over a period of hours, to maximize time with family. Today, we will learn how to make homemade pasta in an effort to spend more time together as a family. And of course . . ." She cleared her throat again. "To honor Kristine's upcoming trip to Rome."

Hannigan whistled. He yanked Kristine over to the pots like a lobster he planned to boil. "We cook here." Then, he dragged her over to an area with colorful plastic mixing bowls. "We create here."

The three of them worked quickly to keep up with Hannigan's instructions, dumping eggs, flour and a variety of spices into the bowls. The chef chose a whisk from his apron collection and whipped the ingredients together, while maintaining a tight grip on Kristine's elbow. Thanks to the motion of his arm, she felt like a kid stuck on a merry-go-round. The ingredients transformed into dough and the chef cried, "Who would like to master the art of the roll?"

"Chloe would," Kristine said, pointing.

As Hannigan raced to be by her side, Kristine approached her mother. "Thanks for doing this tonight. It's really sweet."

June sniffed. "You're welcome."

"I'm sorry I missed the past few weeks." She kept her voice quiet. "The store's been busy."

"Work is the excuse Kevin is using with you," June said. "Don't you dare use it with me."

"Mom . . ." Kristine sighed. "Look, what you did to Kevin was completely unacceptable. Our marriage is not your business."

June eyed her over those purple frames. "If it involves you, it *is* my business."

"You made me look like a child. Can you imagine what would happen if I talked to . . ." She wracked her brain. "Chloe's dean? Without her permission?"

June's eyes looked guilty. "I only—"

"You only wanted to butt in. I'm begging you, butt out." Kristine reached up and tugged at the knot in her hair. Pulling it down, she rearranged it and tied it up again. "Seriously. I don't need your help. I need your support."

"Kristine, I know that things have been difficult for you and Kevin lately."

Kristine looked at her mother in surprise. Even though June had made her concerns about Italy more than clear, Kristine hadn't realized her mother knew that things had been strained with Kevin. On the other hand . . . maybe it was just that obvious.

Reaching out, June smoothed back a strand of Kristine's hair, just like she'd done when Kristine was a little girl. "And because things are difficult, I don't think you should go. You're putting yourself in a bad position. But . . . it's your life and your decision. I just want you to go into it with your eyes open."

Kristine shook her head, irritated at her mother's insistence that something had to go terribly wrong. "Everything's going to be just fine."

"Helloooo." Chloe waved at them from across the kitchen. Hannigan was draped over her, demonstrating how to cut noodles. "What are you two talking about?"

"I was updating your mother on your new boyfriend," June called. To Kristine, she whispered, "They've been seeing each other a lot in the past few weeks. Did you know that he's the grandson of Rue, from my mahjong group? Rue and I just made the connection."

"You're kidding." June loved the ladies in her mahjong group. "Does that mean that Chloe found someone you might actually approve of? I thought that was an impossible feat."

The first time Kristine brought Kevin home, she had expected her mother's disapproval. What she had not expected was how much that disapproval hurt. Now, she wondered why June had given them such a hard time. Maybe it was because . . . she let out a slow breath. Maybe even back then, her mother had seen that the differences between Kristine and Kevin would eventually tear them apart.

"I think it's wonderful Chloe found someone," June said. "I think she's falling in love."

Hannigan seemed disappointed. "You're in love?"

Chloe gave the chef a mournful look. "If only we'd found each other first."

Without missing a beat, Hannigan glommed onto Kristine instead. "Come here, pretty lady." He tugged at her hand. "Let's cut the pasta and make a beautiful meal together."

When the pasta was finally cooked and served, the chef declined their invitation to dinner. "No, no. The meal is for the family." Clearly, he was disappointed to not yet be a member of the family.

"Ah." June was delighted. "Then it must be time for you to leave." After paying Hannigan his fee, she ushered him toward the door.

"Whew." Kristine pulled out a seat at the kitchen table. Sliding off her shoes, she tucked her legs underneath her. "That guy was a handful."

"You mean, we were a handful." Chloe laughed. "He was like an octopus."

June swept back into the kitchen, a look of indignation on her face. "Do you know what just happened?" She smoothed her hair, as though still trying to believe it. "That slimy little man just tried to kiss me. He tried to *kiss* me. At the door. Can you imagine?"

Chloe's jaw dropped. "What did you *do*?"

"What do you think I did?" June said. "I slapped him across the face. Then I told him that I have a collection of knives that extends well beyond the kitchen. And if he tried something like that again, I would cut off his weiner."

"You didn't." Kristine gasped.

"I most certainly did." Sitting down at the table, June folded her napkin and took a bite of pasta. Kristine and Chloe stared. "Oh, please. If I didn't know how to stand up to the pasta man, what am I supposed to do when we take tango?"

The three of them burst out laughing. Chloe laughed so hard her curly hair bounced, something that made June laugh even harder. Wiping tears away from her eyes, she passed around steaming plates of linguini.

Kristine stuck her fork into the pasta and brought it to her lips. It was dripping with olive oil, and gooey Parmesan cheese melted in her mouth like chocolate. "Wow." She closed her eyes. "Amazing."

"Made with love," June said. "A meal meant to be shared with family."

Chloe waved a fork at Kristine. "Even the pasta in Italy won't be this good."

"The company won't be as good," June corrected her. "The pasta will be just fine."

# Twenty-five

Chloe's cell phone rang on the El train. To her delight, it was Geoff. He'd called a couple of times in the past few days, but she'd been at her internship or in class. Then, he'd missed her return calls because he was always with a patient.

"Hi," she shouted. "Sorry it's so loud. I'm on the train." The El clanked and vibrated as the city rushed by the window in a metallic blur.

"Would you like to join us at the park?" Geoff shouted back. "In about twenty minutes?"

"I can't." Disappointed, her eyes fell on an abandoned newspaper on the train seat. An ad was facing up, with a happy couple jogging together along the beach. "I've got to prep for midterms."

"What's the topic?" In the background, Mary Beth screamed something about ice cream.

"Intervention methods." Chloe splayed her fingers like Whiskers sometimes did with her paws. Her hands were sore. Probably from writing too many papers.

"Ah, yes." Geoff's voice was warm. "I can intervene with the best of them." She smiled, cradling the phone against her ear. "Come to the park," he said. "I'll give you a private lesson."

Chloe studied her reflection in the door of the train. She was carting around a huge book bag and her hair fell in a frazzled ponytail, but her eyes were bright and lively. Geoff's words came back to her, from that day in his office: *Slow down, enjoy your life.*

"Okay," she said, surprising herself. "But only if we can get ice cream."

Chloe raced the few blocks from the train to the popular playground, her book bag banging against her side. Geoff looked completely out of place in a tweed jacket, but this time it was Mary Beth who took the cake. She was wearing a white party dress and a pair of white patent leather shoes, completely inappropriate for the dirt and dust of the park.

"Wow." Chloe nodded. "Are we going to an open call for *Toddlers & Tiaras* after this?"

Geoff turned. To her surprise, he looked exhausted, with a five o'clock shadow and dark circles under his eyes. "She wouldn't stop screaming until I let her pick the outfit. I finally had to give in."

"Good tactic." Chloe laughed. "I should have tried that on my mother when I was a kid."

The summer after kindergarten, Chloe had begged Kristine to let her pick out her own outfit for school. She had the perfect vision in mind: a hot pink swimsuit, rubbery yellow rain boots and her favorite pair of bedazzled fairy wings. She'd failed to negotiate the swimsuit or the rain boots but Kristine did let her wear the wings.

Geoff smiled at the story. "Your mother sounds very understanding."

"She's great, but . . ." Chloe pretended to cringe. "She was right to try and rein me in."

Geoff got the message. "You've seen how that goes. I can't do it."

"Of course you can." Chloe nudged him. "You're a psychologist. Duh."

The *duh* dropped out of her mouth like a piece of chewing gum and immediately, Chloe felt stupid. Luckily, Geoff seemed too dazed to notice.

"Theory versus practice," he said. "Last night, it took me three hours just to get her to go to bed. She slept for five hours and had me up at six this morning." Mary Beth ran back and forth across the top of a bridge on the jungle gym, no exhaustion in sight. "Honestly, I'm too tired to fight her."

"Can I ask . . . where's Mary Beth's mother?"

Geoff set his jaw. "California."

Chloe stared at the patches of sun on the ground and the way they made long shadows out of the playground equipment and group of kids. One thing she'd learned in her psychology classes was that typically people would talk if you'd just let them. With that in mind, she waited.

Eventually, Geoff let out a small sigh. "In my professional opinion she suffered from postpartum. She wouldn't hold Mary Beth and didn't want anything to do with her. But in my personal opinion . . ." Pain etched across his handsome face. "Maybe she left because she wasn't in love with me anymore."

Chloe's heart ached for both of them. Watching the little girl run back and forth, she couldn't help but wonder what it would be like to grow up without a mother. It was impossible to imagine. Between Kristine and June, Chloe had more mother than she knew what to do with.

Chloe had always been lucky enough to have a family that cared about her, which was part of the reason she went into art therapy. It broke her heart to see kids who were neglected, unloved and abused. The chance to coax these kids into a safe place, to help them express their feelings with a paintbrush or markers or even chalk, made her feel like she was giving back the love her family had given to her.

"It's been a very difficult time," Geoff said. Turning to Chloe, he put a hand on her arm. "I know seeing each other might be slightly complicated, but I'm delighted you're giving me a chance."

Chloe was surprised. "Uh, I'm the one who's . . . delighted. You're kind of a big deal."

Geoff smiled. "And you're beautiful."

"I'm a mess," she said, embarrassed. "I haven't slept in days, my hair's all frazzled . . ."

"You look beautiful," he repeated. Looping an arm around her shoulder, Geoff pulled her in close. Chloe thought he was going to kiss her, but Mary Beth made short work of that idea.

"*Daddy!*" Ripping off a patent leather shoe, she flung it at Geoff's face. It hit him square in the jaw, just missing Chloe.

The other kids at the park gave up a collective gasp. Mary Beth was obviously In. For. It.

Dropping Chloe's hand, Geoff took a step away. "I'm so sorry. Mary Beth must feel threatened." Walking toward the jungle gym, he called, "Honey, let's go get that ice cream."

Ice cream seemed to be Geoff's go-to parenting move. And it was all wrong, as the women at the park were quick to point out.

"Ice cream? *Hell* no." A heavyset mother glared at Geoff. "Don't you set a bad example in front of *my* kids." The woman shook a thick finger at her daughter, as if her daughter had done something wrong. "You don't *get* ice cream after that."

The other parents nodded. Delighted to have everyone's attention, Mary Beth took off her other shoe and whipped it at Chloe. Catching it, she considered her options.

Kids needed security. They needed boundaries. Even though Chloe wanted Geoff to like her, letting Mary Beth run wild wasn't helping anyone. Especially not Mary Beth. "Geoff, can I please have your permission to get your daughter under control?"

"Fine." His expression was as petulant as Mary Beth's. "I don't know what to do anymore."

"You're doing good," Chloe fibbed. "I'm just going to talk to her." Turning toward the monkey bars, she roared, "Young lady, you get over here *this instant.*"

Instinctively, the other kids scattered to the far side of the play area. Mary Beth remained on the jungle gym. She tugged at her tights as though planning to whip them at Chloe, too.

"I am going to count to three," Chloe warned. "If you are not down here in three seconds, you will be in *huge* trouble. One . . ."

Mary Beth cocked her head.

"Two." Chloe took a menacing step forwards. "Two and *a half* . . ." She frowned at the young girl. "Mary Beth, if I get to three, you had better believe you'll regret it."

"Just go," a little brown-haired kid whispered. He glanced over at a woman who must be his mother. She was sitting on a bench and watching him with a no-nonsense look on her face.

"Two and *three quarters* . . ." She moved toward the bars. Mary Beth let out a squeal. Sliding down a metal pole, she stalked up to Chloe.

Chloe pointed to the shoe lying in the dirt. "Go pick it up."

Mary Beth let out a huff but walked over and picked it up. Chloe snatched it away.

"Now, little girls who throw shoes do not get to wear them until they apologize. Go sit on that bench." She pointed at a seat next to the stern mother. "When you're ready to apologize, you come over and talk to me." Facing Geoff, she murmured, "Do not look at her until she comes back over here."

Out of the corner of her eye, Chloe watched as Mary Beth took a seat on the bench. She kicked her feet against the ground until the mother next to her gave a warning look. Mary Beth huffed and watched the other kids playing. Finally, she got up and walked back over to them.

"I'm sorry I threw the shoe at your head, Daddy." Mary Beth tugged at her party dress, her lower lip practically hitting the ground.

Geoff's eyes were surprised. "Thank you. For your apology."

"Mary Beth, what else are you sorry for?" Chloe asked, her voice gentle.

Mary Beth rubbed her hand across her nose. "That I threw a shoe at *your* head." She turned her attention back to her father and gazed up at him with big green eyes. "I love you, Daddy."

Geoff bent down and pulled her into a hug. "I love you, too."

To her surprise, Chloe felt a lump in the back of her throat. Swallowing hard, she glanced around the playground. The other mothers were nodding.

"Alright." Chloe patted Mary Beth on the back. "It's alright."

Beaming, Mary Beth ran to the monkey bars and played with a new vigor.

The admiration in Geoff's eyes was genuine. "That was impressive."

"Kids want boundaries." Chloe shrugged. "You just have to give them some."

He cleared his throat. "Would you like to go for dinner with us? After this?"

She had at least four hours of reading to do and a paper to write. But for the first time in her life, all of that seemed less important than the person standing right in front of her. "I'd love to," she said. "But if Mary Beth's good, I want to get her a cookie, first. But no ice cream."

Geoff gave her a sly look. "Positive reinforcement for my little serial killer?"

Chloe grinned. "You got it."

# Twenty-six

The weeks leading up to Rome seemed to fly by. The night before her trip, Kristine sat cross-legged on the floor of her bedroom, reorganizing the suitcase that she'd packed weeks before. It was such a thrill to pull out everything and double-check, just to make sure she hadn't forgotten anything.

Kristine's hands hesitated over the lace underwear sets she'd tucked into a side compartment. She'd thought it would be fun to bring them along, considering Italian women probably wore something more glamorous than white cotton under their clothes. Kevin wouldn't even be there to see them. What was the point?

The thought prompted her to scoop up the entire collection and dump it back into a drawer. Pressing her palms on top of the dresser, she stared at herself in the mirror. The king-size bed she and Kevin shared loomed behind her, like some reminder that everything would be just fine. But when?

Before flying out for work the night before, her husband had given her a quick kiss on the lips and a smack on the bottom, like she was his workout buddy or something. "Have fun in Rome, Firecracker," he said, grinning. "Give 'em hell."

Hardly an inspiring *bon voyage*.

Walking back over to her suitcase, Kristine focused on checking off items on her packing list. Had she remembered the notecards for the speech she'd give at the Valiant luncheon? Yes, of course, but maybe she should . . . Her cell phone rang, interrupting her train of thought.

"Hey, Mom. What's going on?" Kristine waited for the inevitable tirade about Rome. That she shouldn't be going without her husband, she should rethink all of this and please, wouldn't she just reconsider? June had been on good behavior but Kristine knew better. Her mother always had something up her sleeve.

"I need you to come over." June's voice was pinched and worried.

*There it was.*

"Of course you do," Kristine sang. "What's wrong?"

"I need your help with a little . . . neighborhood matter."

"Let me guess." Kristine perched on the edge of the bed. "Your neighborhood needs me to sit in the house with you until the plane leaves for Italy. Without me on board."

"I do not appreciate this cheeky attitude." June's voice trembled slightly. "If you don't want to help, I suppose I'll be forced to handle it on my own."

Kristine hesitated, looking at the phone. June did sound upset. Either her acting skills had improved or something really was wrong.

"Mom . . ." Kristine glanced at her watch. It was only eight, but she had to be at the airport by ten in the morning. "I'm leaving tomorrow. I'm not exactly dying to drive back into town right now . . ."

"Damn," June said, sounding truly distressed.

"Damn that I'm leaving," Kristine asked, "or damn that you won't be able to call and torture me for a whole week?"

"Damn that you're leaving. I'll miss you this week, but have fun." June sounded distracted. "Alright, I love you. Get some rest. I'll call Bernice."

It wasn't a trick. June really did need help. Zipping up her suitcase, Kristine got to her feet. "Hang tight, Mom," she said. "I'll be right there."

Throwing open the door, June said, "You made it!" In the light of the hallway, Kristine could see that her mother's hair was rumpled, her eyes slightly manic. Without giving her a hug or even a second look, June did a U-turn and stomped back down the hallway and into the kitchen.

What on earth was going on? She hoped Charley hadn't done anything too out of line. The time he'd planted those black tulips, June had paced the house and plotted revenge tactics for a week.

In the kitchen, Kristine stopped short. The kitchen table, the stove and the counters were covered with camouflage clothing. Sweatpants, sweatshirts and stocking caps. There was even a camouflage tent in the center of the room. June stood at the kitchen window, clutching a pair of gigantic binoculars and spying on Charley.

"Mom . . ." Kristine was baffled. "What the heck?"

Setting down the binoculars, June thumbed through some items on the counter, then thrust a pair of camouflage coveralls at Kristine. "Put these on. We're going on a mission."

"Hold on just a second." Kristine dropped the coveralls onto the table. Their metal buttons clicked against the wood, then they swished onto the floor. "I'm not going anywhere until you tell me exactly what is going on."

Who knew what type of crazy scheme June was hatching? Kristine was not about to do something that could get them both arrested the night before she was supposed to leave for Italy. In fact . . . maybe that was June's plan. She would not put it past her mother to get them both locked up in a jail cell "for Kristine's own good."

"Mother," she said. "I am going to Italy tomorrow. Whether you like it or not."

"For heaven's sake, stop being so self-centered." June's voice was sharp. "You love to travel. Go to Italy. See if I care."

Kristine looked at her mother in surprise. "Then . . . what on earth is going on?"

"I am *trying* to stop a great tragedy." June handed over the heavy binoculars. "Take a look."

Baffled, Kristine walked over to the window. She turned the cold metal dials of the binoculars until the scene across the way blurred into view. Her mother's friend Rose stood in Charley's kitchen, radiant in a turquoise pantsuit. She fluttered around Charley like an exotic bird.

Something warm and hopeful flickered through Kristine's chest. "Mom, do you have a crush on this man?"

When Kristine's father died, June had been so devastated that she swore she'd never love anyone ever again. Whenever Kristine brought it up, June just laughed. "Why would I waste my time cooking and cleaning for some man?" she always said. But June's obsession with Charley seemed a little beyond neighborly concern.

"Mom." Kristine kept her voice gentle. "It's been a long time. Dad would want you to be happy."

"What are you *talking* about?" June's arms flapped up and down. "You are missing the point entirely! This is a neighborhood matter. You see, Rose has wanted to live on this street for years." Flouncing over to the table, June yanked on a pair of camouflage hunting pants. They were at least two sizes too big and she rolled up the cuffs. "I would not put it past her to marry Charley Montgomery just to get her hands on that house."

"I see," Kristine said. Peering out the window, she squawked, "*Aack!* They're kissing."

"*What?*" June dashed across that room so fast that she could have set a world record. She took the binoculars out of Kristine's hands and trained them on the kitchen. After a long moment, she scowled. "That was not funny."

"No. It was very telling."

"You are getting the wrong idea," June said, pulling a black cap over her head. "I simply want to know what is going on. I can stomach Rose in small doses but not as a neighbor. I would rather cash in my grave reservation today."

Kristine laughed. "Well, don't do that." Reaching for the binoculars, she surveyed the situation. "No offense to Rose, but she has had a ridiculous amount of plastic surgery. I can't imagine Charley would go for her."

"Rose is a slut and Charley is a man." June sniffed. "I can't imagine that he wouldn't."

"Mother, come back here." Kristine's whisper was high pitched with worry. "I don't like this!"

June rolled her eyes. She had successfully hung a rope ladder over the edge of Charley's fence and was in the process of climbing over the wall and into his garden. There was no turning back now.

"Seriously," Kristine insisted in a voice much too loud for a covert mission. "This is not safe."

The only thing that could possibly make this unsafe would be if Kristine blew her cover. "Keep your eyes peeled," June whispered. "If they look like they're coming outside or even looking out the windows, just whistle."

The night was a little bit chilly, so June doubted that Charley would, in fact, bring Rose outdoors. There was no telling, though. The man was a sycophant. He might get a sudden urge to impress her by showing off his feeble flower garden.

"I can't whistle," Kristine said. "Can I just snap?"

*For heaven's sake, was it really that complicated?*

"Just let me know if they're coming," June whispered. She lowered herself to the ground, her exposed ankle brushing against the sharp thorns of a rosebush. Stealthily, she moved across Charley's garden, letting the light from the kitchen window be her guide.

The outline of Charley's fountain was her first marker. When June reached it, she stopped and placed her hand on the cold stone, breathing heavily. She relished in the sensation of standing in the center of his garden, the scent of jasmine in the air. It was just like the good ol' Garden War days.

*"Mother,"* Kristine called again.

*"Shh!"* June ducked behind the fountain, tugging her cap lower on her head. Honestly, where had Chloe been when she'd called? June flattened her body against trees and bushes, creeping her way toward the open window. Suddenly, Rose's laugh rang out through the night.

Bull's-eye.

Ducking underneath the window, June scrunched up her lips and listened.

"You were a pilot?" Rose crooned. "That is simply fascinating. I find pilots incredibly attractive."

"Oh, you flatter me." Charley chuckled. "Most women I know believe pilots are cocky."

"I like a cocky man," Rose said.

June sniffed. A cocky man indeed. If only she had a tape recorder, she would play back this shameful conversation for everyone they knew.

"Oh, dear." Rose's tone became low and intimate. "Why are you rubbing your shoulders? I understand you do quite a bit of work on your garden. Does that make you sore?"

There was the sound of a chair being pushed back across the linoleum floor. Frustrated, June stared up at the high ledge of Charley's window. What could she . . . *Aha!*

A white plastic bucket was tucked neatly into the bushes by

the door. Grabbing it, June flipped it over, climbed up on top and peered over the edge of the windowsill. For the briefest of moments, she caught a glimpse of Rose kneading away at Charley's shoulders. Although the man had a slightly bewildered look on his face, he certainly had not bothered to push her away.

A coldness settled in her chest. Just as she'd determined that she'd seen all she needed to see, the plastic bucket started to collapse beneath her. The movement was slow at first, then it seemed to buckle and sink. June felt a hot clutch of panic in her heart. She was going to fall.

Desperate, she fumbled for the nearest thing she could reach. This happened to be a rake, the very one that Charley leaned against the edge of the sliding glass door each evening before he went inside. Unfortunately, it wasn't stable.

The rake swayed and teetered beneath her grip. June stumbled off the bucket, the rake dropping to his low brick patio with a loud clatter. At the motion, lights blazed across the yard like something out of a prison movie. From across the garden wall, Kristine snapped frantically.

"What was that?" Rose's voice was frightened.

June heard heavy footsteps cross the kitchen floor. "I'll go find out."

There was no time to run. Instead, June pressed herself against the side of the house, next to the drainage pipe. If Charley were to step out of his back door and look around the yard, he would most certainly see her. The camouflage she was wearing would do little to help her blend in.

The back door scraped open. June squeezed her eyes shut tight. *Oh, dear.* If Charley caught her sneaking around his house, she would have some serious explaining to do. The man was so close she could practically hear him breathe. After a moment, he gave a little chuckle and went back inside.

"Well, aren't you going to go out there?" Rose asked.

"No, no. It's most likely a wild animal playing outside. That happens a lot around here."

"It could be a burglar," Rose pressed.

*Listen to the man!* June wanted to shout. *He said it was nothing.*

Charley's voice was amused. "I'm not concerned."

As the sound of his voice became muffled, June realized he'd turned away from the door. She was amazed to discover her heart was actually jackhammering in her chest. A heart attack would not be good. Especially on Charley's back porch.

"Oh, Charley." Rose's voice was silky. "You're so incredibly brave."

June rolled her eyes.

"Thank you, Rose," he said. "For your compliments and the dinner. It was lovely but I do have to confess, it's getting awfully close to my bedtime."

"My goodness, you're right!" June could easily imagine Rose making a big deal out of looking at her diamond-encrusted Rolex. "You simply must call me a car."

June knew the exact layout of Charley's kitchen, from a few too many spy missions with the binoculars. His phone was connected to the wall on the opposite side of the windows, so that meant he would have to face the other direction to place an order with the cab company. Even though the motion lights were as bright as the sun, June knew this would be her best chance to make a run for it.

Grabbing the smashed bucket under her arm, June darted across the yard. She paid no attention to the proper path, trampling goldenrods and jack-in-the-pulpits with every step. At the edge of the fence, she whispered, "Catch," and threw the bucket over the fence. With a speed that would make a squirrel proud, she scrambled up the ladder and over the wall.

"Mother, what happened?" Kristine ripped off the camouflage sweater and straightened her shirt. Her eyes were wide and frightened. "Did he see you? I was snapping as loud as I could."

"Of course he didn't see me." June worked to catch her breath. "But I will tell you this. Rose sounded desperate and Charley is not interested. I don't think she'll be moving in anytime soon." And because June was happy she had accomplished her investigation without getting caught, she gave a little victory dance.

Kristine laughed, pulling her into a hug. "What on earth am I going to do with you?"

# Twenty-seven

Mary Beth fell asleep at dinner. The restaurant they picked was a busy hamburger place and the food took forever. As they waited, Mary Beth scribbled on paper place mats with a packet of crayons and sipped at an apple juice. By the time her macaroni and cheese showed up, she took a couple bites then nodded off on the table.

"Being good can be very tiring," Chloe said, rubbing the little girl's back.

Once Mary Beth had nodded off, Chloe and Geoff spent the meal talking about intervention methods, so that she didn't feel so guilty about missing her review. Chloe loved watching the way Geoff bit his lip and looked to the side, thinking hard about whatever question she asked him. The more she got to know him, she realized that the tweed jackets and ascots hid a shy, thoughtful man, not some scary powerhouse psychologist, like she'd once imagined.

After dinner, Geoff scooped his daughter into his arms with a fluid motion. "Would you like to come over for a little while?" he whispered.

Chloe thought of the stacks of work waiting for her at home. "I can't. I still have so much to do . . ."

Geoff smiled, revealing three laugh lines in his left cheek. "That's part of the fun. You can play hooky." The wind rifled through his hair, making it—for a split second—as unkempt as Ben's.

Chloe thought about going back to her apartment. There, she'd have to worry about whether or not she'd bump into Ben, since things were still so incredibly awkward between them. After such a relaxing afternoon, that prospect did not sound appealing at all. "Let's do it."

Geoff hailed a cab and it screeched to a halt. She admired the easy way he slid in with the weight of Mary Beth in his arms. "You're pretty good at that."

"Thank you." Geoff looked down at Mary Beth's sleeping face and smiled. "I might need some help once in a while but it doesn't mean I don't enjoy being a father."

Geoff's building was all glass and metal and very sleek. The doorman was dressed in a gray uniform and smiled at Chloe as they walked in. As the elevator pinged to a stop on Geoff's floor, Chloe noted the pale blue carpeting of the hallway and that, somehow, everything smelled like lavender.

"This is beautiful." Geoff's corner unit afforded a spectacular view of the city. "And so . . . clean."

She had kind of expected his apartment to be in shambles, with toys and clothes thrown everywhere, but it was pristine. The decorations were very masculine, all black leather and silver accents. Chloe felt like she was in a high-end furniture display room, not the home of a four-year-old.

"I have a housekeeper." Geoff headed toward the back hallway with Mary Beth draped over his arms. "She leaves food in the fridge, picks up after Mary Beth. She's basically my surrogate wife."

Chloe nodded, but inside she was floored. What would *that* feel like, to have someone do her cooking and cleaning for her? It dawned on her that, in some respects, she knew. Ben was more than happy to cook for her, whenever she wanted. It was only recently that all that had changed.

Geoff strolled back into the room. "What's the frown for?"

"Not a thing." Chloe gazed down at the lights of Navy Pier. The Ferris wheel was turning, leaving a trail of golden light in its wake.

"I was thinking about what you said about our families knowing one another." Geoff got down on his knees and considered his wine cabinet. "I had the oddest feeling that I'd met you before, when I first saw your eyes." Looking over his shoulder, he smiled. "They're quite memorable."

Geoff poured them some wine and sat on the couch, patting the seat next to him. Feeling like Whiskers, Chloe perched where he'd told her to sit. He handed her a glass of wine and undid his ascot.

Pointing at it, she grinned. "Can I ask?"

Geoff laughed. "My grandfather wore ascots, my father wears them and now, me. It's tradition but it's also a conversation piece. A great icebreaker at the office."

Chloe was impressed. "I'll have to think of something like that. When it's my turn to open my place. *If* I ever open my place."

"You will." Geoff nodded. "With your ambition, you'll go far." Picking up his glass, he toyed with the stem. "I still feel guilty about that day in my office. I was intimidated by you, I think."

Chloe laughed. "Come on. What a line." The famed Dr. Gable was probably hoping to get her into bed. Remembering those green sweatpants, she blushed. The prospect was hardly unappealing.

"It's not a line, it's true." He turned to her, his handsome face earnest. "You were brave enough to come to me and ask for an endorsement for an incredibly advanced grant. I was impressed."

Chloe ran her hands over the stiff leather sofa. "Really?"

He nodded. "I used to be like you, ready to take on the world. Then real life got in the way. You remind me of that time, that optimism."

"I'm not optimistic," she admitted. "I'm just overworked. I haven't had a good night's sleep in . . ." Really, the last time she'd had a good night's sleep was during those two days where she'd hidden in her bed, so worried that she'd told him off. "Well, in a long time."

"Hopefully our relationship will invigorate you." He touched her hand. "The way it's invigorated me."

Chloe swallowed hard. Relationship? She thought of Ben's rude words at the club.

*Yeah,* she wanted to tell him now. *Geoff* is *my boyfriend. So there.*

Biting her lower lip, she looked up at him. "I'm glad . . . we're doing this."

"Me, too." Leaning forward, Geoff hesitated before touching his lips to hers. "May I kiss you?"

"Yes," she said. "But only if you never ask me that question again."

A startled look crossed his face and then he smiled. The kiss was soft and warm, just like that night at the piano bar. But this time, it left her toes tingling.

# Twenty-eight

Kristine bolted awake at 6 a.m.

*Italy, Italy, Italy!*

The thought sang through her head like a favorite love song. Leaping out of bed, she raced for the shower. As the coconut-scented shampoo ran down her body, she mentally ran through the list of what she'd packed, wondering whether there was time to double-check it before the cab arrived.

Ethan was already at the airport when she got there, sprawled out in a lobby chair. Spotting her, he got to his feet. "You look . . ." He blinked. "Incredible."

June had always insisted that it was critical to look good in three situations: on an airplane, at the doctor's office and when getting hit by a cab. So, Kristine was decked out in a pair of fitted designer slacks and a soft-as-the-clouds cashmere sweater. The sweater clung to curves that she normally kept hidden. She'd even taken the time to blow out her hair and it fell in vibrant waves around her shoulders.

At Ethan's obvious admiration, she flushed. "Sorry I'm late," she said, dragging her enormous suitcase behind her. "I thought I lost my passport, the cab was late, traffic was ridiculous . . ."

Ethan put a warm hand on her shoulder. For the first time all day, Kristine felt herself relax.

"*Buongiorno,*" he said.

At the word, Kristine's heart practically burst with joy. "*Buongiorno!*"

Ethan took the handle of her suitcase and lifted the carry-on bag off her shoulder. "Let's check in."

"Passport?" Ethan said, when it was their turn at the kiosk.

Handing it over, she admired how deftly he navigated the screen. Within moments, the machine had shot out their printed tickets. "Voilà. We might even have time for a snack in the lounge."

As they headed toward security, Kristine glanced in the window of a gift shop. There were all those magazines Chloe loved, waiting in the window. A nearby headline screamed, *All Alone!*

Embarrassed, Kristine looked at her boarding pass instead. "Oh, my gosh." She stared at it in surprise. "Ethan, you must have written one heck of an essay. These are in first class!"

He gave her a sly smile. "Or upgraded our tickets."

Kristine's heart sunk. For years, she'd not only fantasized that she and Kevin would see the world together but that, thanks to his millions of airline miles, he would upgrade their seats. It was a blow to think that a man she barely knew had fulfilled this fantasy instead.

Off her stricken expression, Ethan said, "Kris, it didn't cost a thing. I have so many frequent-flyer miles that I don't know what to do with them." He adjusted the worn leather satchel he'd tossed carelessly over one shoulder. "Besides, Italy's much too romantic for coach. We can relax, have some champagne . . ."

"Thank you." She shook her head. "I appreciate it. You really didn't need to do this."

"You deserve the best. Besides, I'm the one dragging you off to Rome in the first place, making you leave your husband for the week."

Kristine's mind flitted back to the reason Kevin wasn't there. Apparently, her husband had no interest in going on a romantic trip with her to a foreign country. He would much prefer a hunting trip with the boys. Standing in the airport, the thought hurt her as deeply as when he had first said it.

"As you know, my husband was invited." Kristine folded her boarding pass and placed it in her purse. "And as you know, he had other plans."

Reaching forward, Ethan brushed a persistent strand of hair out of her eyes. "Well, I think it's a good thing he didn't come." His dark eyes held hers, intent.

Kristine's heart caught in her throat. "Why?"

"Because." Ethan smiled. "He'd be sitting in coach."

That made her laugh.

"Let's hit security," he said, placing his hand at the small of her back. "For some reason, I have a feeling you'll want to spend time in the duty-free shops."

After shopping, they only had a short wait before pre-boarding began. Kristine loved walking up the special, first-class carpet. As the steward pushed back the curtains and led them to their seats, she looked around in shock. "This is ridiculously nice."

The area was spacious and the tan leather chairs absolutely pristine. A complicated-looking control could actually transform the chair into a bed. As she studied the control, a steward said, "Enjoy your flight, Kristine," and handed her a flute of ice-cold champagne.

"Maybe they'll throw my luggage in the ocean and have a set of Louis Vuitton waiting for me at baggage claim," she murmured.

Ethan smiled. "Sign me up."

They laughed and clinked glasses.

Kristine was having so much fun, but couldn't help but feel a tiny pang she wasn't experiencing this with Kevin. It would be nice to hold hands with her husband when the plane took off but . . . She sighed, making a conscious decision to keep disappointment out of her head. Looking around, she knew full well that the only thing she should feel was lucky.

Ethan was busy checking his email about a potential assignment, so she flipped through the *Time Out Rome* guide.

"Ladies and gentlemen," the steward's voice crackled over the PA system. "There will be a small delay."

The passengers on the plane groaned. Kristine and Ethan just looked at each other and smiled. Maybe it was the champagne, sitting in first class or the fact that she was finally going to Rome, but Kristine felt perfectly happy to be patient.

"Since we have time . . ." Ethan leaned over and put his arm around her. As his body shifted close to hers, her eyes widened. Time for what? With a start, she realized that he was pointing his camera phone at them. "Smile."

Relieved, she teased, "You're not going to use your fancy camera?" The worn leather bag filled with costly equipment was safely stowed somewhere above their heads.

Ethan pulled her even closer. "Nope. This is a spontaneous shot."

Kristine leaned her face against his and smiled, a big, cheesy, happy-to-be-going-to-Italy-and-sitting-in-first-class grin.

"Perfect." Ethan uploaded the picture to a site. "Valiant wanted me to do a few social media posts, so this is our first one. The essay contest winners, living a life of luxury out on the tarmac."

"I love it," Kristine said.

Ethan went back to checking his email and she to reading. Eventually, the cabin got a little too warm and Kristine felt sleepy. She let out a yawn.

"Get comfortable," Ethan said. "We've got plenty of time until Rome."

After snuggling up with her travel blanket and pillow set, courtesy of The Places You'll Go, Kristine dozed off with the fans whirring overhead. Eventually, the plane started to taxi toward the runway, rocking like a big ship. By the time the wheels lifted off, she was fast asleep.

# Twenty-nine

June was sitting at the wrought-iron table in her garden, just finishing up a piece of toast with raspberry preserves, when Charley's back door slid open. Before such late evenings with Rose, the man had been in his garden every morning at eight o'clock on the dot. Today, it was nearly nine.

Not that she was paying attention.

As June took a sip of tea, she heard a sudden clank of metal.

"Ahhh," Charley cried. "Help. Help!"

For heaven's sake, what had happened? June leapt up and rushed over to the fence. Charley was lying on his bricked patio in a crumpled heap.

The blood drained from her face. "Charley," she cried. "Are you alright?"

At the sound of her voice, he lifted his head. June practically collapsed against the fence with relief.

"I tripped over that darn rake." He pointed at the very same rake she had knocked over the night before, when she'd crept into his garden to spy on him and Rose. "I can't believe it."

In an effort to not look as guilty as she felt, June stuttered, "Well, why . . . why on earth do you keep a rake lying across your patio anyway?"

"I don't." His face was etched with pain. "Squirrels must have knocked it over." Gingerly, Charley pressed his hand against the top of his white socks. "Ooph." He flinched. "I think I might have twisted my ankle."

"Stay right there," she clucked. "I'll be right over."

Gathering up her breakfast plates, June rushed inside. She dumped everything on the counter, grabbed her keys and rushed out the front door. She practically sprinted (a feat she had not accomplished in years) down the front steps.

"Hold on, Charley," she shouted. "I'm on my way."

June ducked into the alley along the far side of the house, where he kept his garbage and recycle bins. The alley was rocky and cool and led to a rusted wrought-iron gate. She had to shove hard against some overgrown ivy, but eventually the gate opened right into his backyard.

"Huh," he grunted. With every step, her boots squished in the dew of the grass. "I should've known that you would know how to break into my garden. I haven't used that gate in years."

"Break into your garden?" June echoed. "Why—" She had half a mind to leave the man for dead, until she saw the rake lying next to his injured ankle. Eyeing it, she said, "Squirrels knocked this over? Are you sure it wasn't a raccoon? It looks pretty heavy."

In the mystery novels she read, it was not uncommon for the criminal to return to the scene of the crime. With a flash of glee, she suddenly understood why. There was something very satisfying about committing a crime and not getting caught.

Charley shook his head. "I'm not so sure about all that. My bucket's missing, too."

"Oh." Her glee faded. "Well, that's unusual."

The night before, June had set the smashed bucket next to her trash can. Kristine grabbed it, saying, "You at least have to make an effort to hide the evidence." She then shoved it in her trunk, like a body.

Pressing a hand against the brick patio, Charley attempted to get to his feet. He groaned, sinking back down to the ground.

Considering June had been the cause of his accident, it was within her best interest to ensure he made it indoors alive. Petty theft was one thing but murder? Quite another. "Grab my shoulder," she instructed, bending down. "Can you do that?"

Awkwardly, Charley wrapped his arm around her shoulder. June was startled to feel how strong it was. Even though she had seen his arms in those light blue gardening shirts he wore, she didn't realize they'd feel so . . . well, thick.

Clearing her throat, she said, "Now, don't dillydally. Let's go."

Charley gave a grunt and got to his feet. He limped to the back door. As they walked into his home, June was hit by the smell of fresh coffee and cinnamon toast.

The kitchen window had a perfect view of the very table where she'd been sitting. June wondered if Charley ever watched her, the way she watched him. According to Kristine, not everyone was as nosy as June but with this type of view, it would be insulting if he hadn't taken notice of her once or twice.

"Shall we call the doctor?" she asked, since Charley was not giving her an ounce of direction.

He shook his head. "Not much can be done for a sprain. I think I'll just sit for a while."

June helped Charley limp into a dark room at the front of the house. It smelled like firewood and black licorice. As her eyes adjusted, she saw that the walls of this room were made of a dark cherry and the built-in shelves were simply crammed full of books.

"You read mysteries?" June was surprised. He'd said it, that day on her front stoop, but she hadn't believed him. Charley Montgomery seemed like a war history type of man.

"All the time." Easing onto a chaise lounge covered in faded gold velvet, he wiggled his foot and winced. "I think it's a good real-life mystery that our neighborhood might have a crime ring."

"One missing bucket does not constitute a crime ring," June informed him.

He shrugged. "I don't know. I might just call the authorities."

June's heart skipped a beat. "Don't be ridiculous." She attempted to adopt an imperious tone, but her hands started to sweat. "I . . ." She cleared her throat. "I wouldn't report a thing."

"Well, we'll see." Charley eyed his ankle. "This was not how I expected to start my day."

"No one ever plans for an accident," she said. "That's why they're called accidents."

Giving her a look, Charley reached behind his back and pulled out a few feather throw pillows. He made a move to put them under his feet.

"Stop right there," June cried. "Charley Montgomery, you take off your shoes this instant!"

Even though this was not her home, she hated to see the man soil such a beautiful chair with muddy feet. If his wife were still alive, she would most certainly feel the same.

"Now, let's just lift your foot up on these pillows," she said once he'd removed his shoes.

When Charley struggled, June reached out and grasped his leg just above the ankle. She had not felt a man's leg since Eugene's and the sensation was quite strange. Charley's skin felt warm beneath her touch, his wiry leg hair brushing against her hand. Quickly, she dropped his foot onto the pillow.

"I'm going to get you some ice," June said, her voice strained. Walking toward the kitchen, she turned and shook her finger at him. "And don't you move. If you need something to read, I'll get it for you."

"June . . ." Charley shook his head. "Has anyone ever told you that you are downright bossy?"

June opened her mouth to argue but then stopped. "Yes." She smiled. "All the time."

In the kitchen, she filled a bag with ice and wrapped it in a kitchen towel. "Put this on your ankle," she instructed him. "I have to go run some errands. Will you be alright?"

Charley leaned back against the chaise lounge. "I'll be just fine. June, thank you." He smiled. "It's been a while since I've had someone to take care of me."

"Well." June hesitated, her hand resting against the wood of the wall. Knocking the wood twice, she said, "Don't get used to it."

# Thirty

Kristine awoke to the sound of Italian voices and the clatter of dishes. Climbing out of the cozy bed, she threw open the shutters and delighted in the damp morning air. It smelled like espresso and dust and history and motorbikes, which was so different from the stale, sprinkler-watered-lawn scent of the suburbs.

"*Buongiorno,*" she called to no one, spreading her arms out wide.

Glancing at the clock, Kristine rushed to get ready. She and Ethan had made plans to meet in the breakfast room at eight, then spend the day sightseeing. The Valiant luncheon wasn't for a few days, and she reveled in the fact that her sole responsibility was to explore.

Stepping out of the elevator, Kristine scanned the tiny dining area. Tourists of all shapes and sizes dotted wooden tables. Ethan sat in the corner, watching the room as though photographing the ambience in his mind.

After waving at him, Kristine walked over to a table filled with cheese, cold cuts and pastries. The tiny bottles of marmalade, shiny sugar rolls and thin slices of meat were so delightfully European that she piled her plate high. Balancing her breakfast and a bottle of water, she walked over to join him.

"No espresso?" he asked, raising an eyebrow.

Kristine grinned. "I'm too wound up already."

After breakfast, they set out for the Sistine Chapel. She couldn't help but beam at one or two people with particularly interesting faces. An Italian with a bulbous nose and deep lines creasing his forehead smiled back.

Ethan nudged her. "Did you see that?"

"See what?" Kristine stopped in the middle of the sidewalk. "The unified architecture, the guy driving by on a scooter or the signs pointing in the direction of the Vatican? Or that pigeon flapping around that lady at the table, trying to steal her biscotti?"

Ethan laughed. "I meant that grouchy old Italian man. When you smiled at him, he turned eighteen all over again."

Kristine blushed, smoothing her cream-colored dress.

As St. Peter's square loomed into sight, she stared up at it, stunned. Not one single picture in the guidebooks did it an ounce of justice. The baroque design was so perfectly symmetrical, so incredibly beautiful, that it was hard to believe that such a place existed as she went about her business on the other side of the world.

"That's . . . This is . . ." Kristine shook her head. "I'm in awe."

Ethan nodded. "Words can't capture it. It's just an emotion for me. Every time." Shrugging out of his black overshirt, he pointed at a street fontana. "Last chance for free water." Kristine was too busy taking everything in to care about something as basic as water.

Digging through her shoulder bag, she pulled out *Walking Tours of Rome.* If she remembered correctly, there had been a wealth of information on how to best tackle the Sistine Chapel. She flipped through the pages and then looked up at Ethan. At the fountain, he was crouched over, taking a long drink of water. Standing up, he wiped the back of his hand over his lips. Tiny drops of water scattered like diamonds in the sun.

"Hey, let me see that book for a minute," Ethan called, striding over to her.

"You should have brought your own," she said. "It's not like you don't work in a travel—"

Before the words had made it out of her mouth, Ethan had grabbed her book, walked over to the nearest trash can and tossed it in.

She stared at him, shocked. "Wait. What did . . . Why did . . . ?"

"Kristine, look around you." He did a slow turn, in the center of the square. Pigeons flew up in a flurry of feathers, then realizing he was not a threat, went back to foraging along the cobblestones. "You don't need a guidebook to see Rome."

Was he crazy? Of course she did! Thousands of people had visited Rome and a clever few had laid out the hows, whys and what fors. Suddenly, she decided she didn't like Ethan at all. What type of person would throw away another person's guidebook? Kevin would never do something like that.

Through her teeth, she said, "I want to get the most out of Rome as possible, in the brief period of time that I get to be here. I need my book."

"You don't need it," he argued. "Use your imagination. Think of the people who have been here before you. The stories they have to tell, the fights they had . . . the love they shared." Ethan studied her for a moment with his dark eyes. "Do me a favor. Close your eyes."

"No." She refused. "If I do, someone will march up and steal my . . . *Shit.*"

A family of Japanese tourists walked up and dumped a collection of gelato cones into the trash. After giving them a heartfelt glare, she rushed over. The guidebook was covered in goopy, creamy glop.

Ethan started laughing and she did her best to stay calm. "Seriously. You better find me a bookstore and get me another—"

"Relax." Walking up, he put his hand over her eyes. At his

touch, she sucked in a sharp breath. He guided her away from the garbage can and said, "Relax. Close your eyes."

Kristine let out a hearty sigh. "Is this going to bring my guidebook back?"

"Shh . . ." he whispered, his voice close to her ear. "Just listen to the sounds of the city. Feel the sunshine on your face. Breathe in the magic of Rome."

Eyes closed, Kristine took in an exaggerated breath. "There. Satisfied?"

"No. Tell me what you smell."

Kristine shifted in her sandals. She was not about to say it, but she could smell him. That sharp, earthy aroma of sandalwood, the musky scent of his body. Desperately, she tried to focus on the world around her. "I smell . . . the city. Grime, like it just rained and there was oil on the ground that couldn't come off."

"Good." Ethan's voice was low, intimate. "What else?"

Kristine took a deep breath. "Tomato sauce," she decided. "Burned meat from that restaurant. Somebody's perfume. And . . . vanilla." It was as though the gelato truck was only a foot away. "I can smell the gelato."

Gently, he caressed her temple with his thumb. "Now, what do you hear?"

Kristine could hear the chatter of the people around her, as though all of the travel guides in her store had come alive and started talking at once. Squeezing her eyes tightly shut, she forced herself to truly listen. She heard the clank of a cab door a few feet away. The whir from someone's camera as the flash found its power. The rustle of a backpack. The click of high heels on the cobblestones. The sound of Ethan's breath.

"Rome is all around you," he said. "You don't need a guidebook to see it."

Ethan lowered his hands and she opened her eyes, blinking like a newborn in the sun. The spires from the cathedral stretched to the sky, its white pillars in perfect uniform. The obelisk in the center of the square stood proud over thousands of people. So many lives with different wants, dreams and desires . . . Kristine wrapped her arms around herself and shivered.

Ethan took out his camera and snapped a few shots. She started, realizing that his camera lens was pointed at her.

Ethan lowered the camera. "That was beautiful."

Kristine's eyes fell to the top of her sandals, embarrassed. After a moment, she said, "I can't believe you threw away my guidebook."

"Guidebooks follow someone else's heart." Ethan packed up his camera. "Now, you can follow your own."

# Thirty-one

Chloe scanned the crowd at Dave & Busters, trying to spot her father. Not a difficult task. Kevin was the only six-foot-two grown man happily firing basketballs at an electronic basketball hoop.

Growing up, Chloe had loved the lazy summer nights she'd spent with her father, playing basketball in the driveway, playing catch in the backyard or tossing around a football. Even if he was disappointed by the fact that her football career would never go further than the front yard, he still tried to instill a passion in her for the game. Each year, he got them season tickets to the Bears.

Chloe loved those games. Feeling the cold metal of the bleachers, snacking on popcorn, drinking hot cocoa . . . The games were a priority and there had only been one time, in high school, where something became more important than that time with her father.

On that day, a friend called and asked her to go to the Water Tower. A boy they both liked was going to be there. Did she want to come? It took about a half-second for Chloe to say yes.

When she told her father she was ditching the game, he looked at her like she was a stranger. "But . . . we're going to see the Bears."

"Dad," Chloe scoffed. "Come on. I'd rather not spend the day bored out of my mind."

The hurt on his face, even though he tried to hide it, pierced her through the heart.

The following week, she joined him for the game. Even though he didn't say a word about the week before, he cheered louder than usual, rattled off even more sports statistics and when the game was over, made a point of buying them matching T-shirts. On the car ride home, he'd ruffled her hair.

The Bears had been a tradition that had lasted just past high school. Chloe wished there was still time to see a game but there just wasn't. Maybe someday, but for now, a quick dinner at a sports bar would have to do.

"Dad," she called, waving.

Kevin glanced over. "Hey! Hold on. Just need to . . ." He made the last three shots. Then he rushed over and tackled her, lifting her high in the air. "How's my girl?"

"Put me down," Chloe laughed. "People are staring."

Kevin dropped her to the floor, chuckling. Mussing her hair, he said, "You look smart. Like you learned a lot today."

Chloe rolled her eyes. She'd stayed up until four studying and only made it through the day with the help of diet soda. "I look exhausted. But I did just take my first midterm. I might have passed."

Thanks to Geoff, the test had been pretty easy. For two nights straight, they'd met at his office and prepared. There had been a few moments of relatively tame hanky-panky on the couch, and she did make him sing some shitty 1930s music, but mainly, he helped her study.

"Good," Kevin said. "I'm proud of—"

An eight-year-old boy with a cowlick pushed past them, shoving money into the basketball machine. As the balls dropped with a clatter, Kevin eyed him like a bug. "Do you want me to physically remove that kid so we can play a few rounds?"

"Dad, stop that." Chloe laughed. "He's just a little boy."

Kevin pretended to glower. "He's a punk. I guess we could play air hockey instead."

Chloe and her father used to play air hockey in their basement for hours, back before Ben broke the table. He'd accidentally dumped an entire cup of Mountain Dew into the console. She had never admitted that to her dad, even though he'd been looking for the culprit for years.

"Can we eat? I kinda have to hurry because I'm supposed to meet my . . ." Chloe coughed. "Boyfriend. After this."

Kevin was already walking over to the hostess stand but he stopped short. "Boyfriend? Is it serious?"

She grinned. "Who knows?"

Her father eyed her for a long moment. "You know, you have to warn me if I'm going to have to pay for a wedding. And I want to meet this guy, first. No running off to Vegas."

Chloe laughed. "Stop it. It's serious, but . . . it's no big deal."

Since most of the dates with Geoff had included Mary Beth, it had started to become obvious to her that he wasn't looking for a short-term fling. Plus, he kept talking about their relationship in future tense. The whole experience was completely different from the college guys she'd dated. Or that disastrous practice date with Ben.

"Huh." Kevin grabbed some menus from the hostess stand, as well as a handful of mints. Squeezing the wrapper on one, he popped a candy into his mouth. "Is he a good guy?"

Before Chloe could answer, a young girl with bleached blonde hair rushed up. She was at least a few years younger than Chloe and wore bright blue eyeliner. "Table for two?"

"Yes, ma'am." Kevin nodded, handing her the menus. "Please."

The young girl stared up at him with adoration. "Yes, *sir*. Follow me."

Chloe's jaw dropped. *Ew!* Did a girl *her very own age* just flirt with her father?!

As they took a seat at the table, Chloe kept a close eye on the situation. The hostess made a point out of touching Kevin's shoulder and telling him again and again to have a good meal. Honestly, Chloe was surprised she didn't just climb into his lap.

"Ugh, I can't believe that," Chloe said when the girl practically skipped away from the table. "She just like . . . *flirted* with you."

Kevin frowned. "Huh?" He looked after the girl, completely oblivious.

Chloe took in her father's ruddy complexion and bright blue eyes. In those moments when his face split into a grin, he really was handsome, in that older, sporty-guy type of way. "Dad, I can't believe I'm about to say this." She flipped open a menu, shaking her head. "The verdict is still out, but I think you've got game."

"Yeah?" He grinned. "Well, be sure to tell your mother. Try and make me look good."

After they placed an order for two burgers, a round of onion rings and Cokes, he drummed his hands on the table. "So," he asked. "What else is going on at school? Scholarship's all good?"

"Haven't lost it yet." Chloe updated her dad on her classes, the internship options coming up in the winter and finally, the news that (supposedly) she was making a good impression on her professors. Her father listened with rapt attention, only looking away when the food arrived. The plates were piled high with juicy burgers and enormous breaded onions.

"That looks great." He groaned, shaking his head. "A heart attack on a plate."

"Hey, how's Mom?" she asked, taking a bite of her burger. "Have you talked to her?"

Kevin nodded. "That first night. It sounded like she had a nice plane ride. That tour company put her in first class."

"I know!" Chloe wiped her hands on her napkin and found her phone in her backpack. "Check out this picture. It's so awesome."

The picture was up on the Valiant travel blog. She figured her dad hadn't seen it, considering he didn't really keep up with technology, unless it was sports related. There was the picture of her mom sitting on the tarmac, beaming into the camera.

"Let me see." Kevin reached for the phone and squinted. "Who the hell is that?" he roared, banging at the screen with his finger. "With her?"

Chloe hesitated. Even though the picture with Ethan was cozy, it was obvious her mother was just trying to fit into the photo frame. Based on the angry flush on her father's face, he did not see it that way. "Dad, that's just Ethan," she said. "The guy from her store."

Kevin glared at the picture, the vein in his forehead a little too prominent. Man, he seemed really pissed. Chloe shifted, suddenly uncomfortable.

"Didn't she tell you she was traveling with—"

"Yeah, she told me. But . . ." He eyed the picture. "She didn't say—"

"That he kinda looks like an international man of mystery?" Chloe hoped that, by making a joke, her father would calm down.

Kevin snapped his head up, his eyes blazing. "She *said* that?" *Maybe not.*

"Dad, of course not." Chloe took her phone and studied the picture. Actually, she could kind of see his point. She wouldn't be jumping up and down if this was a picture of Geoff and another woman. Still, she said, "Mom told me that she didn't find this guy attractive. Not in the slightest."

"Huh." Kevin took an angry bite of his burger.

"Besides . . ." Chloe nudged him. "Unless I'm missing something, she already has a guy. Who just happens to be the father of her perfect, wonderful, fabulous daughter."

"Yeah." His voice was gruff.

They sat in silence for a moment.

"So." He took a drink of his Coke and set the glass down with a crash on the table. Picking up his burger, he said, "What else is going on?"

"Just school." Chloe told him about the writing cramps she got from jotting down her feelings after each and every session. "They make us keep these journals to make sure we're handling everything okay," she said. "Sometimes, I think it might be fun to make something up to freak out my professors, but I don't think that would go over too well."

"Yeah," Kevin said. "Probably not."

Chloe chewed her burger, watching him. Even though he was still laughing at her stories, passing the ketchup and stealing her onion rings, his eyes kept drifting back to her cell phone.

It was obvious that his mind was half a world away.

# Thirty-two

Every time June thought about the way Charley had tripped over that rake, she felt guilty. He could have hit his head. Or had a heart attack. Or a stroke! June wanted to do something to make it up to him.

"Oooh, you're going to bring him a casserole?" Chloe asked when she'd heard of June's plan.

"No, not a casserole." She sniffed. "I am not one of *those* women."

"Well, you almost killed the guy," Chloe said. "Bring something good. And dress up. Don't go over there looking like you worked in the garden all day."

At promptly 6 p.m., June showed up on Charley's doorstep carrying a bag from the corner market. It was filled with a Cornish hen, a half pound of mashed potatoes, some well-cooked green beans and a pecan pie. Smoothing her hair, June considered what she was wearing. She had certainly not dressed up because she didn't want Charley to get the wrong idea. However, she had donned a simple tweed dress with a pair of red high heels, then spritzed on some orange-scented perfume.

June pressed the doorbell, noticing the stained-glass etching along the edges of Charley's door. When Eugene died, Kristine had forced June to buy a new door with no windows other than the peephole. "It would be so simple for a criminal to smash that glass, Mother." It had broken her heart, but Kristine would not take no for an answer.

Charley's door swept open. It took a moment for her to register that Rose was standing in the entryway, her hands on her hips. "Can I help you?" she asked, as though June were some kid trying to peddle magazines.

"Hello, yourself." June pushed past Rose and surveyed the situation. The last time she had been present in Charley's home, the place had smelled like a man. Now, it smelled like lavender bathwater. Turning to Rose, she said, "What are you doing here? Again?"

Rose pressed her manicured mauve nails into June's shoulder. "I was speaking with Charley on the phone and he told me all about his accident." Leaning forward, she murmured, "Just between you and me, it sounded like a cry for another casserole, but he really is feeling quite blue."

June swept past her and into the den. Charley was stretched out on the chaise lounge, looking anything but blue. He was wearing a pair of silver reading glasses and flipping through the pages of a classic Sherlock Holmes novel.

"June!" Charley slid off his glasses. "How nice of you to drop by."

"It looks like you already have company." She had to make an effort to keep the annoyance out of her tone. "However, I've brought you some more food."

Rose clucked. "The casserole is already in the oven. If we would have known you were coming . . ."

"Yes, June." Charley grinned. "If *we* had known you were coming, we would have asked you to bring dessert."

June flushed. "I did." Setting the brown bag down on a wooden end table, she rifled through it and pulled out the pecan pie. "Here you are."

"My goodness." Rose folded her hands. "Is that . . . store-bought?"

"I think it looks delicious," Charley said. "Pecan pie is my favorite."

June was surprised to hear this. Pecan pie was her favorite, which was why she picked it. She had pegged Charley as more of a peach pie type of man. "It is indeed store-bought," she told Rose, "but that particular store is serviced by the finest bakery in town. I imagine it will taste much better than a strudel."

"Does this mean you're staying for dinner?" Charley asked.

Rose narrowed her eyes. "I really don't know if we'll have enough food . . ."

The doorbell chimed. They all looked toward the entryway, and Charley seemed genuinely puzzled.

"Now, who in the world could that be?"

"I'll get it," Rose and June chorused. Glaring at each other, they strode out of the den and into the foyer. Rose's high heels clicked across the hardwood floor like a horse trying to win a race.

In the hallway, she stopped abruptly in front of the mirror. Pinching her cheeks pink, she turned and glared at June. "Now, you listen to me." Her voice was practically a hiss. "You may as well save your breath. Charley is as good as mine."

"You can have him," June said, exasperated. "I don't even like the man."

"Oh, please." Rose made a face that could have been a frown, but with all of that Botox, it was hard to tell. "Sneaking in like you have nothing at stake. Don't think you're going to be the one who walks away with the silver fox."

"The silver fox?" June echoed, bewildered. "What is he, a holiday ornament?"

The doorbell chimed again. With a toss of her red-dyed hair, Rose pushed past June and opened the door. "What on earth are *you* doing here?" she gasped.

Rose sounded so genuinely distressed that June was certain it had to be Rose's ex-husband. He was a distasteful man, with a rather strong passion for the drink. June pulled Rose out of the way, ready to give the man a piece of her mind. Charley or no Charley, no one messed with her friends.

To her surprise, the person on the front stoop wasn't Rose's ex-husband. In fact, it wasn't a man at all.

It was Bernice, eagerly clutching a casserole.

# Thirty-three

Kristine leaned back in her black metal chair at a corner cafe. The hotel was right next door, a charming structure made from dark gray stone. Next to it loomed a building that had to be at least eight hundred years old, with its stained yellow walls and faded blue shutters.

"I love it out here," Kristine told Ethan. "In fact, I think I love everything about Rome." Kristine had been having the time of her life but something was happening, something between her and Ethan. Maybe it was the fact that she was spending so much time with him or because being in Italy felt like her life back home didn't exist, but Kristine had found herself becoming more and more attracted to him. After all, he was paying attention to her in a way that her husband hadn't in years. It made her feel uncomfortable but at the same time, bold and adventurous, in a way she'd always wanted to be.

Kristine shook her head. Reaching for the carafe, she refilled her wineglass. As the last drops of ruby liquid dripped into her cup, she said, "Looks like we should order another."

A slight smile lifted the corners of Ethan's mouth. "Something about that sounds delicious."

A waiter darted from the inside of the restaurant back out into the street, balancing plates of steaming spaghetti carbonara, penne arrabiata and wild mushroom scallopini. Ethan caught his attention and, after dropping off the plates, the waiter brought more wine.

As he poured, Kristine watched a group of tourists rush past on the sidewalk. She wondered if any of their guidebooks were from her shop in Lincoln Park. Even with a good memory for her customers, it was doubtful she'd recognize any of them, since she was so far from home.

Kristine herself felt unrecognizable. That afternoon, she'd had it with her long, boring hair. Ducking inside a Roman beauty parlor, she made the universal motion for "chop it off." When the hairdresser was finished, short, wispy tendrils framed her face and brushed the top of her shoulders. Ethan said, "It was like watching Michelangelo chip away at the marble until the angel came out."

Now, he took her hand in his and caressed her palm with his thumb.

Kristine ran her tongue over the roof of her mouth, tasting the sweet aftertaste of the wine. Her breathing was shallow. She squeezed his hand, then pulled hers away.

Ethan's eyes held hers for a long, questioning moment. "Come on," he finally said, gesturing at the dance floor.

The dance floor was a partitioned area out in the middle of the street. White lights were strung overhead and a street band played from a small wooden platform. Couples of all ages moved their bodies to the music, under the looming neighborhood hotels.

Kristine hesitated for just a moment but got to her feet. She smiled as Ethan pulled her close to him, and she relished in the feeling of her body against his. He was an experienced dancer, guiding her in and out of turns. Each moment they touched, her entire body tingled. She found herself pressing against him, drawing out the moments, before he'd spin her out into a turn.

Slowly, the music ebbed into a gentle rhythm. Ethan put his

hand at the small of her back and guided her close to him. They were both wet with sweat and Kristine closed her eyes, trying to fight against the attraction growing inside of her. The tingle in her stomach turned into a full-on shudder as Ethan buried his face in her hair and inhaled deeply.

Pressing her hands into his shirt, Kristine blocked out everything but the feeling of his body against hers. She took in slow, steadying breaths as his thumb traced the exposed skin on the back of her arm.

*Stop this*, her conscience screamed. *You shouldn't be doing this!*

But it felt too good to stop. She was just dancing, enjoying the feel of the air, the sight of the white lights swaying above her and the friendly face of the mandolin player bobbing along with the music.

There was a low wolf whistle from the side. Kristine's eyes opened and she looked over, embarrassed. But the young Italian with slicked black hair, his red shirt open at the collar, was not whistling at her. He was tapping his hands against his knees and staring at a dark-haired woman undulating in the center of the floor.

Ethan reached up and, ever so slowly, moved Kristine's hair away from her shoulder. As the singer wailed about lost love over the microphone, Ethan lowered his full, warm lips to her skin. "*Come sei bella*," he whispered. "Let's go back to the hotel . . ."

They were only steps away and she hesitated. It was obvious her husband had lost interest in her a long time ago. Was she really going to spend the rest of her life waiting for something to change?

Ethan spun her around. Leading her away from the dance floor, he kissed the soft skin on the inside of her wrist. They stopped for a moment on the front steps, gazing at each other in the yellow light of the ancient streetlamp. Gently, he reached forward and tucked a strand of hair behind her ears.

Leaning in, he brushed his lips against her ear. "I told you," he whispered. "You're the woman in the cream-colored dress."

He reached for the door handle and pulled it open. Her heart was beating in quick little starts and she took a deep breath, trying to find the right words to put an end to the evening. Suddenly, as her eyes focused, she felt her heart thud to a heavy stop.

There, in the red couch facing the front door, sat her husband.

# Thirty-four

Kristine stood stock-still, stunned. What was Kevin doing here? What had he *seen*?

Without a word, he stood up and strode toward the stairs.

"Kevin, wait!" She dropped Ethan's hand and rushed after him, up all three flights of stairs. Her legs burned with the effort, her heart pounding in her ears. "Kevin," she begged. "It's not what you think."

Her husband didn't look at her, just keyed into her room. The door remained open behind him and she stood in silence, trying to compose herself. The thought that he had been right next to where she'd had dinner, right next to the dance floor . . . A brackish taste filled her mouth. She took a few deep breaths, trying to calm the icy waves crashing through her heart.

Walking into the room, Kristine locked the door and dared to look at him. Kevin avoided her gaze, ducking into the bathroom. He left the door half open and there was the sound of running water. She bit her nail to the quick, waiting. She jumped slightly as he walked back out, wiping his face with a towel.

Kristine dropped her gaze to the luggage rack, where his suitcase was neatly set out. "That's amazing." Her voice came out high pitched, a little drunk. "In the U.S., I can't even talk to the credit card company without your authorization but here, you're welcome to just move in." She felt panic settling in. What was she saying? What had she *done*? "This room is too small for two people. We'll need to get something bigger."

"The room's fine." Kevin walked over to the window and threw open the shutters, staring outside. The scent of garlic and onions filled their room from the restaurant down below. The smell made Kristine's stomach turn. She wondered if Ethan's window was open. His room was by the alley, too. Would he hear the conversation they were inevitably about to have?

Kevin turned and studied her for a long moment. His eyes were dull, like the ocean after a storm. "You cut your hair."

Kristine flushed, bringing a hand up to touch it. "I did."

Dishes clattered downstairs. Absently, she reached for the hair that was no longer there as though to twist it into a tight bun. Frustrated, she dropped her hands.

Why wasn't he saying anything? It all felt so unfair. Kristine had been loyal for twenty-five years, without exception. Could Kevin say the same? There had been so many times when he was away on his business trips that she couldn't help but wonder. Had he ever gone for a drink, flirted with a stranger, considered breaking their vows?

In her heart, she'd always trusted him. The same way he'd trusted her. At the thought, a tiny headache pulsed behind her eye.

"I'd like to go to bed," she said. "I'm tired."

Kristine wasn't tired; her stomach was churning with shame. But turning off the lights, climbing into bed and falling asleep sounded like a welcome relief. Much more appealing than having a knock-down, drag-out fight about something she didn't yet understand.

"I'm sorry," Kevin said.

At first, she thought her husband meant, *Sorry you're tired, but I'm going to talk and you're going to listen.*

He surprised her by adding, "I'm sorry, Kristine. I should have come with you. When you asked."

Kristine squeezed her hands in confusion. Where was the anger? The accusations? She moved her mouth as though to speak but nothing came out.

"But I'm here." His voice was quiet. "It's what you wanted, so I . . ." He stopped, as though realizing her wants might have changed completely.

"Yes," Kristine said quickly. "It's what I wanted. I'm glad you came."

Kevin pressed his palm against the windowsill and stared into the night. She followed his gaze to the building across the street. It was the one with the stained yellow walls and faded blue shutters, the one she'd admired from the restaurant. The lights were off in most of the rooms.

Kristine took a seat on the edge of the bed. The mattress was small, which Kevin wouldn't like. He'd hang off the ends of the bed like an extra appendage that didn't belong. The thought made her unspeakably sad.

"Please." She willed her voice not to tremble. "Let's just go to bed."

Kevin continued to stare out the window. A motorbike drove by outside. As the sound faded into the distance, her husband said, "Did you sleep with him?"

The question hung in the air between them like exhaust. It was a question that, in all of their twenty-five years of marriage, they'd never had to ask.

Kristine ducked her head. "No."

Her husband let out a loud breath and buried his face in his hands. He was silent for such a long moment that she didn't know what to think. Finally, she heard a slight snuffle.

"Are you crying?" Kevin hadn't cried in front of her in ages.

"When I saw you walk in, holding that guy's hand . . ." Lowering his hands, he turned to face her. A tiny tear glistened beneath his lower eyelash. It sparkled in the low light of the room.

Kristine felt a lump in the back of her throat. Grabbing for the tiny bottle of water on the bedside table, she took a desperate, cleansing sip. "Kevin, it wasn't what you—"

He shook his head. "I've really fucked this up. Haven't I?"

"It's not you, it's . . ." Once again, she reached for her hair, desperate to twist it on top of her head. But it wasn't there anymore. Kristine was so frustrated, her eyes filled with tears. "We don't see each other enough to talk or just . . ." Her voice trailed off.

Back when they were first married, they'd spent every moment of free time together biking along Lake Michigan, exploring Thai restaurants in search of the perfect curry, taking a boat out with friends . . . When had all of that fallen away? Kristine had spent more time with Ethan this week than she'd spent with her husband all year.

"We're just not like we used to be," she said.

"No." Kevin wiped the back of his hand over his eyes. "I guess not."

Downstairs, someone yelled, *"Bellissima!"* There was the sound of glasses clinking.

Turning, Kevin closed the window. After a moment, he walked over to her and took a seat on the bed. The mattress dipped, causing her to fall against him. He reached for her hand. Kristine gripped his like an anchor.

"I love you, Firecracker." Kevin said the nickname slowly, as though it was a foreign word. "I know we haven't been what you wanted for a while now but that's going to change. I promise you that."

Kristine let out a small, shaky breath. She'd waited to hear him say those words for such a long time. But now that he had, the ice that had formed over her heart did not break free and float away as she'd once expected. Instead, a little voice inside her head said, *We'll see.*

"I don't even know what to say about tonight," he said, staring down at their hands. "I . . ." Looking up at the ceiling, he breathed in sharply through his nose.

Kristine squeezed his hands as hard as she could. "Nothing happened. Kevin, look at me."

Kevin turned to face her. Her heart ached to think that she had caused him so much pain. It was so hard to believe that he was here, in Italy, just like she'd wanted, but that these were the moments they were sharing.

"I love you." Her voice trembled. "I'm so sorry."

"I love you, too." The words came out in a rush.

Kristine tried to release his hand, patting it gently, but he held on tight. Kevin leaned in as though to kiss her.

For years, Kristine had entertained actual fantasies about kissing her husband on foreign soil. She imagined a passionate embrace beneath the Eiffel Tower, a stolen moment in a cab in Cairo or even a simple snuggle under the bright lights of Tokyo. But never once had she imagined sharing this kiss on a night when she'd walked into a hotel with another man.

Kristine put her hand on his shoulder before their lips could touch. "It's been a long night. Let's just go to bed." Standing up, she found her pajamas and walked to the bathroom to change.

# Thirty-five

After a movie date with Geoff, Chloe spent the night at his place for the first time. When she woke up, she was surprised to find that the expensive sheets were rumpled but he was no longer in them. Drawing the comforter up to her chin, she felt slightly embarrassed. It wasn't like they'd had sex, but things had progressed to a new level.

"You're up," Geoff said, sweeping into the room. He was carrying a tray filled with breakfast. Setting it onto the comforter, he gave her a firm kiss on the lips.

"Yum. What's all this?" Chloe was delighted. Eggs, bacon, toast . . . Then, she looked toward the door, whispering, "Isn't Mary Beth going to freak out when she sees me here?"

"Mary Beth is at dance class," Geoff said. "So, enjoy this little meal that my illustrious housekeeper cooked for you—I'm not going to lie and pretend I cooked it myself—then before I go in to the office, I think I'd like to revisit what we were doing late last night."

Chloe's eyes wandered over his body. The night before, she'd loved running her hands over his chest and kissing just above that trail of hair she'd seen that day in his office. "Hmm," she said. "I can't quite remember?"

Geoff smiled. "Maybe I should remind you."

Leaning down, he pushed back the comforter and buried his face in her chest. Chloe's eyes widened. It was obvious that, without his child in the house, his intentions were a little more adult. Pulling back, Geoff looked at her with a wicked gleam in his green eyes. "Unless," he whispered, "you have somewhere to be?"

Chloe glanced at the alarm clock. Eight a.m., more than two whole hours until she had anywhere to be. Pushing the breakfast tray aside, she said, "I think I'm more than happy to stay right here."

"This is scandalous." June was sitting outside, whispering into her cordless phone to Chloe as bees buzzed around her. Rose and Bernice were *both* at Charley's house sharing lunch with him. He had shouted over the fence, "June, join us," but she had pulled down the rim of her enormous derby-style hat and turned up her nose.

"It's disgusting." She took an angry sip of iced-tea. "I have never seen such a shameless display." Over the phone, June could hear the sound of dishes clanking and people shouting. "Where are you?" she demanded. "I'm hearing all sorts of background noise."

"At a restaurant. With Geoff." Chloe's voice practically danced with delight.

"Oh," June said, depressed. Kristine was in Rome, Chloe was on yet another date and here she was, in her garden all alone. A bee buzzed over the top of her zinnias and June followed it with her eyes.

"I've got news," Chloe said suddenly. "Did you hear? That Dad went to Rome?"

June sat straight up in her chair. *Well. This* was *news.*

"When did this happen?" she asked.

"After I showed him a picture of Mom and Ethan sitting together on the plane. Dad had a fit." Chloe laughed. "He's going for ten days and extending her ticket, which I'm sure will make Mom very happy. Annie's handling everything at the store."

June didn't know whether to feel delighted or offended. It was bothersome that Kevin hadn't taken *her* word for it but she was just happy that he'd gone. "Good. It's about time your father . . ." She bit back her words, not wanting to upset Chloe. "Took a vacation."

"Oh, I should hang up," Chloe said. "Mary Beth looks like she's about to have a meltdown."

"Well, have fun." June fought back a wave of loneliness. She wanted to ask Chloe to come over for dinner, but she knew the girl was much too busy. "Tell Geoff I said hello." She watched a hummingbird dart around a flower. "And that I very much look forward to meeting him."

"Hang in there, Grandma," she said. "Don't let ol' Charley get you down."

"Oh, I won't." June removed her gigantic hat and set it on the table, fluffing her hair. "I just can't believe that women who are supposed to be my friends are spending time with that man." The group across the fence was joking and laughing as though he were hosting a dinner party.

Chloe paused. "Are you jealous?"

"No," June cried. Charley looked over and she lowered her voice. "I am just disgusted to see my friends once again competing over a man. A man such as Charley Montgomery, no less."

"Enjoy it," Chloe said. "It should be like watching a good tennis match."

At that very moment, Rose bent over the table. Her purple taffeta blouse gaped open just enough to draw Charley's attention. Stepping forward, Bernice made a big show of "accidentally" spilling iced-tea down Rose's blouse, who then shrieked in outrage.

"Oh, it is." June's voice was wry. "But to tell you the truth, I'm not rooting for any of them."

# Thirty-six

Kristine was confused to wake up in Kevin's arms. Their bodies were slick with sweat, the heat of the room too much between them. She wondered at what point they'd reached for each other and who had initiated it, considering they hadn't slept this way in ages.

Slowly, Kristine ducked out of his grasp. Pulling the sheets up to her chin, she stared at the stucco ceiling. What had she been thinking the night before? It had all seemed so simple, in the moment, but it had been so wrong. Yes, things had been difficult between her and Kevin but he was her *husband*. How had she let herself get so swept away? As much as she hated to admit it, her mother had been right. What had that note said? The one that she'd left in the store? *Circumstances can, on occasion, make us question the choices we've made.* It was true. Walking through the streets of Rome, Kristine had felt stimulated in ways she hadn't in years. As though she had become a brand-new person or, in some ways, the person she'd always wanted to be. But the person she'd been last night . . . that had been something else entirely.

From across the room, Kristine's cell phone buzzed in her purse. Quietly, she slid out from the sheets. The text was one simple word. *Breakfast?* She imagined Ethan sitting downstairs in the community room, his plate filled with fruit and bread.

Closing her eyes, she let out a breath. As much as she wanted to pretend the whole thing had never happened, she at least owed him the courtesy of an explanation. She would go talk to him. Quickly.

Just before slipping out the door, she wondered if she should leave Kevin a note. A loud snore slipped out of his mouth. *No*, she decided. She would just have to be quick.

Her husband would never even know she was gone.

Stepping out from the elevator, Kristine breathed in the now familiar scent of the breakfast room. Ethan sat at their table in the corner, wearing a black shirt and tight black jeans. Embarrassed, she remembered how his lips had felt pressed against her skin.

As she walked across the room, Ethan's eyes swept over her as though trying to gauge whether or not she'd spent a night of passion with her husband. Raising his espresso in greeting, he said, "Will he be joining us this morning?"

Kristine hovered at the edge of the table. "He's asleep."

Ethan's eyes searched hers. After a long moment, he set his espresso on the table. "I take it you didn't know he was coming."

"It was a nice surprise. We'll probably head off on our own, if that's okay."

Picking up a roll, Ethan broke it in half and spooned marmalade into the center. "No worries. I'll head to the Amalfi coast. I have some friends there."

"Ethan, I—"

Out of the corner of her eye, Kristine saw a hulking figure step out of the tiny cage of the elevator, looking around.

*Shit.*

Spotting her, Kevin rushed across the restaurant and hugged her tightly against him. His body was a little too warm, as though he'd leapt out of bed. "Morning." Deliberately, he gave her a loud smack on the lips. Then, he turned to glare at Ethan.

"Kevin," she warned. "Let's go back up—"

Kevin gave her a conspiring wink. "I'm just gonna have a quick chat with our little friend."

Kristine's heart jumped. "No." She gripped his strong arm, which was practically vibrating with anger. "Kevin, let's just—"

Ethan got to his feet. "Kris, it's—"

That was the only excuse Kevin needed. Lunging toward Ethan, he planted one hand on the wall behind him and pressed the other down hard on his shoulder. "Stay the fuck away from my wife," he growled. *"Capisce?"*

The conversation in the breakfast room came to a halt. The hotel guests stared and whispered, while the man in charge of making coffee stepped out from behind the bread table. He spoke in loud Italian to another man and Kristine felt very afraid.

"Kevin." She grabbed him by the back of the shirt and pulled. The fabric stretched under her hand like a rubber band. "We're leaving. Now."

Kevin dropped his hands from the wall, still glaring at Ethan. Even though she could feel everyone in the breakfast room staring, she didn't dare look back. The elevator doors clanked open and she dragged her husband inside.

In the sudden silence, she took in a deep breath. Even though her hands were shaking, there was an odd part of her that felt hopeful. She felt a sense of appreciation that Kevin would literally fight for their relationship, instead of just walking away.

Turning to him, she touched his arm. "I'm sorry. I just—"

"What the fuck, Kristine?" Kevin shook her hand off. "Do you want to be with that guy? Because if you do, I can leave right now."

"Of course not. Ethan won us this trip." Her voice was quiet. "At the very least, I owed him the professional courtesy of telling him I'd be spending the rest of the time with you."

"You don't owe him anything!" Kevin slammed his fist into

the wall of the elevator. The cage rattled dangerously. *Great*. Her husband was going to break a machine that had to be hundreds of years old and they'd be stuck. This was just great.

"You need to calm down," Kristine practically shouted. "You're scaring me."

They stood in tense silence the rest of the way up to their floor. The elevator creaked and groaned its way up to their floor and finally, the doors clattered open. Kevin just stood there, as though debating whether or not to ride back down to the lobby and get on the first plane home.

"I want to be with you," Kristine said. "I always have."

Her husband didn't answer. Instead, he turned and stomped down the hallway toward their room, his large frame practically bumping against the narrow edges of the walls. "Come on," he said. "We have to grab the bags."

Kristine's heart sunk. "Kevin, no. I'm not going home. You can't—"

"We're not going home." A look of pride crossed his face. "I'm taking you to Venice."

When the train finally arrived at the Saint Lucia station, Kevin sat as still as a stone as the other passengers got off the train. Finally, he looked at her. He got to his feet, reached out and took her hand.

"Venice," he said, as though he were the conductor.

Kristine felt sick. The stuffy quarters and rocky motion of the train hadn't helped the headache she was nursing from the emotion and the wine the night before. Climbing down the steps and onto the platform, she stopped in surprise.

Venice spread out before her like a memory. She stared at the bright green water of the canal, the rickety boats clustered together at the dock, the wooden posts sticking out like coordinates in the water. Taking in a deep breath, she put her hand to her chest. "Oh, my gosh." Her voice was soft with wonder. "It smells like . . ."

Kevin gave her a shy smile. "College."

The air was thick and humid, tinged with salt and something else sharp but subtle. The inside of an empty crab leg, the vague hint of brine, the wet rust of metal . . . It sparked something in her. A tiny piece of history, a moment.

She remembered standing at the water's edge, with Kevin's arm wrapped tightly around her. Her body was raw with the newness of love, her heart filled with a sense of profound possibility for the life they hadn't yet lived. They'd stared out at the old bridges and mismatched pastel houses that lined the docks and watched the sun reflect in the ripples of the water, then Kevin had reached for her and—

Kristine gasped. So many years later, she felt his strong arms wrapping around her once again. As her feet left the ground, the world bobbed and swayed beneath her.

"Hey," she squawked. "What are you . . . ?"

Kevin's lips crashed over hers. They tasted like the salt from the air and his cheeks smelled musky and familiar. Momentarily, she froze. Then her body dissolved into an unexpected warmth. Tentatively, she parted her lips and kissed him back. Soft at first and then deeply, as though the act could somehow undo the last few days, the past few years.

As the kiss stilled, Kevin pressed his forehead against hers. Out of the corner of her eye, she saw their luggage dropped in a jumbled pile at their feet.

Tourists streamed past and a woman in a cream-colored dress stopped to stare. Kristine looked past her to the canal. It sparkled in the sunlight, just like it had so many years ago.

# Thirty-seven

The next morning, June woke up early. She still felt guilty about Charley, every time she thought of him tripping over that rake. The idea that he could have really hurt himself kept coming back to haunt her. As well as the fact that if he was gone, she would most certainly miss him. She leaned against the counter, staring out at his garden across the way.

Even though the man drove her absolutely insane, with his ridiculous inability to pick out flowers that were meant to thrive together and his reluctance to take her advice, she had gotten used to having him next door. She had even started to look forward to seeing him day to day. It made living in this big old house just a little less lonely.

*Apologize, June,* said a little voice inside her head. *Make friends with him.*

June walked to the refrigerator and poured herself a glass of juice. Taking a sip of the sweet nectar, a slow smile tugged at the corner of her lips as the perfect idea came to mind.

When Charley opened his sliding glass door, June was hiding in the shadow of his gazebo. She had just finished planting a yellow rosebush in his yard. It had taken some serious work to uproot that thing and transplant it over, but she'd managed. The roses were looking bright, cheerful and very much alive.

Partially hidden by a Japanese maple, June spied on her neighbor. He was carrying a plate of what appeared to be egg whites and toast, with the paper neatly tucked under his arm. As she watched, he strode back into the house, a spring in his step. He returned with a steaming mug of coffee.

Charley looked as fresh as always, his silver hair neatly combed and his face tanned from the sun. In fact . . . June narrowed her eyes. He seemed to be the very picture of health.

"Hold it right there." June stepped out from behind the tree.

Charley jumped, coffee spilling over the edge of the mug and onto the ground. Blowing on his hand as though he'd burned it, he set the mug on the table and peered in her direction.

"June?" His voice seemed deliberately frail. "Is that you?" The man took a couple of hobbling steps in her direction. On his *left* foot.

Yesterday, and all of the preceding days, his injury was on the right.

"Charley Montgomery," June roared. "You're not blind. And you're not injured anymore, either. You stop faking that limp this instant."

Charley seemed to consider whether or not to press his luck. Then he smiled. Standing up straight, he strolled over to her with his chest puffed out like a peacock. "No, June. I certainly am not."

Just then, she saw him spot the yellow rosebush over her shoulder. "You gave me one of your rosebushes?" he asked.

June gave a little shrug, pleased at the expression on his face. He rushed forward, admiring the rosebush from every angle. Bending close to a particularly flouncy bud, Charley breathed in deeply.

"My goodness, June," he said, standing up straight. "This is really something special."

June sniffed. "It is yellow, for friendship. But you'll be lucky if I don't rip it right back up by the roots. If your ankle is better, why on earth have you been acting like you're still hurt? I have been worried about you for days."

Charley put his hands in his pockets. "To be honest, I didn't want you to stop being nice to me."

A bird started singing in the tree and the sun rose up over the trees.

"Nice to you?" June said, surprised. "Whatever are you talking about?" Her hands were still covered in soil from the planting. Mindlessly, she brushed them off on her gardening pants.

Charley studied her with those clear blue eyes. The bird in the tree chattered away. "June, I think you gave me that plant because you felt sorry for me," he said. "You've never done anything that kind before."

June felt her face color in shame. She hadn't been a good neighbor to him ever since his wife died, but it wasn't her fault. Being around him unsettled her so. Even now, standing in the back of his garden with no escape, she felt decidedly out of her element.

"Or . . ." he said softly, watching her face. "Maybe you gave me that plant not to be nice, but because you felt guilty."

"Why on earth would I feel guilty?" June demanded.

"Because camouflage doesn't blend so well when you're not hiding in the forest."

June flushed down to her gardening socks. Had Charley seen her that night? As she stuttered, trying to think of a decent excuse, the man took a step toward her.

"I saw you, June," he said. "Standing outside my window. You were spying. You wanted to see what Rose and I were up to."

"I most certainly was not," June said, outraged.

Charley's eyes twinkled. "Didn't you just get mad at me for lying to you?"

June had heard enough. Stalking by him in a huff, she was startled when Charley Montgomery caught her gently by the wrist. She didn't resist, but allowed Charley to pull her close to him. "June, have you been spying on me?"

"No, I—" Her eyes flickered up to his. "Don't be ridiculous."

Even though June was fuming, her breath was coming in short, little gasps. This was a very unfamiliar feeling, having a man holding her this close to him. She wondered if, perhaps, she should call for help. But all she could do was stare into Charley's bright blue eyes.

"You have been spying on me for months. I've seen you at your kitchen window, with your binoculars." His voice dropped. "You don't know how many times I almost came over to your house and knocked on your door. Would you have let me in?"

"No," June said. "I certainly would not have let you set foot inside my front door."

"So, you see . . ." Charley gestured at his ankle. "I had to figure out a way to get you to step through mine."

"You don't mean . . ." June's eyes widened. "Charley Montgomery, did you fake that sprain?"

Charley started laughing. "I most certainly did, June. I most certainly did."

"Why, you . . ." She pulled back her wrist as though to hit him, but Charley was much faster.

Pulling her close, he pressed his lips against hers. They were soft and firm, and June was startled at the sensation; it was one she had not felt for more than twenty years. As Charley's arms tightened around her, June heard birds chirping, bees buzzing and—she would swear to it—rose petals opening in the sun.

# Thirty-eight

The hotel room in Venice stunned Kristine into silence. Luxury permeated the space, from the lush, pale blue carpet to the gilded lamps and mirrors lining the walls to the stately antique chairs in the sitting areas. French doors led out to a balcony overlooking the canal, draped by sheer white curtains waving like sails in the breeze.

Surprised, Kristine looked at her husband. "This must have—"

He shrugged. "Amazing what a billion hotel miles can get you."

Slowly, she walked into the room. She ran her hand over the pale blue velvet covering the backs of the furniture and her eyes darted to the bed. Twice the size of any bed she had ever seen, it was tucked into a nook of the room, as though playing hard to get. A silver tray was set up on the duvet, offering up a treasure of Italian chocolates, champagne and red roses.

"What's all this?" she asked, swallowing hard.

Kevin didn't answer. Instead, he took off his sunglasses and laid them neatly on a side table. Then he walked to the bed and removed the tray of champagne and roses. As he touched the light switch on the wall, the room descended into darkness.

Kristine's palms started to sweat. In the light from the canal, she could see her husband striding over to her. Without a word, he scooped her up into his arms and deposited her onto the duvet. She braced herself for a gentle, questioning touch, one that she wouldn't know how to answer. But to her surprise, he grabbed her body and pulled it roughly to him.

"I'm just going to warn you." His breath was ragged in her ear. "I'm not exactly in the mood to be a sensitive guy."

Without waiting for her response, he pushed down the straps of her sundress and buried his face between her breasts. Kristine felt a sweet longing flood through her. His hands were everywhere, exploring her body like he used to, back when it seemed as though there would never be enough time to be together.

*Kevin, Kevin, Kevin . . .*

Pressing her body up against him, Kristine grabbed the back of his head and pulled him in for a kiss. It felt almost angry as he possessed her mouth with his. She bit his lips, thrusting her tongue in his mouth and tasting his skin, until he gave a low groan.

Desperately, she fumbled for his belt buckle and yanked down his pants. He lowered himself on top of her, the hair from his body coarse against her legs. He grabbed her hands and brought them over her head, pinning them against the mattress.

Poised just above her, his breath ragged, he gazed into her eyes. His expression was fierce, his eyes dark and questioning. In response, Kristine arched her back, brushing her body against him. Then, with a sharp thrust, he buried himself inside of her.

She held perfectly still, giving herself time to absorb him, to remember how this was. Then, with a sudden rush of feeling, the pain melted into pleasure. He made love to her with an intensity she hadn't felt in years, and Kristine gripped his shoulders tighter and tighter, until she shattered against him.

Kevin let out a roar as he came, collapsing on top of her in a heap of sweat and emotion. They lay there together working to catch their breath, the duvet kicked aside and slipping to the floor. Kevin leaned forward and held her tight, wrapping his arms tightly around her.

"I love you, Kristine," he whispered. Then he kissed her as though he would drown.

# Thirty-nine

While her mother was in Rome, Chloe had one responsibility: to keep an eye on June.

"Take care of her," Kristine said before she left, squeezing Chloe just a little too tight. "I know you're busy but June's just not used to being on her own."

Chloe's intentions were good but she got so caught up with school, midterms and Geoff that before she knew it, three days had passed without hearing from her grandmother. The moment she realized this, Chloe called her six times and even stopped by her house, but June didn't answer the door. Troubled, Chloe headed to her shift at Tiny Tumblers but checked her phone every hour, on the hour.

June never called back.

The moment her shift was over, she rushed outside and called Ben. Her mouth tasted like metal, but she knew just hearing his voice would help. He'd say, "Clo, everything's okay. I'll be right there," but his phone rang and rang before finally going to voicemail.

Chloe fought back a wave of panic. There was a very real possibility that something bad had happened. It just wasn't like June to not call for three days. And to not return a phone call? Never.

Even though Chloe hated to drag Geoff into all this so early in their relationship, she made the call. "I'm so sorry to bother you at work," she said, her voice breaking. "But I'm too scared to go over there alone."

"I'll call Rue on the way," he said. "See if she's heard from her." After getting directions to June's house, he said, "Don't worry, Chloe. I'm sure she's just fine."

Traffic was jammed, so instead of jumping into a cab and begging the driver to go ninety, Chloe ran the five blocks to June's apartment. Her book bag banged against her shoulder with every step, her heart pounding frantically. What if June was lying there with a broken hip, abandoned for days? Those stairs up to her bedroom were much too steep. She easily could have taken a tumble. Or what if . . . Chloe shook her head, refusing to think of the alternative.

She blinked hard, hating herself for being so irresponsible. It wasn't like her mother had asked her to check on a hamster or a goldfish. June was her *family*. Why, oh why, had she gotten so caught up in her boyfriend? What kind of person *was* she?

Rounding the corner, she ran smack into a man. It was already dark, and she almost screamed. She realized it was Geoff and collapsed against him.

"Thank you so much for coming," she said. "I'm sorry. I'm so scared."

Geoff put a finger under her chin and lifted it gently. "Chloe, look at me," he said, his voice calm. "It's going to be fine. And if it's not, we'll deal with it, okay? We'll handle it together."

She nodded, letting out a shaky breath. Leading the way, he walked up the steps to June's house and pounded on the door.

Chloe's heart was in her throat. She prayed that, at any moment, June would throw open the door and say, "What on earth is all this racket about?" But the house remained dark, the door tightly closed. With trembling hands, Chloe handed him the spare key.

As they walked in, he turned on the lights in the hallway. She cringed, expecting to see June crumpled in a heap at the bottom of the stairs, but the path was as clear as always. Chloe tried to push past him, but Geoff's arm blocked her way. "Please. Let me go first." His voice was grim. "Just in case."

Slowly, with Chloe right behind him, Geoff searched the entire house from top to bottom. Nothing. In the kitchen, he walked over to the counter and eyed an apple on the cutting board. "This seems . . ." A note of hope crept into his voice. "Decently fresh." He held it up. The apple was cut in half and only slightly brown at the edges.

Chloe's heart pounded with relief. There might still be time to save her.

Geoff's eyes darted to the window. "I think I just saw something move outside."

Of course! June would have been working in her garden. Maybe she'd fallen out there. Chloe rushed for the back door. It was dark outside and she couldn't see a thing, but she could hear the faintest muffle of laughter. "Grandma?" she called.

Abruptly, the laughter stopped. There was the sound of shuffling and nervous whispers. Chloe squinted. Through the dark night, she could swear she saw Charley Montgomery dart across the lawn. But he wasn't wearing a shirt. And his hands were crossed in front of his . . .

Chloe froze. Her eyes fell on the wrought-iron table where her grandmother typically ate her breakfast. A checkered gardening shirt was neatly draped across it like a napkin. A few feet away, something white was suspended over a rosebush. Chloe put her hands over her mouth.

It was a brassiere.

She gasped in horror. *No. This couldn't be . . .*

Geoff rushed into the yard, the beam of a flashlight bobbing in front of him. "Did you find her?"

With one hand, Chloe shielded her eyes. "Yes," she whispered. "But something terrible is happening. Please turn off the . . ."

"Chloe?" June called, her voice high pitched and nervous. "Is that you?"

Geoff shined the light in the general direction. June was peeking out from behind a tree, a branch pulled over her form. Even though the tree was covering her, it was perfectly obvious that she was naked.

Chloe dove for the flashlight, turning it off. "Oh, no." She clutched it in her fist, maintaining eye contact with Geoff, afraid of what else she'd see if she dared to look away. "Oh, no."

"Chloe?" June called again. The leaves on the tree rustled.

"Don't," Chloe shrieked. "You stay right there!"

Geoff's eyes widened as he, too, finally figured out what was happening. "Oh, no."

Chloe closed her eyes, shaking her head. "Apparently," she said, "my grandmother is not dead. Not even close."

There was silence. Out in the garden, both June and Charley chuckled.

"Sorry," June sang. "Didn't mean to scare you. We just . . . um . . ."

"Got attacked by fire ants," Charley said. "Had to wash the clothes out. But I think everyone's okay now."

"Yup." June's voice was cheerful. "Doing just fine."

A small smirk settled at the corner of Geoff's mouth. "Fire ants," he said. "Is that what the kids are calling it these days?"

# Forty

Kevin lowered himself into the gondola. It swayed from side to side in the water and sank slightly underneath his weight. "I'm gonna capsize this thing," he said, pulling Kristine in close.

"If you do," she said, "I'll jump in and save you."

"I'm almost tempted," he teased, "just to see how you'd haul me back in."

The gondola driver, dressed in the traditional black-and-white-striped shirt and straw hat, pushed the boat away from the dock and they drifted onto the canal. Kristine breathed in the sultry aroma of the sea and snuggled even closer into the crook of Kevin's arm. The gondola ride was the perfect way to end their time in Venice, even though she was incredibly sad that it was over.

It had been so passionate, so romantic. After that first night, she and Kevin stayed in the hotel room for three days straight, only venturing out to grab food at quaint little cafes on the water. Then they went straight back to each other's arms. They made love in that glorious bed, the gigantic tub in the bathroom and on the balcony overlooking the canal, the stars of Venice shining above them.

Late at night they talked for hours, touching on topics they hadn't delved into in years: their feelings about getting older, their daughter's remarkable ambition, their hopes for the future. Kristine explained how lonely and disconnected she'd been feeling, with Kevin always on the road. He made a vow to try and spend the little time they had together at home with her, doing something special. He even promised to spend time at the store.

Kristine's heart had not been this full in years. She felt that they had finally reconnected on the levels that mattered so desperately to their marriage. The memory of all that had pushed them apart seemed very far away.

As they floated down the water, they passed buildings that were centuries old. Her favorites were the ones with the ornate loggias, because they reminded her of miniature castles. Everything around them seemed so beautiful, even the algae creeping up the base of the buildings. Bright green, it was the canal's version of a tree-lined street.

"I can't think of anything that would make this more perfect," she said.

As if on cue, the Rialto Bridge loomed into sight. The sun was setting and pinks and purples streaked across the sky. The color, coupled with the burnt orange of the rooftops off in the distance, emphasized the pure white of the stone bridge. The portico at the top was lit like a cathedral.

As they approached the bridge, the gondola driver started to sing. His voice lilted through the night as easily as the laps of the oar against the water. Joy bubbled up in Kristine and she turned to kiss her husband once again.

"So . . ." Kevin's hand brushed her face. "I've been thinking a lot this week. About how much I love you. And how little I've done to show it in the past few years."

The song the gondola driver was singing hit a crescendo and they cruised under the cool shade of the bridge. She could hear the tourists above them, laughing and talking in the evening. "Kevin, it's okay. Let's not—"

"We should have celebrated our anniversary," he insisted. "We should have been together. I've just been so . . ." He shook his head. "Look, I'm a hard worker. You know that. And when I lost my job and couldn't find another one, it scared the shit out of me. I don't ever want to be in that position again."

Kristine touched his hand. "It was the economy. Not you."

"Yeah, but . . ." He gazed at her. "My job is my job, Kris. You're my life." The gondola floated out from under the bridge, back into the open water. Gently, he brushed a strand of hair out of her eyes. "We made it twenty-five years. It was so stupid to not celebrate that with you."

Kristine swallowed hard, thinking back on that night. "I wanted so badly to be with you," she whispered, reaching up and touching his soft cheeks.

"I know I pissed you off with that IOU . . ." He smiled. "But hopefully, this will make up for it."

Reaching into the pocket of his fleece, he pulled out a navy leather box and flipped it open. There, cradled against white satin, was the most beautiful diamond ring Kristine had ever seen. Tiny, antique and surrounded by ornate gold, it sparkled in the light from the lamps at the edge of the water.

"Happy anniversary, Firecracker." Shyly, Kevin handed her the ring. "I love you."

Up until that moment, Kristine thought diamonds didn't matter to her. That she would rather have pieces of jewelry that were exotic and ornate, crafted in some place far from home. But staring down at this perfect, gleaming piece that her husband had picked out for her, she changed her mind.

"Hurry, put it on," Kevin joked, indicating the murky water. "I don't want to hit a speed bump and have you drop it or anything."

The gondola was cruising along at maybe two miles an hour.

Kristine laughed. "I think we're gonna be just fine." Still, he reached over and helped to slide the ring onto her finger.

"Over twenty-five years ago," he said, taking her hand in a way that seemed oddly formal, "I gave you an engagement ring and later, a wedding ring. In honor of that time, I have a question for you." Taking a deep breath, he said, "Kristine, will you renew your vows with me?"

Kristine blinked. "You want to renew our vows?"

"Yeah. I thought it might be . . ." Kevin looked at her. His eyes were the exact color of the water. "Meaningful. You know?"

The gondola driver finished his song. The night suddenly seemed a little too quiet. Kristine looked down at the ring, blood pounding inside of her ears. She felt herself begin to panic.

This week with Kevin had been wonderful. It had been perfect. But it had been a vacation.

What would happen when they got home? In spite of their conversations and the promises they'd made, maybe nothing had changed between them. And if this new intimacy couldn't sustain, if everything slipped back to how it was, she would be more brokenhearted than ever. Trying to find the words to explain this, she choked up. "Kevin . . ."

His face clouded over. "You don't want to?"

"I would love to." She shook her head, cradling the hand with her new ring. "It's such a romantic, wonderful idea but I'm just afraid that we'd be doing it for the wrong reasons."

"I'm in love with you," he said. "I have been in love with you since the moment I first saw you. Is there a better reason than that?"

"No, but . . ." Kristine gripped the edge of the boat. "I only want to do this if we can stay like this. Be *together* again like this. Not just plan to renew our vows and hope everything gets better."

Kevin sat in silence, staring out at the water. Another gondola passed with an older couple snuggled up together, drinking from plastic cups filled with champagne. They seemed like they didn't have a care in the world.

The muscle in Kevin's jaw pulsed. "Kristine, do you love me?"

"Of course I do. Why do you think I'm so upset that we never spend any time together?"

"I love you, too." His voice was earnest. "More than anything in this world." Turning to the gondola driver, he said, "Buddy, will you please sing something?" The gondola driver seemed confused, so Kevin belted out, *"When the moon hits a guy, like a big pizza pie . . ."*

*"Bene, bene,"* the driver cried. With renewed vigor, he started to sing.

Kevin grasped her hands. "Kris, I love you." His eyes burned as brightly as the lights along the shore. "I have been in love with you from that first moment I saw you standing there on the deck, wrapped up in that big, ol' ugly sweatshirt. We were both young and innocent and had no idea what we were in for. It's been a ride and it hasn't always been easy. But we built a *family* together."

Kristine nodded, feeling the warmth of his hands. They felt as familiar as her own, as much of a part of her body as his. The gondola driver sang louder, his voice carrying through the night.

"I know we have some things to figure out," he said. "I know that our relationship isn't perfect. But I want to grow old with you. Yes, I might get wrinkled and craggy and forget who I am and what this life has meant, but I will never forget that the most important person on the planet is the one sitting right in front of me. I love you, Kris. Let's promise to stay in this thing. Together."

There was nothing she wanted more than to believe that it was possible to have a love that would last forever. Yes, the past few years had been hard. But that was no excuse to give up.

Feeling her heart swell, she found herself nodding. "Yes," she said, grabbing her husband's hands and holding them tight. "Let's renew our vows."

# Forty-one

Chloe's parents were due back from Italy any moment. For a welcome home dinner, June had cooked her famous chicken potpie, and with Chloe's assistance put together a salad, a side of green peas, baby carrots and rolls. As they cooked, June kept humming.

Even though Chloe had given her a Look more than once, they had not discussed the incident in the garden. Her grandmother had tried, but Chloe held up her hand like a stop sign. "Things we do not speak of. Move on."

In spite of that little incident, Chloe and June still had plenty to discuss. Geoff was coming to dinner that night to meet both her and Chloe's parents. "This is serious," June kept saying. Chloe just smiled.

It was so strange to think that it had only been six weeks since she'd been on that silly practice date with Ben. She'd spent so much time with Geoff—meeting him for impromptu study group at his office, grabbing a quick dinner downtown, sleeping over at his place—that she already felt like they'd been together for much longer.

"You think Mom and Dad will like him?" Carefully, Chloe poured olive oil into a container, waiting for June's answer.

June dropped a handful of garlic croutons into the salad bowl. "Geoff is Rue Gable's grandson. What's not to like?"

To be honest, Chloe wasn't worried whether or not her parents would like Geoff. She was worried about whether or not he'd live up to June's standards. Based on a few bits and pieces of stories she had heard over the years, June had been extremely reluctant to welcome her father into the family. Although their relationship had eventually improved, Chloe knew that disapproval had hurt her dad. Besides, Chloe knew firsthand how much it hurt to have June disapprove of someone who she loved.

Over the years, June had been more than clear about not wanting Chloe to end up with Ben. Obviously, that was never even going to happen, but still it hurt her that her grandmother refused to recognize all the good qualities in him. It was almost as though Chloe's devotion to Ben automatically put him on June's watch-list. She didn't want to see the same type of thing happen with Geoff.

"I'm serious, Grandma." Chloe set the dressing dispenser on the counter and pulled her hair off her neck. The kitchen was hot and the stress of the evening was already weighing on her. "I really need you to be nice to him. Even if you don't like him."

"My precious girl, you have nothing to worry about," June said. "I'll adore him. According to Rue, he likes you very much."

"I knew it." Chloe couldn't help but smile. "I knew the mahjong group simply could not go on without gossiping about our relationship."

The fine lines around June's mouth twitched. "It's what we do best."

"Good," Chloe said, suddenly hopeful. If the mahjong group approved, maybe June would, too. "Just don't say anything weird when you meet him. You can talk to him about Rue and that connection, but don't put him on the spot about the future or anything like that. And do not, *do not* mention that one night in the garden."

Wiping her hands on her red gingham apron, June said, "If this young man truly wants to be a member of the family, he is going to have to accept the slings and arrows of true conversation. I am not going to censor myself. I will say whatever pops into my mind, as always."

"Fine." Chloe shrugged. "I'll tell Charley you used to spy on him."

June turned pink with pleasure. "Go ahead. Charley and I have no secrets."

Chloe laughed. "Mom's going to freak out, you know." She tried to picture her mother's response to the fact that June was dating. "Have you told her anything yet?"

June let out a sound that might have been a giggle. "We thought about putting on some skit to fool her. Charley would stop by and demand I cut back my maples. Then I would get really angry, pull out a gun and shoot him. With fake bullets and a ketchup packet, of course." June's voice got low and dramatic. "He'd fall to the floor gasping for breath. I would cry, *Oh, what have I done?* and start to weep. After kissing him on the lips, pledging to love him if only he would come back to me, he would open his eyes." June licked her lips in satisfaction, as though imagining the scene play out. Finally, she grinned. "What do you think?"

"I think Mom would think you actually shot him." Chloe's voice was dry. "And then she'd citizen's arrest your ass."

The doorbell chimed and June stood up straight. "Well." She took off her apron, folded it carefully and placed it in the pantry. "This must be your young man." With the tips of her fingers, she smoothed her wavy blonde hair.

"Grandma." Chloe had one final moment of panic. Rushing over, she grabbed June's arm. "Seriously. Be nice to him. Okay?"

"Of course." June was already making a beeline for the front door. "Nice is my middle name."

June gave a secretive little smile. Of *course* she was going to be nice to Rue Gable's grandson, especially if he was in love with

Chloe. There were only two things she wanted in this world: for her daughter and granddaughter to be happy. If Geoff Gable could do that, then June would roll out the red carpet.

Throwing open the door, she stopped in surprise. Geoff had the same sharp nose, high forehead and handsome coloring as Rue. "My goodness," she said. "You and Rue could be twins."

Geoff rubbed his five o'clock shadow. "Don't tell Rue that. She'll book an appointment to get her face waxed tomorrow."

June burst out laughing. "Young man, I think I just fell in love with you."

Linking her arm with his, June led him into the foyer. She watched as his eyes sought out her granddaughter. He rushed over to greet her with a kiss and June's heart gave a silent cheer.

Dr. Geoff Gable was most certainly The One.


Kristine and Kevin walked up the sidewalk to June's brownstone, their hands entwined. Stopping, Kristine stared up at the house with suspicion. It was lit from top to bottom, and through the window she could see June chatting with a man she didn't recognize.

Their flight back from Italy had arrived early that afternoon. Kristine and Kevin had spent the day in bed wrapped in each other's arms and drifting in and out of sleep. It had taken three phone calls from June to get them up and on their way. Even though she was excited to see her mother, Kristine was a little too jet-lagged for a welcome home party.

"Should we run?" she asked as they trudged up the front steps.

"Only if she's serving Italian." Kevin pushed open the door. "I'm ready for a good old-fashioned burger."

"I hear our guests," June cried, sweeping into the foyer. Grabbing Kristine, she practically smothered her with kisses. "Don't ever leave me like that. Oh! What did you do to your hair?"

"Looks good, huh?" Kevin reached over and ruffled the new do.

Spinning her around in a full circle, June said, "It looks marvelous." With a conspiring smile, she added, "But of course you look good. You're *my* daughter."

Stepping forward, Kevin opened his arms. "Come here, cupcake." As June squealed, Kevin pulled her into a tight hug. Laughing, she shook a finger at him. "How was Italy? Did you love it?"

Kevin nodded. "I hate to say it, June, but you were right."

"Oh, pish-posh." June patted her hair. "It doesn't matter who's wrong or right. What matters is that you two were together. Now, follow me."

Kristine and Kevin trailed behind her, exchanging baffled looks. "Maybe they had to medicate her," he murmured. "Because you were away."

In the dining room, the lights were turned down low and the table practically glowed with candles. Chloe stood next to it, a huge smile on her face. Someone who could only be Dr. Gable stood next to her wearing a tweed jacket, button-up shirt and a navy ascot.

Chloe rushed forward and hugged them tight. "Mom and Dad, I want you to meet my *boyfriend*." Kristine could tell her daughter loved saying that word.

As Geoff kissed her cheek, Kristine noticed that he smelled like spearmint, as though he'd been using breath spray or chewing on mints in preparation for their arrival.

"It's so nice to meet you," he said. "Chloe has told me so much about you."

Kristine smiled. "It's nice to meet you, too."

Kevin, on the other hand, eyed him like a bug. "You a Bears fan?" he growled.

"Yes, sir." Geoff shook his hand. "I'm from Chicago and—"

"Do you have a job?"

"Dad." Chloe giggled.

Geoff nodded, looking as serious as ever. "I own my own practice. Psychology."

Kevin smiled, his face splitting into a grin. "Alright. Then you and Chloe might get along."

The chime of the doorbell rang through the house like wedding bells, startling all of them.

June flushed. "Now, who could that be? Kristine, would you mind getting the door?"

Even though she would have much preferred to pull up a chair and get to know the man who was clearly making her daughter so happy, she headed out to answer it. To her dismay, Charley Montgomery stood on the stoop, clutching a bouquet of yellow roses.

"Kristine." His blue eyes sparkled. "Do you mind if I come in?"

Charley had always seemed so kind, but inviting him in would not go over well with June. "I'm sorry," she said. "Let me check with my . . ." Turning, she saw that everyone was standing in the foyer, and June was grinning like a cat with a mouthful of feathers.

Kristine's mouth dropped open. "Mother . . ." She looked back at Charley, who was smiling, too. "Seriously?" she cried in delight.

Sweeping forward, June announced, "Kristine, I would like you to meet *my* boyfriend. The ultra-handsome, unbelievably charming Charley Montgomery."

Kristine couldn't believe it. "That is wonderful! Charley, I . . ." Reaching out, she clasped his hand and squeezed it tight. "I don't know what happened here. I left the country and everyone went crazy."

"Not at all," June said. "You left the country and . . ." She gave a meaningful look in Kevin's direction. "We all came to our senses."

# Forty-two

Watching her parents together from her spot at the dinner table, Chloe breathed a sigh of relief. They were finishing each other's stories, sharing inside jokes and even holding hands. They both seemed happier than they had in ages, especially her mother.

"Attention, please." June got to her feet, tapping her fork against her wine goblet. The delicate crystal hummed and the various conversations died out around the table. "Can I have your attention, please?"

Charley took June's hand and kissed it. "You always have our attention, my love."

Chloe exchanged a quick look with her mother. Kristine mouthed, "Cute."

"I just wanted to say . . ." June flaunted her sassy smile, her eyes sweeping over the group. "I am delighted to have my family back together in one room. Kristine and Kevin, our lives are not the same without you."

"Here, here," Chloe said, raising her wineglass.

"And . . ." June nodded at Charley, who also got to his feet.

"As you know," Charley said, smoothing down his light blue button-up shirt, "June and I have been seeing each other."

Geoff raised an eyebrow at Chloe. "Fire ants," he muttered. She coughed to keep from laughing.

"So, the other day, as we were sitting out in the garden, we got to talking." She produced a single white rose and held it up. "Kristine, Chloe, do you know what this is?"

Chloe squinted. "It's from one of your rosebushes, but . . ."

"Nope." Neatly, June tucked the flower behind her ear. From that angle, Chloe could see that the petals were dried and browned at the edges.

Of course! It was one of the flowers from the wedding where they'd all caught that bouquet. The dried rose was exactly like the pink one hanging on Chloe's refrigerator. She felt a tiny pang, remembering how Ben had pretended to give it to her at the beginning of their date. Luckily, that memory soon passed.

"This summer, I caught a bouquet at a wedding," June said. "We *all* caught a bouquet at a wedding. And . . ." Dramatically, she stuck out her weathered hand. A stately diamond ring sparkled from her ring finger. "The bouquet was right!"

"Wait, what?" Chloe could barely process the statement. "*What?*" She looked at her mother. Kristine's eyes were wide. She moved her mouth as though to speak, but nothing came out.

"Congratulations," Chloe shrieked. She leapt to her feet, jostling the table. Wine danced back and forth in the glasses. "Grandma! Oh, my gosh. I can't believe it!"

Rushing over to June, Chloe grabbed her hand and studied the ring. It was a simple emerald cut on a platinum band. Completely different from the extravagant one Chloe's grandfather had given her so many years ago. That ring now sparkled from her grandmother's right hand.

For some reason, Chloe thought back to the time when she was in undergrad, when June had called her at all hours of the night. She had chalked it up to her grandmother being wild and ridiculous but in her heart, she'd always known the truth. June needed someone. And finally, she'd found him.

"Grandma, this is so perfect," Chloe said. "*He's* perfect!"

Charley bowed his head. Suddenly, it struck her—this man

was going to be her *grandfather*. She'd never had a grandfather, because Eugene died before she was born and Kevin's father left his family when he was little. At the age of twenty-five, she would finally have a grandfather.

Kristine put a hand on her mother's shoulder. Chloe stepped aside as she hugged June tight. "This is such good news," she whispered. "Dad would have wanted this for you."

"Well, I think this is bizarre." Geoff's voice rang through the room and Chloe turned to him, surprised.

"Bizarre?" she echoed. It wasn't bizarre that her grandmother was getting married. It was wonderful. "What do you mean?"

Geoff's handsome face creased in a smile. "The last thing I expected tonight was for your grandmother to announce her engagement. It's actually rather odd."

Chloe watched her father eyeing Geoff, as though reevaluating him altogether. Kristine's forehead was wrinkled and even Charley looked a little perplexed. June was the only one at the table still smiling, as though waiting for a punch line.

Blushing furiously, Chloe walked over to him and murmured, "Geoff, seriously. I think you've probably had too much to . . ."

"I haven't had too much to drink. I just have something to say." Tugging at his ascot, Geoff took in a deep breath. "Chloe, we've only known each other for a few months but I feel like I've known you forever. I love you. Your warmth, your humor and your ability to put me in my place with one word."

*Love?* Geoff actually said *love?* Chloe's mouth dropped open.

"I didn't expect to do this here in front of everyone." Geoff gave an apologetic look to Kevin. "I'd rather planned to talk to your parents first and do this the old-fashioned way. But given your grandmother's announcement I have to admit I'm a bit swept up. Chloe . . ."

Right there on the green Oriental rug in the dining room, the rug Chloe had played on since she was a little girl, Geoff got down on one knee. "From the moment we met," he said, reaching for her hand, "I have thought of nothing but spending the rest of my life with you. Chloe, will you marry me?"

To her complete and utter shock, Dr. Geoff Gable IV reached into his tailored jacket pocket and produced a light blue box. Snapping it open, he revealed a shiny diamond ring. Apparently, a diamond ring meant for her.

Chloe had never been so surprised in her life. A hundred different memories ran through her head. The moment she'd first seen Geoff speaking on stage, that time in Tiny Tumblers when he'd first said he liked her, and, for some odd reason, the moment Chloe's and Ben's eyes met after they'd kissed.

"You barely know me," Chloe whispered, gripping the edge of the oak table. "This is crazy."

Geoff smiled. "I'm a psychologist. I think I've earned the right to do something a little crazy."

June clapped her hands in delight. "Ha!"

"Imagine our future together." Getting to his feet, Geoff stepped forward and closed the small gap between them. "Can you see it?"

A series of abrupt images skipped through Chloe's head. Sharing a practice with Geoff, discussing their work late into the night, Mary Beth running up and hugging her legs . . . Actually, she could see it. Chloe sucked in her breath. She could see it very clearly.

Looking around the room, Chloe took in the sight of her family. Her mother's lips were pressed tightly together and both Kevin and Charley seemed impressed. June's eyes were wide with delight. *Don't be foolish*, her expression seemed to say. *Say yes!*

"Yes." Chloe's voice sounded disembodied. "Yes," she said again, louder. "I would love to marry you."

As Geoff leapt to his feet and pulled her close, Chloe felt removed, as though the moment was happening to someone else. Then there was chaos. Hoots and hollers and hugs and kisses.

Her father was shaking Geoff's hand, Charley was clapping Geoff on the back and June had unearthed a camera from somewhere and was taking pictures. Her mother was the only one standing off to the side, looking pale and confused.

"You know I don't like to share the stage . . ." June rushed forward, hastily filling a champagne flute. "But for this, I will. To two weddings!"

"To two weddings," Chloe breathed. Suddenly, a burst of cold sweat covered her body. They were getting married. *Getting married!* Chloe couldn't wait to tell Sally and all of her friends. Except Ben. She had a sneaking suspicion that he would not see the romance in all this. Not one bit.

Kevin cleared his throat. "I have something I'd like to say." The celebration stilled and he smiled at Chloe. "I, too, am a very happy man. In Italy, your mother and I—"

*"Kevin,"* Kristine said, her voice sharp.

Chloe knew that tone. It meant, *Drop it right now.*

"Honey, it's not taking away from their thunder. It's just adding a little lightning." Looking around the room, he grinned. "While we were in Rome, Kristine and I decided . . ." He lifted her right hand. A new diamond ring sparkled from her finger. "We decided to renew our vows."

"Oh, my gosh," Chloe cried. *"Really?"*

"While you two plan your weddings"—Kevin kissed Kristine's forehead with a loud smack—"this beautiful lady is going to be plotting out our vow renewal ceremony."

"Love is in the air," Charley sang.

"And I thought *I* was the only one with news," June cried.

"Wait!" Chloe cried. A wild idea had just hit her. "Mom, Grandma . . . since we're all getting married, what if we did it together?"

For probably the fifth time that night, everyone in the room fell silent.

"Absolutely not." Kristine shook her head so hard her new

haircut swung back and forth. "I'm sorry, but I want your wedding to be about you, not about us."

"A wedding's about love," Chloe said. "And I love you two more than anything."

"That's true." Geoff put his hand on her back. "I see nothing better than all of us celebrating together."

If there had been a flicker of doubt in Chloe's mind about saying yes to Geoff's proposal, that statement sealed the deal. Taking his hand, she held on tight. "I love you," she said for the first time ever in her life.

Geoff smiled, squeezing her hand. "I love you, too."

"Love is a wonderful thing and a very compelling reason, but . . ." June looked vaguely distressed. "There is one tiny problem. It simply might not work to share a wedding."

"Why not?" Chloe demanded.

"You see . . ." June's hands fluttered and her eyes met Charley's. He flashed a perfect, gleaming white smile. "Our time line's a little different than yours. We would like to have a shotgun wedding."

"Are you pregnant?" Chloe gasped. Off her mother's look, she held up her hands. "Look, nothing would surprise me with her."

June beamed. "Of course not. It's just that . . . well . . ."

"We're old," Charley said. "We could drop over dead at any moment. Why waste time?"

June and Charley looked at each other and cracked up. They laughed so hard that they had to grab on to each other to stay upright. "Well, it's the *truth*," June said once she realized everyone was staring at them in horror.

"It's not funny," Kristine said.

Chloe nodded. The thought was not funny at all.

"Oh, but it is." June waved her hand. "It's like the sixties all over again. Back then we lived every day like the world could end because of the war. But this time . . ." She giggled, poking her fiancé. "We have to do it that way because we're *old*." Once again, Charley and June laughed like loons.

Kevin finally chuckled, too. "What?" he said. "They make a good point."

"Life is short," Geoff agreed. "I'd walk down the aisle with this girl tomorrow."

Chloe's heart danced. "Tomorrow?" She beamed. "Really?"

He nodded. "Really."

"I just don't know," Kristine hedged. "A triple wedding?"

"Come on, Kris," Kevin said, squeezing her hand. "You'll love this. Come on."

"Yes, Kristine," June echoed. "I'm the bride and I want you to do it."

"*I'm* the bride," Chloe said, "and I command you to do it!"

Kristine gave a tight smile. "Then it's decided. I guess we'd better start hunting for a church."

Part Two

# Forty-three

Kristine walked into the pantry off June's kitchen, shutting the door behind her. Her mouth was dry and she felt dizzy. There were too many things to take in.

June's engagement was a wonderful surprise. The fact that June and Charley had fallen for each other . . . well, nothing could seem more natural. Chloe, on the other hand . . . Kristine put her hand to her chest just thinking about it.

Yes, Geoff seemed poised and earnest, but he and Chloe had just met! They'd only known each other for *two months*. Yes, Kristine wanted her daughter to find love and get married but this was much too fast. How long was it going to take for Chloe to really think about this and panic? Or maybe—and Kristine could only hope—her daughter had accepted the proposal out of courtesy, planning to break it off when there weren't so many people around.

Or maybe Chloe and Geoff really were meant to be. Maybe they would get married and live happily ever after. But did happily ever after even exist?

Even after the magical time she and Kevin had shared together in Venice, she still had questions about their relationship.

It was one thing to be romantic on vacation. But at home? With this triple wedding—a *triple wedding*, for heaven's sake—she would be solidifying a vow to accept him the way things were, for better or for worse. Even if nothing changed.

"Shit," Kristine said softly. "Shit, shit, *shit*."

"I certainly hope you are not cussing out my dry goods," a familiar voice said from behind her.

Kristine turned to face her mother. "No, no." She pasted on a smile. "Not at all. Mom, I'm so happy for you."

June waggled her ring finger. "Can you believe it?"

"Yes, I can. But *you* told me you hated that man," she teased. "That the very sight of him made you break out in hives. That you thought he'd bury your body in the garden."

June grinned. "Well, I was wrong." Pulling the pantry door shut behind her, she whispered, "Have you noticed how handsome he looks in his gardening shirt?"

Kristine laughed. "That will be your engagement photo. The two of you dressed alike, in gardening gear." Out of the corner of her eye, she noticed that a few of June's canned goods were out of order. Quickly, she put them back into place.

"Kristine." June laid a hand over hers. Their hands were exactly the same. But Kristine's hands were still young and smooth, while June's were spotted with age. "You're upset about Chloe's engagement, aren't you?"

Kristine hesitated and her shoulders slumped. "She hardly knows him. It's so risky. It's—"

"Chloe deserves to be happy. It's not your job to judge the situation. It's your job to guide her to make the best decisions within the framework of what she's decided to do."

Kristine eyed her mother. Where had this new, enlightened version of June come from? Maybe falling in love had changed her. Or maybe (more likely) she approved of the match.

Shaking her head, Kristine pressed her fingers into the tender area around her nose. It was painful to the touch and she wondered if she'd caught a cold on the plane. "I don't know," she said. "I just don't know if I can get behind this."

"I know you're worried. But he's lovely." Her mother seemed to consider something. "I've heard that his little girl, on the other hand . . ."

"I forgot about that," Kristine groaned, sinking against a shelf. "Chloe's going to be a mother? She's not ready for that."

"Chloe loves children," June said. "Especially the naughty ones. The universe has a way of giving us what we ask for. Maybe she just forgot to be specific."

Kristine shook her head. Against her will, tears pricked at the edge of her lashes.

"Kristine, don't cry," June pleaded. "Sweetheart, this is a happy time. I promise you."

Maybe because she was tired from the flight or the uncertainty of it all, she gave over to her tears. "Come here." Her mother pulled her in tight. "It's going to be okay."

"I'm sorry." She sniffled. "I don't mean to ruin things. I'm really happy for you guys. For all of us. But I just . . . I don't want to see Chloe get her heart broken."

June patted her on the back, just as she'd done so often when Kristine was a little girl. When the tears finally stopped, June handed her a napkin shaped like a turkey. It was from a plastic bag sitting on the shelf, and Kristine had a vague memory of seeing these napkins at Thanksgiving a few years ago. It had been just Chloe, Kristine and June celebrating. Kevin was stuck in Denver or somewhere, thanks to a snowstorm.

"You don't have to worry about Chloe," June promised. "Geoff's not going to break her heart."

"Are you sure about that?" She pressed the napkin to her eyes, thankful that she wasn't wearing mascara. With the other hand, she pushed open the pantry door and scanned the dining room.

Chloe was telling a story, gesturing wildly. Her new ring glinted in the candlelight. Kevin and Charley were chuckling as Geoff gazed at her in adoration.

June peered over her shoulder. "To be honest," she murmured, "Chloe's much more likely to break his."

# Forty-four

Sally's face flushed pink with pleasure. "Bollocks," she screeched. Everyone in the ice-cream shop turned toward their table. Sally gestured at Chloe, her voice at a fevered pitch. "She's getting married. With her entire family!" As the other patrons went back to their sundaes, Sally beamed. "This is brilliant. Truly brilliant."

Chloe selected a nut resting gently on top of the whipped cream and popped it into her mouth. "I thought you were going to say the opposite," she admitted. Putting on her best British accent, she said, "You can't be serious. You're going to share a wedding with your mother and grandmother? Oh, and didn't you just meet that guy?"

"Who cares when you met him?" Sally pounded the table in excitement. "If it's love at first sight, why second-guess yourself? Honestly, I think it's about time you did something crazy. All you do is work and study. This is great!"

"It is. Right?" Setting down her spoon, Chloe stared down at her ring. It sparkled like a suncatcher in the fluorescent light of the ice-cream shop. "I'm really glad to hear you say that. To be honest, I have been freaking out. Just a little bit."

"Why?" Sally demanded.

"I don't know . . ." Chloe hesitated. "It's so sudden. Who gets engaged after two months of dating? It's crazy. Who does this? I'm not the type of person who does this."

"Don't you dare try and ruin the romance." Sally looked so much like a petulant doll with her blonde ringlet curls, round face and rosy cheeks that Chloe couldn't help but smile. "You met your prince and he proposed. The end."

"True." Chloe touched the ring. The sharp edges felt new and strange against the pad of her thumb. "But you know what it is? It's Ben." Just saying his name made her stomach drop. "I'm freaking out about telling Ben."

"Wait." Sally stared at her. "You haven't told Ben? He's your best friend. You should have told him, like, right away."

"I know." Chloe dragged her spoon through the thick caramel at the bottom of her ice-cream dish. She hated to think what Ben was going to say when he found out. It was not going to be short and sweet, she knew that much. Every time she had the conversation with him in her head, she pictured him staring at her with a baffled look on his face. *"Funny,"* he'd say. *"But did you seriously think I'd believe you'd do something so outrageously stupid?"*

Sally licked a bit of ice cream off the spoon. "Right," she said. "Well, he can hardly complain. Geoff clearly adores you, considering he proposed, and you obviously adore him, since you said yes."

"Yes, but Ben will . . ." Her voice trailed off.

"He'll have a hard time with it." Sally nodded. "That you're marrying someone else."

"Huh?" Chloe was surprised. "No. He'll be upset that he didn't even get to meet the guy first. And that I'm rushing into things. The time line is going to be a major problem for Ben."

"Oh."

The two fell silent, and Chloe listened to the nearby clinks of the spoons hitting glass bowls. Through the window, she watched as weekend shoppers raced by. They moved as though trying to grab something just out of reach. Feeling slightly sick inside, probably from all the sugar, she said, "Please don't tell me you are another person who truly thought I was going to marry Ben."

"I always thought it was a possibility." Flipping her spoon backwards, Sally spooned up some ice cream and put it in her mouth. Pulling it out, she said, "But who knows why people end up together? I didn't think that I'd end up with someone like Norman, but he couldn't be a better match for me. Holy hell, if I'd married that rocker guy from college . . . What was his name—"

"DeAndre."

"Yes!" Sally squealed. "If I would have married that guy, who knows where I'd be. I'd probably be living in Vegas or something, in a one-bedroom apartment with bad lighting and flying cockroaches. It's obvious that Geoff is really good for you. You look relaxed for the first time in, like, two years."

"He is good for me," Chloe agreed. "You know, the whole thing is good. Ben and I could never get married, anyway." She smiled suddenly, imagining it. "Can you imagine? He'd want to design our own invitations and the placards on the table and have some weird, avant-garde band at the reception just to confuse people . . . No, no." She shook her head. "Marrying Ben would be a lot of work."

"Yup." Sally nodded. "Geoff is exactly the type of man you need. Successful, loves his daughter . . . Wait. Does he—"

"Yes," Chloe said. "He wants to have more kids, especially after seeing me with Mary Beth. The love's there but the discipline is not." Sometimes Mary Beth was good and, as the storybook said, sometimes she was simply horrid. "But I can change that. I'll have her under control in six months."

"I can't wait to meet him." Lifting up her sundae dish, Sally clinked it against hers. Chloe must have had a funny expression on her face, because Sally said, "Oh, no. What?"

"Nothing." She grinned. "The clinking sound just made me think of hundreds of champagne glasses coming together in a toast."

Sally laughed. "Spoken like a true bride to be."

# Forty-five

The clock on the top of the desk seemed to tick in time with her heart. Kristine sat in her black rolling desk chair, her feet drumming against the tile of the floor. The office felt too hot, as it always did during the first few days of winter while the staff tried to find a temperature that worked. Seventy might be perfect one year and boil them the next. She wished she could take off her sweater but wasn't certain what shirt she was wearing underneath. Considering Ethan was stopping by, she felt an irrational desire to remain covered up.

*Knock knock.*

"Hey." Ethan walked into her office and shut the door behind him, a slight swagger to his step. He took a seat in the chair across from her and crossed his legs. "It's good to see you."

Kristine gave a sharp nod. Squaring her shoulders, she resolved to get this conversation over with as quickly as possible. "Thanks for coming in."

At her brisk tone, Ethan seemed startled. Then, he gave her a wry look. "I take it the rest of your trip went okay."

Kristine felt her cheeks color. "It was great." She picked up a pen and fidgeted with it, trying not to look at him. "My husband

and I went up to Venice. We spent a week there, just like when we were younger. It was very special."

"The canals." Ethan gave a slight smile. "A never-ending maze of mystery."

Why did he have to say things like that? Kristine gripped the pen and licked her lips. They suddenly felt a little too dry and she considered reaching into her desk drawer and applying some gloss, but changed her mind. She didn't want to give the impression that she was trying to . . . impress him.

Staring at the pen, she clicked it. "Ethan, I asked you to come in today because . . ." *Click-click. Click-click.* It sounded like a heartbeat. "I don't think it's a good idea for you to continue working here."

"Ah."

Kristine shifted in her chair. "I'm sorry."

"I'm sorry, too." His brow was furrowed, his face serious. "I've really enjoyed getting to know you, Kristine."

Quickly, she got to her feet and crossed her arms. "I have to get back to work."

"Wait." Ethan pulled out a small wrapped package from his jacket pocket. Handing it to her, he said, "I brought you something."

Kristine hesitated, her eyes glancing at the door. What if Annie walked in?

"Open it." His voice was low and intimate. "Please."

With fingers that still trembled, Kristine untied the red string around the plain paper. A black-and-white photograph stared up at her from a frame. She remembered the exact moment it was taken in St. Peter's Square, right after Ethan threw her guidebook away. She'd turned to the camera with a look that was both dark and inviting.

"That's how I see you," he said. "I really hate to think that I'm losing that."

For a brief moment, she held tightly to the frame. It was so hard to believe that the wild, beautiful woman in the picture was her. Then she handed the gift back to Ethan.

"I'm sorry." Her heart felt as heavy as lead. "I just can't."

Ethan studied her for a long moment. Then, tucking the photograph under his arm, he turned and walked out the door.

## Forty-six

Sitting in front of the mirror at her vanity table, June touched the perfume dauber to her neck. The bright, citrusy scent did not match her dark mood one bit. Setting down the bottle, she frowned at her reflection.

"Maybe I should call in sick," June told Charley. "I just know they're not going to want to see me at mahjong."

Charley was busy looking out the window with a pair of binoculars. "June. Don't be foolish. You never miss your group."

"Yes, but . . ." Her hands hovered over the earrings she'd planned to clip on. They were yellow daisies, trimmed with white enamel. They seemed much too bright for the way she was feeling. "I'm afraid. Isn't that ridiculous?"

When June and Charley had started seeing each other, Rose and Bernice simply stopped returning her calls. The snub very much hurt June's feelings. Besides, everyone was saying that Rose had started to date a young man she'd met while spending time with Charley at the golf course. How could she possibly be angry at June? Bernice, on the other hand . . . well, June could understand.

"They'll get over it," Charley said, scanning the backyard, "as soon as they see how happy you are." Turning away from the window, he trained the binoculars on her. "I can see that pretty clearly. You're glowing."

"Oh." June's hands fluttered to her face. She was certain those binoculars picked up every wrinkle, each imperfection. "I most certainly am not." When the binoculars remained trained on her face, she shook her finger at him. "Charley Montgomery, you stop that this instant."

Chuckling, he walked over to her and rested his chin on her head. Gazing at their reflection in the mirror, he said, "I have never seen anything as beautiful as you. Not the plume of a bird or the petal of a flower. Your friends couldn't possibly be mean to something so lovely."

"I don't know." June frowned, although she very much liked the sight of Charley's face hovering above hers. "These women certainly don't like to lose."

"You don't like to lose, either." Charley winked. "And for that, I will be forever grateful."

June scrunched up her lips. "Do you really think you could have married Rose?"

He chuckled. "Rose is a lovely woman. And she makes a delicious strudel. But marry her? No. Most certainly not."

"What about Bernice?"

"Bernice . . ." He thought for a moment. "There's something very sweet about Bernice. Actually, I wouldn't mind setting her up with one of my friends. I might know just the fellow."

June's eyes widened. "Really?" She clasped her hands in delight. "Oh, Charley. That would be wonderful. Then maybe she'd forgive me."

"Well, don't get too excited. He's down in Florida now and won't be back until the spring but . . ." Charley tapped his finger against his lips. "I think those two would hit it off real well."

June let out a happy sigh. "Now, if only Bernice will speak to me, I can tell her that."

He just shook his head, watching her.

"What?" June clipped on her earrings. "What is it?"

"You're just a remarkable woman, June. I've never met anyone who wants so badly for everyone around her to be happy."

June studied her hands, feeling guilty. It was nice of him to say but she certainly didn't feel remarkable. Not in the slightest. "That's not true," she admitted. "I would have died if Rose or Bernice ended up with you."

"That never would have happened," Charley said. "I had my eye on you from the beginning. And I didn't even need to use these." He patted the binoculars.

June smiled, thinking of the way she used to spy on him.

"Now, you've all been friends for a long time," he said. "They'll come around. And if they don't . . ." He lifted his chin, trying to look tough. "You just give old Charley a call. He'll go ahead and give them a talking-to."

"Ah-ha," June said, her eyes dancing. "Turns out, I am not a nice person at all, because . . ." Getting to her feet, she rested her cheek against Charley's chest. "That's something I'd really like to see."


June hovered at the edge of Nina Lowenstein's wood-paneled library, twisting her hands. The low-lit room with its long bro-cade curtains, wall-to-wall first editions and ornate antique ta-bles suddenly felt cold and intimidating. Groups of women were clustered together, whispering, their backs to the door. It did not escape June's notice that not one of the women looked her way.

Oh, dear. This was worse than she suspected.

Just as June was about to make a run for it, Rue swept up to her side, gripping her elbow. "Hello, darling family," she crooned.

Conservative as always, Rue was dressed in an elegant pantsuit with her hair done in a neat bob. Considering she was from one of the oldest families in Chicago, June had always been slightly intimidated by her, until the day June paid her a visit to discuss Geoff's intentions with her granddaughter. Rue had been so de-lighted to learn that the two were seeing each other that she and June had their first good talk ever, lasting late into the afternoon.

Now, June smiled at her in delight. "Isn't it something? You should have seen your grandson. He got down on one knee as though he were an old pro."

Rue raised a well-groomed eyebrow. "Darling, he is something of an expert. He's been married once before, you know."

June laughed. "Yes," she said. "That experience must have come into play."

Rue's tongue touched the edge of her mouth, as though waiting for June to say something else. Finally, she said, "You little devil. You're going to make me ask about it, aren't you? Fine. Is it true that you will be in the wedding, too? Not as a bridesmaid but as a bride?"

A smile leapt to June's lips. "It's true," she sang, pulling the faux fur wrap she was wearing tightly around her. "I'm marrying Charley Montgomery, my darling neighbor. I'm very happy but . . . I think Bernice and Rose are angry at me."

The two had their heads together and were in a very animated conversation. On one hand, June was happy to see them finally getting along. On the other, it was disappointing that they seemed to be bonding over a mutual dislike for her.

Rue's eyes flashed. "I will most certainly take care of that right now. As a matter of fact, why don't you come with me?"

Rue strode across the thick carpeting. Clapping her hands, she announced, "Ladies! Before we get started today, I have something to say. This bride-to-be is about to join my family and I am simply delighted for her. If there is anything any of you have to say about the issue, I'd appreciate it if you'd say it in front of me."

Rose stepped forward, her blue taffeta dress crunching with the effort. Putting her hands on her hips, she studied June with those cold, cat-like eyes. "I certainly have something to say."

Bernice nodded, taking a step toward June. "Something to say, indeed."

The room suddenly felt quite tense. June swallowed hard, wondering if she'd have to call in Charley's assistance after all.

"Alright," she said, lifting her chin. "What is it?"

Rose and Bernice looked at each other, then shouted, "Congratulations!" The women in the mahjong group cheered and applauded, stepping away from the table they'd been crowded around. There sat a cake in the shape of a silver fox. In bright pink script, the cake read: *Congratulations, June! You always win the prize.*

June's mouth dropped open. She stared at the cake. "Oh, my," she breathed, clasping her hands against her chest. Suddenly, the room felt quite hot. "Oh, my."

Rue patted her on the back. "It appears, darling, that everyone is, in fact, quite pleased."

"I'm sorry I was a shit," Bernice said, rushing over and giving June a tight hug. In spite of their proximity, her voice was as loud as ever. "You deserve all the happiness in the world. Congratulations."

"Out of the way, Bernice," Rose said, pushing her aside. "It's my turn." Shaking her head, she said, "I have to admit, June. I am quite relieved about all this."

"Relieved?" June said, surprised. "Why?"

"Charley was simply exhausting to court. The only thing he ever wanted to talk about was *you*." Giving her a kiss on each cheek, Rose smiled. "I'm happy for you."

June's heart was brimming with joy. Not only had she been blessed with the gift of love for the second time in her life, she was blessed with wonderful friends to celebrate with. Giving a big smile, she said, "Well, what are we waiting for? Let's eat cake."

# Forty-seven

The next afternoon, Chloe met her mother and grandmother at the Drake for an afternoon tea. The hotel was only a few blocks from June's house and Chloe loved it. They'd been going there ever since she was a little girl and as they entered the lobby, she felt nostalgic.

"What's wrong?" her mother asked, nudging her.

Chloe took in the flower arrangement on the table and the enormous chandelier that dangled overhead. "I don't know," she said. "It's like, in the past few days, I suddenly started seeing things differently. Like a grown-up, instead of a kid."

"A diamond will do that," June said. "This is just the beginning. Next, you'll probably start wearing dresses and putting on makeup." She said this while eyeing Chloe's jeans with disdain.

"These jeans were very expensive," Chloe lied as they walked into the tearoom. "They'll fit right in."

Of course, they didn't. Everyone was dressed up but, honestly, Chloe didn't have time. She'd slept over at Geoff's, went straight to class and then worked a shift at Tiny Tumblers. Still, she *had* started to think about her appearance in the past few days, particularly her nails. Every time she caught a glimpse of the diamond on her finger, she resolved to go get a manicure.

"So, you feel different?" Kristine said as a waiter whisked away her coat. "More mature?"

"Let's not get crazy," Chloe said. Even though she wanted to appear as stately as the harp player or as the coiffed women sipping tea at the tables, she still had a childlike urge to run around the room screaming, *I'm engaged, I'm engaged, I'm engaged!* "I think my maturity level is right on par to where it's always been."

"Maturity is highly overrated." June settled into her chair and reached for a menu. "Maturity requires hormone creams."

"Gross." Chloe laughed. "TMI."

Kristine looked puzzled. "TMI? What is that?"

Chloe and June exchanged a look. Together, they chorused, "Too much information."

June looked incredibly pleased with herself as she flipped through the menu.

While Kristine and June tried to decide on a flavor of tea, Chloe studied her ring. She'd noticed that it always looked different, depending on the light. At home, it had a crystal glint. On the walk to school, it sparkled with purples and blues. And here, in the tearoom, it flashed with deep golden tones.

Chloe sighed. The artistic nuances of the diamond ring were something she'd love to share with Ben. That, of course, would require her to tell him that she was engaged, which she still hadn't quite worked up the nerve to do.

"Earth to Chloe," June said, waving a hand in front of her face.

She snapped back to the present. "Yes. What?"

"We're about to plan a wedding," June said. "Will you take notes? As the student of the group, I feel you're the one who is most capable."

"Sure." Fumbling through her backpack, Chloe unearthed a notebook. She felt guilty, somehow, as if thinking about Ben at a time like this had been inappropriate. Pen poised, she cleared her throat. "Go for it."

"Alright." June adjusted her red felt hat and pursed her lips, as though deep in thought. "To start, I have engagement photos booked for us this Saturday afternoon. I'll need Kevin and Geoff, of course, so—"

"Stop right there." Chloe held up her hand. "That's two days from now. You have to give me more notice. I'm booked for, like, three months—"

June gave her hand a small squeeze. "Don't worry, my darling. It will take two hours. I'm thinking sunset, by the lake. Then you're back to whatever it is you have planned."

Mentally, Chloe ran through her schedule. She was working until four so, even though it would be tight, it would work. Still . . . "You have to give me more notice," she grumbled. "From now on. Deal?"

June sighed. "I'll do my best, but the next few months will be very busy. I want this wedding to be the most impressive thing Chicago has ever seen. Imagine . . . the snow glistens from the ground. Lights shine from every tree. The city still sparkles with the magic of Christmas and—"

"Wait, what?" Kristine cried. "You want to get married in two months?"

Chloe's eyes widened. Two months? There was a lot on the roster in the next two months: exams, internships, not to mention homework, Tiny Tumblers and actually having a relationship. How on earth was she going to fit in a wedding?

June flicked off a piece of lint nestled on her dramatic velvet cuff. "For heaven's sake," she said, looking back and forth between Kristine and Chloe. "Why are you two acting so surprised? I told you I wanted to get married quickly."

"Yes," Kristine said, shooting a worried look at Chloe. "But come on, Mom. We can't plan a wedding in two months."

June waved her hand. "Nonsense. Your father and I were married in a matter of weeks, when he was called to Vietnam. It most certainly can be done."

Chloe considered this. "I guess a lot can happen in two months. I got engaged in two months."

"Yes." Her mother's voice was tight. "I'm well aware of that."

June shot her a look. "Unnecessary."

Chloe looked at her mother in surprise. "Wait . . . What?"

Since when did her mother have a problem with her engagement?

"Mom," she pressed. "Come on. What is it?"

"I just . . ." Tapping her fingers against her mouth, Kristine turned to watch the harp player by the fountain. The woman's fingers were moving across the strings at lightning speed. "The engagement was fast. That's all."

Chloe was surprised. For years, her mother had been saying she needed to hurry up and find someone. Now it was *too* fast? That wasn't fair. Besides, it felt good to do something romantic and spontaneous, instead of being "closed off to love," like Ben had said that night in the bar.

"Why does that even have to matter?" Chloe asked.

"It's just . . ." Kristine turned back to the table and arranged the silverware in a neat pattern. "Marriage is something to commit to for a lifetime. I'm afraid you're trying to— *Ouch!*" Glaring at June, she said, "Mother, don't kick me. I have every right to my opinion."

"This is a celebration tea." June took off her hat and set it on a chair, smoothing her ash blonde waves. "You can save your opinion for another time."

A silence fell over the table. The waiter walked up, perfectly cheerful. He set a tiered tray filled with finger sandwiches, scones and desserts in the middle of the table and explained each item in detail.

When no one reached for anything, he gave a confused smile. "Alright, ladies. Let me know if you need anything else."

Chloe could think of a couple of things that she needed. Like a more understanding mother.

"You know what, Mom?" The steam from her tea was hot on her face, so Chloe pushed it away. "I said yes to Geoff's proposal because I'm tired of working so hard to make everything happen. For once in my life, something came easy for me. I met someone, he loves me, he proposed. The end."

With that, Chloe reached for a sandwich and took a bite.

"But it's not the end," Kristine insisted, looking down at her wedding ring. "Chloe, it's just the beginning."

June snatched a scone from the tray. She scooped up whipped cream from the bowl and dumped it on her plate, banging her spoon loudly against her dish. "Sometimes, I just don't understand you, Kristine. Didn't you get angry with me? When I said these types of things to you?"

"That was a completely different situation, Mom." Kristine wrapped her hair into a bun and held it there. "You didn't like Kevin."

*Geez.* This tea was revealing all sorts of tidbits that Chloe would rather not hear.

After all, it wasn't a secret that her father and June had butted heads over the years, but Chloe had always assumed it was in good fun. She'd never realized that June hadn't *liked* him. Chloe turned to her grandmother, waiting for some sort of an explanation.

"Chloe, I adored your father," June said. "I was simply worried that your mother wasn't ready to get married. For heaven's sake, she met him in college. She was very young."

"Yes," Kristine said, dropping her hair. It fanned out above her shoulders. "I was young. But we'd known each other for quite a long time before he proposed."

At school, Chloe had learned that sometimes it was best to ask questions directly.

"Mom, do you want me to marry Geoff?" she asked. "Yes or no?"

Kristine hesitated. "Honey, I want you to be—"

"Happy, I know," Chloe said, her voice dry. "Yes or no?"

Kristine fidgeted with her wedding ring. After a long moment, she looked up at Chloe with her clear blue eyes. "Yes. I want you to marry Geoff, if that's what you want. You'll have my full support."

"Great!" June said, clapping her hands. "Then can we please plan this wedding?"

June picked up where she'd left off. She explained the strings she'd pulled to book them a church two days after Christmas, her ideas for food, music, decorations . . . There were so many little details to think about that Chloe had to write quickly to keep up.

"Okay, hold on," Kristine finally said. June had just revealed a plan to release doves with rose garlands dangling from their beaks. Taking the notebook out of Chloe's hands, she scanned through three pages of notes, her forehead wrinkling more and more after each page.

June watched her in surprise. "What are you doing? Is there something I missed?"

"Mother . . ." Kristine said slowly. Setting down the notebook, she looked off into the distance as though trying to choose the right words. "I'm very excited about all of this and so happy for you. But . . ."

June took a sip of tea, patiently waiting for the caveat.

"I'm concerned about some of your suggestions," Kristine said. "This all feels a little over the top, especially considering that Kevin and I will be paying for two of the three weddings in question."

June's laugh tinkled as brightly as the harp. "Darling girl, please don't tell me we're going to start *that* whole thing again.

We've been through this before, a quarter of a century ago. I'm not going through it again."

"Mother, seriously." Kristine glared at her. "*I'm* not going through it again. So, don't even try it."

"Try what?" Chloe asked, taking a bite of an egg sandwich. The filling practically melted in her mouth. "This is good," she said, holding it up. "What's she not supposed to try?"

"When your parents got married," June said, "your father did not want me to pay for the wedding."

"Mother." Red splotches crept up Kristine's neck like flames.

"Your father is incredibly proud, you see. It took some pressure on my end to help him to understand that, if he wanted to marry my daughter, he was going to do it in style." June gave a little smile. Reaching for her scone, she took a bite, then waved it as she talked. "*This* time, I will not even tolerate that conversation. This is *my* wedding, my daughter's vow renewal and my granddaughter's wedding. I will pay. End of story."

Kristine's eyes surveyed the groups at the other tables, as though wishing to sit somewhere, anywhere else. "I'm not going to debate this with you right now," she said. "Not here."

"There's no debate." June's voice was firm. "I have been investing the money to use for Chloe's wedding before she was even born. Now that the opportunity is here, I have more than enough to give her the wedding of her dreams. What's wrong with that?"

Kristine pressed her fingers into her temples. "You know what's wrong with that." Her pretty eyes looked troubled. "Kevin's not going to like this. Please, just let us take care of it."

Picking up her teacup, June extended a pinky and turned to Chloe. "Darling, why don't you decide?" June's expression clearly read, *Your mother is being unreasonable.* "Do you want your father to work himself to the bone to pay for this wedding? Or do you want to use the money that I won't need when I'm cold, dead and lying in the ground, but would bring me such incredible joy to use today?"

Chloe thought for a moment. Ever since her father lost his job and started this new one, he'd seemed pretty stressed out about money. He worked all the time, and he was always asking about her scholarships. Last year, he'd even mentioned something about wanting to move back into the city but owing too much on the house to do it. The last thing Chloe wanted to do was put more of a burden on him, especially if June was so eager to pay for the wedding.

"I vote yes." Chloe finished her sandwich in one bite. At her mother's groan, she shrugged. "Sorry, but Dad works too hard. Let's give him a break."

"Your father loves to work," Kristine said, shaking her head. "You have to understand that. He's not going to go along with this. I can tell you right now, it's just going to cause a big problem."

"It will be fine." June patted Chloe's hand. "Everything, including this wedding, will be just fine. Not just fine. Spectacular," she said, fanning her hands out like a stage performer.

Chloe bit her lip. "I hate to tell you this, especially after all your big plans, but I don't want my part to be spectacular. I want to keep it pretty basic. So does Geoff."

After getting engaged, she and Geoff had a long talk about the wedding. Since he'd been married before, he wanted her to plan whatever she wanted, as long as it wasn't over the top. Considering Chloe had never wanted a big wedding, she was perfectly happy to keep it simple.

"Simple?" June seemed baffled. "Who wants a *simple* wedding?"

Kristine raised her hand. "I wanted to get married in your garden. I was so scared at the idea of walking down the aisle, all those people looking at me . . ." Her freckled face flushed at the memory. "But you insisted on having some big old wedding in a big old church. I almost passed out."

June picked up a fork and pointed it at her. "Kristine, your wedding was wonderful. Frankly, I'm shocked you didn't appreciate it."

"My wedding was wonderful and I *did* appreciate it." Kristine recited this as though she'd said it many times before. "But it was a little out of hand. And so were you."

"I most certainly was not." June stabbed her fork into a sandwich.

"Ha!" Turning to face Chloe, Kristine said, "Did you know that she swapped out my flowers at the last minute? Without even *asking* me?"

Chloe's jaw dropped. "Grandma. You did *not*." Although, to be honest, the move sounded exactly like something June would do.

June sniffed. "My selections were lovely."

Kristine let out a sound that could have been a squawk. "I walked into my reception on my wedding day and I thought the flower company had made a mistake! Instead of violets and baby's breath, there were these gaudy birds-of-paradise. Everywhere. It looked like a funeral home in Hawaii."

"It most certainly did not," June said. "The violets would have looked wimpy. They would not have filled up the room. The birds-of-paradise, on the other hand, were gorgeous. They received several compliments."

"Because *that's* what matters. Compliments." Kristine sat back in the chair and glared at her mother. "This time, if I am seriously sharing a wedding with you, I am the one in charge of the flowers."

"Sorry." June actually did look apologetic at this. "Charley and I fell in love over flowers. We'll be in charge of that."

"Fine." Kristine wrinkled her forehead, as though trying to think of something, anything, that June would let her do. "Then . . . Then in my bouquet, *if* I even carry one, I'm going to have violets!"

"You tell her, Mom." Chloe nodded. "Get it all out on the table."

"Let's not get it *all* out." Kristine gave June a wry look. "I don't want to start World War Three."

June's eyes bugged slightly. "What *else* could I have possibly done to ruin your wedding day?"

Eagerly, Chloe leaned forward. This was just like sitting in on family therapy. Typically, when the conversation got this heated, the therapist suggested the family take a moment and cool down. But that was not about to happen at this table.

"The speech," Kristine said, then folded her hands and waited.

"Oh, please." June sat back in her chair. "Tell me something I haven't heard."

"I haven't heard," Chloe sang.

"Apparently," June explained, "your mother and father did not appreciate my wedding toast. However, that was simply because they did not understand it. One day, they will and—"

Kristine's face was thunderous. "We most certainly will not."

Chloe was fascinated. "Grandma, what on earth did you say?"

June thought for a moment. "I said—"

"No." Kristine held up her hand. "Don't you dare. I do not want that repeated in front of my daughter. It was the most rude, insulting thing I have ever heard."

"Don't be ridiculous." June fanned herself with a napkin. "You simply misunderstood."

Chloe was amazed. She could imagine the two of them back then, planning out the nuances of Kristine's special day. It was so strange to think that one day, Mary Beth could be sitting here as an adult, listening to Chloe and Kristine discuss the same issues.

Kristine must have caught the expression on her face, because she said, "Chloe, we're not trying to upset you . . ."

"I'm not upset." Trying to laugh, she told them what she'd been thinking. "I'm about to become a mother." She pointed at Kristine. "That makes you a grandmother." Turning to June, she said, "And that makes you . . ."

June smiled. "Pretty darn great."

Eyeing the display of scones, Chloe reached for one and

absently broke off a corner. "Do you think . . ." Popping it into her mouth, she swallowed it over a lump in her throat. "Do you think I'll be a good mother?"

Kristine nodded. "Absolutely."

"Better than me," June said, her voice mournful. "Apparently, I was a terrible mother."

"Oh, give me a break." Kristine's bright blue eyes scanned the room. "Alright, I've had enough. Where's the waiter? I think I'm going to need something stronger than tea."

"This does not bode well." Chloe laughed. "Day one of wedding planning and Mom already has a drinking problem."

"It'll only get worse," June said. "Marriage is a tricky thing. And it all starts with the wedding."

# Forty-eight

Kristine planned to wait until Kevin was home before getting into a serious conversation about the fact that June wanted to pay for the wedding. It wasn't a topic to discuss over the phone, that was for sure. Even though June's intentions were good, Kristine knew that he wouldn't see it that way.

Kevin had always had a strong sense of responsibility for providing for their family. Instead of seeing June's gesture as what it was—a way for her to control the wedding—he would see it as a slight. He would take it as proof that June didn't have faith in his ability to give Chloe the wedding she deserved. It was ridiculous, but that's just how he was.

This worried her, especially since things had gotten so much better between them. Even though Kevin was still on the road all the time, he'd promised to talk to his boss about working from the satellite office or traveling only half of the time. Things were definitely looking up, and Kristine did not want anything to threaten that careful balance they'd found with each other. So, when he got back into town on Friday, she gave herself permission to enjoy one night with him without bringing it up.

Instead of talking about the wedding, they took a long walk around the neighborhood, cooked dinner together and, as they had practically every day since Italy, had amazing sex. As they lay in bed, Kevin held her until they both drifted off to sleep. It had been such a perfect, promising evening, but when she woke up on Saturday, she knew there was no more time to avoid the issue. That afternoon, while getting ready for the engagement photos, Kristine steeled herself for the conversation.

As Kevin walked out of the bathroom in a cloud of steam, straightening his tie, she said, "Hello, handsome." He was wearing a simple navy suit that fit him perfectly and smelled like lemongrass and musk. "You look nice."

"Yeah?" Kevin grinned. "Hot and sexy?"

Kristine wrapped her arms around his broad shoulders. "Very." She stood up on her tiptoes to kiss his ear. Seeing their reflection in the mirror, she made a face. "Do I look like a bridesmaid?"

Kristine was wearing a fitted navy dress with a cowl neck, courtesy of June. The dress alone was a perfect lead-in for the conversation.

"You look gorgeous," he said. Looking down at the tie, he shook his head. "But I'm still trying to wrap my mind around the fact that I will be dressed exactly like two other grown men."

"That's June," Kristine said. "There's nothing she likes more than controlling a wedding."

On Friday morning, both the navy dress and the navy-and-silver-striped tie had been delivered in a neatly wrapped package from Ferragamo. The note inside the box explained that June had been hit with inspiration and that they should all plan to dress alike for the photograph. *Since we're not having bridesmaids*, the note said, *this will be the big "dress-alike" moment in our wedding. LOL!*

"Oh, she means well." He smiled. "Isn't that what you always say to me?"

"Yes, but . . ." Kristine applied some coral lipstick, then set it down on the dresser with a clunk. "Kevin, I'm worried. She's running the show, just like she did back with our wedding. Chloe doesn't seem to mind, but . . ." Kristine smoothed down a damp strand of her husband's hair, hating that the next words out of her mouth might hurt him. She hesitated. "There's something I haven't told you. Something big."

Kevin cocked an eyebrow. "June wants me to ride down the aisle on a pony?"

"She wants to pay for the whole wedding," Kristine told him. "Her part, our vow renewal and Chloe. She wants to pay for Chloe."

Kevin's blue eyes widened and his cheeks flushed. It was the same look he used to get before running down the field and tackling someone. Great. This was just the response she'd expected.

Quickly, she said, "Look, it's only because she wants to make the wedding some big extravaganza. I told her that you would say absolutely not, that we'll pay for our daughter, but she's insisting. I really don't know what to do. She's not taking no for an answer."

Kevin swallowed hard, the muscle in his jaw pulsing. "I—"

"Honey, I know." Gently, she touched his cheek. "You've worked so hard to be able to do things like this. June's not trying to take it away from you. But she has the money, she wants to be in charge and with everything happening at the last minute, it's going to be incredibly expen—"

"Kristine, it's okay." He shook his head. "It's fine. Let's just let her do it."

Kristine dropped her hand in surprise. "Really?"

"Why not?" He let out a sharp puff of air. Reaching for her hand, he said, "If it will make her happy, then let her go right ahead. We can use Chloe's wedding money for something else. Something special for us."

Kristine didn't know what to say. To be honest, she was shocked. Where was the bulging vein in his forehead? The angry proclamation that he was the provider for his family, no matter what? She waited for some type of tell. A rude remark, a frown, something. But the only thing he did was reach down and smooth his tie.

*Huh.* Maybe he didn't want to ruin the careful balance they'd recaptured, either.

"June's got money." Flipping over the tie, he indicated the designer label. "Let her use it."

Kristine felt slightly suspicious. The easygoing response wasn't like him. "What are you not telling me?"

Kevin seemed to jump. "What do you mean?"

"I don't know." She studied his blue eyes. They seemed guarded. "I feel like you're taking this too calmly. Did you already put the deposit down on the church or something? You beat June to it?"

"Kris, no." Glancing at his watch, he said, "You about ready? There might be traffic." She was still eyeing him and he said, "Look, it's not a big deal. We're a family. If it's important to you and it's important to her . . . I really don't mind."

"Thank you," Kristine emphasized. "I really appreciate that."

"What am I supposed to say to you?" Kevin reached out and stroked her face. "I'm kind of defenseless, considering the fact that you're an absolute knockout." Leaning forward, he kissed her on the mouth and ran a hand up her leg. Suddenly, his hand stopped and a funny look crossed his face. "What the hell are these?" he said, tugging at her pantyhose.

"Wait. Kevin, those are—"

Too late. Kevin had already grabbed the thin material between his thumb and forefinger and stretched it out from her leg. With a little pop, the pantyhose snagged.

"Whoops." His face split into a grin. "You didn't really want to wear those anyway, did you?"

"Shit!" Kristine examined the tear. "Yes, actually. I did."

They were taking pictures down by Lake Michigan and even though it was only November, the breeze would be icy cold. Clear nail polish might stop the snag, but she had no idea where her nail kit was.

"Great. Now I'm going to freeze. *Stop*," she said when he tried to run his hand up her leg once again. "Seriously. It's going to be . . ."

Kevin reached for her hands and held them. Using the strength of his legs, he guided her toward the bed and gently pushed her down. Leaning in close, he examined the tear. She could feel the warmth of his breath as he studied it, then the heat of his mouth as he pressed his lips over the exposed skin of her thigh.

"Stop," she said, batting at him. It was futile. Like trying to fight off a bear on a hunt for honey. "Kevin, we have to go . . ."

Slowly, he traced the outline of the tear with his tongue. She felt a slight tingling in her stomach at his touch and a sharp tug as Kevin took the sheer material in between his teeth. Slowly, he ripped them all the way up her inner thigh.

"Kevin, stop," she groaned, but her commitment to be on time was definitely starting to waver.

It wavered even further as Kevin slipped a thumb under the thin material of her white cotton underwear, found her center and pressed down. She tried to wriggle out of his grasp but every time she moved, it just increased the sensation between her legs. Slowly, he lowered his mouth back down to her thigh and lightly bit into her skin.

"This reminds me of the last time we did engagement photos." He chuckled, reaching for her.

Back when Kristine and Kevin got married, June not only took charge of the invitations, the guest list and the location of their wedding, she also orchestrated the engagement photos. The instructions were precise: The photos would take place at the country club. Kristine was to wear light blue and Kevin was to wear a khaki suit with a light blue tie. Kristine was to look slightly weepy, while Kevin was to stare at her in adoration. Kristine was to lean against him and Kevin was to place a hand on hers. The list went on and on.

The only way Kristine and Kevin got through it was sneaking

off to the bathroom and having sex in a linen closet. Kristine had walked out with her hair all askew and June had shrieked in horror.

Kristine smiled at the memory. Stretching out a languid arm, she ran it over Kevin's back. The material of his suit jacket felt as smooth as water against her fingers. "Maybe this time," she said, "we should just skip the photos altogether."

Kevin buried his face in her neck. "If it wasn't for the fact that our daughter will be there with her fiancé, that is exactly what we'd do." Sitting up on one elbow, he gave her a wicked look. "I would keep you here and fuck you senseless for the rest of the night."

"Oh, honey." Kristine kissed the tip of his nose. "How did you ever get to be such a sensitive guy?"

Chloe stepped out of the cab, her dress flapping in the wind. June had decided that the engagement photos should be shot on the beach, just off Lakeshore Drive. The skyline loomed in the background, the sun bouncing dramatically off the buildings.

From where she stood, Chloe could see that her parents, her grandmother and Charley were already there. Geoff was nowhere in sight. She was surprised. He had promised to get Mary Beth a sitter and be there on time, since the odds were good that Chloe would be running late. Luckily, she wasn't. After racing home from a midterm to change into the navy silk dress June had sent, she'd paid the cabbie extra to put the pedal to the metal and get her there on time.

June rushed forward to greet her. "Chloe, you look darling," she crooned, kissing her hard on each cheek. "Weren't these dresses a great idea?"

"You're wearing it best," she said, admiring her grandmother. "People are going to look at your picture and be like, 'It's a shame that one's off the market.'"

June did look awesome. Whether it was due to face creams, those crazy hats she wore or just good genes (Chloe crossed her fingers on that one), her skin was luminescent. Her hair was perfect, her eye makeup perfectly applied (certainly no makeup chart required) and large diamonds sparkled from her ears.

"Seriously, Grandma," Chloe said, nodding. "You're a hottie."

"Charley's the hottie." June gave a coquettish smile. "Just look at him."

Charley was standing down by the water, chatting with the photographer. He wore the navy suit, a light blue button-up and the silver-and-blue-striped tie. His silver hair glinted like something out of a yacht ad. Spotting Chloe, he gave a friendly wave.

Chloe laughed. "Leave it to you to find him."

June beamed. "Oh, I know quality when I see it."

"Hi, honey," Kristine called. She was walking toward them in her bare feet, her shoes dangling from her hand. Pulling Chloe into a tight hug, she gave her a loud smack on the cheek. "I can't believe we're taking your engagement photo!" Beckoning to Kevin, she said, "Can you believe this? Our baby's old enough for an *engagement* photo."

Chloe blushed, giving a furtive look around. She might be old enough for an engagement photo, but apparently, she wasn't smart enough to have a groom that could get there on time. Where the hell was Geoff?

"You look good, kid." Her father walked up and ruffled her hair. Looking from Chloe to Kristine to June, his face split into a grin. "I hit the jackpot. I'm surrounded by beautiful women."

"Alright, we should get started." June pointed at the sun, which was starting to dip in the sky. As though Geoff's absence had just struck her, she said, "Chloe, where on earth is your fiancé?"

"Um . . ." Chloe scanned the beach, as though she'd just noticed that he was missing, too. Fumbling for her phone, she said, "Give me just one second."

June bit her lip, her brown eyes watching her closely. "He *is* coming, isn't he?"

"Yes, of course," Chloe said. "Don't be silly." But inside, she was starting to panic. He should have been here by now. Hopefully, he hadn't forgotten. "Let me just see where he is."

Adjusting her dress, June straightened her shoulders and headed over to the photographer. "Tell him to hurry up," she called over her shoulder. "I want that sunset!"

Geoff answered on the first ring. "We're on our way."

Taking a few steps away from her parents, Chloe said, "Wait. You're bringing Mary Beth?"

The beach was practically deserted, if you didn't count old seaweed and the occasional water bottle. She didn't see a nanny service hanging around, just waiting to keep an eye on a four-year-old. Not to mention a four-year-old who had the capacity to ruin an entire photo session.

"Geoff, who's going to watch her?" Chloe asked, as Mary Beth screamed something in the background. "We're all going to be in the picture."

"It was short notice," Geoff said. "The babysitter couldn't—"

A solution popped into her head. "Take her to Tiny Tumblers," she instructed. "Tell them it's an emergency."

"I can't . . . You," Geoff's voice crackled over the line. "Sor . . . See . . . A minute."

Chloe hung up the phone. Sand whipped around her, stinging her skin. Letting out a deep breath, she turned to her parents. "He couldn't get a sitter," she called. "It looks like Mary Beth is coming."

"Oh, good!" Stepping forward, Kristine smoothed back a strand of Chloe's wild hair. "That's great news. We've all been dying to meet her."

"Don't get too excited," Chloe warned, trying to not look as worried as she felt. "It sounds like she's in one of her moods."

. . .

"I want to be in the picture," Mary Beth cried, stomping her feet.

June was horrified. Sand flew up around Geoff's child like some sort of natural disaster. The girl sniffled and heaved, staring at them with clenched fists, as an unsightly strand of snot ran down the front of her face.

Typically, June made it a rule to avoid children but for her future grandchild, she thought she could make an exception. Heavens, she'd thought wrong. Mary Beth had done nothing but cry and carry on since she'd arrived. Chloe had wasted several precious minutes of their photography session trying to calm down the girl, while the sun continued to dip lower and lower in the sky.

"We need to keep shooting," June called, running her tongue over her front teeth. "Chloe, please come stand here with us."

The group had its back to the water, while small waves crashed gently against the shore. Every now and again, a tiny spray of icy water slapped June on the legs but it was worth it. The pictures would be gorgeous, *if* they actually had enough time to take them.

As soon as Chloe rushed back to the group, June said, "Okay. Now, everyone smile."

Mary Beth wailed, kicking sand in their general direction. Some of it landed on June's shoes.

Geoff must have heard her huff, because he turned those pretty green eyes on her. "I'm sorry, June," he said. "I am so sorry about all this."

June sniffed. If Geoff were truly sorry, he would have called an emergency nanny half an hour ago. At this point, sorry wouldn't cut it. She wasn't trying to be selfish, but this engagement photo meant the world to her. Not only was it with her entire family, but it was June's first engagement photo ever.

It was hard to believe that she and Eugene had skipped this important step but back then, it had seemed like the right thing to do. There simply wasn't time for such a thing. With him slated to ship out, they were lucky to get the wedding preparations completed. In the interest of both time and money, they decided to skip it.

June had regretted that decision for years. There were moments where she would have given anything to look through a photo album and revisit that magical period, just before she and Eugene had become husband and wife. The fact that this time she had the opportunity to share the experience of marriage with her entire family . . . Well, that was a blessing too precious for words. June was determined to take full advantage of each and every detail and, finally, have the wedding of her dreams.

However, this bothersome child was quickly turning her dream into a nightmare.

As though on cue, Mary Beth screamed, *"Wahhh!"* from her place in the sand.

"Mary Beth, honey," Chloe called, her voice strained. "Look at your daddy smile for the camera."

June let out a hearty sigh. Fluffing her hair, she breathed in the soothing scent of the tea rose perfume she had worn for the occasion and pasted a beatific smile on her face. She hoped that, when the pictures were printed, her eyes would not betray the fact that she found the situation ridiculous.

Feeling a tap on her shoulder, June turned to see a pleading look in her granddaughter's gray eyes. "Why don't we just let her be in one picture?" Mary Beth's cries had become borderline hysterical. "Seriously. It won't hurt anything."

Hearing this suggestion, Mary Beth stopped crying. Instantly.

*What a little fraud.*

"Absolutely not," June said, forcing her voice to remain cheerful. "Mary Beth, when *you* get married, you'll have your very own engagement photos. And . . . everyone smile!"

"I want to get mawwwwwwwied," Mary Beth bellowed. *"Ahh-hhhhhhhh."*

The pitch was at a frequency that made even the photographer cringe. June put a finger to her ear and was grateful that Charley didn't wear a hearing aid. The sound might have brought him to his knees. As it was, the top window of one of the nearby sky-scrapers undoubtedly had a hairline crack.

"Geoff, we need to—"

"Chloe, just smile for the—"

"June, why can't we just—"

*"That's it."* Charley's voice boomed across the beach like dyna-mite. "That's enough!"

Everyone, including Mary Beth, fell silent.

"Mary Beth, get over here," Charley ordered. "Right now."

June preened. Finally. A man who could take charge of the situation.

Mary Beth stuck her thumb in her mouth and stomped through the sand toward Charley. She stood in front of him, her eyes bright and teary. He bent down to one knee without any trouble, which is something June loved about him. The man was fit. No doubt about that.

"Do you want to be in the picture?" Charley demanded.

Mary Beth nodded.

"Well, come on then." Charley lifted her up and put her on his shoulders.

June's mouth dropped open. "But . . . But Charley," she sput-tered. "This is *not* what I planned for. This is—"

"This is life, June. Sometimes, you've just got to work with what you got," he said. "Now, everyone smile! We want that sunset."

As the photographer snapped away, June was devastated. Had

she not made it clear that Mary Beth was *not* to be in the picture? Yes, the girl had finally stopped crying but her shoes were swinging back and forth, practically kicking sand into June's face. Oh, everything was ruined. Ruined! Didn't Charley understand?

Just as she was ready to call off the whole thing, Charley leaned forward and brushed his lips against her ear. "It'll be okay, June," he said, his voice gentle. "Trust me. You just have to be patient."

Well, if it didn't just turn out that the man was right. Just as the sun started to set, Mary Beth got bored with it all and decided she would rather play in the sand. The little girl skipped away from the group and started to build a sand castle. The photographer burst into action.

"Quickly. Quickly, please," he shouted, directing the group to line up along the shore.

Charley pulled her close. "You see?" he said, giving her that perfect smile. "Sometimes old Charley knows exactly what to do."

Spontaneously, June turned to kiss him as the photographer fired away.

# Forty-nine

That night, lying in bed, June could hardly sleep. The idea of having a real engagement photo had left her too excited for words. The moment the proofs were ready, she planned to get copies framed for all three couples and commission a painter to put the entire scene on canvas. Maybe even large enough to hang over the fire. Rolling over, she smiled in anticipation.

"June," Charley groaned. He reached out a hand and placed it on her shoulder. "Are you alright? You're flipping around like a fish in a frying pan."

"Oh, good." June was delighted. "You're up. Shall we make breakfast?"

Charley's arm reached for the alarm clock. In the moonlight shining through the window, June could see the silhouette of his arm hair. For some reason, it struck her as a beautiful sight.

"Breakfast," he murmured, then let out a sigh. "I don't know that 4:38 in the morning is my ideal breakfast time, June. We might not want to sell my house. It sounds like I'm going to need somewhere to sleep."

June snuggled up against him, delighted to feel the warmth of his body pressed against hers. He'd been so wonderful today. So strong and handsome, handling Mary Beth the way he did.

"I'm sorry I'm keeping you up," she told him, "but I'm just so excited. The pictures were wonderful and I'm just so happy this is all coming together. The wedding's going to be perfect."

"Yes," Charley mumbled. "Let's go to sleep. Let's dream about it."

"You know . . ." June reached over and rubbed his back. His muscles were firm beneath her hands. "It's so strange to think that Kristine has already been married for twenty-five years. I feel like I was just watching her walk down the aisle. Time is a funny thing, isn't it?"

June thought back to the sight of her daughter as a young girl, stepping so nervously into the church. Kristine's neck had been bright red and splotchy with nerves, but the moment she laid eyes on Kevin, a glow seemed to light her from within. She'd walked down the aisle, her eyes locked onto his.

"Things seem to be going well for those two." June turned onto her back and stared up at the ceiling. "I'm glad I talked to him. He made the right choice going to Italy with her."

"He sure did." Charley's voice was half asleep.

June nodded, her feather pillow shifting with the movement. "But I almost strangled Geoff today. He's been so good for Chloe, but after seeing something like that . . . I'd hate to think I had a hand in orchestrating something that wasn't quite right."

Charley opened one eye. "What do you mean, orchestrating something?"

*Oops.* June had not meant to tell Charley—or anyone—that tiny little fact about Chloe's engagement.

"Oh, nothing." June rolled over, pulling the high-thread-count sheets up to her chin. "Is it really four in the morning? We should get some rest."

There was a pause and the bed shifted. Charley leaned over and clicked the chain of the bedside lamp. The light was as bright as any police interrogation room.

"June . . ." Charley's eyes were tired but serious. "Did you have a hand in that engagement?"

Fiddlesticks. The man was too smart for his own good.

June let out a huge sigh and sat up in bed. "Not a *hand*. But I might have . . . planted the seed."

*"What?"* Charley roared.

For heaven's sake. How could a man who claimed to be exhausted achieve that type of volume?

"You don't need to get so worked up about it," she said. "I just . . . When I realized who Chloe was dating, I might have mentioned to Rue that Chloe had fallen in love with her grandson. There's nothing wrong with that."

"Is that all?"

June wiggled her toes under the blankets, wondering if she should get up and end this conversation this instant. "Well . . . I might have . . ."

"You might have *what?*"

Goodness, the man was pushy.

June sighed. "I might have *mentioned* to Rue that it would be a good idea for him to propose or that Chloe might move on. But I certainly didn't think he'd do it that quickly. I think that must have been Rue's doing."

"June!" Charley sounded shocked.

"What?" She fidgeted. Her fiancé was giving her a look that she didn't like. "The man would have proposed to her with or without my help. He clearly adores her."

"You don't know that." Charley's forehead was lined with worry. "Why rush things? Why did you have to butt in?"

"Because I like Rue," she said.

"June, it doesn't matter who *you* like. It matters who Chloe likes."

"Chloe likes him," June insisted. "She's engaged to him!"

"Because of you." Charley grabbed the glass of water he kept on the bedside table at night and took a drink. Shaking his head, he set it back down. "That poor girl."

June's heart rate seemed to increase. "Charley, it will be fine," she insisted, feeling her palms start to sweat. "Sometimes people need a little something to push them along. This is a good thing. It . . ." June's voice trailed off. Oh, dear. Charley was looking at her as though she were a stranger.

"Charley." June panicked. "Do you still love me?" The thought that he might not made her entire body go weak with fear.

"Of course I do!" Charley pulled her close, and she pressed her face against the strong outline of his chest. "June, you are a remarkable woman," he said. "But you are a meddler. You've meddled enough. You need to let your family make their own decisions."

June shook her finger at him. "You have no right. You cannot tell me what I can and can't do when it comes to my family."

Charley caught her finger. Gently, he lowered it. "I most certainly can and I most certainly will. Because, unless I am mistaken, they are my family now, too."

*Well.*

"I want you to ask yourself," Charley said, "if this is the best situation for Chloe."

"Of course it is," June cried. "She loves him. Charley, she said yes."

Charley shook his head. "He proposed to her in front of her family. It was spontaneous and romantic. I think it would be difficult for any young woman to say no to that."

June felt sick inside. "Should I tell Chloe?" she whispered. "Let her know the truth?"

"Don't you dare," he said. "It would break her heart."

Reaching over to the bedside table, he flipped off the lamp. The room descended into darkness. For some silly reason, tears pricked at the back of her eyes. Reaching out, she fumbled under the blankets until she felt Charley's hand, strong in hers.

Charley gave her hand a firm squeeze. "June, I want you to make me a promise," he said. "I need you to put the trust and confidence in your family that they are capable of doing the right thing. That means you have to stop making decisions for them. You need to stop meddling. Do you promise?"

"I promise," she whispered.

June thought about her granddaughter. The way her gray eyes had gotten big at the Drake as June soared through the plans for the wedding. She hoped that Chloe sincerely loved Geoff and wasn't just caught up in the excitement, like Charley seemed to think. If that was the case, her granddaughter would be facing a life of unhappiness and it would be all June's fault. The thought made her heart ache.

Leaning against Charley once again, she whispered, "Please tell me everything's going to be okay."

"I most certainly will not," he said. "I don't know that and I'm not going to lie to you."

Just as June felt like her heart might break into a million pieces, he reached over and gently touched her face. "But I can promise you one thing." His voice was strong and serious. "No matter what happens, I'll be there. You can always count on that."

# Fifty

Standing on the sunny sidewalk, Chloe cupped her hands over her eyes and peered into the window of the cake shop. That afternoon, June had scheduled a cake tasting for the three brides-to-be. Chloe gaped in delight at the five-tiered creations with dramatic turrets of whipped cream.

"I can't believe they actually let you just come in and eat cake. For *free*," Chloe said. "Geez, if I would have known that, I would have slapped on some cubic zirconia and pretended to be engaged a long time ago."

June laughed. She seemed to be hovering a little close to Chloe's elbow. "You alright?" Chloe asked, giving her a funny look. Her grandmother was staring up at her with dark, troubled eyes. "Do I have something on my face?"

"Everything's fine." June fiddled with the bright pink cashmere balls dangling from her scarf. "In fact, that's what I wanted to ask you. Are things going well? With you and Geoff?"

"Of course." Chloe turned back to the window. The scallops of pink frosting looked particularly delicious. "He's busy, I'm busy, Mary Beth's a handful . . . the usual. Why?" As June cleared her throat, Chloe got the picture. "You want gossip to take back to your mahjong group! Forget it. My relationship with Geoff is my business. It's private."

"Yes, I know that," June said. "I certainly don't want to meddle."

Chloe snorted. *That would be the day.*

"I just . . ." June's voice seemed troubled. "I just wanted to make sure you're happy."

Chloe peered at her. Her grandmother looked unusually distressed. Behind her carefully applied makeup, her eyes looked drawn and tired. "Grandma, is . . . is everything okay with you and Charley?"

"What?" June demanded. "Please. We're like carrots and peas."

"Hi, guys," Kristine called, rushing down the sidewalk. Her camel-colored wool coat billowed behind her like a cape. "Sorry I'm late! Things were busy at the store." She kissed them both on the cheek. "What did I miss?"

"These cakes," Chloe said, pointing.

Kristine looked at the cake in the window. "Oh, my gosh," she laughed. "They didn't let you do this type of thing when your father and I got married."

"Me neither," June said. "Back in my day, we had to think about whether or not our husband would even return to us alive, not what kind of cake we'd eat. The three of us are very, very lucky. We should respect this experience."

A somber silence fell over the group. Then, June grinned.

"And just so you know . . ." She lowered her voice and gave a furtive look around. "There are all sorts of bakeries in this city. This doesn't have to be our only stop. We can hit each and every one."

Kristine laughed, linking her arm with Chloe's. "Sounds like a plan."

Inside, the scent of buttercream and spun sugar infused the air. Chloe stopped and breathed it in, before taking an eager look around. The shop was brightly lit, with a glass-covered pastry display case up by the cash register and extravagant photographs of all different kinds of wedding cakes lining the walls.

Chloe felt a twinge of disappointment. When June had first

told her about the appointment, she described the bakery as something out of *Willy Wonka & the Chocolate Factory*. This looked like a normal bakery.

June spoke to the girl at the front desk and then beckoned. "Come on," she said. "They're ready for us."

A woman in a white apron and chef's hat stepped out from a swinging door that must have led to the kitchen. The woman's cheeks were rosy and the patch on her apron read *Carolyn* in blue embroidery. "You must be the three brides here for the tasting," she said, smiling at them. "Follow me."

Pushing open a door with a floral mural painted on it, the three of them followed the pastry chef into a side room. As they walked in, Chloe felt a flash of excitement. *Yes.* This was exactly what she'd imagined.

The room was painted a pale cotton candy pink, with bright lavender accents and shabby chic pastel chandeliers hanging from the ceiling. Display tables filled the room, covered with white tulle that spilled to the floor like spilt containers of sugar. On top of the display tables sat the most extravagant wedding cakes Chloe had ever seen.

The most impressive one sat in the center of the room. A seven-tiered cake with white frosting, it was embellished with gold-embossed trim, pastel fondant and fresh roses. It looked like the very cake that would have inspired Marie Antoinette to blurt out her famed quote.

"Wow . . ." Chloe breathed, looking at her mother. "Have you ever seen anything like this?"

Kristine smoothed back her red hair and surveyed the room. Chloe could almost see her wondering if she needed a guidebook to navigate a place like this. "No," she said. "This is a first."

"Isn't it marvelous?" June's eyes were bright. "I was half tempted to have our ceremony here." Off Kristine's eye roll, she said, "I know, I know. You're right. Everyone would be too busy admiring the cakes to pay attention to the brides."

Kristine exchanged a look with Chloe. "That's not exactly what I was thinking," she murmured, "but I'll just let her keep living the dream."

"You ladies look around and enjoy," Carolyn instructed, wiping her hands on her apron. "I'll go prep the samples."

As Chloe's eyes struggled to find somewhere to settle, they landed on a cake in the far corner. It was an oval creation with elegant ivory frosting. Understated white piping added flair to the bottom of each layer, while a forest-green ivy fondant wove up to the very top, to meet a lush bouquet of fresh red roses.

"Grandma," Chloe said, walking over to it. She pointed. "This cake's perfect for you. Roses, the garden . . . I think this might be your cake."

June rushed over and studied it with a critical eye. "Maybe . . . maybe . . ."

"Chloe, look at this," Kristine called.

Tearing her eyes away from the rose cake, Chloe headed over to see what her mother was looking at. On the way, she gaped at everything they passed. There was a gorgeous white cake with cornelli lace frosting topped off with a veil; a pink and silver heart-shaped cake standing upright and draped in red silk ribbon; a stately pulled sugar creation with pillars and votive candles propped between each layer . . . The options seemed endless.

"That's adorable," June said, admiring the cake Kristine had discovered.

"Isn't it darling?" Kristine said. "Chloe, it's perfect for you."

The cake was three simple square layers with an elaborate fondant bow at the top. Its frosting was a pale Tiffany blue . . . just like the box that had held her engagement ring. Chloe smiled and said, "I should take a picture and text it to Geoff."

"Take a picture?" June said, fondling the bow. "I'd just as soon eat it."

"Mother." Grabbing June's hand, Kristine removed it from the cake. "You're not supposed to touch anything."

"Who says?" June demanded.

"Well, *I* don't know." Kristine gestured wildly at the tiny placards placed on practically every table. In neat black calligraphy, they read, *Please refrain from touching the cakes.*

As Chloe laughed, a tiny sparkle over by the window caught her eye. Taking in a sharp breath, she rushed over to it and stared. A dramatic waterfall of pastel flowers cascaded down the side, but the thing that had caught Chloe's attention was the fact that, when the light fell just right, its frosting sparkled with a pinkish blue, iridescent glow.

"That's it," she breathed. "That's my cake." As June and her mother approached, studying it in confusion, Chloe said, "This is it."

"I don't know . . ." June squeezed her hands together, making a face. "It's pretty basic. I was thinking . . ."

There was a squeaking sound as Carolyn pushed a rolling cart into the room. It was weighed down with a lavish assortment of miniature cupcakes. "Here we are," she sang.

"Carolyn, before we go any further," Kristine said, "which cakes can you make sparkle?"

The pastry chef squinted. "Oh. We can do that to any of them. It's very simple."

Chloe's heart danced. "Alright," she said. "Get me a cake that sparkles and everything else is completely up to you, Grandma. And you, Mom."

Kristine gave a half-smile. "Oh, I think we all know who's running the show."

June was busy examining a life-size cake in the image of a bride. At their laughter, she looked up. "What? Did I miss something?"

Carolyn set up the bite-size cupcakes on the white wicker table at the corner of the room. "I've brought out a variety of different flavors for you to try. The cupcakes are labeled, so keep track with the list on the notepad by your plate."

Eagerly, Chloe took a seat at the table, followed by June, then her mother. The pastry chef had set out a glass of water for each of them, along with a napkin and a full place setting. To the side of each plate was a small silver bucket. It looked just like a spittoon at a wine tasting but Chloe had no idea what it was for.

"The bucket," Carolyn explained, noticing her confusion, "serves as a receptacle. Many brides choose to take a tiny bite of cake and discard the remainder."

June's mouth dropped open. "They spit out the cake? Why?"

"They spit it out because they don't want to get sick, Mom," Kristine said, tucking a strand of red hair behind her ear. Chloe loved her mother's new haircut. It made her look more fun, somehow. More relaxed.

Carolyn nodded, handing them each a piece of paper with a small pencil. "Use this to keep track as you go. If there's a flavor combination you like, just give it a tiny star."

Chloe looked down at the paper. In the chocolate column, there was a lengthy list: milk chocolate, dark chocolate, white chocolate, German chocolate, black forest and hazelnut. Below that, the options were angel food cake, butter cake, pound cake, tres leches and (oddly) wedding cake. The specialty flavors included carrot, tiramisu and red velvet.

Many of the cupcakes were frosted with buttercream, whipped cream or raspberry chocolate. The carrot and red velvet cake were, of course, frosted with cream cheese.

Chloe's eyes scanned the options eagerly. She hadn't eaten any breakfast, in preparation for this little extravaganza. Suddenly, an idea struck her.

"Hey, Grandma," she said, kicking June under the table. "Want to see who can eat the most without spitting?"

June already had a cupcake halfway to her mouth. Her face lit up. "I'll most certainly win."

"Chloe, we are not at the county fair," Kristine said. "We are selecting cake for your *wed*dings."

Chloe waved her fork. "Mom, you can either sign on as a judge or vacate the premises."

June's eyes surveyed the assortment of cupcakes. "I say we battle for the right to plan the bachelorette party. If I win, Bernice is doing it."

A bachelorette party thrown by June's friends? Even though Chloe's grandmother was cooler than most, it didn't mean her friends knew how to throw a good party. What would they do, knit?

"No way," Chloe said. "My friends are in charge of that. Your friends do not know the first thing about throwing a bachelorette party."

"Then you'd better win," June cried.

Chloe grinned. "Done." Dramatically, she reached for a square of dark chocolate cake. The cake was slightly spongy, with an earthy richness. The whipped cream frosting melted like a roasted marshmallow in her mouth. "Yum . . ."

June's sharp eyes considered the cupcake in her hand, and she consulted with Kristine. "Should I stay away from the rich ones? Until she's full?"

Chloe sank her teeth into the piece of tiramisu, sighing happily. "Doesn't matter what you do, Grandma. I can eat cake for days." The powdered cocoa on the tiramisu melded with her tongue like a kiss. It suddenly struck her that Ben would have enjoyed this tasting, since he liked tiramisu so much. Too bad they still weren't really talking or she might have just brought him a cupcake.

"Pace yourself," Kristine warned. "Old age and treachery beats youth and enthusiasm every time."

June nodded. "That's a fact."

Chloe scoffed. "Keep telling yourself that." She surveyed the cakes, trying to decide which to try next.

June reached for a piece of red velvet. "That's strange," she said after biting into it. "I thought it was going to taste like strawberries, not cocoa."

Kristine was in the middle of dropping the remainder of a vanilla cake into her bucket. Hesitating, she said, "It's red velvet. Why would it taste like strawberries?"

"Because it's red," June said. "Duh."

Kristine raised an eyebrow. "That's like saying it should taste like ketchup."

Chloe nodded. Through a bite of cake, she said, "Or blood."

Reaching for another piece, she hummed a little tune. The dark chocolate cake dissolved in her mouth like a piece of fudge, then she tried a spongy-type thing. It was all delicious. So rich.

Kristine wrinkled her freckled nose. "I'm getting sick just watching you."

Carolyn nodded. "I've never seen anything like this."

Chloe considered the plate of cupcakes and suddenly, she hesitated.

*Oh.*

She *was* starting to feel a little ill. The sugar had set in and her vision was a little less focused than it had been moments before, but June's expression was gleeful. It was not the time to start slowing down.

Reaching for the hazelnut, Chloe took a deep breath and bit down. It tasted like burned caramel or the smell of wood. Taking a sip of water, she reached for the tres leches. Smooth and creamy, but wow. Super sweet.

A little too sweet.

"Yum," Chloe cried. Discreetly, she wiped her forehead with her napkin. For some reason, she'd started to sweat.

"Delicious," June proclaimed.

*Ugh.* Chloe's head had really started to pound. Would the carrot cake be lighter than the buttercream? The cream cheese frosting might be heavy. There was also a texture risk. If she felt a carrot or a piece of zucchini in her mouth right now, there was a very real possibility that she might gag.

Reaching for the buttercream, she brought it to her lips and hesitated. "Grandma, what number are you on?"

June looked down at her checklist. "Nine."

Damn. Chloe was only at eight. Squaring her shoulders, she brought the cake up to her mouth.

"Oh, is that the buttercream?" June chirped. "It's very rich. Like chewing on a stick of butter."

*Gross.* Chloe's hand shook. She forced herself to bring it to her lips.

"It's like drinking a Crisco milk shake," June said. "Like biting through a melted crayon."

"*Ugh.*" Chloe dropped the cupcake into the bucket and laid her head on the table. "I can't do it." Grabbing for a napkin, she dipped it into the glass of ice water and pressed it against her face.

June cheered. "Say it," she cried, pounding the table with glee.

Chloe groaned. "You win."

As June did a little victory dance, Kristine laughed and shook her head. "Told you," she said. "Age and treachery. Every time."

June flopped down at the table, fanning herself. "I think I need a salad. I might be in a diabetic coma."

Flustered, Carolyn jumped to her feet.

"She's kidding," Kristine said. "She's doing just fine."

"I can't believe I lost." Chloe buried her head in her hands. "Our bachelorette party is going to suck."

June smiled. "Oh, I guess we'll just see about that."

# Fifty-one

After the cake tasting, Chloe stopped by her apartment to grab some clothes and to see Whiskers. When Chloe started dating Geoff, she'd bought an automatic food dispenser and a self-cleaning litter, but Whiskers still needed love. It had to be lonely, staying in that apartment without anyone to play with.

Chloe hoped it wasn't going to be a huge issue when the time came to move her across town. Geoff had already dropped a comment or two about Mary Beth maybe being allergic. Chloe had nodded, saying, "Oh, that *would* be a shame. I'd hate to live apart from you until Whiskers died." There was no way she was leaving her cat behind, no matter how perfect Geoff was.

While keying into her apartment, Chloe glanced over at Ben's door. It seemed pretty quiet and she was disappointed. Still high from all the sugar, she finally felt brave enough to tell him about the engagement.

When she walked in, Whiskers streaked across the room and practically tackled her, purring and rubbing her head up against her leg.

"Hi, baby," Chloe crooned, rubbing her ears. "Oh, I miss you."

After giving the cat a thorough rubdown and some snacks, Chloe started going through the huge collection of mail she'd pulled out of the box downstairs. Flipping through the ads, her hands stopped on her *Star* magazine. Maybe she should stick it under Ben's door with a note saying, *Check out this celebrity wedding. Oh, and did I mention I was getting married?*

Chloe's phone rang. Peering at the caller ID, she said, "Hey, Sally." For some weird reason, she'd thought it was going to be Ben. "What are you doing?"

"I am so sorry." Sally's voice was low. "I am a terrible, awful friend."

"Why?" Chloe asked, sifting through the rest of her mail. It was so strange to think that, in just a few months, the bills would be for an entirely different home altogether. And, it suddenly dawned on her, it was not likely Geoff would make her responsible for them at all.

"You might want to check on Ben," Sally said. "I've been calling him but—"

Just then, bass boomed through the walls. Whiskers cocked her head, the bell around her neck jingling. This just added another note to the music, which was definitely from the movie *Braveheart*.

"What's wrong with him?" Chloe asked, worried. "Is he sick?"

"I got drunk a few days ago and let it slip," Sally wailed. "That you were engaged."

*"What?"* The drums pounded through the wall like a death march. "Sally," she whispered, as if he could even hear her over that music. "I said don't tell *anyone* until I told him."

"I'm so bloody stupid," Sally cried. "But he was there and we were all talking about it and—"

"Shit." Chloe gripped the magazine tight.

"Will you ever forgive me?"

"Of course," she said. "But right now, I've got to go."

Hanging up the phone, Chloe bolted out of the kitchen and into the hallway. There, the music was even louder. It pounded the walls so hard she was surprised the peeling yellowed paint didn't just drop off in strips. It wouldn't be long until the crabby lady downstairs called the police.

"Ben," Chloe cried, banging on his door. "Open up!"

The rare occasions that Ben got upset, he had been known to work on a design project and let it take him over for days. He'd put every ounce of anger and energy into whatever he was creating and forget about silly little things like eating, sleeping and bathing. Ben joked that it was his artistic temperament, but Chloe found nothing funny about watching her best friend sink into oblivion.

Based on the pounding music, she knew he was doing exactly that. Sally told him about the engagement, and he was hurt Chloe hadn't said anything. She could picture what was happening behind that apartment door. Stacks of design journals would be out, the computer would practically be smoking and Ben would be tugging away at his hair, at least fifteen cups of coffee in.

"Ben," Chloe called again. "Open the door. Don't make me go get my key!"

The lock rattled and the apartment door flew open. Chloe was hit with the smell of burned coffee and old pizza. Walking in, she saw that the shades were drawn. The room was as dark as a tomb, other than the glowing white light of Ben's computer. He was standing in front of it, pacing like an artist in front of an easel. He was wearing a pair of tight gray jeans and a fitted blue T-shirt, practically vibrating with raw energy. She couldn't help but think that he looked even better than he did on the night of their date but just as quickly, she pushed that thought away.

Ben turned to her. "Welcome to the cave of creation," he cried.

That's when Chloe noticed the two streaks of black under his eyes. Like he was a football player or tribal warrior.

Or a total psycho.

Chloe marched over to the windows and threw them open. A gust of icy air shot in the room and she wrapped her arms around herself, feeling the material of her sweatshirt turn cold and stiffen. She stalked over to the stereo and flipped off the music.

Ben put up a hand to shield his eyes. "What, exactly, do you think that you're doing?"

"What do you think *you're* doing?" Chloe demanded. "How long have you been holed up in here? When was the last time you ate something besides . . ." She eyed the tower of empty pizza cartons that were stacked up on his coffee table. They were, of course, arranged in an artistic pattern. "Cardboard and grease?"

"Cardboard and grease." Ben nodded enthusiastically. "I like that." He turned back to his computer. Chloe took a few steps forward and saw at least five windows open on the screen, each with detailed graphic designs. As always, they were brilliant.

"That's a little better than your face paint," she said. "What's up with that, by the way?"

Ben ignored her. He continued to pound away at the keys like some crazy pianist. She noticed that he was unusually tan. Hopefully, he hadn't been outside, running in the cold with his shirt off.

"You are acting like a psycho." Chloe nudged him with her toe.

Hitting Save, he closed the computer. "Why do you even care?" he asked, turning to her.

"Why do you think, you dumb ass?" she cried. "Because you're my best friend."

Ben glared. She half expected him to tackle her, with those stupid black streaks on his face. Instead, he stalked over to the coffeemaker and refilled his cup. Chloe noticed that instead of plugging the coffeemaker into the wall, it was attached to an extension cord that led to the kitchen. "Why," she couldn't help but ask, "didn't you just plug that into the wall out here?"

"The coffeemaker is a part of the kitchen," he said. "The cord is symbolic."

"Please tell me you're drunk."

"Stone sober."

"Ben," Chloe groaned, sinking down into the couch and burying her head in her hands. "Do I have to call your mother? Tell her that you've finally, officially, lost your mind?"

Ben's blue eyes blazed. "*I've* lost *my* mind?" he demanded. "You busted into my apartment, ruined the flow I had going, froze me out with your attitude and your . . ." Suddenly, he seemed to notice that the windows were open. After some sort of angry grunt, he stomped over to them and slammed them shut. Chloe jumped at the bang. "Seriously," he said, turning to her. "Why are you here?"

"Because. I have something to tell you."

"I've already heard." Ben leaned against the wall. He linked his fingers in the loops on his jeans and eyed her. "Everybody has. You are about to marry a complete stranger and didn't even bother to tell me. So, who's the one who's gone crazy here?"

"It's not crazy," Chloe protested. "I love him." For some reason, the sentiment sounded completely ridiculous in Ben's apartment.

"You don't love him." Ben ran his hands through his hair. He needed a cut and it stood up at wild angles. "You were too scared to go on a date with him. So, I don't really understand why, when he shoved a diamond ring in your face, you didn't just say no. Considering you don't even know the guy."

"I do know him," she said. "We've spent every second together since we met." *Except that one night,* she thought, *when I went on a date with you.*

Ben glared at her. "Oh, okay. Now you've got time to spend with people?"

"I . . . I made time." She puffed out her cheeks. "Love is important."

Once again, the sentiment sounded ridiculous. Maybe it was

because of the way Ben was watching her, his body coiled and tense. Letting out a slow breath, he shook his head. "Chloe . . . doesn't this guy have a kid?"

"Yes. So what?"

Ben pressed his lips together, but didn't say anything.

"What?" she demanded.

"I can't believe you're being so stupid," he said. "Everything you've worked for, everything you've wanted . . . You're just going to throw that away to be someone's mother?"

Chloe stared at Ben in horror. "I'm not throwing anything away." Her stomach clenched at the very idea. "Geoff supports my career. He doesn't expect me to be a full-time mom. No way."

"It just seems awfully convenient," Ben said. "This guy can't handle his kid, you come along and make things better, then all of a sudden, he proposes in two days? I don't like it."

Furious, Chloe leapt to her feet. "You think the only reason someone could fall in love with me is so that I could be their *nanny*? Is that what you think of me?"

Ben's face flushed beet red. "*No*. I'm . . . I'm just saying—"

Chloe let out a strangled cry. "I can't believe you!" A red burst of rage clouded her vision. Stomping toward his pizza boxes, she swung at them. They clattered to the ground in a crash of crumbs. "You think he can't just *hire* a nanny?" she demanded. Turning to face him, tears clouded her vision. "You really think that's a reason to *marry* somebody?"

"I'm sorry," Ben said quickly. "That's not what I meant. I just don't understand why you wouldn't just talk to me before—"

"Look, I get it," she cried. "Maybe I'm tall and gangly and too nerdy to fit your profile of what a perfect girl should be, but the fact of the matter is, there are some men in this world who do see me as something special."

Ben rushed over to her. "Chloe, that's not what . . ."

"Isn't it?" She wiped away the tears clouding her vision and drew herself up to her full height. "Do you realize that after we went out on that *stupid* date, you barely talked to me for weeks? Why do you *think* I didn't tell you about getting engaged? Because after we kissed—and trust me, that's something I truly regret—you totally stopped being my friend."

"Chloe, I—"

"No," Chloe poked him in the chest as hard as she could. "Don't you dare"—poke—"act like I"—poke—"should have come to you!"

"Let me just explain." Ben grabbed her hand. An electric current seemed to pass through her and she yanked her hand away.

"I can't believe," she said, her voice low, "that you still haven't said the *only* thing you should be saying."

"Oh, yeah?" he demanded. "And what's that?"

Chloe stared at him. His eyes were locked onto hers, with an expression she didn't understand. "Congratulations."

Ben stepped close to her, reached out a hand and placed it on her arm. His hand was warm and strong. The same scent she'd smelled the night that they kissed seemed to engulf her and she caught her breath. "Congratulations." His voice was quiet. "Congratulations on making the biggest mistake of your life."

"You'll get to know him. You'll like him," she pleaded. "It's not like . . ." Even though he had hurt her, the idea of not having him as a friend was too painful. It was like imagining life without her parents or June. "It's not like he could ever replace you."

Ben's mouth dropped open, then he started to laugh. "Wow, Chloe. You really don't get it, do you?" He pulled his hand away and crossed his arms. In a painful flash, she remembered how those arms had felt that night, wrapped around her.

"Get *what*?" she whispered.

Ben's eyes darkened dangerously and he looked down at her lips. Her body flushed with heat and she had a sudden, horrifying realization that he was going to try and kiss her. Again. The memory of his body pressed against hers sauntered through her brain, followed by the memory of how he had pushed her away the very next day.

Well, it was her turn.

Tearing her eyes away from his, Chloe practically ran for the door.

# Fifty-two

June sat on a chair in her bathroom, watching as Charley buried his head under the faucet of her bathtub. The faucet had been dripping for weeks, with an annoying, *plink-plink* sound against the smooth porcelain of the tub. She had been doing a decent job of ignoring the sound, but Charley had spotted the small rust-colored area surrounding the drip site the moment he went into her bathroom. He insisted on fixing it right away.

After a quick trip home, Charley returned with a box of tools and a can of Comet. He turned off the water in the bathroom and went about disassembling the faucet as easily as laying out parts to make a sandwich. June was very impressed.

"I think it's remarkable you know how to do that." This was said from her perch on a wooden chair, which she had dragged in from the bedroom. June had done this because she was not about to sit on the toilet in front of her fiancé. Discretion was the key to a happy marriage. "Chloe claims anyone can learn how to fix anything with the assistance of the Internet, but . . ." She waved her hands, dismissing the idea. Even though she knew her way around YouTube, watching a how-to video sounded like some sort of a punishment. Old clips of *Murder, She Wrote* were much more her style.

"Chloe's a smart one," Charley said, his voice muffled. "Are things still going well with Geoff?"

320 · Cynthia Ellingsen

"As far as I know," June said. "I have made an effort not to meddle."

Charley stopped working. Sitting up, he gave her a skeptical look. "You have?"

"Of course," she said, surprised that he was surprised. "Charley, I made you a promise. I don't plan on breaking it."

At this, his face softened into a look of appreciation that she had come to love. "Thank you," he said. "That means a lot to me."

Even though leaving her family to their own devices had already proven to be incredibly difficult for her, June did plan to honor Charley's request. In her opinion, the reason that she and Eugene had always had a happy marriage was because they'd respected each other. Yes, they'd gotten on each other's nerves now and again, but if there was something the other felt strongly about, they would do their best to abide.

As Charley went back to fixing the faucet, she said, "Besides, I think everything will be just fine. Chloe can handle herself. She's a smart girl."

"She's very good in school, isn't she?" Charley asked, his voice once again muffled.

"Yes." Ever since Chloe was a little girl, she'd always had her nose buried in some book or another. "I thought it was wonderful that she cared so much, but on the other hand . . ." June sighed. "Kristine and I really would have liked to see her try and enjoy herself more."

Chloe had always been more interested in reading a book by herself, learning how to throw a football with her father or playing video games with Ben than participating in all of the things that made it fun to be a young girl. Dance recitals, parties, dressing up . . . She simply wasn't interested. It was only when Ben turned into an attractive young man that June saw her granddaughter start to struggle with the fact that she wasn't like the girls he was dating. It was obvious that Chloe had developed a crush on her best friend, and it broke June's heart to see that those feelings were never returned.

June was thankful when Chloe finally went to college. There, her tomboy tendencies weren't enough to stop a crop of boys from beating down her door. In spite of her sloppy ponytail, baggy sweatshirts and jeans, Chloe had turned into a tall, willowy knockout. Even though she'd never taken anything but her career goals seriously until Geoff, June hoped that time had at least given her granddaughter some confidence as a woman.

"Either way," June said, "she's certainly turned into a remarkable young lady."

Charley nodded. "When she meets Harriet, I think those two will really hit it off."

June had seen pictures of Charley's granddaughter, a fiery-looking thing who worked for the Peace Corps. She was living in a hut somewhere in West Africa. When Kristine heard this, she'd pumped Charley with so many questions about his granddaughter that June finally had to intervene, saying, "You can ask her when you meet her." She wouldn't be able to get home for the wedding but would come to visit in the spring.

Charley's son, on the other hand, would be at the wedding. June had seen pictures of him and he was the spitting image of Charley, with bright blue eyes and a perfect smile. He worked as a schoolteacher in Michigan and had been married as long as Kevin and Kristine.

"Alright, June." Charley held up a warped piece of plastic. "How long has it been since you've had this washer changed?"

June laughed. "Since Reagan was in office. Or maybe Nixon." Fiddling with the tiny pearls surrounding her watch, she said, "Charley, what on earth made you fall for an old woman like me?"

He thought for a moment. "The rabbits."

"Be serious."

Charley chuckled. "I am. It was the rabbits that did it. I fell in love with you the day you dropped those rabbits in my backyard."

Biting her lower lip, she dared to ask, "Were they terribly hard to catch?" June had experienced many hours of amusement in the days when she disliked Charley, imagining him chasing those rabbits around the yard with a net.

"Not really. Rabbits like carrots." He smiled. "And flowers."

June tsked. "I was certainly a terrible person before I fell in love with you."

"Truth be told, you were the worst neighbor I'd ever had." Charley gave a very manly grunt as he turned the wrench. "But I liked your spunk. I think that's what I really fell in love with. Watching you out there in your garden. The way you managed it . . . You were a species of woman that I didn't understand." He smiled as she opened her mouth to protest. "One that I never fully expect *to* understand."

"Did you understand Claudia?" She thought of the brief moments she had met Charley's wife, out on the sidewalk or in passing at the local market. June remembered her as pretty and petite, dressed in proper sweater sets and pearls.

"Oh, I tried. But I failed, more times than not." Charley's eyes were wistful. "She was a wonderful woman. I miss her every day. Sometimes, I think that the reason this thing between us works so well is that you two are opposites. I certainly didn't plan to get married again. The idea felt disloyal. But you are . . ." He rested the wrench on the edge of the bathtub. "You are a different woman entirely."

June nodded. "I know what you mean." Even something as simple as watching Charley down on the floor in the bathroom, changing a washer instead of placing a phone call to get it done, demonstrated the marked difference between Charley and Eugene. "Eugene didn't like to get his hands dirty," she said. "Not in the yard, not in the kitchen . . . not anywhere. But he was so good with people. I always admired the way the man could talk to a brick wall."

Charley's eyes sparkled. "You have that talent as well, June."

"Oh, not always." She thought back to Eugene's incredible ability to hold court at whatever dinner party, event or dance they attended. He had a gift for making everyone in the room feel special, her included. "I was such a shy little thing, just like Kristine when she was growing up. I had no idea why someone like him could possibly be interested in someone like me. He probably thought he could get away with talking all the time. I had to learn to speak up. It was my only defense." She was quiet for a moment. "He was a wonderful man."

"He'd have to be," Charley said, "to pick you."

"I was so lucky. And now to have you . . ." June shook her head and looked up at the skylight. The sky was bright blue in the afternoon light. "Sometimes," she admitted, "I don't think that it's fair that I should have so much."

With careful hands, Charley replaced the final piece of the faucet, turned the water back on and tested it. The dripping had stopped. Getting to his feet, he wiped his hands on the roll of paper towels he had brought up from the kitchen. Then he walked over and knelt on the floor in front of her, taking her hands in his.

"June," he said, "I believe we're meant to have good things in this life. We're not meant to be unhappy."

"I am happy," she said, surprised. "I have such a wonderful family, my history with Eugene, this beautiful house and now you. I just . . . It all makes me feel rather guilty. That's all."

"Why?" Charley's handsome face was troubled as his blue eyes searched hers.

"Because I haven't done anything to deserve it. I haven't given anything in return."

"Oh, I don't know about that." His eyes crinkled around the corners. "I can already think of a couple of people in this world, myself included, who would say you do quite a bit in return."

"I *do* donate to several charities," she clarified. "Every year, I—"

"That's not what I meant." He looked up at the skylight and

smiled. "Sometimes," he said, "I can't help but wonder if Eugene and Claudia are up there together. Conspiring to make us happy."

June tsked so that he couldn't see he'd almost made her cry. "Charley Montgomery," she said, pulling him in close. "Sometimes you do say the most foolish things."

# Fifty-three

Chloe took Geoff's arm as they stepped inside the Asian fusion restaurant. "I am so excited for you to meet my friends!"

"I hope they approve." Geoff stopped, giving himself a critical look in a decorative mirror. Straightening his sweater, he eyed his reflection. "I look good, right? Not too old and stuffy?"

Chloe laughed. "You're hardly old and yes, you look perfect."

Before leaving the house, she'd convinced Geoff to ditch the ascot in favor of slacks, a plaid shirt and a navy sweater. Even though his outfit looked like he'd just stolen it from a Michigan Avenue mannequin, it beat the heck out of those stupid tweed jackets. In exchange, Chloe had put on a simple red dress and left her hair long and wavy. Geoff had already told her three times how pretty she looked.

Geoff's phone buzzed and he checked the number. "Sorry," he said. "I don't recognize this. Why don't you go sit and I'll be right in, okay?"

Chloe nodded. Since Geoff owned his own practice, he didn't have the luxury of ignoring his phone, as it could be a patient in a crisis on the other end of the line. She looked forward to the day where she couldn't afford to ignore her phone, either. "No problem," she said, giving him a quick kiss on the cheek. "Go do what you do best."

Following the hostess to their table, Chloe admired the bright red walls, black lacquered decorations and the golden symbols coloring the walls like graffiti. The low pulse of bass filled the air and her heart beat a little faster. She was excited her friends were finally meeting her fiancé and she hoped they would approve, especially after that disastrous conversation with Ben.

Spotting her, Sally leapt to her feet. "Where is the lucky guy? And don't you look hot!"

"No, I don't." Chloe blushed. "He's right behind me. He just got a phone call. Probably a patient."

Dana, the final part of her college trio, gave Chloe a kiss on the cheek. "I know how that is," she said. "Brad just got called in, too. He sends his apologies." An OB-GYN, it wasn't uncommon for Brad to bail on their plans at the last minute.

"You've got me, though," said Norman. "So, that more than makes up for those two losers."

By "those two losers," Norman was adding Ben to the equation. Normally, he'd be the third guy in their group. Sometimes, he brought a date, sometimes he didn't. But tonight, he'd been conveniently booked up.

Chloe smiled at Norman. "You're right. You more than make up for—"

Norman leapt to his feet. "That's gotta be him," he whispered to Sally. Then he called, "Hey, Geoff."

Chloe turned and gave her fiancé a nervous once-over. His green eyes were bright and his hair gelled neatly into place. In fact, he was the picture of perfection, and she shook her head, wondering how on earth she'd ended up with him.

"Sorry about that." Geoff gave the group an apologetic smile. "Work."

There were handshakes all around. Sally and Dana both gave giddy, approving looks but Norman took his time sizing him up. He was probably trying to gauge whether or not Geoff would be any fun or, more likely, he was supposed to bring a full report back to Ben. Either way, Chloe was grateful she'd talked him out of wearing an ascot.

Once they'd all taken their seats, Sally raised her drink. "Cheers, everyone," she cried. "Geoff, we are so excited to meet you and so excited about the wedding. It's right around the corner."

"Yeah." Norman eyed him over the rim of his beer glass. "Why so fast?"

"Well . . ." Geoff's phone rang again. "Sorry." He gave Chloe a conspiring look, as though saying, *Please tell them I'm not really this rude.* "Same number. It was dead air before." Touching her shoulder, he got to his feet. "I'll be right back."

Geoff strode toward the hallway where the bathrooms were. Standing underneath a red lantern, he put the phone to one ear, a hand to the other and answered. He looked startled and quickly turned to face the bathroom hallway. By the sudden tension in his shoulders, it was easy to see he was upset. Chloe sighed, hoping it was a patient and not the babysitter. More than once, Mary Beth had misbehaved so badly they'd had to come home early.

"He's adorable," Sally squealed. "I love his green eyes. They are dreamy."

"Dreamy?" Norman demanded, turning to her. "Did you seriously just say dreamy?"

"Well, they are," Dana said. "He's a much older man, sexy-intellectual doctor type."

Chloe blushed. "He's not old. He's only thirty-six."

"But he's still a sexy-intellectual doctor type," Sally echoed. She giggled hysterically as Norman tried to muzzle her.

The waiter interrupted the impromptu wrestling match between Sally and Norman as he approached with a tray of appetizers. It was piled high with fried calamari, ahi tuna rolls, pot stickers and some type of veggie roll. It smelled wonderful and Chloe's stomach growled.

"We ordered some apps," Sally said, reaching for a piece of calamari. "We can figure out entrées in a minute, can't we?"

"Yes, and . . ." Dana popped a pot sticker in her mouth. "We have to discuss a certain something with Chloe."

"Oh." Sally snapped to attention. Forgetting the food, she leaned forward on her elbows. "So . . . are you going to ask us?"

Chloe looked at them, confused. "Ask you to . . ."

"Be bridesmaids," Sally squealed, grabbing her hands.

"Oh." Chloe was surprised and a little bit embarrassed. The bridesmaid thing had barely even crossed her mind. She'd been too busy to even think about it. "You guys, I'm so sorry. I should have said something. We're not doing bridesmaids. Since we have three brides, we thought there wouldn't be anyone left to watch us get married."

Sally stuck out her lower lip. "Bloody hell," she said. "Seriously?"

Dana shoved another pot sticker into her mouth. "Damn. I'm officially old, married and boring." She wiped her mouth with her napkin and straightened her glasses. Shaking her head, she said, "Whatever happened to the good old days of being a young, single and slutty bridesmaid?"

Sally nodded. "I just needed one last hurrah before being tortured with motherhood."

Chloe gasped. "Are you pregnant?"

Making a face, Sally held up her drink. "*No.* But it's out there." Warily, she eyed Norman.

He nodded, grinning. "We're going to have a soccer team. I can't wait."

Sally rolled her eyes.

Chloe glanced back at the hallway. Geoff was pacing anxiously and she wondered if it was, in fact, something to do with Mary Beth. "Well, I'm about to have a kid," she reminded Sally, "so you better learn to like them."

Groaning dramatically, Sally said, "Fine. But I'm only going to be nice to her if she'll let me play with her Barbies."

Catching Chloe's eye, Geoff said his good-byes and came back over to the table. "Sorry," he said, pulling out his chair and placing his napkin back in his lap. "Won't happen again."

"Everything okay?" she asked, reaching for his hand. To her surprise, his palm was damp with sweat. She looked at him, startled. "It's Mary Beth, isn't it?"

Geoff pulled his hand away and wiped it on his pants, his cheeks flushed. "Tell you later," he murmured, draining his glass of ice water.

"So . . ." Sally passed him a plate full of appetizers. "I think the fact that you are getting married with Chloe's family is going to be hilarious. How on earth did she talk you into that?"

"Chloe did not have to talk me into a thing," Geoff said. "I have no problem doing it the way she wants."

Norman laughed. "Good attitude, old chap. It'll keep you out of trouble."

"Either way, the wedding won't be how I want it," Chloe said cheerfully. "June's pretty much running the show. If I could do the wedding how I *want*," she said, taking a sip of water, "I'd go down to city hall. I've never wanted something big and fancy. But it looks like that's exactly what I'm going to get."

"It's karma," Dana cried. After cutting into a pot sticker, she pointed her knife at Chloe. "You made fun of me for years because I had a big, fancy wedding."

"Only because your wedding required vaccinations," Sally sang.

Off Geoff's confused look, Norman said, "Dana got married in Malaysia. No vaccination required. But your fiancée got confused and . . ."

Sally pretended to shove her fork into her arm like a needle and they all laughed.

The whole vaccination debacle had actually been Ben's fault. On a hot summer day, four weeks before Dana's wedding, Chloe and Ben had spent the day drinking on the beach. When it got too hot outside, they finally moved into one of the bars on the River Walk with the fans and misting machines. There, Ben started telling complete strangers about the wedding and how cool it was that he'd get to see Mauritania. The guy he was talking with freaked out.

"You're going to *Mauritania*?" His eyes bulged. "Look, I'm a med student. You have to get vaccinations. Like, today."

Considering Chloe's fear of needles, they decided to go do it right then, while they were still intoxicated. That way, she wouldn't feel it. Ben held her hand the whole time. The next morning, he showed up at her apartment with a bottle of aspirin and the wedding invitation.

"The good news," he said, scratching his head, "is that we won't be getting Yellow Fever anytime soon. The bad news . . ." He pointed at the destination.

Malaysia.

"So, then." Norman nudged Geoff, who looked lost in thought. "What's the worst wedding story you've got?"

"I don't know." Geoff took a drink of water and glanced at his phone. Chloe wondered who on earth it was that had called and upset him. "All the weddings I've been to have been fine."

"Any hitches at your first wedding?" Norman asked, rubbing his hands together.

"Hmm." Geoff frowned. "Well, really just the fact that I got a divorce."

The group fell silent. Sally's face flushed and she said, "Right! Well, that'll do it."

The waiter approached the table and opened his book. "Everyone ready?"

"Yes." Geoff gave an apologetic smile. "Unfortunately, we're in a bit of a hurry. I'm so sorry, everyone." He gestured at his phone. "Something unexpected did come up."

Dana smiled at Chloe. "So it begins."

As everyone ordered, Chloe leaned in close enough to smell Geoff's hair gel. "What's going on?"

"That was my ex-wife on the phone," he said. "Apparently, she's moved back to Chicago."

The next morning, Chloe was awake before her alarm went off. Reaching over, she touched Geoff's hair, which was still perfectly smoothed in place. "What time is it?" His voice was thick with sleep.

"Early." Chloe kissed his forehead. "Go back to sleep."

Peeling herself out of the warmth of the bed, she pulled on her running clothes. Every once in a while, she met her father down by the water for a jog. They would get in five miles before most people were even awake. Chloe loved these mornings with her dad and when he'd texted her yesterday, she'd been quick to say yes, but now she regretted it. She and Geoff had stayed up way too late last night and she was still processing everything he'd said.

By the time she managed to trudge her way to the beach, Kevin was already there. He was dressed in a pair of gray jogging shorts, an oversize Detroit Lions sweatshirt and a pair of beaten-up tennis shoes. She couldn't help but smile, watching his great, hulking figure stretch on the sand.

"Short stack!" His voice bellowed across the misty beach. "Over here."

In junior high, her father called her "short stack" when she sprouted up past all the other girls and felt like a total outcast. "I'm a beanpole," she'd complain, embarrassed. Her father would rumple her hair and say, "Nah. You're just a little short stack to me."

Sprinting across the sand, Chloe gave him a hug. It felt good to feel her father's arms around her after the drama of last night. Pulling away, she smiled up at him. "You sure you don't want to skip this? Let me go back to bed?"

He laughed. "Not a chance." Dropping to the ground, he started doing push-ups. "Did you do something wild last night? Is that why you're dragging ass this morning?"

"Not wild, exactly." Chloe sat on the cold sand and pulled her knees to her chest. "I took Geoff to meet Sally and Dana and that whole crew but . . ." She picked up a handful of sand and let it sift out through her fingers. "We had to leave early because Geoff's ex-wife moved back to town and called him. He was really upset."

Her father paused mid-push-up. "Yeah?"

Chloe nodded. "It was not expected." She fiddled with her laces. "Geoff was afraid she was going to show up at the apartment and talk the babysitter into seeing Mary Beth or something."

"He's not going to let her see the kid?"

"No, he will," Chloe said. "Eventually. She doesn't have custody or anything, but he will." She shook her head. "He just wasn't ready to do it last night. The whole thing kinda caught him off guard."

That was an understatement. Even though Geoff did his best to charm her friends for the short time they were at dinner, he went silent the moment they were alone in the cab. Back at the apartment, he poured himself a drink and walked out to the balcony. It was freezing, but Chloe went out to join him. She had a lot of questions. Things like: What was the ex-wife doing in town? What did she want? And . . . was there any chance that he was still in love with her? But Chloe didn't ask any of these things. Instead, she just put a hand on his back. They stood in silence until his drink was gone.

Hearing the story, her father shook his head. "You think it's going to be a problem?"

Chloe shrugged. "It could be hard on Mary Beth."

Her father clipped a bottle of water to his running belt. "I meant, will it be a problem for you?"

Chloe looked down at her ring. "I don't know," she said honestly.

Even though she didn't want to be, she was worried. What if Geoff saw his ex-wife and decided that he still had feelings for her? It was very possible. They did have a child together, after all. And she was the one who left him.

"Well, it shouldn't be." Her father took a sip of water. "It's like this. She flaked out on him and his kid. He's not going to go running back to her just because she showed up."

In a way, she knew her father was right. When they'd gone to bed, Geoff had kissed her more tenderly than ever before. They'd made love and he'd fallen asleep, cradling her body against his. But still, the situation was going to complicate things. It was going to cause drama between the two of them, which she didn't want. And it was going to be hard on Mary Beth.

This thought concerned her the most. Mary Beth had really started to warm up to her. It had taken time, energy and a lot of love, but the little girl had started throwing fewer tantrums and was reaching for her hand without coercion. Once she even brought a storybook over, climbed into her lap and said, "Read." Very slow bonding steps, but at least they were happening.

Throwing an ex-wife into the equation could set them back in a big way.

"Come on," Kevin said, holding out a hand and pulling her up. "Let's get your blood flowing. It'll make you feel better." They started to run, her father setting the pace. Immediately, Chloe's limbs started to ache. "So, what does Ben think of all this?" he finally asked.

Chloe blew out some air, her heart pounding with exertion. "Ben and I don't really talk anymore. He was kinda pissed when I got engaged."

"That sucks," Kevin said. "Jealous?"

Chloe stared straight ahead. "No." Her breath was coming in painful gasps. Man, she was too tired for this. The run, the conversation, all of it. "Why on earth would he be jealous? He has hundreds of girlfriends."

"Maybe." Her father shrugged. "But he's only got one Chloe."

# Fifty-four

"Get ready, ladies." June peered out the window, rubbing her hands together in excitement. Kristine and Chloe were walking up the steps, all decked out for the bachelorette party. "They're here!"

Bernice ran up behind June and peered out the window. "They're in for the wildest night of their lives."

"I can't believe they said old ladies don't know how to party," Rose agreed, fluffing her freshly dyed hair. "We'll show them."

After the cake-eating contest, Chloe had gone on and on about how June and her friends had no idea how to throw a bachelorette party. June had been so offended that she wracked her brain, desperate for a revenge tactic. It finally hit her in the middle of the night.

Even though the real bachelorette party was scheduled to take place in two weeks at an elegant spa, Kristine and Chloe had received an invitation to a bachelorette party of their very own. The purpose? To embarrass the pants off them. Of course, they had no idea they were the only ones invited.

Throwing open the door, June cried, "Welcome, bachelorettes!" She whipped out a hot pink feather boa and wrapped it around Kristine's neck, followed by an electric blue boa for Chloe.

"Grandma, what the hell are you wearing?" Chloe laughed.

June spun around. "A French maid's outfit," she cried. "Isn't it wonderful?" She'd had a heck of a time tracking one down on such short notice, but eBay was a remarkable thing. The cleavage was low and daring and the skirt puffed out like a fan. "I thought I should dress appropriately, in case the night got a little wild."

"Chloe, this is for you." Bernice clipped a gaudy white veil to her head.

Kristine laughed. "I want pictures."

Rose pulled out a pair of black fishnet stockings and a pair of three-inch silver platform shoes. "And Kristine, these are for you."

Kristine's mouth dropped open. "Scratch that. There will be no pictures."

As they struggled to put on the accessories Rose and Bernice were handing over at a rapid-fire rate, June clapped her hands. "Are you ladies ready to see the games we have for tonight?"

"Please," Chloe said, adjusting her veil.

As Bernice scampered off to the kitchen, Rose led them to the basement door. She yanked it open to reveal a life-size poster of a completely naked man. Tanned and oily, there was a thought bubble above his head that read, *Come to Papi.*

"Uh . . ." Chloe stared at the picture, stunned.

Just then, Bernice darted into the room, carrying a piñata that looked like a very large pink banana. "Isn't it frightening?" she said, shaking it. "I can't wait to whack this thing with a baseball bat."

Kristine looked shocked. "Um . . ." She exchanged a look with Chloe. "Listen, I appreciate the effort you put into all this, but I do have people coming who I work with. Maybe we should tone it down? I don't know that all this is appropriate."

June smiled. With the assistance of Annie, she had enlisted a few of Kristine's friends to pretend they were attending the party but of course, they were not.

"I'm sure they'll understand," June said. "After all, it's a bachelorette party."

Rose nodded, eyeing the poster. "Everything's appropriate."

Chloe fidgeted with her hair. "Uh . . . I can kind of see Mom's point. Maybe we could lose . . . the poster. At least."

"But I don't understand," June said, her voice sweet as sugar. "I thought you wanted a wild bachelorette party?"

The doorbell rang. Right on time.

"Oh, goody," she cried. "Our first guest." Ushering the group back to the living room, she said, "Chloe, could you please do the honors?"

Fluffing her veil, Chloe straightened her shoulders. Throwing open the door, she said, "Welcome to our . . . Oh, shit."

"Ma'am," said a low male voice. "Someone in this neighborhood contacted us about a disturbance. Do you care if we . . ." He cleared his throat. "Come inside?"

Chloe turned to face June, her gray eyes wide and panicked.

"What is it?" Kristine asked. "What's wrong?" Spotting the man at the door, she froze. "Mother, *no*."

Rose blasted an air horn. "Let them in, let them in!"

The three best-looking men June had ever seen in her life stepped into the foyer of Bernice's home. They were dressed in tight police uniforms and wearing sunglasses, even though it was pitch-black outside. Rose squealed and clapped her hands. Bernice was already sitting on the couch, her legs crossed and a drink in hand.

"Ladies," the blond one said, waving his nightstick at Chloe and Kristine, "we're going to have to ask you to take a seat."

Just as June had hoped, her granddaughter looked absolutely mortified.

"Chloe, what's wrong?" June called.

"You *said* you wanted a wild bachelorette party," trilled Rose.

"In fact," Bernice said, "I believe you said we didn't know how to throw one."

The blond officer slapped the nightstick against his hand. "It's pretty obvious these ladies know how to throw a party. Now, are you going to let me in, or am I going to have to use force?"

Chloe turned nine different shades of purple. Slinking over to a chair, she buried her head in her hands, muttering something about needing therapy.

Giving a huge smile, June cried, "Hit it!"

The group of handsome policemen turned to face the women.

"Mother," Kristine said, through clenched teeth. "There is a line and you crossed it."

Slowly, the men lowered their sunglasses to the tips of their noses.

"No . . ." Chloe moaned. "Oh, no."

The men cocked their hips. Then, in perfect pitch, they burst into a full barbershop quartet performance of Louis Armstrong's "I Ain't Got Nobody." They snapped their fingers, did some shimmies and even threw in some perfectly timed doo-wops. June was very impressed.

Chloe stared at them in horror. June watched as it finally sank in that the men were not going to take off their clothes. And even better, that they were singing the very same song Geoff had been singing when he and Chloe first met.

"What do you think?" June asked, beaming.

Chloe turned those wide gray eyes on her. A slow smile crept across her face. As the group hit a particular high note, she burst out laughing. She laughed and laughed, burying her face in her mother's arm. "Grandma, you are awful," she said, shaking a finger at her. "I thought they were strippers!"

At that, one of the singers had the dignity to look offended.

June leapt to her feet and gave Rose and Bernice high fives. "We got them," she cheered. "We got them!"

As Rose sounded the air horn, June pulled her daughter and granddaughter in tight. They collapsed onto the sofa in a heap of fishnets, bridal veils and the crunchy satin of a French maid's outfit. Snapping their fingers in time to the music, they sang along with the barbershop quartet at the top of their lungs.

The group of handsome men sang and shimmied, but they did not take off one single item of clothing—not even their sunglasses.

June chuckled. Not know how to throw a bachelorette party, indeed.

# Fifty-five

Kristine sat in her office, going over the numbers for the week. The store was turning a profit and at this rate . . . She leaned back in her chair, surprised. The Places You'll Go was almost at the point where it could bring in a tiny income. It would only take—

*Knock knock.*

Looking up, Kristine's heart skipped a beat. A large bouquet of violets was walking through the door, followed by none other than her husband. He was dressed in his work clothes: a navy blazer, a light blue button-up shirt and a pair of khakis.

Leaping to her feet, she cried, "What are you doing here?"

"Surprising you." It only took one gigantic step for Kevin to pull her into his arms and kiss her, the flowers mashing in a fragrant mess between them. "You taste so good." He smacked his lips. "What is that? Lip gloss?"

Kristine pointed at the coffee cup sitting on her desk. "Hazelnut creamer." Swatting at his broad chest in delight, she said, "I'm so happy to see you. I thought you were in Arizona."

"I was." After giving her another quick kiss, he stuffed the violets into a cup of water on her desk. "But I had to come see you because . . . I have something exciting to tell you."

Kristine's heart started to pound. There could only be one thing that Kevin would need to tell her in person. Taking a deep breath, she whispered, "You told your boss that you can't travel anymore. They're finally letting you come in off the road!"

Oh, it would be so good to have her husband back. No more lonely nights, no more weekends in front of ESPN, no more wondering when their life was really going to begin . . .

He coughed. "Uh, not exactly. Something . . . even better."

"Better?" Kristine was confused. "What could be better than that?"

"A promotion!" Kevin shoved his hands into his pockets and jingled some loose change. "The mother of all promotions, actually."

"Kevin, that's great." Maybe they were letting him run the satellite office here in Chicago. Maybe they could finally sell their house and move back into the city. "What is it?"

"National territory director. It's practically a forty percent salary increase, a better 401(k) plan, some more vacation time . . ."

Kristine tried to ignore the sinking feeling in her stomach. "You were regional manager before. So, are you overseeing everyone from corporate or . . . ?"

Kevin's eyes darted to the pictures on the desk, of them together as a family. In that moment, she got it. Her husband was excited about a job managing the entire *country*, not just an eighth of it.

"You're staying on the road." Gripping the edge of her desk chair, she sank into it. There was a pounding like a rush of water in her ears. She blinked and blinked, trying to process what was happening.

"Firecracker, just hear me out." Kevin took a cautious step toward her. "Yes, it will mean more travel but—"

"*More* travel? No!" Kristine was so angry she slammed her hand down on the desk. Her ring cut into her finger and she gasped, cradling her hand against her chest.

"Kris." Rushing over, he reached for her hand.

Yanking it away, she leapt to her feet. The desk chair rolled backwards and hit the wall. "You promised. You told me you would try to *stop* traveling so much, not get a job that will put you out there even more!"

"You've got to understand . . ." Kevin's cheeks were flushed, his eyes guilty. Shutting her office door, he pleaded, "This is a major move. A lot of money. I don't even have an MBA. Do you know what a huge accomplishment this is?"

Kristine cradled her hand, which was pulsing with pain. "Kevin, money doesn't matter. Our marriage matters. If you want money . . ." She grabbed the store financials from the desk and threw them at him. Papers fluttered to the ground like confetti. "Here. The store is doing just fine. In a year, it might be doing really well."

"The store is a hobby," he said. "Not a career."

Her jaw dropped. "Ex*cuse* me?" She had worked harder at this store than she'd worked at anything in her entire life. "This is certainly more than a 'hobby.'"

"I don't mean it like that," Kevin said with a sigh. He eyed the papers scattered on the floor, shaking his head. "I know you work hard, Kris, but you do it because you love it. This place isn't going to pay the bills. Please," he begged. "Let's be a team. Let's work together and figure out how to make this happen."

Kristine hated it when he tried to use "team" terminology on her. Especially since, "Let's work together and figure out how to make this work" apparently meant "let's work together and figure out how to make it work for Kevin."

Slowly, she shook her head. "No. I don't want you to do this. Turn it down."

Kevin crouched down into a squat, as though doing calisthenics. "Kris," he groaned. "I *knew* you would react like this. I just knew it." Getting to his feet, he said, "You're not being realistic—"

"In what way?" she demanded. "Chloe's almost done with

school, June's paying for the wedding, the store is starting to pay for itself . . ." Kristine glanced down at the store financials littering the floor, still in disbelief that her husband had so little respect for her work that he wouldn't even acknowledge them. "We have a savings, we have a home. Why do you need so much more?"

Kevin leaned against the desk, his eyes serious. "Kris, if I learned one thing from being unemployed, it's that opportunities are far and few in between. It would be foolish to turn this down."

"But you promised me." She waited for her voice to waver, for the tears to come, but nothing happened. Her voice was as steady and cold as a glacier. "In Venice, you promised me that you would at least try to stop traveling so much."

"I know, but—"

"So, don't come in here and put on some big show when this is *exactly the opposite* of what I want." With a flick of her wrist, she indicated the bouquet of violets drooping listlessly in the water.

Stepping forward, he reached for her hand. "Kris, you're hurt."

When she'd hit the desk, the diamond from her ring had bit into her skin. A tiny trickle of blood ran down her finger. Irritated, she grabbed a tissue and wrapped it around the cut.

They stood in silence for a long, tense moment.

"I have to take this," he said. "It's too good an opportunity to pass up."

With as much dignity as she could muster, Kristine got down on her hands and knees and gathered the papers up from the floor. She felt light-headed when she stood up. Taking a seat, she pressed her fingers into her temples.

"Things are going to be okay," he said, his voice gentle.

Kristine wasn't so sure of that. Sick with disappointment, she stared down at her hands. The tissue she'd wrapped around her finger, once so bright white and perfect, was stained with blood.

"We need to get you a Band-Aid," he said. "Right away." Reaching for her hand, he put pressure on the cut. "Does it hurt?"

"Nope." Kristine shook her head. Her hand, like her heart, was numb. "To be honest, I can't feel a thing."

# Fifty-six

Chloe stood in front of an office door, finishing a diet soda and crossing her fingers. Earlier that week, the head of the department had called a meeting with her to discuss "her future." She had no idea what that meant and hoped that it wasn't a euphemism for "considering another field altogether."

The past few weeks, it had been so difficult to manage her time. For the first time ever, she found herself skipping study groups and class reviews in favor of racing across town to meet with June about invitations or thank-you notes or the type of shoes they would wear at the reception. It was hard to say no to all of June's requests, and managing that, coupled with spending time with Geoff and Mary Beth, had made her worry that her work was slipping.

Taking a deep breath, Chloe knocked on the door.

Dr. Jacobs barked, "Come in."

Stepping into his well-organized office, she gave a weak smile. "Hello, Dr. Jacobs. Thank you so much for seeing me." She glanced at the stately wooden desk and his floor-to-ceiling shelves of books, reports and medical journals. At his indication, she took a seat in the red leather chair across from his desk.

Dr. Jacobs was sifting through a report at lightning speed. Finally, he set it down and gave her his full attention. "Chloe McCallister." Behind round tortoiseshell glasses, his dark eyes seemed to smile. "How do you feel this semester is developing for you? Things are good?"

Inside, she groaned. This meeting *was* going to be about her work. *Crap.*

"It's been an interesting few months," she admitted, setting her backpack on the ground. "Typically, I expect much more from myself but this semester, I let some personal distractions get in the way. I plan to do more in the winter term."

Dr. Jacobs leaned back in his chair, running a hand over the precise lines of his beard. "Interesting," he said. "When I was your age, I was hard on myself, as well."

Chloe looked up, surprised. "Hard on myself?"

The doctor smiled at her. "Chloe, your work is fine. Better than fine."

At his words, she felt a profound sense of relief. In spite of the wedding, she had not lost sight of her goals. She still planned to own her own practice by thirty and to make a name for herself in the world of art therapy. It was good to know she was still up to the challenge.

"Chloe, there are some big opportunities coming up next semester that I think would be perfect for you," he said. "There is an internship at the children's hospital . . ."

Immediately, her heart started to pound. She was very aware of the position he was talking about. The students had been circling around the topic for weeks, trying to determine the best way in.

". . . actively looking for assistance." Dr. Jacobs peered at her from over the rims of his glasses. "This internship has a strong focus on research and it's highly competitive. Does that interest you?"

Nodding enthusiastically, the office seemed to bob around her head. "Yes! Very much."

"The position starts in February," Dr. Jacobs said. "However,

I'm confused about your statement regarding personal distractions."

Chloe blushed. "I'm getting married. Right after Christmas."

Dr. Jacobs hid a smile. Suddenly, she wondered if he'd seen the engagement announcement in the paper. Or . . . Oh, geez. He and Geoff knew each other. What if they were actually friends? It felt strange to imagine that, in a few short weeks, there was a very real possibility of ending up at a dinner or a social outing with the head of her department.

"I will be fine when it's all over," Chloe said. "Participating in a wedding is a big commitment."

Dr. Jacobs held up his left hand to display a wedding ring. "So is marriage."

Chloe smiled. "That's the rumor."

They both sat in silence for a moment. "You'll have to meet with the hospital," Dr. Jacobs said with a nod, "but my recommendation will weigh heavily on their decision." He leaned back in his chair. "Chloe, I'm very impressed with your work. If you want my recommendation, it's yours."

Chloe leapt out of the chair. "Oh, thank you," she cried. "Thank you! I am so excited."

Dr. Jacobs got to his feet. Stepping out from behind his desk, he shook her hand. "Stop being so hard on yourself. You have the ability and vision to achieve great things. Now, get out of here."

As Chloe raced out of the office, she let out a happy shriek. It wasn't a real job or anything, for heaven's sake, but it was a very big, very important step in her career. She couldn't wait to share the news with Geoff.


To her surprise, Geoff was less than enthusiastic. Chloe saved the news until they were sitting out on the balcony later that night, shivering in the chilly air and drinking mugs of hot apple cider. The lights of Chicago stretched out before them and the wind brightened their cheeks.

"What's that face for?" Chloe asked after telling him the news. She was wearing his wool-lined jacket and felt incredibly cozy. "I thought you'd be more excited about it than that."

"But it's an enormous internship." Geoff's green eyes seemed worried. "It typically leads to a job at the hospital. That's why they don't offer it every year."

"I know." Beaming, she lifted her mug and clinked it against his. The sharp smell of spiced apples wafted up, warming her. "Why do you think I'm excited?"

Geoff didn't say anything. He just gazed out at the buildings. Across the way, she could see someone vacuuming an office, the fluorescent light bright in the night. His silence stretched on, until she could hear the faded sounds of cars rushing by, on the street so far below.

"I don't understand," she said. "What's wrong?"

Geoff shook his head. "I'm concerned. Taking on an internship like that, you won't have the time to devote to Mary Beth. She's going to need your attention, Chloe. Your love."

Chloe swallowed hard, thinking back on Ben's words. *He just wants you to be a nanny.*

They both sat in silence for a moment, then he let out a sigh. "I have something to tell you. I . . . I took Mary Beth to see Miriam today. My ex-wife."

Chloe's eyes widened. "You did?" She felt surprised that he'd waited so long to tell her. "How was it? How did it go?"

"Surprisingly well." He turned the coffee mug around in his hands, avoiding her eyes. "It was emotional. To see her again. They, of course, bonded right away."

Chloe felt a pang of jealousy. "That's good." Mary Beth hadn't bonded with her yet. Not really.

Geoff glanced at her, as though realizing the conversation might be upsetting. "Should we talk about this? Or is it . . ."

Chloe shook her head. "Sure," she said, waving her hand like June always did. "Of course we can."

"Thank you." He set down his mug of cider and took her hand. "It was all so strange. Mary Beth was shy at first, but she warmed up to her right away. And now that Miriam is back to normal, she's eager to invest time with Mary Beth."

"How do you feel about that?"

Letting out a sigh, his eyes settled on their hands, which were woven together. "Not great. It's almost too much, the plans she has. Mother and daughter classes, outings . . . I know I should let them spend time together, but I don't want Mary Beth to get it confused. You're her mother now." He squeezed her hand, as though to punctuate the words. "These are things you should be doing, not her."

They sat in silence for a minute, the wind blowing harder around them. Sometimes, being this high up was frightening. There were moments where Chloe thought that, if the wind hit just right, it could carry her away.

"Regardless, you can do the internship," he said, as though giving her permission. "Just please be aware of how it will affect Mary Beth. I'll need you to be there for her, Chloe. That's why I asked you to be my wife."

"Um . . ." She blinked hard, the wind tugging at her contacts. "I thought you asked me because you love me."

"Well, *duh*," Geoff said. Giving her a cautious look, he added, "Isn't that what you always say?"

Chloe burst out laughing. "Wow," she said, shaking her head. "You just duh-ed me. Taking on the vernacular of the fiancée." For some reason, this made her inexplicably happy, in spite of their conversation. Scooting her chair closer to his, she snuggled up against him. "I might like this new you."

Geoff reached over and touched her face. "Well, I *love* you. Your ambition, your gorgeous body . . ."

Chloe blushed. Until Geoff, she'd never once thought of

herself as being gorgeous. He said it so often, though, that she finally had to admit to herself that, okay, maybe she was attractive. Leaning over, she gave him an appreciative kiss on the nose.

"But the thing I like about you most," he said, "is that you value family. And children. I know that you would never . . ." He stopped suddenly, his jaw clenched. His voice low, he said, "I just don't ever want Mary Beth to be pushed aside like that again. Not ever again."

Chloe felt sad, thinking of the little girl. "I know."

"Good." He nodded. "I want to build a family together, Chloe. Something that will last for years to come. And I want to do that with you."

Linking her hand in his, she rested her head against his shoulder. Together, they sat in silence, staring out at the night.

# Fifty-seven

June bustled Kristine and Chloe up to a dress shop, saying, "This is the most exciting thing that's ever happened to me. I get to pick out a wedding dress for the first time in my life and I can't *wait* to see what you two choose."

Kristine swallowed hard. It had taken everything she had to get out of bed that morning, meet Chloe and June for lunch, then traipse over to the fancy wedding boutiques. Given her current state of mind, the last thing she wanted to do was shop for a vow renewal gown. What she really wanted to do was take the time to think about whether or not she should participate in the ceremony at all.

"You're not picking out a wedding dress for the first time in your life," Chloe told June. "I've seen your wedding pictures. You're not nude."

"I wore a hand-me-down," June said, lifting her chin. Her dark eyes were wistful, and Kristine could imagine her as a young girl, standing on the edge of the life she had ended up living. "It was my sister's wedding dress. It was beautiful but it had a few holes that we had to patch up and . . . Well, it wasn't *mine*." She gestured at the window of the boutique. "Who would have guessed that, fifty years later, I'd get to pick out something I want?"

Kristine smiled. "Good, Mom. You deserve it."

"Yes, I do. My dress," June said, raising her hand to the sky, "will be the most amazing creation anyone has ever seen!" Letting out a battle cry, she rushed up the stairs and into the store, the door clanking shut behind her.

Chloe giggled. "Get ready, Mom. I hope you took the whole day off. This is going to be an extravaganza."

Nodding, Kristine glanced at her watch. It was eleven, which meant the travel bookstore would be absolutely slammed right now, as it always was during the middle of November.

Shaking her head, Kristine looped an arm around her daughter's shoulders. Chloe looked especially pretty today. Her long hair was down and she was even wearing mascara.

"I want you to remember," Kristine told her, "today's not just about June, it's about you, too. We're going to find you the perfect dress and we'll take as long as we need."

Chloe gazed at the dress shop. "It's so strange," she said, brushing back a strand of hair. "I can't believe I'm actually getting married. When did this even happen?" There was a tremor in her voice, which surprised Kristine.

"Are you getting nervous?" she asked.

"Not nervous, exactly." Chloe looked down at her sneakers and kicked at a loose stone on the sidewalk. "Just overwhelmed. Everything's changing. It's weird. But it's good. Just . . . weird."

"What's weird, exactly?" Kristine pressed.

"I'm just trying to process some things Ben said to me." She slid an elastic band off her wrist and pulled her hair into a ponytail. "I didn't get a chance to tell him about the engagement before Sally did and he was pretty upset." She hesitated for a moment, as though choosing her words carefully. "He said some really shitty things."

"Like?"

Chloe shrugged. "Oh, you know. That Geoff only wants to marry me to have someone to take care of his daughter."

After the engagement photo session at the lake, Kristine

had left wondering the same thing. Kevin, of course, had thought she was being ridiculous. "What do you mean? Geoff loves her," he said, as though personally offended. "He's lucky to have her."

"Honey . . ." Kristine put a hand on the sleeve of her daughter's sweatshirt. The material was soft and well worn. "Do *you* feel that way? That Geoff only wants you to be his nanny?"

"No, no. Of course not." She twisted her engagement ring. Blowing air into her cheeks, they puffed out. Releasing a slow breath, she said, "But did Dad tell you? That Geoff's ex-wife is back in town?"

Kristine was surprised. No, Kevin hadn't told her. Apparently, he was too busy getting promotions to tell her something that could seriously affect her daughter's relationship.

"I feel like I have to compete or something," Chloe said. "She just met with Mary Beth and . . . I don't know. It's making things complicated. Geoff says I'm the mother, I'm the priority, but it's just a little too much drama. It was a lot easier when she was still living out in California."

Kristine was at a loss for words. "Maybe . . ."

Chloe shook her head. "Please do not say Geoff and I should take more time and think this through. It's not going to change anything. I'm just going to have to learn to deal with it and move on. Who knows? Geoff married her. She could be a lovely person. Maybe we could even be friends."

Kristine gave her daughter a look. "Really?"

Chloe laughed, the sun dancing on her face. "No. Doubt it."

They stood in silence for a minute. "We should go in," Chloe said. "I'm sure June's tearing that place up."

Kristine took in a chilly breath of air. Down the block, she could smell almonds roasting in cinnamon. She wished there was time to just go have coffee with her daughter, alone. Talk about this a little more. "Honey, I . . ."

"Mom." Chloe shook her head. "It's fine. Not a big deal."

Actually, it was a big deal, but if there was something she had learned about Chloe over the years, it was that she only talked when she wanted to. She was a lot like Kevin that way.

Kristine glanced at the display window. "Shopping for a dress can be a little overwhelming."

Chloe nodded, obviously relieved at the change of subject. "Throw June into the equation and it's absolute madness."

"Don't let her pressure you into something you don't like, okay?"

Chloe grinned. "Is that what she did with you?"

"Nope." Kristine picked at a piece of black paint on the metal railing. "I let her plan the reception, choose my invitations and, apparently, my flowers, but I would not budge when it came to my dress."

The white lace, vintage dress that Kristine had married Kevin in was the most delicate, beautiful thing she'd ever seen. It tied up the back with pale green and pink velvet ribbons and the silk bodice gave her a shape that her body had not seen before or since. The best part about it, though, was the old-fashioned lace, rippling down her body and swirling across her ankles like the froth of the sea.

Kristine had loved that dress. But her mother hated it. June hated the fact that the dress didn't have a train, a veil or a designer label. She hated that it was made from silk and lace and had ribbons that weren't white. But most of all, June hated the fact that her daughter insisted on the dress—just like she'd insisted on her groom—regardless of what she thought.

"So, I was thinking . . ." Chloe blushed. "Last night, I was actually thinking it would be awesome to find a way to make your wedding dress fit me."

Kristine gripped the stair railing, surprised. "Really? You'd want to do that?"

Chloe looked down at her tennis shoes. "I thought it would mean something, you know?"

Kristine put her hand to her heart. She thought back to the moment she stood in front of the mirror for the first time, wearing that dress. The dress, in that moment, symbolized a moment of infinite possibility. In spite of the problems with her and Kevin, passing the dress down to their daughter would be such a special thing.

"I would be honored," Kristine said. "That would mean so—"

A look of regret crossed Chloe's face. "Mom." Her voice was gentle. "I just meant I'd thought about it. It wouldn't work. We'd have to add on, like, a five-foot extension at the base, since I'm such a beanpole. Matching that lace would be almost impossible. And to bring in the chest and . . ." She shook her head. "There isn't time to do all that. I just wanted to let you know I'd thought of it."

"Chloe, we can do it," Kristine said. Rapidly, she calculated just how far away the wedding was. Could a seamstress make those changes in a few short weeks? Digging in her purse for her cell phone, she said, "Let me just call a tailor and . . ."

"Mom." Chloe put her hand on hers. "There's not enough time."

Kristine was surprised at how disappointed she felt. Shaking her head, she said, "You know, I'm so glad you're sharing a wedding with your grandmother but—"

"And you." Chloe nudged her. "A vow renewal still counts."

Kristine swallowed hard. "It's just that all of this is going so fast. Are you . . . Are you *sure* you want to rush into this? You could get married next year. You and Geoff could—"

Chloe sighed. "I thought we just talked about this."

"Right." She fidgeted with a button on her coat. "I just—"

"Mom, everything is fine with me and Geoff," Chloe insisted. "Besides, I don't need a long engagement. This is perfect for me.

I show up and everything's done. Yes, it might have been nice to wear your dress but . . . Next time, right?"

"Next time?" Kristine was shocked.

Chloe grinned. "You know what I mean."

June banged on the window. She was holding up two different dresses, one with holes in the bodice and the other lined with sequins and leather.

"We better get in there before she decides on a last-minute theme or something," Chloe said, rolling her eyes. "I am *not* getting married dressed like Cleopatra."

Kristine let out a pent-up breath. Even though she wanted to grab her daughter's arm and insist that she stop and give this some more thought, she didn't do it. Kristine didn't want to be like June, always trying to run everyone else's life.

Shoving her hands deep into her coat pockets, she followed her daughter into the store, ready to help pick out a wedding dress.


The bells on the door jingled as they walked into the store.

"Welcome to Garters," said a young salesgirl. "My name is Ashley."

Bustling forward, Ashley took both of their coats and whisked them off to a closet. She returned with two small bottles of sparkling water, her long blonde hair swaying with every step. "Congratulations on your engagement," she said, dutifully admiring both Kristine's and Chloe's rings.

"Aren't they beautiful?" June crooned, sweeping up and hugging them. "The rings *and* my family!"

Ashley laughed, obviously charmed by June. "Yes, absolutely."

"Thank you," Chloe said, looking around the store.

Based on the sparse selection of wedding dresses, it only took a second to classify the store as very expensive. Suddenly, she felt nervous. She'd never been good at picking out clothing and she didn't have the slightest idea what to look for in a wedding dress. Luckily, June had it under control.

"Come on, come on," June said, snapping her fingers. "I already have you all set up in a room. I found the perfect dress."

"I thought you were shopping for you," Chloe said, nudging her.

June's dark eyes sparkled. "Oh, we have all afternoon for that." Gesturing at the dressing rooms, she said, "Go. Get back there!"

The tiny dressing room smelled like roses and was partitioned with pink silk curtains. Sweeping them back, Chloe marveled at the romantic setup. The fitting room was decked out with an antique fainting couch, a small bureau made of mirrored glass and an oddly tasteful fluffy white rug. There were several pairs of designer shoes lined up against the wall, as well as ivory hooks offering up a variety of high-end strapless bras.

"Wow," Chloe said. "This is nice." Considering she hadn't voluntarily set foot in a clothing store in ages, it was fun to walk into one like this. Reaching over to the little candy dish on the mirrored bureau, she unwrapped a chocolate-covered mint.

"Are you ready to see the dress?" the salesgirl asked.

"You only picked one?" Chloe asked her grandmother. Kristine cocked her head, equally surprised.

June smiled. "You'll see."

Ashley did in fact return with just one dress. She was flanked by two salesgirls, who threw open the curtain with a loud swish. Ashley hung the single dress on an ivory hook, tossing her long blonde hair. "Here it is."

"That's it?" Chloe said, feeling slightly disappointed. Even though she didn't have a lot of experience shopping at boutiques, she thought it might involve trying on hundreds of options.

She'd model and dance around, then eat pizza like they did in *Pretty Woman*.

"We'll do several, of course," Ashley said. "But with your body type, your grandmother thinks this will be the only dress you'll need."

Kristine peeked around the corner. "Oh," she gasped, touching the material. "Yes. I can see this."

Chloe squinted. How? It was just some white material on a hanger. How on earth could any of them even begin to guess how it would look? Fashion was an art form she just didn't understand.

Ashley and two assistants stood there, waiting for something. Chloe stared back, completely confused.

"Good heavens, girl," June finally said. "Take off your clothes!"

Praying that she was wearing a decent underwear set, Chloe slid out of her jeans and sweatshirt. Ashley and her team got to work tugging and yanking to fit her inside the dress. For something that looked soft and flowing, it certainly did have a lot of things inside of it that had to be adjusted.

Kristine and June stood by during the process, talking in low, excited tones. Once the dress was on, Kristine turned to her and gasped.

June clasped her hands in delight. "This is it!" Rushing forward, she circled around Chloe, fluffing and smoothing fabric.

"I hate to say it," Kristine murmured, "but June might be right. You look amazing."

"You hate to say that I look amazing?" Chloe teased.

Kristine laughed. "No, I hate to say that June is right."

"Well, can I see it?" Pointedly, she looked at the blank walls of the dressing room. "I wish there were mirrors in here." She tried to catch her reflection in the mirrored bureau, but the drawers made it impossible.

Ashley fluffed out the train. "Chloe, we don't want you to base your selection exclusively on your perception of how you look in the dress, but the reality of how you feel in it. So, before you even take a look at your gorgeous self, how do you feel?"

"Um . . ." She had no idea how to answer that question. "Hot? I mean, there are a lot of us in one little dressing room."

"Do you feel comfortable?" Kristine asked. "Could you wear this all day and all night?"

Chloe thought for a moment. She felt some sort of a firm bodice around her stomach and bust, but it seemed to be hugging her gently instead of biting into her. The rest of the material was soft and flowing, like spun silk. "Yeah. I mean, it's really comfortable. To be honest, it feels very expensive."

"Perfect," Ashley said, with a flash of her perfect white teeth.

One of her assistants threw open the curtains. Together, they lifted the train off the ground, as Ashley took Chloe's hand and guided her hand up three pink-carpeted steps. There, Chloe stood in front of a three-way mirror. And stared.

It was a white strapless dress with a fitted silk bodice. The lines of the shape seemed to point upwards, drawing attention to the sharp bones of her shoulders. Scalloped material at the bust gave Chloe a shape for the first time in her life and below that, the material was gathered together in a crisscross that tightened her waist, just below an elegant crystal-encrusted jewel. Where the crisscross pattern ended, the cloud-like skirt began. Sheer white silk seemed to sway with every movement, making her feel as though she were walking inside a cloud.

"Wow," Chloe breathed. The girl wearing the dress looked just like a girl in a magazine. She reached out and touched the mirror, watching as her finger left a small print. "Is that really me?"

"I think she likes it," June said, her tone gleeful.

"I love it." Turning toward her mother, she said, "Mom, what do you think?"

Kristine's eyes were damp with tears. "When did you become so grown-up?"

"Oh, stop that." Chloe blushed furiously. She sneaked another peek at herself in the mirror. "I look beautiful." Her voice was quiet, disbelieving. "I look like a bride."

June nodded. To Ashley, she murmured, "I think we've found the dress."

# Fifty-eight

Seeing Chloe in that dress was the strangest thing. Kristine felt as though her daughter had *just* been toddling around in diapers, wearing rubber ducky boots to first grade, winning first place at the science fair . . . When had she gotten so big?

Kristine looked at June, wondering how she felt about it all. It must be twofold to watch a daughter have a child and then see that child grow up. It was strange to think that soon Chloe would have a daughter of her own.

"What are you thinking about?" June asked, linking an arm in hers. "You're looking awfully weepy."

They were sitting in the waiting area, waiting for Chloe to get changed. After that first dress, she'd tried on several more, but she put the first dress back on and said, "What can I say? I love it."

"I'm just thinking about the circle of life," Kristine said.

June made a silly face. "Well, wrap your mind around something that matters." Reaching out, she tucked a strand of hair behind Kristine's ear and smiled. "We still have to find something fabulous for you."

Kristine avoided her mother's eyes. "Absolutely. But let's just worry about you first. I can't wait to see what you find. We're not stopping until we find you the dress of your dreams."

Once they'd put Chloe's dress on order, it became obvious that June planned to take Kristine's words seriously. She took them on a whirlwind tour of every wedding dress shop in Chicago, trying on dress after dress, debating their merits endlessly. There was the one with the empire waist, the brocade train, the fur on the sleeves . . . Even though they'd stopped for sandwiches at one point and then coffee, Kristine's enthusiasm started to waver. Finally, at their tenth stop, she took a seat in a chair and accepted a glass of champagne from the salesgirl.

"Mom," Chloe said, sidling up to the chair. "What's wrong with you?" She stared down with a face that looked just like her father's.

Instantly, Kristine felt guilty. "I'm fine." She got to her feet. "Does June need help?"

Chloe glanced in June's direction. She was in the dressing room once again, surrounded by a handful of salesgirls. Her thin shoulder was poking out of the curtain. "Oh, she needs help alright, but not the way you're thinking."

June cackled. "I heard that!"

Kristine suppressed a tiny sigh.

Chloe gave her a confused look. "What's wrong?"

"Nothing," she said, quickly. "I just . . ."

It wasn't that she didn't want her mother to find the perfect dress. It was just hard to keep up her enthusiasm for all this today, especially now that they'd been at it for hours. As the day progressed, Kristine couldn't stop thinking about Kevin's promotion and how it would affect their lives, their marriage and . . . well, the wedding.

"I'm just not feeling well," Kristine lied, touching Chloe's shoulder. "I had a glass of champagne. It made me sleepy."

"Do you want a diet soda?" Chloe asked, fumbling with her backpack. "I have one."

Kristine felt a rush of affection for her daughter, followed by a flash of pain. If Kevin took this job and their marriage continued to unravel, she couldn't bear to think how it would affect their daughter. She'd be devastated, that much was for certain.

That thought alone made Kristine feel a renewed flash of anger at her husband. What was he thinking? Why was he doing this?

Just then, June burst out of the dressing room, decked out in a form-fitting white dress completely covered in feathers. She looked like a bird about to take flight. Waving her arms up and down, she laughed hysterically and Chloe joined in. Kristine felt nothing but exhaustion.

"You know what?" she whispered. "I think that champagne got to me. I'm going to go."

Chloe eyed her with concern. "Okay. Call if you need us?"

"Of course."

# Fifty-nine

Chloe was so busy with the wedding, Geoff, Mary Beth, her job and her internship, that she had little choice but to stay up until four in the morning to finish the final term paper for her Theories in Psych class. After a few precious hours of sleep, she raced across town to turn it in, hating the fact that her professor wouldn't just let them submit by email.

As her chapped red hands hovered over the basket, Chloe hesitated. Was the paper good enough? She was too exhausted to be objective anymore. Her grades were good enough but in her heart, she didn't want to be good—she wanted to be great. At this point, she just had to cross her fingers and hope for the best.

Dropping the paper in the basket, she made a mental promise to do everything possible to prepare for the final exam. That was the score that could *really* make a difference. Unfortunately, she had to break that promise as quickly as she made it.

A group of students were filing into class for a final exam review but she had to duck right back out. Today was the only day Geoff had available to help her register, so after repeated phone calls from June asking her to get it done, she figured it was now or never.

Chloe waved at his doorman as she raced toward the elevator, her backpack banging against her arm. The ride up was calm, with the elevator seeming to lose all oxygen as it sped toward the upper floors. It was almost like meditation. Of course, the peace and quiet was shattered the moment the elevator doors slid open.

"No, no, no, no, no!" Mary Beth's screams were accompanied by the sound of tin clanking against the ground. It was a wonder the neighbors didn't call the police.

"What the heck?" Chloe rushed for Geoff's door. It was already half open, in anticipation of her arrival. She rushed in to find her fiancé cowering in the kitchen as Mary Beth systematically threw pieces from her tin tea party set against the ground.

Other than the tea set, the apartment was as immaculate as always. Lacquered black tables that were perfectly polished. Windows sparkling in the morning sunlight. The city of Chicago looming beyond them like some shining fortress.

"Hey." Chloe rushed across the room and scooped up Mary Beth. Not in a hug, but in a sleeper hold. "What on earth is going on here?"

Mary Beth let out a piercing scream, and Chloe carried her over to the couch and stared her down until she stopped. Finally, Mary Beth stuck her fingers in her mouth. "Daddy won't take me to the park."

"Daddy *can't* take you to the park. Because it's cold outside and because Daddy and I have to register for our wedding presents. *But*," she said, watching the fingers come out and that little mouth open in preparation for another scream, "if you're a good girl today, I can get you a present, too."

Geoff came striding out of the kitchen as though he hadn't spent the last few minutes under attack and kissed Chloe on the top of her head. "Hello."

"Hi." Chloe's eyes widened, and she hoped she didn't look as tired as she felt.

"I actually have a surprise for the both of you." Geoff cleared his throat and folded the cuffs on his tweed jacket. "You two get to go shopping together!"

Chloe looked at him, confused. "Geoff, that won't work.

We're going to be around china and crystal. That's not gonna go well, if you know what I . . ." Her voice trailed off. "Wait. What do you mean, by 'you two'?"

"One of my patients is in crisis." He shook his head. "I'm sorry but I have to go in."

"Honey, you should have called me." She looked at her watch. The exam review had started fifteen minutes ago. It would be another dash, but she still might be able to catch the end. "Alright." Grabbing her backpack, she headed for the door. "Mary Beth, we'll have to go shopping another day. Geoff, when do you want to reschedule?"

Geoff's face flushed. "Chloe . . ." With raised eyebrows, he indicated his daughter. She got the message. He hadn't called to let her know about the change in plans because he'd expected her to be perfectly happy about the idea of watching Mary Beth.

Maybe she was overly tired, but she suddenly felt so defeated. It was one thing to work together as a team, to raise his—their— daughter, but geez. It was obvious that Geoff saw his job as more important than anything she could possibly have to do. Instead of calling a sitter, he expected that she wouldn't mind the fact that he not only broke their plans, but chose to pawn Mary Beth onto her, as well.

"Geoff, I have a huge final coming up." Chloe's ponytail swung back and forth as she shook her head. "I'm missing the review, like, right now. If we can't register, I have to—"

Striding over, he pulled her into his arms. "I'm sorry," he whispered. "But Mary Beth's been having such a hard time. I didn't want to leave her with a stranger. Please." Geoff took her hands and smiled, his eyes crinkling in the corners. "I'll help you with the final. We'll have our own study group. Later."

Chloe sighed. "Okay, but when are we going to register? June needs us to do that."

"*June* needs us to do that?" He adjusted his ascot, giving her a half-smile. "Am I marrying June?"

Actually, yes. He might not know it yet, but he was. She had a feeling her father could attest to that.

"All of her friends have been asking," Chloe said. "Hasn't Rue said anything to you?"

"Yes, of course she has," he said. "But I've already done all this. The wedding thing."

"The wedding thing?" She drew back as though he'd slapped her. "What's that supposed to mean?"

"The parties, the invitations, the registering . . ."

"It's your wedding, too," she said slowly. "Doesn't it matter to you at all?"

Geoff looked over at Mary Beth. She was sitting in silence, watching the scene unfold with fascination. "Listen." He took Chloe's hands. "The wedding is very important to me but it's more important to me that *you* enjoy yourself. I'm sorry I can't go today. I really am."

Reaching into his wallet, he passed over a platinum credit card. "Call up your mom and June. Go out there and have a good time."

"Um . . ." Chloe stared at the card. "Registering doesn't mean you purchase the gifts. Typically, the guests purchase them for you."

"You're so funny." He kissed the top of her head again. "Buy your mom and June lunch and have a wonderful day. Then tonight, I'll take you out to that Italian place you like so much."

Chloe felt a small pang in her chest, remembering the last time she had been to her favorite Italian restaurant. "I won't have time for any of that." She handed the card back to him. "Look, I'll take Mary Beth for a few hours, but after that I'm going to need to go register. For both of us. Okay?"

Geoff looked relieved. "Thank you for understanding."

Chloe nodded. But she didn't understand. If he didn't want to go through the whole "wedding thing" again, why get married at all?

Pressing her fingers into the area under her eyes, she reminded herself to keep it in perspective. To slow down, to relax. Considering she'd only gotten four hours of sleep, this situation probably seemed much more intense than it was.

Turning to Mary Beth, Chloe gave her a big smile. "What do you say, kid? Let's go have some fun."

By the time Mary Beth was bundled up in her pink puffy coat, purple knit hat and matching gloves, Chloe had lost the desire to keep things in perspective. She was fuming. Geoff didn't even say good-bye. He headed straight for his office to make business calls before meeting the client in crisis.

The moment she and Mary Beth were outside the apartment, Chloe got down on her knees. Mary Beth's nose was bright red from the cold and her brown curls framed her face. "I have a secret to tell you," Chloe said. "One that you can't tell your dad."

Mary Beth hopped up and down. "What's the secret? What's the secret?"

"The secret is . . ." She let out a deep breath. "We're going ice-skating!"

Chloe and Ben had been ice-skating together every year since the rink had been open. At first, Ben had to talk her into doing it. She was scared to put all her weight on a thin little blade, convinced she'd snap an ankle. But once he showed her how to balance and start gliding, she fell in love. It was something she looked forward to every year.

"Oh! I can't wait until you and Daddy get married," Mary Beth said. "We can play all the time."

"Yup." Chloe nodded. "That will be lots of fun. Give me just one second, then we'll go."

Getting to her feet, she pulled her phone out of her purse. Taking another deep breath, she dialed. "Hey," she said, surprised he actually picked up. "What are you doing? I could really use your help."

Chloe felt him before she saw him. Walking up behind her, Ben clamped a hand down on her shoulder and gave it a firm squeeze. "Hey, stranger," he said.

For some reason that she didn't understand, Chloe felt her eyes fill with tears. "Hey," she said, turning to face him. "Thank you so much for coming."

Ben's blue eyes sparkled and his lips turned up into a half-smile. "Couldn't handle the little one on your own? Needed an expert?"

Without waiting for her answer, he walked over to Mary Beth and tugged on her skate. "I bet I can skate faster than you."

Mary Beth looked at Chloe, confused.

"This is my best friend, Ben," Chloe explained. "I've known him since I was just a little older than you."

Mary Beth stuck her mitten in her mouth. "I can skate faster than you," she said, giving him a sly look.

Ben tweaked her nose. "No. I can skate faster than *you*."

"I can skate faster than *you*!" Mary Beth shouted, then dissolved into giggles.

Chloe was impressed. "Wow. You really do have a way with women."

Ben shrugged, his wool coat moving up and down with his shoulders. "It's a gift." Extending his hands, he pulled Mary Beth to her feet. Smiling at Chloe, he said, "Let's do this."

They walked out onto the smooth surface of the rink and Chloe slid forwards a couple of feet. She loved the sound of the metal blade cutting through the ice and the feeling of the wind on her cheeks. Turning, she beckoned to Mary Beth. "Come on," she said. "Skate to me."

It took some help from Ben but Mary Beth did it, her hand fixed carefully on the wall. Studying the other kids flying past her around the rink, the little girl dropped her hand and said, "I want to do that."

"Go ahead," Chloe said. "You can do it."

Mary Beth took a couple of plodding steps, then started to get the hang of it. A little boy tried to hold her hand. She pushed him away.

"Wait until she gets really good," Chloe told Ben. "She'll trip him."

Ben laughed. Companionably, they leaned against the wall. Chloe tried not to think about the last time they had seen each other. The way it had ended in a fight.

"It's funny to watch you with her," he finally said. "It's pretty obvious that she adores you."

Chloe laughed. "Thanks, but that's not true. She only likes me when I do what she wants."

The thought made her sad. She'd always been so good with kids but for whatever reason, Mary Beth was not attached to her in any way. Yes, they were making progress, but it was frustrating to think that there were kids at Tiny Tumblers who cared about her more than her soon-to-be daughter did. Chloe knew they had a lot of work ahead of them before they'd achieve any sort of unbreakable bond, but if that were the case, they'd just have to keep trying.

"So . . ." Ben nudged her. "How's everything going? Are you happy?"

"Sure." Chloe noticed that the tip of her nose was frozen. The year before, she and Ben had competed to see whose nose could get the absolute coldest. Of course, he had cheated, dipping his nose into a Coke and then standing there in the wind.

"Good," he said. "I'm glad you called."

Ben walked onto the ice and skated a few feet, the sweet spice of his cologne floating after him like the essence of a ghost.

"I miss hanging out with you," Chloe said. "I . . . I miss you."

Ben stopped skating. After a moment, he clomped over to her and held on to the wall. "Things have changed, you know?" Pointedly, he eyed the ring. "We can't be the way we used to."

"Why not?" she demanded. "If we're really friends, why can't we just—"

Ben took a step toward her. "Because," he said. "It doesn't work like that."

"We kissed." Chloe looked down at her hands. "Big, freaking deal . . ."

"It was," Ben said, his voice quiet.

As a slow flush crept from her head to the tips of her toes, Chloe knew he was right. She thought back to the kiss. The hunger behind it, the need. Their friendship would never be the same.

"Come on," he said. "Let's go hang out with the little one. I've gotta get out of here pretty soon."

"A date?" Putting her hands to her mouth, she blew on them in an effort to stay warm.

Ben took off his gloves and handed them to her. "Yup," he said. "I guess you know me pretty well."

As Mary Beth did yet another round on the ice in the kid's section, Ben slid over to an empty corner. There, he performed a series of twists and turns they'd perfected over the years. Chloe took a careful step toward him.

"Go for it," he called. "Do a turn."

"No." Chloe hesitated. "I think I'm just gonna keep it simple."

The wedding was close. She didn't want to get hurt.

Kristine rushed into the homewares section at Macy's. Colorful china sets were on display from floor to ceiling, positioned alongside polished silver. Chloe stood in the center of all of this, looking completely lost. She was dressed in her typical jeans, backpack and sweatshirt.

Spotting her, Chloe's gray eyes lit up with relief. "I'm so glad you're here." Rushing forwards, she said, "I have absolutely no idea what I'm doing."

As Kristine hugged her daughter, she could feel Chloe's ribs through the sweatshirt. "Honey," she scolded. "I don't care how busy you are. We're getting dinner after this. Steaks."

"Mom, you sound like Dad," she scoffed, pulling away.

The words pained Kristine. Ever since Kevin told her about the promotion, she had been filled with so much guilt, confusion and anger that she'd barely been able to speak to Kevin on the phone. Then, when he'd come home for his midweek break, he tried to touch her but she pushed him away. Kevin had looked at her, his eyes a mix of hurt and anger, then he'd gone back to his refuge in the basement.

"Besides," Chloe said, snapping Kristine out of her reverie, "eating is the least of my worries."

Pointedly, she eyed a couple across the way. They wandered through the china section, consulting with each other on practically every piece. The guy had his hand on the girl's lower back and she giggled at everything he said.

"I mean, where do these people come from?" Chloe demanded. "I bet they're not even a real couple. I bet the store hires them to coo over each other all day and make the rest of us feel like shit."

Kristine looked at her in surprise. This attitude wasn't like Chloe, not at all. She was normally very even-keeled. Hoping to get to the bottom of whatever was going on, Kristine said, "Tell me again why Geoff couldn't come."

"He had to go into the office." Chloe shrugged. "He's got a client in crisis."

"But doesn't he know he has a fiancée in crisis?" Kristine said, hoping for a smile.

It didn't come. Instead, Chloe picked up a white plate and ran her finger over the silver-plated pattern on the edge. "Look, his job isn't easy. Someone could have tried to commit suicide or something. Who knows? I don't blame him for going."

"Right . . ." Kristine said slowly. "But why isn't he here now? Does a crisis last all day?"

Chloe set down the plate. "It's an excuse. Obviously." She sighed. "He's already been married. He's done the whole 'pick out a china pattern' thing. I totally get it."

Kristine had always admired her daughter's empathy. She had such great insight into what made people tick. On the other hand, there was such a thing as being too empathetic. If Geoff didn't want to invest time in the wedding, he probably wouldn't invest time in the marriage, either. "Chloe, I—"

"Do you like this?" Chloe picked up a teacup and regarded her with those gray eyes. "Cool, right?" The cup was white bone china, with a pink design cut through it. It dangled precariously from her fingers.

"It's a little trendy," she said, careful to keep her voice gentle. "You might want to look for something—"

"Am I making a mistake?" Chloe blurted out. Her face crumpled and immediately, tears began streaming down her face.

"Oh, honey." Surprised, she pulled her daughter into her arms. "Honey, calm down. It's going to be okay."

A salesclerk made a move to approach them but Kristine gave a sharp shake of her head. The woman winked. *Ah, yes. The registration meltdown,* her face seemed to say. Subtly, she pointed to an area just around the corner. There was a tiny nook with a couch, some magazines and no shoppers.

"Here." Kristine guided her daughter to the couch. "Have a seat."

Chloe flopped down, putting her head in her hands. Kristine's heart ached. Chloe looked awful. Exhausted, stressed out. Maybe registration meltdowns were common, but this was obviously about more than just picking out pots and pans.

Silently, Kristine rubbed her back, wondering what to say. It had been so much easier to council Chloe when she was younger. The problems were so much simpler. A bad grade, a losing shot in the basketball game, a junior high crush . . . These pains were easy to fix with a walk around the block or a bowl of ice cream. But relationships were so much more complex.

"You okay?" she finally asked.

"No," Chloe mumbled, sniffling. "I'm embarrassed. The only time someone should cry at Macy's is when there's a good sale."

Kristine bit her lip. There it was, the Kevin humor shining through. He'd much rather crack a joke than deal with real emotions. Chloe had picked up the same defense.

"It's okay to cry," she said. "You know, you and June always make fun of me for it but it's a heck of a lot better than trying to keep all of your emotions bottled up inside."

Chloe nodded, letting out a huge sigh. "I know."

"You have so much going on, honey." Kristine touched her knee. "I don't know how you handle it all." She glanced at her daughter's engagement ring. The diamond was cloudy and needed to be cleaned. "Does Geoff do things like this a lot?" she asked. "Make plans with you and break them?"

Chloe dabbed at her eyes with her sweatshirt. "No."

Kristine reached into her purse and found a packet of tissues. "Here. Blow your nose."

Chloe gave her a look. "Mother, I'm not five." But she still blew her nose.

After a long moment, she wadded up the tissue. "Geoff doesn't break plans at the last minute. It's just . . ." She played with the tissue for a moment, then twisted it around her finger. "He's always pushing Mary Beth on me. I understand. I mean, I'm going to be her *mother*." Her lower lip trembled. "But it's too much. When I've got school and planning this wedding and . . ."

"Have you talked with him about it?"

"Yes, kind of." Chloe shook her head, glum. "But now that Mary Beth's mother is back, he's all worried that Mary Beth will get confused and he really wants to solidify my place in her life. Which is *great*, you know? But it's just too much to handle right now. I wish I could just take it at my own pace."

The salesclerk poked her head around the corner. "How's it going back here? Did you have any questions about china?"

"No." Chloe chewed on her top lip. "Just a few questions about marriage."

The salesclerk smiled. "I understand. We get that a lot around here."

"And what's the verdict?" Chloe gave a little laugh. When the salesclerk made a move to answer, Chloe shook her head. "I'm just kidding."

The salesclerk didn't laugh. She had to be in her late fifties, with light brown hair and a carefully made-up face. "You know, there were many years where I wondered why I ever got married. And then, why I bothered to stay the course." She shrugged and her tailored pink blazer moved up and down with the motion. "But if I've learned anything, it's that you don't have to figure it all out right now. Life is long and love has a way of working itself out."

"And if it doesn't?" Chloe stared straight ahead, her hands gripping her knees.

"Well." The salesclerk thought for a moment. "Then I guess you'll leave the marriage with half a set of really nice china."

Chloe looked at her in surprise.

"That is," the salesclerk said with a smile, "if I do my job correctly."

That made Chloe laugh. She threw back her head and laughed and laughed, until Kristine and the salesclerk finally joined in, too. "That's more like it," the woman said, handing her a registry gun. "This is the fun part. Save the serious stuff for the chapel."

# Sixty

Kristine was sitting in bed, reading an article on Japan, when Kevin walked in. He was dressed in his sweats and carrying a glass of water. He set it down on his nightstand and switched on the lamp.

He gave her a cautious look. "Hi."

"Hey."

Kevin stood there, chewing his lip. His eyes were troubled.

"What are you doing in here this early?" she asked, pulling the sheets up around her.

"I don't know." Kevin's meaty face looked slightly bewildered, as though he didn't quite know what he was doing in their bedroom either. "I thought I'd come in here with you. Read for a while."

Kristine looked over at his side of the bed. On his nightstand, there was only the water, a box of tissues and an alarm clock. "Do you have a book?"

"Nope." He gave a small laugh. "I was hoping you could point me in the right direction."

"Oh." Even though there were so many things wrong between them, they couldn't ignore each other forever. In some ways, she was still desperately hoping that he would come through. That he would turn down the promotion or if he accepted it, somehow find a way to prove to her that it was the best choice, that he had a plan to make it all work.

"A book you'd like . . ." She thought for a minute. He wasn't much of a reader but he seemed to prefer biographies on sports figures or world leaders. "A biography?"

"I don't know." Kevin made a move to crack his knuckles. She tensed in preparation, then he dropped his hands to his side. "Action?"

Throwing back the heavy comforter, Kristine padded into the living room. She ran her fingers over the spines until she found what she was looking for. Walking back into the room, she handed him a mystery thriller she'd been stupid enough to read on a night when he wasn't home. "Courtesy of June. It scared the crap out of me. Maybe that will do it for you."

"Great." He stood there, holding the book, as Kristine slid back under the covers. She read a few pages, then noticed he was still standing there, looking at her.

Letting out a sigh, she took off her reading glasses. "What is it?"

Kevin opened his mouth, then closed it. "Nothing." He walked over and sat on his edge of the bed. The mattress shifted slightly under his weight. "You look beautiful tonight. I just wanted to tell you that."

"Oh." Kristine's voice was dull. After worrying about their marriage, juggling the events for the wedding and staying on top of the holiday rush at the store, she did not feel beautiful. She felt tired, old and more defeated than she'd ever thought she'd be.

Kevin gave her an awkward smile and climbed into bed. They both sat there for a moment. Her book was half opened, the pages fanning out in front of her. His book was still closed, resting on his lap.

"Do you . . . care if I read?" she finally asked.

"No, no. Let's read." Kevin cracked open his book. He read a page and turned it. Then he shook his head and gave a little laugh.

She looked over at him in surprise. "What are you laughing at? I thought it was a thriller."

"Us." He gestured at them. They were both tucked in under the covers, the lights on the nightstands fired up and their books neatly lying in their laps. "When the hell did we get so old?"

Kristine shook her head. "I have no idea. But I ask myself the same question every day."

After a moment of pretending to read the book jacket, he set it aside altogether. "Kris, are we going to make it?" His eyes were worried, his voice low and earnest.

She stared down at the pages, watching the words blur in front of her. "I don't know," she finally said. "To be honest with you, I really don't know."

# Sixty-one

The doorbell chimed and June wiped her hands on her apron. Kristine was working at the store and Charley was at the country club for his poker game. June wondered if it was a deliveryman, with yet another present. Even though she and Charley had not registered, it seemed that everyone in town had decided to send over a token or a trinket anyway.

At first, June had considered sending the gifts back. This was the second marriage for each and they certainly didn't need anything. She hated for people to waste their money. But as the silver picture frames, monogrammed hand towels and wine goblets arrived, she found something very special about each item. They symbolized the life that she and Charley were building together.

Sliding open the peephole, June was surprised to see her son-in-law standing on her doorstep. He was wearing a heavy brown coat, jeans and a pair of tan worker boots. The navy stocking cap pulled low over his forehead made him look like a criminal, not a successful plant manager. June shook her head. No matter how he tried to play it, Kevin was a worker. That's who he'd always been.

June eased open the door and kissed him hard on each fleshy cheek. "Kristine's not here. She's working at the store."

Kevin's face was ruddy not just from the cold, she saw, but from emotion. "Actually, June," he said. "I'm here to see you." He bowed his head, the muscle in his cheek working. "I . . ."

June pulled her sweater around her, surprised. Kevin rarely came to visit her. In fact, she couldn't remember the last time. A cab drove by on the street, honking angrily at another car blocking his way. Stepping aside, she gestured at Kevin.

"Come in, come in." She stepped back into the hallway, watching as he closed the door behind him. The move was hesitant, as though he wanted to leave it open for a clean getaway. Finally, he pulled it shut and locked it. "Would you like a drink?" she asked. "I could make coffee?"

Kevin shook his head. Peeling off his cap, he stuffed it into the pocket of his jacket. Then, he made his way to the parlor, where he collapsed in a Taurean chair much too small for his frame.

June bustled over to the couch and took a seat. Her son-in-law sat in silence, clearing his throat. His mouth worked to say something again and again, but the words wouldn't come.

"The longer we sit here, the older I get," June chirped. "Let's move it along."

He let out a hearty sigh. "June," he said, running the heel of his hand over his eyes. "When I first met you, I didn't like you very much. In fact, I didn't like you one bit."

"Oh?" She shifted, suddenly uncomfortable. "I'm sorry to hear that."

"No, I'm sorry," he said. "Because as the years went on, not only did I grow to like you, I grew to respect you."

She let out a tiny breath. *Good.* He'd frightened her for a moment.

"I appreciated the way you always told it how it was. I'm here today"—Kevin adjusted his form and the chair creaked—"because I need you to tell me exactly how it is."

June was stunned into silence. This proud, hulking man had come to her for advice? This, after years of insisting that she butt out and let him run his family his own way?

"Hmmph," she said. "I rather don't know what to say." She took a tissue out of the pocket of her wool vest, folded it neatly, then put it right back into her pocket.

"Wouldn't that just be the icing on the cake." Kevin ran his hands over his face. "For the first time in the history of man, when I actually come to you for advice, you have nothing to say."

June raised her eyebrows. "What's on your mind?"

Pulling his hat out of his pocket, he rolled it over and over in his hands. "I need you to tell me what to do. Because . . . Because I love your daughter more than anything in this world and I don't want to lose her. And I'm about to lose her, June. I know I am."

As much as June wanted to debate this point, it was more than obvious that something was wrong with Kristine. She'd been pale and agitated ever since Kevin had gotten this new promotion. She wouldn't go so far as to say that Kevin was about to *lose* Kristine but . . . maybe he knew something June did not.

"Kristine told me about your job," she said carefully. "Congratulations."

Kevin didn't say anything. He just looked at her.

"I understand that you want to provide for your family, Kevin. I understand that you have some enormous responsibilities, with Chloe in school and Kristine running that store. But why do you insist on making your work more important than your family?"

Kevin opened his mouth to speak, but June was not quite finished. He had asked her a direct question and she was going to answer it.

"If you were *my* husband, I would be very confused," she said. "On one hand, you tell me you love me. On the other, you put work before your family. Why would you do that, unless . . ." June put her hand to her mouth. It was like that moment when she'd solved one of her mysteries. Suddenly, she knew exactly what was going on. "Of course."

June thought about the ease at which Kevin accepted her offer to pay for the wedding, the jokes he made about Chloe keeping her scholarship, the panic that crossed his face every time Kristine mentioned that store.

"It's money." She lowered her hand, staring at her son-in-law. "You're in a terrible spot. Is that correct?"

Coughing to cover up his emotion, he nodded.

June's heart sunk. This from the man who had always been too proud to ask for anything. The man who had gone above and beyond to make sure that he could provide for his wife on his own. She couldn't believe it.

"Kevin, what happened?"

He shook his head. "I was just trying to catch up. And everything went to shit." He tugged at the cap. "When I couldn't get a job, we dug into our retirement account. Then, when I got a job—*finally*—I asked our guy to make some big moves. To get us caught back up." Kevin wiped his hand across his face. "The market crashed and . . ." He blew out a deep breath. "That was the end of that. I was so stupid."

"You certainly were not stupid," she said. "*Everyone* lost a lot of money. You did nothing wrong."

"I did, though," Kevin insisted. "I should have been patient. Just done some honest work, for honest pay. But I got greedy. And . . ." He closed his eyes, as though in pain. "I never told her. I was so afraid she was going to lose that store. She'd just opened it and . . ."

June looked at him in astonishment. Kristine didn't *know*? This man had been going through all this and his wife didn't even know? For heaven's sake.

"When were you planning to tell her?" June demanded.

Kevin wrapped the hat around his hand like a tourniquet. "I was going to, but . . . You know how that is. You don't say anything when it happens and then it's too late. And I was fixing it. I *am* fixing it . . ." A flash of pride crossed his face. "I had built everything back up pretty good but then this promotion came along. Huge salary, huge 401(k). It's exactly what we need."

June raised her eyebrows. "Is it?" she asked, her voice quiet.

He looked at the floor.

June studied her son-in-law for a long moment. "I'm disappointed in you, Kevin. Not because you lost money, as everyone else did during that time, but because you didn't trust Kristine enough to let her go through this with you. The whole richer or poorer thing? That's in there for a reason."

"I didn't want her to think of me like that," he growled. "So weak. Such a loser."

"Kevin," she snapped, "wake up. You want me to tell you like it is? It's like this: I have watched you spend your entire marriage trying to prove to Kristine that you are better than the guy she married. But there was a *reason* she married you. She loved you. *You.* Not the person you wanted to become, but the man who you've always been."

He looked surprised. "You really think that about me, June?"

"If you simply must fish for compliments," she said, "then yes. Yes, I do."

Kevin's face worked with emotion. He cleared his throat.

"If you don't want to lose your wife," June said, "you need to be honest with her. Talk to her. Tell her everything that's happened and find a way to meet in the middle. But you better do it quickly because I'll tell you this much . . ." She swallowed hard. "I've never seen my daughter so unhappy. If you don't work things out, I have no idea how much time the two of you will have left."

"Are you going to tell her that I was here?" he asked. "What I said?"

In the past, yes. June would have called her daughter immediately and repeated his every word. But now, she planned to honor the promise she'd made to Charley. That she would let her family solve their problems on their own.

"No." June reached out and patted his hand. "No, I am not." Oddly, it felt good to say this and mean it. "You can fix this, Kevin. I know you can. You don't need my help."

They got to their feet and he hugged her. "Thanks, June," he said. "I'll do my best."

"Now." She straightened. "You're staying in town? Until after our engagement party?"

Kevin shook his head. "Flying out tonight, coming back the afternoon of the party."

June paused. "Oh. I thought . . ."

Kristine had specifically asked Kevin to not fly in that same day. With the weather, it was too risky that his flight would get delayed. She didn't want him to miss the party.

"It'll be okay," Kevin said, as though reading her mind. "I'll be there, Cupcake. You can count on that."

After giving her a kiss on the cheek, Kevin left her house as quickly as he came. June picked up a coffee cup and placed it in the dishwasher. Walking around, she couldn't help but notice that the house suddenly seemed very empty without him.

# Sixty-two

Chloe was spraying down the mats at Tiny Tumblers with a mint-scented disinfectant, when the owner walked in. Tall and lanky, Albert wore his thinning gray hair in a comb-over. He always walked around with a bewildered expression on his face, as though surprised to find himself working with children.

"Excuse me, sir." Chloe got to her feet. "We're closed for the day. I'm going to have to ask you to leave."

Albert squinted at her, confused. "Chloe, it's—"

"Albert, I'm just teasing you."

Walking over to him, Chloe set the bottle of disinfectant on the cash register counter. She dropped the dirty paper towels in the bright red wastepaper basket. "So, what brings you to this neck of the woods?"

Albert lived out in Lake Forest and rarely made in-town visits.

"Ah, well, I've come here with some rather unfortunate news," he said. "Have a seat."

Worried, Chloe perched on one of the blue chairs in the waiting area. "What happened?" She hoped it wasn't one of the kids. Asher had been out with the flu for a week. Maybe it had turned into something more serious.

Albert fidgeted with the latch on his briefcase. "You've been with Tiny Tumblers for a long time. But, Chloe, this is a family establishment. It's come to my attention that you have started a rather inappropriate relationship with one of our clients."

Chloe's eyes widened, then she laughed. "Oh, don't worry. It's not anything scandalous." Holding up her left hand, she said, "Albert, we're getting married. I would have liked to invite you to the wedding but thanks to my grandmother, the guest list was pretty packed already."

"Congratulations." He pursed his lips. "But please do not be coy."

"Coy?" She was totally confused.

"Your relationship started here." He pointed at the blue and red mats. "At Tiny Tumblers."

Chloe felt a tiny prickle of concern. "I didn't meet him here. We knew each other before and . . ." Realizing this was irrelevant, she cut to the chase. "What's this all about?"

Albert let out a hearty sigh. "You signed a code of ethics when you took this job. Having an affair with one of the parents is unacceptable."

"It wasn't an affair," she said. "We're getting *mar*ried."

"Nonetheless, we're going to have to let you go." He handed her a plain white envelope. The type of envelope that her checks had always arrived in. "I'm sorry."

Chloe was stunned. "What? But . . . "

He took advantage of this moment to get to his feet and usher her to the door.

"Don't look so surprised." Albert collected her coat and purse and handed them to her. "You have to understand, this sets a bad example with the other parents. Considering you are planning to work with children, that may be something for you to keep in mind as you move toward the future." He waved around his hands as if trying to shoo her away. "Good luck."

Chloe trudged out of the building. Quickly, he shut and locked the door behind him.

Left out in the cold, she stared at the big picture window in shock. She could see Albert striding around the room, finishing up the tasks she had expected to do. She felt a wave of confusion and then, as the realization of what had just happened really hit her, a wave of despair.

Fumbling through her purse, she picked up her phone and called Geoff. "I got fired." She almost choked on the words. "I'm, like, totally stunned right now."

After telling him the story, there was a lengthy pause. Finally, he said, "Chloe, it's for the best. You'll have that internship to handle, which is going to take up all of your time. Plus, you'll have Mary Beth. You already know she's a full-time job. Tacking that onto your current responsibilities, while trying to hold down a part-time job . . ." He sighed, as if the thought was too much for him to handle.

"But I loved my job," Chloe said. Tiny flakes of snow melted across her phone and smeared down the face like tears. "I loved the kids. These were happy kids, without problems and bad things happening to them and . . . it helped pay for school and my rent and I liked it. I liked being there."

She stared at the building, distressed to see that Albert had pulled down the shades on the front window. So much for a last longing look inside.

"Chloe." There was a smile in Geoff's voice. "You're not going to pay rent anymore. You'll be living with me."

The thought of packing up her cozy apartment and moving downtown suddenly seemed exhausting. She wanted to stay where she was. For everything to stay the same.

"Are you still there?" Geoff sounded concerned.

"Yeah. I'm just upset," she said. "He acted like I'd done something horrible, but we're getting *married*. It's not like I'm, like, going on dates with the par—"

"Chloe, I have a patient coming in right now." Geoff's tone was gentle. "But tonight, we'll celebrate this. Mary Beth will be so excited to hear that she'll get to see you more."

Chloe snorted. "But will Mary Beth be excited to hear that she's never, and I mean ever, going back to Tiny Tumblers? Even if it's the last place left to play on earth?"

Geoff laughed. "Spoken like a true ex-employee. Hang in there, I'll see you tonight."

"Wait." She shook her head. "I can't do anything tonight. I *have* to go to my apartment. I have no clean clothes, the place is a wreck and I just . . . I just need to put my life back together."

"That's fine," he said. "I'll see you tomorrow."

After they hung up, Chloe gave Tiny Tumblers one last look. She had walked in and out of that door so many times in the past few years. It was impossible to count all the hours she'd spent there. Chloe's gaze shifted to the garden next door, where she and Geoff had shared their first date. It seemed like just yesterday that the sun had been shining down and the flowers were in full bloom. Today, the trees were bare and the ground was covered in dirty snow.

It was hard to believe everything could change so quickly.

# Sixty-three

Kristine hovered by the cash register, staring off into space. Not ideal, considering the holiday rush was happening all around her. The normally cheerful staff was shooting her looks to kill.

There was a loud bang from upstairs and she jumped. The landlord had started doing construction in the space above the store, just in time to add more chaos to the holiday season. She had the Christmas music turned up loud, but in between "Holly Jolly Christmas" there was the whir of the drill or a steady banging. The whole thing was giving her a headache.

"Where are the rest of the Spanish Santa cards?" Annie demanded, swooping up to the counter. She was wearing a deliberately ironic snowman sweater, complete with carrot noses made out of felt. "I know we haven't sold through all of them."

"Um . . ." Kristine blinked, trying to remember. "In the office. I put the extras back there to make them look more in demand. Do you want me to—"

"I've got it." Annie took off her glasses and quickly cleaned them with a tissue. Sliding them back on, she said, "But if you could just refill the coffee pots and put on some more mint cocoa, that would be a big help."

"Okay." She nodded. "Absolutely."

Normally, the holiday season was her favorite time of year. Not only was business booming, but she loved the smell of the fresh-baked cookies that they served from morning until night and the thrill of helping people find that perfect gift. This year, though, Kristine couldn't concentrate. She was so confused.

Kevin was doing his best to fix a bad situation, that much was for sure. She had been receiving cards in the mail from him, little love notes saying things like, *Can't wait to see you again, Firecracker!* or *I love you more than honey-roasted airline peanuts.* But just like the last-minute trip to Italy, it all felt just a little too late. Years ago, she had loved getting cards from him. Now, it just wasn't enough.

On a late-night phone call, where Kristine suspected he'd been drinking, Kevin insisted that things were going to be fine. That he had some news that would make her "very, very happy." Kristine had just rolled her eyes. She was so tired of talking, so tired of being alone.

The bells on the door jingled and she forced herself to snap to her senses. Straightening her shoulders, she walked over to the coffee display. She threw away the paper cups that were lying around and loaded the gigantic carafe onto a cart. Wheeling the cart back toward the utility room that served as a makeshift kitchen, she even managed to smile and say hello to a few regular customers.

At the door to the kitchen, Annie stopped her. "Listen," she said, frowning behind her black-framed glasses. "I'm sorry if I sounded short. I've just been worried about you."

Kristine pasted on a smile. "Annie, I'm fine."

"Kris, be real with me." Annie put a hand on her arm. "The big triple wedding is right around the corner. I mean, I know mothers who have lost their mind just handling one wedding. Like, stone-cold nuts. So, the fact that you're trying to deal with three?" Annie raised her eyebrow, her eyebrow ring winking. "That's enough to push anyone over the edge."

Kristine bit her lip. "Yeah. It's . . ." She sighed. "It's a handful."

"Are . . . Are you and Kevin having problems?" Annie blurted out.

Kristine flushed, surprised that her friend would be so blunt. "Every relationship has problems." She forced herself to keep it light. "But that's life, right? We'll work it out."

Annie hesitated, as though debating on whether or not to tell her something. There was another bang from upstairs.

"What is all that noise?" Kristine demanded, looking up. "It's so annoying."

"Things aren't always what they seem, Kristine." Annie's eyes were intent behind her glasses. "Hang in there. I promise you everything is going to be okay."

# Sixty-four

As Chloe trudged up the steps to her apartment, she took it all in. The heavy cement porch railings. The steep stairs. The familiar onion smell of the lobby. It was so strange to think that she'd be leaving it behind.

The hallway was quiet as Chloe pulled out her keys. She stood at her door a little longer than necessary, jiggling the lock. If Ben was home, he didn't bother to come out to see what all the commotion was about.

Pushing open her apartment door, Chloe shuddered to think of the mess that was waiting for her. Dishes in the sink, laundry scattered everywhere and Whiskers' self-cleaning litter certainly needed to be changed by now. On top of that, Chloe hadn't dusted or cleaned the bathrooms in months.

Oh, well. It was time to suck it up and get caught up. One day soon, she was going to have to pack up her apartment and clean it for good. For some reason, the thought made her incredibly sad.

Walking in, she stopped in surprise. "What?"

The place did not smell like cat litter; it smelled like Lemon Pine-Sol. The kitchen counters were bright white, clear of any dishes or clutter. The trash had been taken out and— she gasped—her laundry was neatly folded in baskets sitting on the couch. It was tagged with a receipt from the local Laundromat.

Chloe put her hand to her heart. Geoff must have sent his housekeeper over to clean. She couldn't believe it. Ever since the registration fiasco, she'd been a little wary. There was so much going on in her life but it felt like his life always took precedence. Sometimes, she wondered how much he really cared. But this—Chloe's eyes swept over the dust-free living room—this was exactly what she'd needed.

Taking out her cell, she punched in his number. "Hi . . ." Mary Beth, of course, was screaming like a banshee in the background. "You are the best fiancé in the world."

At the sound of her voice, Whiskers came bounding out of the bedroom. Purring and meowing, the cat weaved in and out of Chloe's legs. She bent down and rubbed her ears.

"Are you home?" Geoff's voice was warm.

Mary Beth screamed a little louder, most likely annoyed to share her father with the phone.

"Yes." Scooping up Whiskers, Chloe strolled into the bedroom. "And I just wanted to say . . . Oh, my gosh!"

Chloe stopped in surprise. On her bed sat a display of six entertainment magazines, a box of caramel and sea salt chocolates and a bottle of red wine. "Wow." Her mood instantly lifted. "I'm going to have to get fired more often."

"Is there something you need?" Geoff asked. "Sorry, but Mary Beth's having a bit of a meltdown."

Setting Whiskers down on the bedspread, she reached for the card on the box of chocolates. "No, I just wanted to call and say thanks."

"For . . . ?"

Chloe cocked her head in confusion. "For . . ." Suddenly, she looked down at the card on the bed. It was homemade, with a brightly colored graphic design on the cover.

Ben.

Chloe almost dropped the phone. "For . . . For being so understanding today."

"Of course," he said. "I love you. I have to go. See you tomorrow, okay?"

"Goodnight." Hanging up the phone, she opened the card with shaking hands.

*Hey, Chloe,*

*Considering the foul odor coming out of your apartment, I had two choices: call the health department or clean it. Since I hate bureaucracy, I decided to give it a little scrub.*

*Consider it a "Sorry I'm going to miss your engagement party" sort of thing.*

*P.S. Whiskers had me get you some wine, some magazines and a pet mouse to make up for it. If the pet mouse is missing by the time you get home, talk to your cat.*

*Missing my friend but happy she's happy, Ben.*

Chloe read the note three times. She touched the collection of magazines and the box of candies. Whiskers, who was stretched out next to it all like the rightful owner, watched Chloe with her wide yellow eyes.

"He cleaned my apartment," Chloe whispered. "And . . ." Blushing, she thought about Ben gathering up her laundry. Thank goodness he'd sent it out instead of doing it himself. She couldn't imagine how much it cost him, though. Probably a fortune.

Whiskers hopped up, stalked to the end of the bed and yawned. For a cat that had been left alone for days at a time, she certainly didn't seem hungry for attention. Chloe watched the easy loll of the pink tongue and the flash of white needle teeth. Suddenly, she got the picture.

"You've been over there, haven't you?" she demanded. "Ben's been taking you over to his apartment to play."

Whiskers stretched, then gracefully started giving her legs a bath. Unbelievable. Just like any female in Ben's company, Whiskers had blossomed.

Jumping to her feet, Chloe padded out of the bedroom, across the hall and to his apartment, her heart pounding in her chest. Whiskers trotted faithfully behind, as though used to the route. Taking a deep breath, Chloe knocked on the door and waited.

Nothing. Not a sound. He wasn't home. Disappointed, she took out her cell phone and called him.

He picked up on the first ring. "You must have seen my handiwork."

Ben's voice was so incredibly cheerful and familiar that a grin stretched across her face. Whiskers rubbed up against her legs and looked at the phone, as though she knew it was him.

"I'm standing here with my cat," Chloe said, "who has obviously fallen madly in love with you."

"It's amazing what a little catnip can do."

Chloe smiled, leaning against his door. There was a silence. Then they both spoke at the same time. "Thank you so much—"

"I hope you don't mind that I—"

There was an awkward pause, then Ben laughed. "I think you were about to thank me."

"I was. That was probably the sweetest thing anyone has ever done for me." She shook her head. "And the U.K. version of *Star*? I mean, seriously. That was just a whole new level of awesome."

"You deserve it." Ben's voice was low, earnest. "I want you to be happy."

Chloe closed her eyes. It struck her then that she was standing across from the exact spot where they'd kissed that one night. A funny feeling started in her gut. It was almost as though . . . It was almost as though she wished it could happen again. Right now. That Ben would walk up those stairs and take her into his . . .

"Clo?" Ben's voice was soft. "You still there?"

"Uh . . ." She looked at the phone in horror. Her hands were sweating. The phone case was actually slightly damp. "Yes, I just . . ."

"What's wrong?"

Chloe didn't know what to say. Maybe it was the pressure. Maybe there was just too much going on in her life and she longed for a simpler time. Or maybe—"I think I'm having a pre-wedding meltdown," she said, giving a strangled laugh. "I really—"

"You really what?"

"I really miss you," she whispered. "I mean, bad."

As Chloe watched, Whiskers scratched at Ben's door, as though desperate to get inside. Whiskers looked up at her as though to say, *Is he coming home?*

"Chloe, I—"

Just then, she heard a distinct female voice on the line. "Babe, are you coming in? The movie's going to start."

"You're on a date." Chloe's heart plummeted into her stomach. "I'm so sorry. To interrupt."

"Do you want me to come home?" Ben asked. "Chloe, I'll come home. Right now."

Yes, it was what she wanted more than anything in the world. To spend her night of silence and solitude with Ben, watching reality television and ordering Thai food. But looking down at her engagement ring, she realized those days were long gone. Her eyes filled with tears.

"Don't come home. Have fun on your date."

"Chloe, seriously—"

"Ben," she practically shouted. "I'm fine! If I need someone, I'll call Geoff. Okay?"

There was silence on the other end of the phone. Chloe could hear the people in the movie theater walking by, talking and laughing. She could picture Ben standing there, with his latest conquest hanging on to his jacket like an accessory.

"Yeah," he said, his voice hurt. "Sure thing. You do that."

"Thank you for everything." Chloe gripped the phone. "Seriously. I . . . I appreciate you."

Hanging up the phone, she stood in the hallway for a long moment. She had this crazy moment where she wanted to key into his apartment and lay down in his bed. To just take ten minutes imagining what it would be like to be a part of Ben's life again. Of course, that would be a total psycho move. Honestly, it was the type of thing that could get her banned from practicing art therapy. Hell, it was the type of thing that could get her arrested.

Shaking her head, Chloe scooped up her cat and walked back to her apartment. She turned the knob on the bath until it creaked, poured a capful of lavender bath gel into the water and flipped on the space heater. Sliding into the water, she felt the tension in her muscles begin to melt away.

All of these crazy thoughts . . . Chloe must just be too tired. She would finish up this bath and go straight to bed. Tomorrow, everything would seem a whole lot brighter.

In just a few short weeks, she was going to marry Geoff. She was happy about this, she really was. It was just fear or nerves or maybe coming back to a place that she used to call home that made her think, for a stupid moment, that she belonged with someone else.

# Sixty-five

The stone lodge Charley's friends had booked for the engagement party bustled with activity everywhere Chloe turned. The guests were three generations of close and casual acquaintances, all thrown together in one room.

The lodge was decorated for Christmas, with boughs and holly lining every spare surface. A fire roared in the fireplace downstairs and the scent of eggnog and gingerbread floated through the air, mingling with a hundred different types of perfume. June and Charley stood in the center of the main room, both completely in their element, but Chloe was finding the whole thing overwhelming.

On top of that, Sally and Dana were hovering around her like the court of a queen.

"Do you need anything?" Sally chirped. "Maybe another cocktail?"

Sally looked so cute. She was dressed in a white sweater dress and red high heels, along with dangly candy cane earrings and a big black belt buckled at her waist. Chloe envied the fun outfit. It looked so much more comfortable than the black taffeta monstrosity June had crammed her into.

The dress had arrived by courier two nights ago, along with a pair of adorable silver shoes. The outfit looked awesome, yes, but the dress itched like crazy and made noise every time she moved.

The shoes were also giving her a blister. Honestly, she would much rather be at home, dressed in her pajamas and curled up with her cat.

"No, I don't need anything." Chloe showed Sally her full glass of Chardonnay. "Thanks."

"What about some food?" Dana asked. "That tapenade looked pretty amazing."

The hors d'oeuvres circulating the room did look delicious, but Chloe didn't want to get anything in her teeth. Every time she turned around, she had to smile at someone and say, "Thank you," as they offered their congratulations.

"No, I'm good." She took a sip of wine.

"Don't you bloody need anything?" Sally demanded.

Chloe laughed, looking back and forth between her two friends. "I'm fine. What on earth is going on? Why are you guys trying to wait on me?"

Sally grinned. "We're pretending to be bridesmaids," she cried. "How did we do, then?"

"Perfect," Chloe said. "You're definitely bridesmaids in my heart." She felt a tap on her shoulder and turning, she came face-to-face with her mother. "Wow," she gasped. "Mom, you look beautiful!"

Chloe's friends nodded in agreement. Kristine looked like some sort of tragic heroine, with her black flared taffeta dress, flawless skin and diamond teardrop earrings. Unfortunately, she also looked a little upset. She leaned in close enough to smell the scent of coconut in her hair.

"I don't know how to say this," she murmured, "so I'll just say it."

"What?" Chloe asked, suddenly worried.

Sally held up her drink glass. "Anyone?" When they shook their heads, she and Dana headed off in search of another round.

Chloe turned to her mother. "What's wrong?"

Kristine pressed her fingers under her eyes. "Your father's stuck in Denver. He's going to miss tonight but he wanted to let you know how incredibly sorry he is."

Chloe's heart sunk. "Oh, no."

"I know." Gently, Kristine reached out and adjusted the ribbon on Chloe's dress. Her hands were shaking.

Even though it was a bummer her father was going to miss the engagement party, Chloe was more worried about the way her mother seemed to be taking the news. "Mom, are you okay?"

Kristine waved her hand. The sparkle from her wedding ring seemed dull in the muted light. "I'm fine. Just disappointed he's not here to see you on your big night. You look beautiful."

"Okay, but . . ." Chloe surveyed the crowded room. So many of the faces belonged to friends of her parents. "This was supposed to be your big night, too. I'm fine, but you must be really upset."

"Oh, things happen." Chloe must not have looked convinced, because her mother went on to say, "Honey, your father and I have been married for a long time. This is a nice idea for us, but it's the real deal for you. I know your father is devas—"

A guest swooped in. It was some friend of June's, and based on her exclamations, she hadn't seen Kristine since she was "this big." Kristine allowed the woman to drag her away, without forcing Chloe to endure yet another introduction. Looking back over her shoulder, she mouthed, "Love you."

"Everything alright?" Geoff walked up and put a hand on Chloe's arm.

"I'm not sure." She nodded, watching the retreating form of her mother. "I think I need to sit down for a minute."

Taking Chloe by the arm, Geoff guided her through the crowd and pushed open the first wooden door he saw. Shutting it behind them, he flipped on the lights. The room was just a tiny nook with a scratchy brown and orange couch and no decorations. But it so was quiet and empty. It was the perfect escape from the chaos of the party.

Geoff gave her a quick kiss. "Tell me what happened."

Peeling off her high heels, Chloe collapsed onto the rough springs of the sofa. Quickly, she narrated what her mother had said. "She's devastated. I could tell by the look on her face."

"It's just a party." His voice was gentle. "It's not the party or even the ceremony that counts. It's everything that happens afterwards."

She bit her lip. "You always say the right thing. Have you thought about a career in psychology?"

Geoff smiled, showing those three lines in his cheek. "I don't have all the answers," he said, tugging at his ascot. It was red and dotted with diamond rings. Even though Chloe wanted to like it, she had to admit it was painfully tacky. "No one has all the answers." Letting out a weighted sigh, he looked down at his hands. "Especially when it comes to marriage."

"I've been meaning to ask you . . ." Chloe picked at a string on the scratchy material of the couch. "Are you feeling any better? About Miriam being back in town?"

Geoff adjusted his ascot. "She stopped by the office today. We chatted for a while."

Chloe blinked. This was the second time there had been some sort of interaction with his ex-wife where he had mentioned it after the fact. As though it was not a big deal.

"Why wouldn't you tell me that?" she asked, her voice cautious. "Like, right away?"

Geoff seemed genuinely puzzled. "You've been in class all day. It's not really something to leave you a message about on your phone. Or to talk about at our engagement party," he said pointedly. The din of the party could be heard just beyond the door.

"Right, but . . ." Yes, she had been in school all day, then at her internship, changed into her dress in two seconds flat, then hopped in the town car they'd shared with Charley and June. Still, for some reason, she wasn't comfortable with the fact that he was just telling her this now. "What did she want?" she pressed. "Why did she stop by?"

"To apologize." Geoff clasped his hands so tightly that his knuckles turned white. His green eyes looked sad. "It turns out, I was right about the depression. She went on medication about a year after she left. She really regrets some of the choices she made and she just wanted to apologize."

Chloe rubbed her lips together. "Did she ask you about us?"

There was a slight pause. "Yes."

"What did you say?" Chloe knew that she sounded like a typical jealous girl, but come on. If she was, in fact, going to invest the rest of her life in Geoff, she did have a right to be a little proprietary.

He looked confused by the question. "I told her about you. Who you are, how we met . . . I showed her a picture. She's interested in knowing who will be raising Mary Beth." He smiled. "She was happy to hear you want to work with children."

Chloe reached down and played with the taffeta ribbon hanging on her dress. It crunched like a dead leaf in her hand. "How do you feel, Geoff? About all this?"

"Surprised." He shook his head. "The conversation was complex. I felt . . ." He thought for a moment, once again smoothing his ascot. "Sad for her. For us."

At the "us," Chloe wrinkled her forehead. "*Us*, like me and you?"

"*Us* as in me and Miriam. It was a very painful time, Chloe." Geoff's eyes were fixed on the black laces of his patent leather shoes. "We were both hurting and didn't help each other. I regret that. Very much." He ran his hands up and down over his thighs. "Before all this, Miriam was a wonderful woman. It's important for Mary Beth to get to know her."

Chloe chewed the inside of her lip. If there was one thing she had learned from her classes, it was to be direct. Clear questions were designed to bring honest answers.

"Do you still want to get married?" she asked. "To me?"

"Of course I still want to marry you!" Reaching out, Geoff pulled her in close. "I'm sorry. We shouldn't be talking about this here. However, you asked and I thought it only fair to answer honestly. I love you, Chloe. I really do."

They sat in silence for a moment, their arms around each other. She rested her cheek against his lapel. The murmurs outside had gone silent. She sat up straight. *Crap.* It was very possible that someone—June—was making a toast.

"We better get back out there," she said, fumbling on the floor for her shoes. She slid her right foot into the silver shoe with the diamond-encrusted broach at the toe, then moved her left foot around, trying to find the other. "I can't find it."

Dropping to his knees, Geoff dug around under the couch. "Aha!" He gave a triumphant smile. "Found it." It had a little dust bunny on it, which he blew off with a quick puff. Then, he held it out, waiting for her to slip her foot inside. "You ready, my princess?"

Extending her foot, Chloe let him slide it on the shoe. Immediately, the sharp leather pinched into the raw skin of her blister and she winced. It was just too tight.

"You ready?" Geoff asked, holding out his hand.

Chloe nodded. Taking his hand, she limped her way back into the party.

# Sixty-six

After the engagement party was over, Kristine went straight home. She took off her dress, deleted the eight messages from Kevin all begging her to call him and went up to the attic.

The space was dusty and freezing cold. Ratty pink insulation hung out from the sides of the rafters and something scurried across the corner. She picked through the well-organized boxes, amazed that twenty-five years in one place could mean such an incredible accumulation of stuff.

In the corner, there was a collection of ski equipment, from the days when they used to take ski trips as a family. Now, they were covered in cobwebs and dust. There were boxes filled with Kevin's baseball card collection from when he was a kid. It was carefully organized. Even though she knew nothing about baseball, she knew he had cards that were valuable because when he'd lost his job, he'd been tempted to sell them. "Absolutely not," she'd said. "Some things are more important than money." Then, of course, there was the section of the attic just filled with Chloe's stuff. Even though Kristine was tempted every spring to throw away the sports uniforms, second grade spelling tests and essays, she could never bring herself to do it. In that way, she was a lot more like June than she wanted to admit.

Walking past the box that held the collection of love notes Kevin had once given her, Kristine found what she was looking for—her wedding album. Holding it in her hand, she looked down at the faded white silk cover. At the party, June had a collection of photos from the ceremony set up on a table, and Kristine hadn't been able to even glance at them, for fear she'd burst into tears. Now that she was home, she gripped the book to her chest and climbed back down the rickety ladder.

Armed with a cup of hot tea, she sat on the comforter of her bed and flipped it open. She gazed at the first picture with a dispassionate eye. It was a photo of her hands gripping Kevin's as they lit the unity candle. Their rings glistened in the muted yellow light, and in that moment, if it were possible, even their hands looked happy.

Slowly, she flipped through the pages, marveling at how young they looked. Kristine's dress was just as beautiful as she remembered, floating around her like some ethereal cloud. Kevin looked strong and proud in every shot, his hand somehow always rested on her body. In one picture, his hand was on the small of her back. In another, it held on to her elbow. In another, he held her hand.

Kristine peered at the picture of the two of them cutting the wedding cake. When it came time to feed each other, they'd playfully smashed the cake into each other's faces. Then they'd kissed and kissed, delighting in the fact that frosting was getting all over their hair and their clothes. She remembered him murmuring, "The sweetest first kiss," before pulling her close once again.

Turning the page, she sucked in a sharp breath. There was a picture of her father dressed in a smart black suit, guiding her down the aisle. He looked exactly the way she held him in her memory: a precise, kind man with freckles on his nose and eyes that seemed to pick up on everything. Oh, what she wouldn't give to have him back right now. She would ask him what she could do to get things back to good. Even though June would most certainly love to offer up volumes of opinion on the topic, Kristine trusted that her father would have known the answer.

Even so many years after the fact, it was so confusing to her that he was really, truly gone.

Her father had died just a few months after the wedding, when Kristine and Kevin lived in an apartment in the city. In those first few, horrible months, she had spent many of those nights at June's house, taking care of her. When she wasn't with her mother, Kristine would come home and lie in bed with Kevin, staring blankly at the rusty fire escape just outside the window. At that stage, she still believed that if she'd just be patient, her father would climb up the fire escape, poke his head in the window and wave. "Not dead," he'd say. "Just a joke." June would pop up along behind him, laughing at the ruse the two had pulled off.

In those moments, Kristine would rifle through her favorite memories of her father. The time he taught her to ride a bike on the sidewalk in front of the house. The trip they took to Washington, DC, without June, exploring the White House and having lunch with a senator. The secret phone calls he made to her at college when June was not be around, just so he could get a word in edgewise. The memories would make her laugh and then, finally, cry.

"You okay?" Kevin would ask, cradling her head against his chest.

Kristine would nod, letting her most recent, favorite memory burn her father's memory even more firmly into her brain. "At least he got to walk me down the aisle. How many girls get to say that?"

It was just two months after his death that Kevin walked into the room and found her staring out the window, yet again. On this particular day, snow was falling and the fire escape was thick with a fresh white powder. Kevin had walked into the room, whistling and carrying a big bowl of popcorn, but he stopped the second he noticed the look on her face.

"Are you thinking about your dad?" he asked, walking over to her.

"No," Kristine said. "I was just thinking . . ." She stared at him as though he could answer the question growing inside her. "This is kind of strange, but . . ."

"What?" Plunking down on the edge of the bed, Kevin shoved a handful of popcorn in his mouth.

She touched her stomach. "I think I'm pregnant."

Kevin's eyes practically bugged out of his head. He choked and as he sputtered, she patted him on the back. "Geez, honey. Are you okay?"

He turned to her, his face bright with excitement. "Are you being serious? Do you think we've got a little baby?"

Kristine looked down at her stomach.

"Yeah," she said, looking up at him in wonder. "I think we do."

The popcorn all but forgotten, Kevin climbed into bed and held her close. Kristine rested her head against his chest, staring out at the fire escape. In the light from their bedroom, the snow seemed to wink.

Over the years, Kristine watched Kevin become the type of father hers had been. For this, she found herself falling in love with him in new ways, as he taught Chloe how to catch bugs, how to throw a ball and, in particular, ride a bike. The fact that he had always been there for their family, just like her father always had, was something else that had made her love him, more than anything.

Tonight, when he had missed out on sharing their daughter's engagement party with her, with their family . . . Kristine closed her eyes, fighting back yet another wave of pain. In twenty-five years of marriage, they had created one thing that mattered even more than their relationship—their daughter. That mattered more than anything. The fact that he was now giving that part of their relationship so little respect, as well . . .

Staring down at the wedding album, she gazed at a picture of the two of them. Their faces were filled with love and promise. It was hard to believe, looking at them back then, that they would ever be capable of drifting apart.

Kristine wanted their relationship to work. She wanted her family back. But after tonight, it had become pretty clear that her husband could not care less.

Closing the book, she set it on the bedside table. She turned off the lights and pulled the sheets to her chin, dreading the night ahead of her and the thoughts that would run through her mind. There was a lot to think about. Particularly, whether to keep fighting to save a marriage so clearly beyond repair.

# Sixty-seven

When Chloe's alarm clock went off, she opened her eyes with dread. It was going to be one of those days. She was booked solid, back to back to back. The thought of rolling over and snuggling up to Geoff's warm body was so tempting, but it was impossible. There wasn't even time to fantasize about playing hooky.

On her way out the door, Chloe poked her head into Mary Beth's bedroom. It was so early that the little girl was still asleep, her stuffed animals carefully arranged around her body. Mary Beth always slept with her arm wrapped around a fuzzy penguin and sure enough, the penguin was in his proper position as her tummy breathed in and out.

Mary Beth looked so incredibly sweet and peaceful that Chloe felt bad about barely having any time to spend with her. According to Geoff, she had already gone to two Mommy and Me classes with Miriam and they seemed to be getting along very well. Chloe was happy for Mary Beth, but selfishly sad. Once exams were over, once the wedding was over, she really needed to make a concerted effort to build a bond with this little girl. It wasn't right that she felt closer to some of the children in her internships than the girl who was to become her daughter.

Racing out of the apartment, Chloe started her marathon day. After meeting with her study group (good, she might actually know her stuff for the final exam), dashing across town for a final fitting (crazy, it was so weird to think she was so close to walking down the aisle), attending her final class on intervention methods (oops, falling asleep at some point for at least ten minutes) and then, taking her first final (yikes, ethical and legal issues), Chloe dashed across town again to complete her final internship hours for the semester (phew!).

After ten straight hours of running hard, Chloe pulled out her phone to check in with Geoff.

"Whoa." To her surprise, there were six missed calls. Worried that something had happened to Mary Beth, Chloe played the messages.

*Hi, it's Geoff. Can you come home for a few hours? Mary Beth scared away another sitter and I've got a full day . . .*

Delete.

*It's me. Where are you? I really need you to take Mary Beth today. It's an emergency. Call me back.*

Chloe went on to the next message.

*I'm starting to get a little annoyed. Where are you?* [There was a bloodcurdling scream in the background.] *Managing this is going to be your responsibility soon enough but I really need your help. Call me.*

The next three were exactly the same, each filled with more screaming from Mary Beth and more of an acerbic tone from Geoff. In the final message, he said, *I contacted Miriam. She's taking Mary Beth for the day. If I'm going to need an appointment to get my fiancée on the phone, I really don't know what the hell it is that we're doing.*

Chloe stared at her phone in disbelief. It was one thing to know that he expected some help taking care of his daughter. It was quite another to realize that meant dropping whatever she was doing so that he could go about his day. And the snide comment about making an appointment? What was *that*?

After staring at her phone for a long moment, she shook her

head. He knew how busy she was. He must have really been freaking out about Mary Beth to say something like that.

Sorry, exams today, she texted. Thought you knew?

Geoff texted back: It's all straightened out.

Chloe stared at her phone, surprised. Where was the "hope it went well" or "know you did great" or even "let's meet for dinner"? She stood in silence, a funny feeling in the pit of her gut.

Hopping on the train, Chloe went straight to her favorite corner bar, which was the bar where she and Ben had made the pact to go on a practice date. Even though it was a Wednesday night, she half hoped to bump into him. Maybe they could drink until it felt like old times, laughing and joking and pretending that the past few months hadn't happened.

Chloe sat at their booth, squeezing limes into her drink and watching the door. After two vodka tonics, she decided there was something she needed to know. Stumbling outside, she hailed a cab. As it cruised toward the destination, her heart pounded with fear.

"What are you doing here?" Sally squealed, throwing open the door. She was wearing a fuzzy white robe and had a light green face mask smeared all over her face. Her hair fell in wet ringlets around her shoulders.

Chloe couldn't quite answer. Instead, she swept inside and slammed the door behind her. The framed black-and-white posters that lined the walls shook. So did Sally's ridiculous collection of wedding crystal. It was a menagerie of colorful animals riding carousels, holding balloons or playing with friends. To this day, Sally found it difficult to articulate exactly what had compelled her to register for something so ridiculous.

"I need you to tell me something." Chloe turned to her friend. "And I don't want you to lie."

"Are you pissed?" Sally demanded. "Come on, Chloe. It's late. I was just about to go to bed."

"It is 11:10 in the p.m." Chloe's eyes settled on the black-and-white clock hanging above the black leather sofa. "Stop being so incredibly"—she searched for the right word—"*married.*"

Sally snorted. "Bloody hell. You are pissed."

"I am not. Do you have anything to drink?" Chloe swept into the kitchen, looking for an open bottle of wine. There was nothing. "Shit."

Sally poured two glasses of sparkling water. "Somebody must have the pre-wedding jitters!"

Chloe paused. It seemed like she had those quite a bit lately.

"Look, I have to ask you something serious." Chloe squinted at her. "Do you like him? Do you like Geoff?" There was a moment of hesitation in Sally's face. "You don't." Chloe hit the table like she had a winning poker hand. "You can't *stand* him."

"I didn't say that," Sally insisted. "You're drunk." Shoving the glass of water toward Chloe, she said, "Look, I think Geoff is fine. He's just not who I pictured for you."

"Who did you picture?"

Twisting a blonde ringlet around her finger, Sally bit her lip. "Come on. I don't know."

Chloe stretched her arms across the table, resting her head on her sleeve. "What did Ben say to you?" she asked. "When you told him about the engagement?"

Sally hesitated. "Why do you want to know?"

Sitting up, she picked up the glass of water and studied it. "I just . . ." She took a long drink. "I just do."

"Ben's in love with you," Sally said. "He has been for years."

Chloe stared at her friend, stunned. Feeling a slow flush creep up the back of her neck, she said, "No. I don't believe you. He's barely spoken to me in weeks. And . . . And he said that the only reason a man would even want to be with me is so that I could be his kid's nanny. Those are not words of love."

"Ben has been in love with you ever since I've known him," Sally said. Giving a hearty sigh, she tugged at a silver stud earring in her right ear. "I was never supposed to tell you that, you know. Ben confessed one night when we were getting high, up on the roof."

"You got high with Ben?" Chloe was shocked. "He can't get high. He's bad at it."

Sally shrugged. "It was just one of those nights. You'd gone on a date and he was . . . having a hard time with it. So, we started talking."

Chloe swallowed hard. "Why didn't he say anything to me?"

"About getting high? Probably because—"

"Sal." Chloe's tone was sharp.

"Ugh." Sally groaned. "I don't want to be put in the middle of this." She tugged on the lapel of her bathrobe. It was monogrammed with her and Norman's initials. Chloe thought about the bathrobes she and Geoff had received as a gift. They looked almost exactly the same. "Ben didn't say anything because you're best friends. There was a risk in ruining that then, wasn't there?"

Chloe looked down at her engagement ring. "I wish he would have just said something."

"Why?" Sally's face was stern. "It doesn't matter. You're getting *mar*ried. In two weeks. Now is not the time to start playing the what-if game."

Chloe looked down at her glass of water. The bubbles were rising to the surface like champagne.

"Unless . . ." Sally reached over and took her hand. Her voice was gentle. "Unless Ben is the person you want to spend the rest of your life with. If that's the case . . . well, then that's a different story."

Chloe shrugged. "You're forgetting something very important. Ben would have to want that, too."

"He does, Chloe." Sally nodded so hard that her blonde curls bounced. "He does."

# Sixty-eight

Thursday night, June received a visit from holiday carolers. The doorbell rang and, since she was expecting Chloe and Kristine, she threw the door open without even checking the peephole. To her surprise, a cheerful-looking group, decked out in antlers and carrying sleigh bells, was clustered together on her stoop.

There was a time, not too long ago, when June would have shooed them away. This year, though, she drew her faux-fox shrug around her shoulders, rested her hand on the doorframe and listened. The woman in the middle was short and plump, with a bright red nose. A soprano, her voice cut right through to June's heart and filled her with an incredible sense of joy.

When Chloe and Kristine finally arrived, June was still slightly giddy. After all, she'd been serenaded by beautiful music, was just over a week away from her wedding and about to spend the evening with the people who she loved.

Throwing open the door, June held her daughter and her granddaughter tight. They were stomping their feet like horses, freezing in the chilly winter air. It was that time of year where Kristine tried to stay off the roads and took the train in and out of town instead, and June was tempted to make her stay over since Kevin was out of town anyway and it was much too cold for her to take the train back home.

"Come in, come in!" Quickly, June helped them to remove

their coats, hats and mittens. "I'm so happy to see you. I have cocoa brewing on the stove and cookies in the oven." Earlier, she had sent a plate of these away with the carolers.

"Oh, it's so cold." Chloe shivered, slipping off her boots. She stomped her feet on the ground. "I think my feet are wet. No wonder."

Kristine peered at her daughter's feet. "You need to start putting plastic baggies over your socks like I taught you."

June tsked. "Like I taught you," she said, smiling.

Leading them into the kitchen, June poured the cocoa, set out plates and eyed her family in delight. "Well. This will be the last Thursday we will have time to meet, just the three of us, before we're married. Or . . ." June winked at Kristine. "Renewed."

"Yay." Chloe's voice sounded weak from the cold.

Kristine nodded. "Yup."

June clasped her hands in delight. "Well, let's all have a seat," she said, her voice practically shaking with excitement. "Tonight, I have a very special, very meaningful activity for all of us."

Chloe gave her a suspicious look. "Why are you all amped up? What, exactly, will we be doing?"

"We . . ." June beamed. "Are going to write our wedding vows!"

# Sixty-nine

Kristine stared at her mother. "I'm sorry. What?"

The *last* thing Kristine felt like doing was writing her wedding vows.

"Yes!" June clapped her hands, the glare of her diamond practically doing the cha-cha in the light from the kitchen. "That's why I asked you the other day if you'd already written them. If you had, then I would have found something else but I have to write mine, so does Chloe and, of course, so do you."

Bustling toward the long dining room table, June took a seat and Chloe followed. Silently, Kristine joined them.

On the table were three stacks of paper, each paired with a gorgeous fountain pen.

"Those are from me." June smiled. "Look at the inscription."

Kristine squinted at the silver pen. It reminded her of the one she'd gotten Kevin for their anniversary. This one read, *With ye I wed* . . . and the upcoming date of the wedding.

Chloe looked about ready to cry. "Grandma, that's . . . that's really special."

"This is *all* very special," June said. "How many women are lucky enough to get married with their entire family?"

Kristine watched her daughter out of the corner of her eye. Chloe looked pale, withdrawn and exhausted. It was as though the prospect of the wedding was too much to handle. Catching her eye, she gave her a look as though to say, "Are you alright?"

Chloe looked down at the table. Then, putting on a brave smile, she gave a sharp nod.

Sliding on her reading glasses, June reached for her notebook. The glasses were red and white striped. Finally, a pair Kristine did not own.

"Wedding vows." June beamed. "Wedding vows started back in the Roman Empire."

"They were created as a way to keep a marriage together via the honor system, instead of through signed documentation. *The Book of Common Prayer* is the first known location where standard wedding vows appeared, as far back as the 1500s. A variation of these vows are used in traditional ceremonies today. However, many brides and grooms choose to write their own personalized version of vows to share with their spouse to create a stronger level of intimacy at the ceremony."

Closing the book, June gave a serene smile. "Isn't that lovely? So. With that in mind . . ." She slid off her reading glasses. "I think we should all get started."

The dining room was filled with the sound of pens scratching across the page, filling the empty space with strong and solid words of love. Kristine stared down at the paper, her mind blank. So many years ago, she and Kevin had written their own vows and read them to each other at the front of the church. They had been so simple but they'd still gotten choked up. As if they couldn't believe their luck in finding true love. Slowly, she brought the nub of her pen to the paper and waited for a wave of inspiration.

Nothing came.

June and Chloe continued to scratch away. Every few words, June would go so far as to let out a satisfied little grunt. Kristine's page remained blank. Finally, as June gave a happy little sigh and pushed her paper away, Kristine slowly got to her feet.

"Would you mind getting me some water?" Chloe's pen was between her lips. "Since you're up?"

Kristine didn't answer, just held on to the edge of her chair. June looked up. As soon as their eyes met, her mother seemed to know.

"Kristine," she said, leaping to her feet. "Please don't do this. You're making a big mistake."

"Do what? What is she . . . ?" Chloe asked. Her voice trailed off, probably at the look on Kristine's face. "Mom." She laid the pen on the table. "What's wrong?"

Kristine thought of the weeks, months and years in front of her, if she chose to stay with Kevin. The loneliness, the desire for something more. She imagined standing up in the front of the church, next to her mother and daughter, as they made promises they meant to keep.

"I can't do it." Kristine bowed her head. "I can't go through with this. Mom, I'm really sorry. Chloe, I'm really sorry. But I just can't do it."

Kristine dared to look at her daughter. She was staring at her with eyes so much like Kevin's. As the realization of what she was saying dawned, Chloe's face flushed a bright red. "Why?"

"Did Kevin talk to you?" June demanded. "Did he tell you what he told me?"

Kristine stared at June. "What do you mean, what he told you?"

"About the money, the . . ." June's voice trailed off. Turning slightly pale, she said, "I guess not."

After years of complaining about June's constant interference, Kevin had sat down and confided in her about something that Kristine obviously knew nothing about? This made Kristine so angry she could hardly see straight. "Mother, what is it?"

June looked out the window toward Charley's house. The lights were on, twinkling merrily. Turning back to Kristine, she looked physically pained. "I'm sorry," she whispered. "I can't tell you. I . . . I gave Kevin my word."

"Tell me." Kristine's voice was low, dangerous. "*Now.*"

June squared her shoulders. "Kristine, I am sorry. I am. But I made him a promise. And I made a promise to Charley that I would let you all start figuring your lives out for yourself. So, you're going to have to just figure it out."

"Are you *kidding* me?" Kristine was beyond furious. After a lifetime of meddling, June was going to start keeping her nose out of other people's business *now*? Kristine shook her head, a bubble of hysteria rising up in her throat.

Unable to speak, she grabbed her purse and darted toward the front door. Quickly working the locks, she threw open the door and ran out into the dark, icy night, forgetting all about pulling on a coat. Huge mistake. The snow and sleet was pelting down. The wind bit against her skin and she was freezing. But she was not about to go back.

"Mom!" Chloe followed her to the front stoop. Her silhouette was dark against the bright light of the hallway. "Come back here!" she shouted. "Let's talk about this."

June was right behind her, wrapping a shawl around herself. "Kristine! Now, just hold on."

Kristine had to grab the railing to keep from falling down the steps. She found her footing and ran as fast as she could, not caring about the way the sidewalk slipped under her feet. She ran until her heart pounded and sent blood to warm her skin. She ran until the only sound she could hear was the panicked huffs of her breath.

Stepping into the street, she turned right, then left. A cab screeched to a halt, just missing her. The cab driver laid on the horn. "Figure out where you're going, lady," the driver shouted.

Kristine nodded. That was exactly what she was trying to do.

# Seventy

"Holy shit." Chloe stared out into the night. "Holy shit. My mother just went bat-shit crazy." She peered down the block in the direction her mother had gone. The snow and ice blew indoors, landing on her bare skin. She shivered.

"Close the door," June said. "Come back inside."

As they walked back into the parlor, Chloe kept looking back at the door. It was freezing outside and she was obviously worried. "We have to go find her." She turned back to the door, her eyes panicked. "Grandma, I'm going to go."

"Just give her some time, Chloe. She'll come back." June took a seat on the couch. "In my experience," she said, "someone running that fast is doing so for a reason. Your mother has some things to figure out right now."

"Like what?" Chloe demanded. "What the hell is going on?"

"Your parents are having some problems."

"Thank you." Chloe's voice was tinged with sarcasm. "Thank you so much for the news flash. You have truly rocked my world."

"Do not take that tone of voice with me, young lady." June folded her hands and eyed her granddaughter. "Your mother is going through a hard time right now. She's always been somewhat of a timid person. But she's always wanted so much."

June thought back to Kristine watching those travel videos as a child, fantasizing about where she was going to go, knowing full well she was not brave enough to go on her own. Then, June thought back to the first time she'd met Kevin and chuckled.

"Your father was the best thing that could have ever happened to her. He was so loud, so out of control . . . In the beginning, I was so scared he would take over her life." She stared at the colorful lights dotting the Christmas tree. "But he didn't. The only thing he did was love her."

Chloe seemed to be listening closely, her gray eyes intent.

"They were best friends. But . . ." June looked up at the mantel. It was lined with photographs of their family over the years. Her gaze settled on the one of Kristine and Kevin, on a ski trip. Chloe stood next to them, just a little girl. "With him gone all the time now, your mother hasn't had any idea how to handle it. She's lost her anchor. And your mother is the type of person who needs to have an anchor."

June looked out at the window. The snow was coming down hard. She said a silent prayer that Kristine would hurry up and come back home.

"We should call my dad." Chloe shook her head. "Get them on the phone. Just get them to talk to each other."

"We have to let your parents handle it on their own," June said. "They can do it. I know they can."

"What are you talking about?" Chloe practically exploded. "You never let anyone handle anything on their own!"

June looked down at her engagement ring. "A wise man told me that it's time to trust that my family has the capability to figure out their own problems. I've really been trying to do that."

"You decide that now? After something like *that*?" Chloe gestured at the door.

Inside, June's heart was pounding. Yes, she was terrified for Kristine. Out there, alone, on a night as cold as this? It was simply foolish. What was the girl thinking? But June was not going to jump in a cab and troll the city streets until she found her, then drag her back home. She had made a promise to Charley. One that she intended to keep.

"I trust your mother," June said. "And you, Chloe. I trust that you will make the right decisions in your life. I can't do it for you."

Getting up, Chloe paced the room. She walked over to the mantel and rested her hand against the garland. After a long moment, she stared at June. "I need to ask you something."

June swallowed hard. Chloe looked angry. Did she know that June had influenced her engagement? She certainly hoped not. If that were the case, June doubted her granddaughter would ever trust her again.

"My dear," she said, smoothing a couch cushion with a nervous hand, "you can ask me anything."

"Why weren't you nice to my father?" Chloe's eyes blazed. "When he and my mom first got married?"

June started. Goodness. Talk about water under the bridge. "I'm not quite sure what you've heard . . ."

"When my father came to meet you for the first time, you wouldn't even let him stay at your house."

"Well, of course not," June said. "I booked him a room at a lovely hotel. I couldn't have him sneaking down the hallway, trying to get into your mother's—"

Chloe held up her hand. "You didn't approve of him. For years."

"So what?" June would make no apologies for that. "Chloe, he wasn't good enough for your mother." She chuckled, reaching for the afghan draped over the back of the couch and settling it over her shoulders. "But I've learned something over the years—no one would have ever been good enough for my little girl."

"You didn't have to act that way," Chloe said. "You did not have to treat him that way."

June sighed. In Chloe's eyes, she could see so much of Kevin. The hurt and confusion that settled there, in those early years. "I made a mistake. But Chloe, when you are a mother, you'll understand . . ."

"I'm getting a degree that is heavily influenced by psychology." Her voice was cold. "I think I understand how family dynamics work. But Grandma, I do have to say this—maybe the way you felt about my father didn't give my mother the permission to love him the way he deserved to be loved."

June's mouth dropped open. "Whatever are you talking about?"

"I know how it feels." Chloe's forehead was scrunched up. Her eyes appeared to be fixed on the angel on the tree. "There was a time when I thought that, if the stars aligned and something crazy happened, Ben and I would end up together. But you made it very clear you would die if that happened."

June scoffed. "I never said I'd *die*. I just said that . . ." Her voice trailed off. A prickle of fear clawed at her spine. "What, exactly, are you saying?"

"I don't know." Chloe shook her head. "I think I'm in love with Ben. I think I always have been."

A million different thoughts ran through June's head. She stayed silent until she could decipher one of them. Finally, she said, "I understand."

Chloe's eyes widened. "You *do*?"

Reaching down, June indicated the broach she was wearing. "Did you know that your grandfather gave me this?" The pin was shaped like a tiny flower. It was a gorgeous enamel, done in purples, blues and greens. "He gave it to me a few days before we got married. And to be honest, I didn't know if I should even accept it."

"Why?" Chloe breathed.

"Because I was having doubts."

Chloe walked over to the couch. Hesitant, she took a seat. "You've said that. You asked your mom to send you to a nunnery."

June squirmed. "That story isn't exactly true. I made that up because . . ." She thought back to that one terrible night with Eugene. To this day, it still filled her with regret. "Because the real story . . . Well, it hurts my feelings, to be perfectly honest." Swallowing hard, she said, "One night, your grandfather and I made the foolish mistake of having a heart-to-heart, just a few nights before the wedding. And he told me . . ." She squeezed her eyes tightly shut, as though she had the power to stop the words. The memory came anyway, as clear as day. "He told me that he was afraid he wasn't in love with me."

Chloe's mouth dropped open. "He *said* that?"

June fussed with the afghan, then finally set it aside. "I'm afraid so. Your grandfather and I got engaged because of the war, you see. His number came up and we decided to just do it. But because of that one stupid night, when we said all the things that we shouldn't, I spent the first few years of my marriage not knowing if my husband was really in love with me." She shook her head. "Boy, we were so young. What did we know?"

Chloe wrinkled her eyebrow and looked out toward the window. Sleet was pelting the windows in a steady, rhythmic crunch. "What are you trying to say to me?"

"I don't want to meddle," June emphasized, "but I know what you're going through right now. You're jumping into a marriage and you're worried that it might not work out. But love is a funny thing, Chloe. It has a way of working itself out."

Chloe fiddled with a beaded bracelet on her wrist. "You still haven't said a word about Ben. I said I could be in love with him and you just ignored me. Tell me." Her granddaughter's face was troubled. "Why don't you like him?"

*Oh, for heaven's sake. If the girl was going to drag it out of her . . .*

"I don't like Ben," June said, "because in all of those years of friendship, he has never bothered to see you as something more. You're an amazing woman, Chloe. And it hurts me that he can't see it."

Chloe stared, her hands folded tightly in her lap. "That's the only reason you didn't like him?"

"Isn't that enough?" June sniffed. "Honestly. You were standing right in front of him for how many years? How could he possibly be dumb enough not to see it?"

"I think I'm going to go," Chloe said, getting to her feet. The poor thing looked dazed. Exhausted, really. "This day has been a little too much for me."

June also got to her feet, her muscles aching. The tension of the day had been too much for her, as well. "Alright." Finding her purse, she unearthed a twenty. "Take a cab. Tell him to drive slow. The roads are slick." She looked at the window, trying to fight back the fear in her heart. "Considering your mother is out there, most likely freezing to death, I want to know that at least one of you made it home alive."

Chloe walked over to June and collapsed in her arms. As they held each other, June kissed the top of her granddaughter's head. "Everything will be just fine," she whispered. "Everything's going to be alright."

The words echoed in her ear as June stood at the front window, watching as her granddaughter hailed a cab, but June wasn't certain she believed them. The moment the taillights faded into the night, she walked over to the phone and dialed up Charley. He was at his house, waiting for her night with the girls to come to an end.

"Come on over," June said, sinking into the sofa, "but be warned. I have an unfortunate feeling that everything is about to fall apart."

# Seventy-one

After leaving her mother's house, Kristine hailed a cab. They sat at the curb for a long moment as Kristine debated. Should she?

Giving the address, she leaned back in the seat and closed her eyes. Heat blasted out from the vents in the front seat and she shivered, wondering if she would ever be warm again. Her heart was aching, her mind torn in too many directions.

Kristine couldn't believe what she'd done. She could only imagine the look on Kevin's face when he got her message and how much it would hurt him. Twenty-five years of expectations sinking to the bottom of the sea. But there were too many problems, too many things that a vow renewal ceremony wouldn't fix.

They didn't *talk*. Not anymore. Why did June, of all people, know some deep, dark secret about their marriage that Kristine didn't even know? Something to do with money, which explained Kevin's intense behavior over the past few years. She would call their financial advisor first thing in the morning and find out.

The thought was so humiliating. The fact that she would have to pick up the phone and explain to someone they'd worked with for years that she had no idea what was going on. Still, that would be the least of the embarrassment they'd have to face. As soon as word got out about the cancelled vow renewal, everyone would know they'd failed. She wondered what people would think. She wondered if they'd say, "We can't believe it, they were so in love" or, "Yeah. Saw that one coming a mile away."

Kristine had always done that. When she heard of a marriage ending, she'd quantify it in her mind, thinking, "Oh, that makes sense because . . ." Or, her reaction had been the opposite, too. Completely taken off guard. Even though it didn't matter anymore, she really hoped that people were surprised when they heard the news about her and Kevin. Otherwise, what had they been doing for all those years?

"Ma'am?" the cab driver said. The windshield wipers were moving back and forth, making a rhythmic sound against the snow. "We're here."

Kristine opened her eyes. She gazed at the large building. The moment of truth. Could she really do this?

Fumbling with her purse, she paid the driver and opened the door. Her clothes were wet and for a brief moment, she'd gotten used to being comfortable and warm. The chill of the wind hit her, even harder than before. She really didn't know what she was doing here.

Navigating the ice on the sidewalk, she looked up. It was hard to see through the thick white flakes that were falling in earnest. But in a vague outline against the sky, she took in the sight of the church where she and Kevin had gotten married.

Kristine hovered in the entryway, staring up at the nave, letting the sudden warmth engulf her. It had been years since she stepped in this church, but the faint smell of candle wax and incense took her right back to her wedding day. She'd been terrified at the idea of walking down the aisle, all eyes on her. If it wasn't for Kevin, holding her hands the way he had, she might have just passed out at the altar.

Taking a few tentative steps forwards, she remembered the way the red carpeting had swallowed the sound of her footsteps and the way the pipes of the organ gleamed overhead. On that day, light had shined like a beacon through the stained glass windows but tonight, with the snow and the darkness, the colors seemed old and faded. Sliding into the hard wooden bench in the back, she bowed her head.

Freeze-frames of her and Kevin clicked through her mind. The moment they'd met, the kiss they'd shared after welcoming Chloe into the world, even some random day when they'd bickered over what security system to buy for their home. There was so much history between them, it was almost impossible to sort out. It was even harder to think of letting it all go.

Opening her eyes, Kristine stared at the place at the altar where they had pledged eternity to each other. She ached for the innocent girl she'd once been. So idealistic, so sure that life and love would give her everything she'd ever wanted. She was marrying the man of her dreams! What could go wrong?

Kristine waited for the inevitable barrage of tears. To her surprise, they didn't come. Instead, her heart was filled with an icy calm, like the sea after a storm. She bowed her head. Reaching down, she slid off her engagement, vow renewal and wedding rings. Snapping open her pocketbook, she dropped them inside like loose change.

"Do you have everything you need?" June asked.

Kristine had arrived back on her doorstep half an hour later, pale and removed. June had brought her inside, drawn her a hot bath and made her a strong drink. It did not escape her notice that Kristine was not wearing her wedding rings.

"I'm fine." Kristine's voice was quiet. "Thank you." She was buried in the bubbles of the bathtub, her head against the blow-up pillow. The delicate skin around her neck was flushed a bright red and finally, she seemed to have stopped shivering.

June nodded. "In case there's any confusion about the matter, you're welcome to stay here," she said. "As long as you need. Until you figure things out."

"I know." Kristine gave her a weak smile. "That's why I'm here."

Shutting the door gently behind her, June walked down the stairs and into the parlor. Charley was sitting in a straight-backed chair with a worried expression on his face. As she walked in, he stood up, as he did every time she walked into a room. She felt a wave of appreciation for this wonderful man. Then, her eyes filled with tears.

"June." Charley pulled her into his strong arms. "Is she alright?"

"No." Impatiently, June wiped at her eyes. "She left him. The man who I begged her not to marry all those years ago, she up and left him. The man who . . ." Her voice caught in her throat. She sank down on the couch, letting her face fall into her hands. Looking up at Charley, she said, "The man who loves her more than anything in the world."

Laying his hand on her back, Charley held her tight. In the safety of his arms, June cried as if the heartbreak were her own.

# Seventy-two

The next day, Chloe took her last exam, had her interview with the children's hospital and went to June's. Letting herself in through the front door, she called up the stairs, "Grandma, are you home?" The Christmas tree was lit and the lights on the tree were dancing but the house was quiet.

"She's at Charley's," Chloe heard from upstairs. "But I'm here."

Chloe gripped the railing, relieved. In between breaks, she had tried to call her mother again and again, but the phone went straight to voicemail. Racing up the steps, she burst into the guest bedroom. Kristine was lying in bed, wrapped in at least five different blankets, listlessly reading a book on Venice.

Perching on the edge of the bed, Chloe felt those familiar springs dip beneath her weight. When she was a child, she used to bounce up and down on this bed. June had probably had the same mattress since the sixties. "Mom, you didn't call me back. I was worried."

"I'm sorry." Kristine slid off her reading glasses and rubbed her eyes. They were vaguely bloodshot and Chloe wondered if she'd even slept. "I thought June texted you that I was here."

"She did. That's why I came." Chloe swallowed hard. "No vow renewals for you and Dad? For sure?"

Kristine didn't answer. She turned a page in the book, studying the pictures. Chloe reached out and took it from her, like taking a toy from Mary Beth.

"Look at me. Are you guys getting . . ." Chloe took a deep breath then forced herself to say the word. "Divorced?"

Kristine fixed her eyes at a point on the wall. Blinking, she said, "Maybe. I don't know."

"Mom, you have to talk to him." Chloe's heart was breaking for her father. He'd been calling her nonstop since that morning, after he'd talked to her mother. Yes, he worked too hard. Yes, he was gone all the time. But he loved his family. He was desperate to figure out what was going on and how to fix it. "He's flying home right now. He'll be here all week, for the wedding. You have to talk to him."

"I will," her mother said. "Just not yet."

"Mom, you have to. You have to work this—"

"We've tried to work it out," her mother said. "I've told him exactly how I feel, I've told him what needs to change." She shook her head. "People don't change, though, Chloe. Relationships just do."

Chloe bit her lip. That was true. In the beginning, her relationship with Geoff had been filled with promise. That changed as time went on and slowly, she realized he was not the right fit. Maybe that's what had happened with her parents, too. The thought made her feel as though she was being torn in two.

"I'm sorry." Kristine took Chloe's hand. "I'm sorry we're doing this now, when you're getting married, when June's getting married. But," she let out a little sigh, "in spite of appearances, it *is* possible to have a long, healthy and happy marriage. You and Geoff will be able to do that. I know you will."

"No," Chloe said. "Actually, I don't think we would have been able to do that. Which is why . . ." She took a deep breath and held up her left hand. "I called off the engagement."

. . .

Breaking off her engagement was one of the most surreal experiences of Chloe's life.

As she walked through the doors of Geoff's building, the attendant said, "Hello, Miss," just like always. This time, though, Chloe noticed things she hadn't seen before. A small mole next to his ear, the way the strap on his hat bit into the skin on his neck, the tiny dent on his brass name tag.

Passing through the lobby, she noticed the sound of her boots scuffing across the floor. The large potted plant placed under the bright white buttons of the elevator and the fact that the fake leaves were perfectly dusted. That, even though the elevator arrived quickly, the clicks up to the fifty-second floor seemed slow and precise.

Time went back to normal when Geoff opened the door. His bright green eyes looked sleepy and confused. "Everything all right?" He was dressed in a pair of striped pajamas, no ascot in sight.

"I'd . . . I'd like to talk for a minute."

Geoff looked at his watch. He nodded and moved aside, then sat next to her on the couch. They studied each other for a long moment, tension thick in the room.

"Your messages yesterday." The words came out sounding much shorter than she'd planned. "They were awful. Why?"

Geoff rubbed his hand against his cheek. Dropping it with a thud, he said, "I apologize. I was frustrated I couldn't get ahold of you but it all worked out. Miriam took Mary Beth for the afternoon."

"Yeah." Chloe nodded. "Which is great. But . . . Geoff. I can't help but notice. Things have been different between us, ever since she's come back."

Geoff turned to her. There was a crease in the middle of his forehead and his green eyes were cautious. "Why are you so threatened by her?"

"I'm not threatened," Chloe said, meaning it. "In fact, I think it's good that she came back when she did." Taking a deep breath, she reached into her coat pocket and placed the box with the engagement ring on the coffee table. "I'm sorry."

Geoff's eyes darted from the box to her naked ring finger, then back to the blue box. He made a sputtering sound before saying, "Now, hold on. What is this all about? I'm not about to let Miriam come back and ruin—"

"It's not about her," Chloe said, her voice quiet. "It's about me." With a pang, she thought back to the first moment she'd laid eyes on Geoff, speaking to her school. The way she'd been so impressed by him, so in awe. "Our relationship . . . it's not going to work."

"All because of a few messages?" he demanded.

A picture of Ben's laughing blue eyes danced through her head.

"It's not the messages," Chloe said. "Or the fact that you expected me to drop everything to take care of your child or that your ex-wife is in town and that you deserve the chance to put your family back together." She thought back to the beginning of their relationship. The way Geoff had encouraged her to get out and enjoy her life. "We were right for each other, for a while," she said. "But not forever."

Geoff sat in silence with his shoulders slumped. His hair was neatly gelled into place, his profile strong and handsome. She remembered how they'd first met, him singing his heart out in his office, wearing just those green sweatpants. If her heart wasn't aching, she might have smiled at the memory.

Reaching over, she touched his knee. "I'm so sorry."

He shook his head. "No, I . . . You're right. I . . . ." Putting his face in his hands, he whispered, "I think I still have feelings for her." He looked at Chloe, his face stricken with guilt.

At his words, Chloe's eyes filled with tears.

Geoff's face fell. "No, please don't cry. I would have married you—"

"No, no. It's . . ." Letting out a shaky breath, she looked out at the skyline of Chicago. There were so many windows, so many lights, so many people. It broke her heart to think that she and Geoff had found each other, shared something special and almost turned it into something so wrong.

Chloe thought of her wedding dress, that moment she'd stood in front of the mirror. She tried to imagine walking down the aisle, saying "I do" to Geoff but she couldn't see it. Not at all.

"We almost made a huge mistake," she said. "For two people who are so smart, I can't believe we almost did something so stupid."

Geoff stared at his hands for a long moment. Then, he reached over and pulled her in tight. The relief coursing through them was palpable.

# Seventy-three

Kristine stared at her daughter. "You did *what*?"

Chloe chewed on her upper lip. "It's for the best. You know it. I know it . . ." She paused for a moment, then picked at the soft white yarn of a blanket. "You've only been asking me to postpone the darn thing from the beginning."

Leaping up off the bed, Kristine paced back and forth. Yes, she'd worried that Chloe's engagement happened too fast. But her daughter was in love with him. She didn't want her to throw that all away just because her parents had set a bad example.

"Call him back." Kristine turned to face her. "You saw me panic last night, you got nervous, it scared you and—"

"*Mom*. This is not about you! Geez, between you and Grandma," Chloe muttered, shaking her body as though shaking off an annoyance, "it's a wonder I can get a thought in for myself."

Kristine stared at her in surprise. *Where was this coming from?*

"In case you're wondering," Chloe said, "I didn't break off my engagement because of what's going on with you and Dad. I broke it off because Geoff and I are not right for each other. He wants his family back together. I know he does. It's going to be hard and painful and all of those things but they deserve a chance to try again. I'm not going to stand in the way of that."

Kristine took a cautious step toward her daughter. "Honey, Geoff adores you. I've never seen anyone treat you so . . ."

"Mom." Chloe grabbed a pillow as though choking it. "*Stop*." Dropping the pillow, she said, "Yes, he treated me well. Which was nice." At the memory, an affectionate smile lit up her face. "But I don't love him."

Kristine paused. "You don't?" She wrinkled up her forehead, trying to process this. "I'm sorry, but . . . for some crazy reason, I thought you did."

Chloe smiled, ducking her head. "Yeah. People do kinda tend to get that impression, when you say yes to a proposal. I just . . . got caught up, you know? From the first moment I saw him, I had the biggest crush on him. Then, when he was interested in me and we started dating and it was so much fun . . ." She took a breath. "Geoff could have given me a lot. But we never would have had the one thing that really matters—love."

Kristine stared at her daughter in surprise. After years of creating milestones, thinking that Chloe wouldn't really be an adult until she finished school, got a job or got married, her daughter had grown up right in front of her.

"Mom." Chloe rolled her eyes, exasperated. "Seriously. You don't have to cry."

"I'm not. I haven't been cry . . ." Kristine brought her hands to her cheeks. Sure enough, they were damp to the touch. Getting down on one knee, she pulled her daughter into her arms.

# Seventy-four

For all of her bravado, Chloe's stomach felt like it was filled with thorns when it came time to tell her grandmother that she would not be sharing the wedding. They sat at the dining room table, the same one where they had spent so many Thursday nights. The words came out very clean and practical, then Chloe burst into tears.

June absorbed the information quietly, her eyes shutting only briefly with pain.

"I'm sorry, Grandma." Chloe reached out and touched her arm. "I know how important this day is to you. I know that you wanted to share it with me and Mom. But I can't marry Geoff. I'm in love with Ben. I always have been."

June looked down at the table.

"I wanted to go through with it," Chloe pleaded, grabbing her hands. "I almost did it because . . . because I wanted to make you happy."

"That's the most foolish thing I have ever heard," June snapped. "I thought you were smart."

Chloe made a face. "Smart, maybe. Brave? No. I just couldn't marry a man I didn't love."

"Well. Of course not." Placing her chin in her hand, June gazed off into the backyard. The garden was covered with clean white snow. "Out of curiosity, would being with Ben make you happy?"

At the idea, an odd picture flashed through Chloe's mind. That moment when she and Ben were both standing on the ice and he told her things between them would never be the same. "Yes," she said. "Nothing could make me happier. But . . ." She shook her head. "That will never happen."

"Why?" June said. "If you feel this way about this young man . . ."

"Grandma, I know we haven't done those dance lessons quite yet," Chloe said, patting her hand, "but I hear it takes two to tango."

Shaking her head, June gave a little sigh. "Well. I got my wish. This wedding certainly is going to be the biggest thing Chicago has ever seen. Think of the scandal. I can see the headline in the society pages now: *Here Comes the Bride. Maybe.*"

Chloe bit her lip. "Is it bad that I want to laugh?"

June gave her a stern look. "I would not recommend it. Not at this moment in time."

Chloe fiddled with the corner of a red placemat. It was woven through with silver sparkles. "Do you think you'll ever forgive me?"

"Darling girl," June said. "This is *your* life. I want the best for you. That is all that I have ever wanted and that I ever will want. Everything else is just noise."

Later that night, June sat in the chair in Charley's den, staring at the fire burning in the fireplace. More snow was blowing outside and tiny pellets of ice tapped at the window. She was perfectly cozy, wrapped in a white blanket lined with faux fur, but her heart was troubled. So much had gone wrong with Kristine and Chloe. June couldn't help but think that, in some way, it was all her fault.

Charley walked into the room, carefully balancing a tray. On it sat two mugs of hot, milky tea and a plate of biscotti. Jumping to her feet, June went to help him.

"You sit back down this instant," Charley told her, setting the tray on the table between them. "Let someone do something for you for a change."

June sat, gratefully accepting the warm cup. The heat helped soothe the arthritic ache that seemed to affect her hands when she wasn't using them every day, out in the garden.

"Now." Charley settled into the chair across from her. "I intend to say something to you and I don't want you to get angry."

June sighed. "Just say it."

"It seems to me . . ." Charley picked up his mug of tea and took a thoughtful sip. "It seems to me that I was wrong."

June froze. "What?"

"I was wrong, June. I thought that your meddling was causing trouble but it was doing just the opposite. It was keeping your family together."

Charley pulled out the drawer on the table between them. Taking out a deck of playing cards, he shuffled with cool precision. Then he dealt them out a game of gin.

"Charley, you don't have to say that." June sighed. It had been so foolish to suggest to Rue that her grandson should propose to Chloe. What a mess that had turned out to be. "It turns out you were right."

"I most certainly was not." Charley was wearing a light blue sweater and a plaid sweater vest. As he said all this, June couldn't help but notice that his eyes were an even brighter blue than usual. "Perhaps some of your suggestions were ill-guided, but your heart was in the right place."

June didn't answer, just picked up his discard.

"At the moment, your family appears to be falling apart." Charley's voice was quiet. "I doubt it's a coincidence. You need to step in."

"Absolutely not." June rearranged her cards. "You told me very clearly that I need to let my family make their own decisions and their own mistakes."

Charley took a sip of tea. "Well," he chuckled, "they've certainly done that. Now, it seems to me that they need some guidance on how to put everything back together."

June considered that. Suddenly, she blinked. The hand she was holding was very heavy on hearts.

"It seems like that Ben is a nice kid," Charley said, his voice thoughtful. "Chloe sure did seem to brighten when she brought him around here."

June looked at him in surprise. "When on earth did you meet Ben?"

"Oh . . ." Charley took a bite of biscotti. "It seems like I might have seen him around here once or twice."

For heaven's sake. Ben hadn't been to this house in . . . at least a year, when he and Chloe stopped by after biking along the lake. She and Charley hadn't even been speaking yet.

"Charley Montgomery," June said, starting to laugh. "How long, exactly, have you been watching me?"

He smiled. "Oh, I'd guess just about the same amount of time you've been watching me."

Goodness, she loved this man. June pressed her lips together to hide a tiny smile. Selecting a piece of biscotti, she dipped it into her tea.

Charley reached out and put his warm hand over hers. "Lead your family, June," he said. "I was wrong to tell you otherwise."

June drew the next card in the deck. The Queen of Hearts, exactly the card that she needed. Laying down her hand, she said, "Ha! I win."

"Well, look at that," he said. "An entire hand of hearts. If that's not a sign, I don't know what is."

June looked down at the cards, then back up at him. "Why, Charley Montgomery." She shook her finger at him. "Don't you think for one moment that I don't know that you stacked that deck."

# Seventy-five

Picking up the phone, June took a deep breath. Her grand-daughter answered on the first ring.

"So," June said, without saying hello. "I've been thinking . . ."

"That you're going to back out, too?" Chloe said.

Hmmph. For someone who just called off a wedding, her granddaughter certainly sounded chipper.

"No," June said, her voice stern. After an appropriate moment of weighted silence, she said, "But I've been thinking. Perhaps you should still bring a date to my wedding. It's too late to cancel the extra plate."

"Oh." By the tone of her voice, Chloe was not expecting that. "I don't know who I could . . ."

"I was thinking you should bring Ben," June said. "You know, I have always thought he was a very nice young man."

There was silence on the other end of the receiver. June stared out at her garden, noticing that the frosted branches looked beautiful against the sky. Finally, she heard Chloe sigh. "Grandma," she said, "I know exactly what it is that you're doing."

"Good." She sniffed. "So do I."

June hung up. Staring at the receiver, she heard the pages of a newspaper rattle, then a soft chuckle. Charley snapped his paper shut and stood up.

"Ah, June," he said, walking over and kissing her on the head. "You might just teach me a few things yet."

. . .

Ben answered the door in his pajamas. His hair was a rumpled mess, as always. So was his bright green T-shirt, which Chloe found to be ridiculously immature.

"What are you doing here?" he asked, surprised.

Chloe swept past him and into his apartment. The shades were drawn and the room was dark. The whole place smelled like Ben.

Turning to face him, she said, "I want you to know that I think your behavior over my engagement was deplorable."

"*My* behavior?" His eyes flashed dangerously.

"I appreciated your gift. But seriously?" She glared at him. "You couldn't even be bothered to come to my engagement party?"

"I don't show up to farces." Ben rubbed his nose. He widened his eyes just slightly, as though trying to wake up.

"Oh, okay. But you'll come to an ice-skating rink?" She rolled her eyes. "To tell me that we can't be friends anymore?"

Ben ran his hands through his hair. It stood up everywhere, like he'd stuck his finger in a light socket. "I didn't say we couldn't be friends anymore. I just told you that things couldn't stay the same."

"You know what?" She put her hands on her hips. "You need to get a haircut."

"What?" He gave a half-laugh.

"And you need to stop being so ridiculously immature," she said. "Because unlike you, I want our friendship to continue." A flash of anger zapped through her heart as she remembered their walk back from the restaurant. The way Ben had kissed her at the door.

"What do you mean, immature?" he demanded.

Chloe glared at him. "Remember our date? The one you used to test the waters?"

Ben opened his mouth as though to speak but closed it just as quickly.

"Maybe my engagement was a farce." She took a step closer to him. "But at least it was honest. I went after what I wanted instead of cowering in the corner. Who would have guessed that a Casanova like you could have been such a chicken?"

Ben looked pained. "Chloe, I—"

"I came over here to tell you that I broke off my engagement." She held up her left hand, as though to prove it. He stared at her finger, his eyes wide. "Maybe I'll have to wait the rest of my life for the person I'm supposed to be with but that's fine. I'll wait. I don't care how long it takes."

The air in the room seemed to crackle between them. "Good," he said, letting out a breath. "I am so glad to hear you say that."

"Well, *great.*" Chloe's voice dripped with sarcasm. "Thanks so much for the support."

"Geoff with a G wasn't right for you," he said. "You would have been miserable."

"Then it all worked out." Chloe gave a little shrug. "My family still loves me and now, maybe I have my best friend back."

"Definitely." Ben's eyes sparkled. "I . . ."

"You what?" Chloe asked. They stood there in silence for a moment, watching each other. Finally, she said, "I feel like I'm waiting for something, here. Like an apology."

"I'm sorry," he said, running his hands through his hair. "I was jealous. I didn't want to lose you to that guy."

"To be honest," she told him. "I didn't see you fight so hard to keep me." Walking toward the door, she reached for the handle. "By the way, you better not be doing anything on December 27th."

Chloe already knew that he was. Sally had told her that Ben was planning to go out to Colorado and stay with his brother during the wedding. He said it would have been "physically impossible for him to stay in town and not show up to object."

"Actually," Ben said, "I was planning on visiting my brother."

"Cancel it," Chloe said. "You're coming with me to the wedding." At the sudden silence in the room, she turned to look at him. "I'm sorry, but you owe me."

"I know." Ben nodded. "I'm just . . . I'm really happy that you asked."

# Seventy-six

It was tradition for Chloe, June, Kristine and Kevin to attend church together on Christmas Eve. June always marched down the aisle with her head held high, decked out in the most dramatic red suit she could find. She sang the holy carols loud and off-key and each year, ended the evening with a full heart.

Except for this year.

Even though it was the first Christmas with Charley by her side, June felt as though her family had gotten smaller. That afternoon, Kevin called the house and asked if he could come to the ceremony with them. Kristine held up her hand before June could even ask the question. "No." Her face was drawn. "Tell him I'm sorry, but I really need this time."

June had been tempted to ignore her daughter's wishes. To tell Kevin he was always welcome as a member of her family. But she didn't dare. If there was any hope of the two reconciling, it was clearly going to have to be at her daughter's pace.

Still, June's heart ached at the thought of leaving her son-in-law all alone on Christmas. Yes, he had missed more than one holiday in the past, thanks to a delayed flight or the typical travel nonsense, but to actually be in town and denied the opportunity to be with his wife and daughter? That just broke June's heart.

After church, June laid out her usual spread of Christmas Eve goodies on the dining room table. Meatballs from the corner deli, served in a sweet sauce. Sugar cookies from that bakery down the street. A bowl of holiday popcorn, fresh and crunchy from Garrett's. Crackers and cheese, chilled cocktail shrimp and, for health, a veggie tray.

Once the snacks were set out, she turned on Christmas music. Settling into her chair in the parlor, she watched Kristine, Chloe and Charley sip on mulled wine and admire the holiday decorations.

"It's so festive in here," Kristine said, her voice quiet.

"I know. I've always loved those stockings," Chloe said. Getting up from her chair, she walked over to touch them. They were crushed red velvet with iron-on patches of Santa and his elves in the workshop. Each family member's name was neatly embroidered at the top. This year, June had ordered one for Charley.

As Chloe touched her father's stocking, she gave June a questioning look. June sniffed, lifting her chin. "Your father is a member of this family, whether everyone in this room believes it or not."

Kristine sighed. She looked out the window as though contemplating an escape.

"Don't even think about it," June told her. "Or I'll fill your stocking with coal."

Kristine shook her head and gave a tiny smile.

Reaching for a meatball from her tiny hors d'oeuvre plate, June wondered if this would be the last year they would uphold their Christmas Eve tradition. Charley had a place in Naples that he migrated to when the snow hit. He mentioned that it might be nice to spend the winters down there, together.

The idea of wintering in Florida was certainly something to consider. June had never dreamed she'd live anywhere other than Chicago, but Charley made Naples sound so lovely. It might be nice to get vitamin C from fresh oranges, learn more about that frustrating game of golf and, of course, start a tropical garden. But if Kristine did not resolve her marital problems, June couldn't leave her all alone.

"Are you excited about our wedding, my love?" Charley was sitting next to her on the couch, his feet up on the ottoman and his hands wrapped around a mug of mulled wine. Placing it on a reindeer coaster, he put a comforting arm around June.

June thought for a moment. "I'm disappointed," she said simply.

Kristine ducked her head and looked at Chloe, who was staring down at her hands.

"Grandma, I'm sorry." The poor girl said this for what very well could have been the hundredth time. "I know that you're disappointed that I'm not going to marry—"

"No, no, no." June held up her hand. The left one, of course, so that her new diamond ring could sparkle. "That is not what I mean." She took a deep breath. "I am simply disappointed that I will be standing up at the altar, without my family by my side. The truth is, it takes a family to make a marriage work. And as the leader of this family, I should have stepped in a long time ago."

Charley gave a slight nod.

June turned to her granddaughter. "I am delighted you are not going to marry Geoff. You didn't love him and marriage is hard enough if you don't have that to hold you together. And as for you, Kristine . . ."

She lifted her pretty blue eyes. "Yes?"

June sniffed. "I think it is absolutely shameful that you will not be standing up there at that altar with me."

"Mother," she protested. "I am not going to talk about—"

"Regardless." June waved her hand, as though to brush away the topic. "I am most certainly looking forward to my wedding. But I will not sit here and say that I can walk down the aisle in good conscience, knowing that my house isn't resolved."

"You can, Grandma," Chloe said. "Mom and I are going to be just fine."

Pointedly, June looked at Kevin's stocking hanging up on the mantel. "Well. It's not you and your mother who I'm worried about."

# Seventy-seven

The next morning, Chloe woke up at the crack of dawn. She'd done this every Christmas morning, as soon as she understood the concept of Santa. "It's like you'd prop your eyes open with toothpicks or something," her dad always said. "The moment the sun was up, so were you. It was impressive."

This morning, it didn't feel impressive. She would much rather be asleep. But the noise in her head was impossible to sleep through.

Sliding out of bed, she pulled open the curtain and looked outside. The window was covered in etched patterns of frost. A new layer of snow had fallen, making the world look fresh and bright. Pulling on her coat, scarf and gloves, she sneaked out of the house and headed for the train.

When Chloe let herself into her childhood home, it was still. Everything was in place, except for an empty container of black olives that was sitting on the counter. Her heart ached thinking of her father sitting alone on Christmas Eve. She'd texted him to see if he wanted her to come over last night, but he'd said, "No, honey. Christmas Eve is important to your mother. Stay with her."

Quiet as a mouse, she threw out the jar of olives and found the coffee. Once the pot was gurgling, she took off her coat and sat on the couch. It took her a moment to realize that the reason her parents' house didn't feel like Christmas was that, for the first time she could remember, there were no decorations. Not a tree, not a garland, not anything.

Wrapping herself up in a blanket on the couch, she closed her eyes. Memories started flashing through her mind and she thought back to a Christmas in the third grade. Her Brownie troop sent each of the girls home with gingerbread kits for a gingerbread-making competition. Her parents got super into it, buying more candy at the drugstore than could possibly fit on the house. Gumdrops, cinnamon disks, bricks of chocolate for the roof . . . Her father kept stealing caramels and popping them into his mouth and her mother kept slapping his hand. Eventually, this simple interaction evolved into a full-out food fight, with pieces of candy and hunks of frosting flying across the kitchen like missiles.

Chloe fell asleep smiling, thinking of the moment her father had pelted both her and her mother with gumdrops, the three of them laughing hysterically.


"Hey." Chloe felt someone tugging at her toe. Opening her eyes, she saw her father standing over her. "What are you doing here?" His face was split into a smile.

Chloe yawned, sitting up. There was a crick in her neck. "What do you mean, what am I doing here?" She rubbed her eyes. "I'm not letting you spend Christmas alone."

The look on her father's face was more than worth skipping June's homemade Christmas brunch. "Thank you," he said, clearing his throat. "Then let's go ahead and get some breakfast on the table."

As they whipped up eggs and bacon, she told her father all about the internship she had waiting for her at the hospital. They had called on Christmas Eve, just before closing up for the holidays.

"It's awesome," she said. "It starts in February and could lead to really big things. I'm so excited."

"I'm so proud of you," Kevin said, ruffling her hair and setting the plates on the table. "I don't get a chance to tell you that enough. And, I've gotta say . . ." He shook his head, his tone suddenly serious. "I'm glad you called off your part in the wedding."

"You are?" She took a seat. "How come?"

"It was too fast," her father said. "There's such a thing as love at first sight but I got the feeling you just did it because it was easy. And typically, you don't do anything that's easy."

"I got swept up." She thought about those early days when Geoff would talk her into skipping out on class to study with him in his office. "I really liked him. I still like him. But I just don't love him. You know? I've felt this huge sense of relief, ever since I called it off."

"What about the kid?" Kevin set glasses of juice in front of their plates. "Are you going to miss her?"

Chloe felt sad, thinking about Mary Beth's pouty little face. "Desperately. I mean, I kept thinking that I needed more time. To get to know her, to spend time with her. But, in the end . . ." She sighed, thinking about the reality of the situation. "It was good that she never really got attached to me."

Kevin looked surprised. "Really? Little kids flock to you."

"Not this one." She shook her head. "Things happen for a reason, I guess and . . ." She thought for a moment. "Maybe it's silly but I'm kinda hoping that Geoff and his ex-wife patch things up. You should have seen his face when she came back to town." She laughed, remembering that night at the restaurant. Geoff had been white as a sheet. "It'll be interesting to see what happens. Mary Beth deserves to have her mother. I think that's the best-case scenario, on a developmental level."

Kevin grinned. "It's good to hear you talking like you again."

"What do you mean?" She smeared jam onto her toast and

took a bite. Her dad hadn't been shy with the butter. It was rich and sweet in her mouth.

"You just weren't acting like yourself." He popped a piece of bacon in his mouth. "You didn't care about school, you got caught up in all that wedding stuff . . ."

"I still cared about school. But Geoff taught me to relax, to slow down." She grinned, thinking of the day he'd said that to her. The day she'd first seen him in those silly green sweatpants. "Yes, things have still been crazy busy but I feel like I'm finally taking time to look around, you know? To see the things that matter." She let out a breath, thinking of all the fun times with Ben she'd taken for granted. "Maybe I don't have a sparkly diamond anymore, but at least I have a life."

Kevin nodded. "I feel a little responsible for all that. For setting a bad example."

"You sound like Mom," Chloe groaned. Reaching across the table, she grabbed his hand. "Whatever happens between you two," she said, trying to keep the tremor out of her voice, "you'll still be my dad. Obviously."

For the second time that morning, she could swear her father choked up. Jumping to his feet, he picked up their dirty plates and rinsed them in the sink. After loading them into the dishwasher, he said, "I love you, too, Chloe. You and your mother." He let out a sigh. "And June."

"It's not too late." Chloe bit her thumbnail. Her mother had seemed so sad last night, so lost. "To talk to her."

Kevin wiped his hands on the kitchen towel. "Oh, I'm gonna do more than that."

"What do you mean?" Chloe sat up straight.

Kevin closed the dishwasher and leaned against the counter.

"Well . . ." He smiled. "Let's just say I've still got a little something up my sleeve."

# Seventy-eight

That morning, after the dishes from the breakfast brunch were put away, June looked at her watch. "My, my," she said. "Is it that time already?"

"What time is that, Mom?" Kristine was reading a book by the fire, her legs tucked up underneath her. She looked so cozy that June almost hated to disturb her. Almost.

"I simply . . ." June's hands fluttered. "I still have one Christmas wish that hasn't been met."

Charley eyed her over the top of his glasses. "Oh?"

June reached over and clasped his hand. "Yes. I would love to do some private shopping at The Places You'll Go. Since Bernice and Rose are going to step in as bridal matrons, as I will be all alone at the altar . . ." She shot her best wounded look at Kristine. "I need to get them a thank-you present."

Kristine slid a bookmark into her book and set it on the table. "Of course." She stretched and looked out at the obviously chilly day. "Did you want to go now?"

June looked at her watch. "Yes. I think now sounds like a great idea."

When Kristine pulled the car into her parking space in the alley, it took some fussing to get everybody out. She watched with affection as Charley got out first, testing to see whether or not the sidewalk was slick, before taking June's hand and helping her. The two clung to each other, shivering, as Kristine unlocked the store.

When they walked in, she stopped in surprise. The place smelled like cranberries and cinnamon. Kristine wondered if someone had left a candle or a potpourri burner on. Or maybe, Annie had decided to ignore the holiday altogether and just do some work. "Hello?" she called. "Is someone here?"

"Hi, Mom," Chloe called. "Merry Christmas!"

*Chloe! What was she doing here?* Kristine had assumed her daughter had gone to Kevin's that morning. Instead, she must have been here, putting together some sort of a holiday surprise.

"You tricked me." Kristine turned and shook a finger at June. "I knew that the sudden urge to shop for presents was a little suspicious."

June gave a tight little smile. "Yes," she said. "Perhaps I did. Now, go see."

"Mom?" Chloe called again.

Shaking her head at their exploits, she followed the direction of her daughter's voice. She wondered what type of present they had pulled off for the store. Maybe it was . . .

Kristine stopped. Her daughter was standing next to the interior door that led to the attic upstairs. "Merry Christmas." Chloe was beaming, her eyes bright and dancing. "Go on up."

"To the attic?" Kristine said. "I don't know if it's safe . . ."

"Trust me," Chloe said. "You'll be just fine."

June nodded. "We'll be right here if you need us."

After a moment's hesitation, Kristine walked up the stairs, intrigued. The smell of cranberry and cinnamon got stronger. She pushed open the door and stared in surprise.

# Seventy-nine

The attic above her store had been transformed into an expansive loft. Hardwood floors from the turn of the century gleamed below whitewashed walls and exposed brick accents. Rows of windows along the far wall looked out over Lincoln Park, the treetops sparkling with snow.

Kevin stood in the center of the room, his hands in his pockets. He was wearing a cream-colored sweater with wooden buttons and a pair of well-fitted khakis. "Merry Christmas," he said, his voice echoing across the empty room.

Kristine stared at him, then looked back toward the door. Was this the surprise? To arrange a meeting with her and Kevin? She wasn't ready to talk to him yet, wasn't ready to face him. There was still too much to think about, to figure out.

Leave it to June to put her in this position.

"I'm sorry," she said, starting to back toward the door. "I'm just not quite ready to—"

"Sorry, Kris." Kevin's voice was firm. "We've gone far too long without talking." He walked over to a table by the window. It was covered with a white cloth and a red candle flickered in the center. Two mugs of what looked like hot cocoa had been placed in front of each seat and marshmallows were floating on the top. Pulling out a chair, he said, "Have a seat."

She stared at him in shock. "Have a seat? Are you kid—"

"No. I'm not." He stared at her with flinty blue eyes.

Kristine crossed her arms. "You're ambushing me," she said. "This isn't fair. This isn't—"

"This is what June has been doing to *me* our entire marriage." His cheeks were flushed, his eyes blazing. "And unless I missed something, you've never had a problem with it before."

"Oh, give me a break," Kristine said. "I always told her to back off, to let us handle things on her own." The statement came out a lot weaker than she wanted. Maybe because her requests to her mother to let them handle things on their own had always been a lot weaker than she wanted.

"Exactly," he said, as though reading her mind. "Have a seat, Kris." His voice softened. "Please."

Considering June was right downstairs, very possibly spying on this conversation and intent on having it go a certain way, Kristine knew that she wouldn't get very far without at least talking to her husband. "Fine," she said. "But let's at least go down to my office. This area isn't mine. I didn't even know the landlord had done this."

It certainly explained the banging over the past few weeks. The owners must have remodeled the entire floor. It looked fantastic and she hoped it wouldn't raise . . .

"You're looking at the landlord," Kevin said. "Rumor has it, he had a wife who was tired of living in the suburbs, so he thought it might be a nice idea to buy the unit and get it fixed up. Kinda bad timing on his part, considering she just left him."

Kristine's heart jumped. "What?" Her eyes flew to Kevin's face. They were still as dark as stone, but they were watching her closely.

"I bought the unit," he said. "With what was supposed to be Chloe's wedding money. You can thank her later, even though we'll probably just have to put this place on the market, when you divorce me." Walking away from her chair, he took a seat at the one on the opposite side of the table. "Sorry it's so cold up here," he added. "The heat's not on yet."

Kristine looked around, stunned. Everything about the space was modern, rustic and cozy. It had a brick fireplace with a rustic wooden mantel and dark brown wooden beams that stretched across the ceiling. The windows overlooking Lincoln Park made it feel like they were up in a tree house. It was exactly the type of place they'd talked about finding when they'd still planned to move back to the city.

"I don't understand." Her hands were trembling, not just because the loft was freezing. "When did . . . How did . . ."

"It was supposed to be a vow renewal surprise," he said. "But that didn't turn out so well."

Slowly, Kristine walked over to the table and took a seat. She looked at Kevin for a long moment, studying the ruddy face that was so familiar yet still seemed to belong to a stranger. It was hard to believe that they had known each other for so long and had drifted so far apart.

"It seems like there's a lot of things that haven't turned out so well," she finally said. "I talked to our financial advisor."

Kevin's face paled. "June told you? She said—"

"No, she wouldn't tell me." Kristine had to fight to keep the bitterness out of her voice. "I had to call our advisor and ask him myself. Humiliating, considering one would think a husband would tell his wife if seventy percent of the retirement account was suddenly gone."

At the words, her stomach clenched, as it had many times over the past few days.

The phone call to their financial advisor had been devastating, even before she'd heard that news. Kristine had asked him for the financial records for the previous five years, as though it were the most natural thing in the world, and danced around his questions about whether or not everything was all right. She'd been shocked to learn that everything was not all right. Apparently, they'd taken a huge hit a few years back, when Kevin had switched their retirement fund to an aggressive approach.

Studying the papers, Kristine couldn't believe what she was seeing. Even though she'd always been diligent about the store's financials, Kevin had been the one to handle their personal finances. And why not? He was the one making the money. Besides, he'd always brought the major decisions to her. She was stunned that, in this case, he hadn't. Staring down at the numbers, his behavior over the past few years began to make sense.

Yes, Kevin had always been a hard worker but his devotion to his new job had been so confusing. He'd said he owed the company for giving him a job at a time where no one else would, but apparently, there was something bigger driving him to stay employed. According to the numbers, if his current job hadn't kept him around, they would have spent the rest of their lives scrambling just to get by.

"For the past few years, I have been trying to understand why you would want to spend so much time away from me, away from our family," Kristine said. "When you could have just told me—"

"I couldn't tell you," he said.

"Why?" she demanded. "I am your wife! I have the right to know if—"

"Because I felt like such a loser," he cried. At the look of raw shame on his face, she stared down at the table. The only sound was his labored breathing. Out of the corner of her eye, she saw that he was clenching his hands so hard that his knuckles had turned white. "I've spent my whole life working hard, trying to make something out of myself. I gave us a good life, then . . ." His voice cracked. "How do you think I felt, when I'd given my whole life to one company and then they let me go?"

Kristine looked at him in surprise. Even though she'd tried, many times, to get him to discuss this, he'd always refused. Now, he was staring down at his hands, the tips of his ears bright red.

"Kevin," she said, her voice gentle. "It was the econ—"

"Bullshit." He ran his hand over his face. Giving a sharp sniff, he looked her in the eye. "There are still lots of guys who used to be my friends who still have their jobs. Why didn't they get let go?"

"Because," she said. "They . . . They hadn't been there for twenty years, they weren't making the type of money you were, they . . ." She didn't know the answer and suddenly realized that maybe there wasn't one. "I don't know," she said. "But it wasn't your fault."

"I did everything right," he said, shaking his head. "But that's the thing that gets me. Because in the end, what did it matter? After all that planning, all that playing it safe, I still found myself struggling to find money to take care of my family. After I got this job, I thought I'd make a big move, make the money we lost back and make you proud of me again. Instead . . ." His voice trailed off and the muscle in his jaw worked, the way it always did when he was too scared to show emotion.

Kristine felt her eyes smart with tears. "I was always proud of you," she whispered. "You gave us such a good life. I can't believe you didn't just talk to—"

He shrugged. "I wanted to tell you. But I was afraid you'd leave."

"You thought I'd leave you?" Kristine couldn't believe what she was hearing. "For *money*?"

"No," he said. "For putting our family at risk."

"I'm your wife," she whispered. "I never would have left you."

Kevin made a sound that could have been a snort. "Oh, really? Unless I'm missing something, yeah. You would."

Silence fell between them.

"This is different," Kristine finally said. When he scoffed, she insisted, "Kevin, it is. I don't know you anymore. I have barely seen you for the past five years. The most time we've had together was Venice and even then, I knew . . ." Her voice trembled and she took a breath, trying to steady it. "I had a feeling that it wouldn't last. I knew that, in the end, you'd still want to spend more time away from me."

"I have been gone because I've been working so hard to fix what had happened, not because I wanted to be away from you," he said. "It's *killed* me to be away from you." The words came out in a ragged whisper and her heart ached.

Desperately, Kristine's eyes scanned the loft he'd designed for them. It was so perfect. She had to wonder, how could he have created something so perfect when they didn't know each other anymore, at all? Looking up at the ceiling, she wished that this could be easier.

"Kevin, I . . ." A sudden chill hit her and she shivered.

Immediately, he was on his feet, shrugging out of his cable-knit sweater. "It's too cold in here." He handed it to her. "Put this on."

The sweater was as big and warm as a blanket. When she made no move to put it on, Kevin walked over to her and gently pulled it down over her head. His scent seemed to engulf her and she felt tears somewhere in the back of her throat. Was this the last time she'd be this close to him? Would this be the moment that she'd look back on, when she dared to think of the times they'd shared? She bowed her head, too pained to speak.

"This isn't the end, Kris," Kevin told her. He crouched down, until they were both eye level, his voice earnest. "I said forever and I meant it."

Kristine shook her head, thinking of the months and years of loneliness stretching out in front of her. "I can't do it," she whispered. "I can't spend the rest of my life all alone in that big house—"

"We can sell the house," he pleaded. "We'll have to, to finish paying for this place. And if we can't sell it, we can rent it. I want to live up here, with you. To be a part of your life, a part of your work . . ."

Kristine tugged at the sweater, half tempted to rip it off. His warmth, his smell . . . It was too much. Too painful. "You'd still be gone. The constant *he's here, now he's gone, he's here, now he's gone*. I can't do it. I just can't." Her voice was close to hysteria. She glanced at the door, wondering if she could get up and leave. Go back to June's and sign up for some cruise that would take her to the other side of the world. Some place far away, where she could forget who she was, where she was from and all of the promises that had gotten broken along the way.

"I have a solution—"

"You had a solution in Venice," she cried. "You told me that you were going to figure out a way to work less, to spend more time with me. Or, if you couldn't work less, then to at least spend quality time with me. Instead, you decided to take a job that would—"

"Listen," he begged. "I talked to my boss about coming in off the road. There's nothing available at headquarters but there is a comparable travel position to the one that they gave me."

*He didn't get it. He truly didn't get it. And he never would.*

"The position is international," Kevin said. "China, Germany, Japan. Occasionally the U.K. I'd only have to travel once every six weeks, for two weeks at a time. But I thought, if I did something like that, it might work. That maybe you'd want to come with me."

Kristine blinked. "What?"

"Yeah. I, uh . . ." He cleared his throat. "I told my boss that I'd give him an answer after the wedding. Guess I'll have to explain that little fiasco to him, unless . . ." Kevin stared at her, his eyes intent. "Unless you wanted to do something like that. You know, see the world. Together."

"But . . ." Her mind suddenly felt like it was traveling at a hundred miles an hour. "You hate going to foreign countries. Everything about it. Kevin, you'd hate that."

"Venice wasn't so bad." He gave a tentative smile. "As a matter of fact, I have some pretty good memories. I'd still have to work," he said quickly, "which means you'd be on your own during most days."

Kristine stared at him, as though he was speaking a foreign language.

"But at night, I thought we could go out," he said. "Explore. Use some of those guidebooks. Speaking of, maybe you could give Annie a promotion, put her in charge of the store a little more often. We've already talked about it a little bit. She's been pretty helpful with this whole loft thing."

Kristine couldn't believe what she was hearing. "Annie knew about all this?" Suddenly, she remembered that day Annie had told her that not everything was as it seemed. Shaking her head, she mumbled, "You really gathered the troops, didn't you?"

"It takes a village," he joked, then his eyes got serious. "Think about it for a moment, Kris." Reaching for her hand, he held it in his. "Imagine us here. Growing old together. Then, every few weeks . . . heading out to see the world together."

Looking around the loft, Kristine imagined waking up every morning with Kevin, gazing out the windows at the trees etched against the sky. Walking past the exposed brick to that staircase, to open up her store. Helping customers plan their trips while knowing that, every few weeks, she and her husband would be flying somewhere new, holding hands as they flew over the ocean.

"Oh, my gosh," Kristine said, as it all hit her. She swallowed hard. "Oh, my gosh."

Kevin cocked his head, watching her in confusion. "Does that . . . Is that—"

"Is that what?" she cried, wrapping her arms around his neck. "The thing that I've wanted for my entire life? Yes. All I have wanted, all I have *ever* wanted, is to be with you."

Kevin's body shook with laughter or emotion, it was hard to

tell. "Firecracker," he murmured, kissing her hair, "you haven't been around me that much in a few years. I can guarantee you're gonna get pretty tired of me, pretty fast."

"Don't make jokes." Gently, she reached out and stroked his cheek. "Not now."

Kevin stared at her, his eyes as blue as the sea. After a long moment, he scooped her up and carried her over to the windows. Setting her gently against the brick sill, he pushed her hair back from her face, leaned in and kissed her. The kiss was soft, gentle and overflowing with love.

Kristine held on to her husband as tight as she could, her body shivering against his.

"Are you still cold?" he whispered, pressing his forehead against hers.

Kristine shook her head. Her body and her heart were filled with a warmth that she hadn't felt in years.

Closing her eyes, she pressed her cheek tightly against his. A strange thought passed through her mind and she sucked in her breath. Pulling away, she looked at him.

"What?" he asked. "What's that look for?"

Kristine held up her left hand. It was glaringly empty. A cloud passed over his face. "Oh." Taking her hand, he flipped it over and studied it.

"I was thinking," she said. "That maybe you should be the one to put my rings back on. Would you . . . Do you still want to renew your vows with me?"

Kevin's face broke into a smile. "Do you?"

"Yes." She nodded. "But this time, I'd like to do it our way."


Later that night, Kristine walked through Charley's garden toward the gazebo. It was decorated with white Christmas lights and piano music played softly over small outdoor speakers. Kristine wore a pair of fluffy white snow boots, her original wedding dress complete with its pink and green velvet ribbons, and she gripped a bouquet of violets in her hands.

Kevin waited for her in the gazebo, dressed in a perfectly fitted black suit. He looked tall, strong and handsome, just as he had so many years ago. Catching her eye, his face split into that familiar grin. The years they'd shared seemed to pass between them in just one look.

"Here comes the bride," June cried. Chloe cheered and Charley clapped. The group was small and intimate, exactly the way Kristine had always wanted. As she stepped into the gazebo, the sudden warmth from the heat lamps made her cheeks flush.

"This is so beautiful," she murmured, looking out at the silent night and the garden, its rosebushes frosted in snow. "Charley, I can't believe my mother ever wanted you to tear this place down."

"Well, I was wrong," June chuckled. Giving a meaningful look at Kevin, she said, "It happens on occasion." Patting him on the back, she said, "Kristine, you made a really good choice with this one."

"Oh, I know." She studied her husband. His ruddy face was neatly shaven, his hair combed perfectly in place. He was the most handsome man she had ever seen.

"If someone would have told me, back on our wedding day, that the time would come where I would love you even more," she told him, "I wouldn't have believed them. But with every day that passes, I do."

Kevin's eyes misted with tears. He started to say something, but was too choked up to speak. He tried to chuckle, but ended up just shaking his head.

Kristine handed her bouquet to their daughter and reached for his hands. This time, it was her hands that steadied his. "I love you," she said. "All I have ever wanted was to spend the rest of my life with you."

The priest stepped forward, opening the Bible. "Are we ready?"

"You sure you want to do this?" Kristine teased, just as Kevin had so many years ago.

He smiled. "More than anything in the world."

"Dearly beloved," the priest began.

Flakes of snow drifted down around them like baby's breath.

# Eighty

Chloe was running late. Her stupid curling iron was broken, so she dragged out an old set of Clairol rollers from the back of the linen closet. They were covered in a layer of dust and even after ten minutes they were barely hot to the touch.

"Dammit, dammit, dammit." Chloe looked at the clock. "Hurry up!" She only had an hour until she was supposed to be at the church to help her grandmother get ready. By the time she tamed her hair, got dressed and called a cab, she would be lucky if she got to the church on time.

Picking up her phone, Chloe called her mother and put her on speaker. "Hey," she barked when Kristine picked up. Grabbing a lukewarm roller, she started wrapping her hair around it. "I might be five minutes late. Or thirty."

"It's a good thing you're not getting married today," her mother sang. "You'd be late for your own wedding."

"Ha-ha." Chloe cringed at the thought. Geez. It really *was* a good thing she wasn't getting married today, in more ways than one. "Alright. I love you. See you—"

There was a pounding at the door and Chloe stood stock-still. The series of knocks were more than a little familiar. Quickly, she said, "Mom? I've gotta go."

Whiskers was already at the door by the time Chloe got there. Reaching out to open it, she remembered the curlers in her hair. *Shit!* Oh, well. It wasn't like Ben hadn't seen her like this before.

Chloe threw open the door. "I'm sorry about my hair," she said. "I look . . ." Her voice trailed off as she took in the sight of him.

Ben was devastatingly handsome in a navy blue suit. His hair was cut close to his head and a slight shadow of a beard covered his face. His eyes were the most radiant shade of blue that she had ever seen.

Chloe gulped. Suddenly, she had no idea what to say. "Um . . ."

Reaching down, Ben pet Whiskers. The cat weaved in and out of his legs, purring like crazy. Dropping a new toy on the floor, Whiskers batted at it in delight. Chloe couldn't fight the smile that stretched across her face. Ben was so good-looking and so . . . *kind* that it just seemed a little unfair. In fact, she wanted to kick him in the shins.

Getting to his feet, Ben grinned. "Should I come back? Give you a few minutes? I mean, I don't know if you're planning on pulling out your makeup chart or . . ."

Chloe laughed. "No, no. Come on in." As he walked past her, she had to put a hand on the wall as though to steady herself or, rather, to not reach out and try to tackle him.

"You alright?" he asked, turning to face her.

Actually, no. The sight of him in that suit was almost too much to handle.

"I'm just happy," Chloe said, her voice a little too bright. "Happy my grandmother's getting married and happy that . . ." Holding his gaze for a moment too long, her bravado slipped. "I'm happy that I'm just a guest at the wedding," she admitted. "And that I'm going there with you."

Ben's gaze melded into hers. "Yeah. Me, too."

Whiskers scampered across the room, the new toy jingling away.

Dropping her eyes, Chloe headed for the bathroom. She chided herself for being so ridiculous. The only way that she and Ben could go back to being friends was if she'd stop acting like some schoolgirl with a crush. Maybe he'd been in love with her at some point, but that didn't mean he was anymore. A lot had happened, a lot had changed. She needed to stop thinking about it and just get on with her life.

She could start by taking the stupid rollers out of her hair.

"Have a seat or something," she called. "I'm sure there are some magazines or something for you to look at. I'll be ready in—"

Suddenly, Chloe felt two strong arms wrap around her from behind. She sucked in a sharp breath as Ben turned her toward him and pulled her in close. Her face was squashed into the sharply starched lapels of his suit, but she couldn't imagine a better feeling. Other than, of course, the hard sinew of his body underneath his clothes and the strength of his thighs against hers. They held each other for a long moment, their hearts beating with the same frenetic rhythm.

"Oh, man," Chloe finally said, her voice muffled. "I don't think I can do this."

Ben's body seemed to stiffen. "Do what?"

"Pretend like this is a fucking friendship hug."

Ben was silent for a moment. The only sound in the room was Whiskers batting at her new toy. "That's good news," he said. "Because this isn't going to be friendly at all."

Taking her face in his hands, Ben crashed his mouth into hers. Chloe felt a jolt of desire more powerful than violence rush through her as he probed her lips open with his tongue and his mouth melted into hers. Her robe fell open and his hands were everywhere as he kissed her face, her neck and her body.

In a tangle of flesh and joy, Ben lifted her up and carried her over the threshold of the bedroom.

# Eighty-one

Kristine looked around in delight. The enormous church where June's wedding was to be held was still decorated for Christmas, just as they'd planned. Garlands draped the pews, while red and white poinsettias dotted the aisles. The wedding planner had added clusters of holly decorated with tulle and bright red berries. White candles glistened from tall holders and a harpist strummed softly, filling the church with music.

Charley, the silver fox, stood waiting at the altar. He was impeccably handsome in a simple gray suit. His back was straight and his hands were folded as he patiently awaited his bride.

Kristine smiled at him as she slid into the pew. He nodded, giving her a slight wink. "I like that man so much," she told Chloe. "He has really brought out the best in June."

"It's bizarre," Chloe said. "Who would have thought *that* tiger could be tamed? If we're not careful, she might expect us to run our own lives."

Kristine thought about that for a moment. "That will never happen," they chorused.

Laughing, Kristine reached out and pulled her daughter into a half-hug. Rue was sitting two pews over and eyeing them with disdain. Kristine let out a little sigh. Subtly indicating Rue with her chin, she said, "Are you doing okay?"

Chloe followed her gaze. Giving Rue a bright smile, she waved. The old woman tossed her head and looked away. "Oh, she'll thank me soon enough," Chloe promised. "Mark my words on that one."

Kristine nodded. Based on some of the things Chloe had said, it wouldn't surprise her if Geoff did indeed get back together with his ex-wife. In some ways, that could be the best thing for everyone.

"Besides," Chloe beamed, "I'm sorry, but . . ." Turning to Ben, she patted him on the knee. "This is the man I love." Looking slightly embarrassed, she said, "Can I say that yet? The whole 'I love you' thing? Or is it too soon?"

Ben, who had been busy reading the program, closed it and grinned. "Dating tip number seven thousand: Only if you are totally confident that the guy you're saying it to is going to say it back."

Chloe considered this. "Okay, so . . ." She grinned. "I love you?"

Ben's face lit up. "I love you, too."

Even though the kids were laughing, Kristine could see that they meant every word. She shook her head, amazed at how things worked out. After so many years, Chloe had finally found the man of her dreams and he had been right in front of her, the whole time.

The first seductive notes of "At Last" by Etta James started to play.

"It's starting," Chloe squealed, and Kristine held her breath.

There was a sound at the back of the church. The heavy wooden doors were thrown open and June took center stage. As she surveyed the church, her ash blonde hair perfectly in place and her jewelry shimmering, Kristine couldn't remember a time when her mother had looked more radiant.

Quickly, she turned toward the altar in order to capture the look on Charley's face. It didn't disappoint. He was shaking his head and smiling at June, as though she were the most astonishing thing he'd ever seen.

"Grandma's so happy," Chloe whispered. "Just look at her."

Kristine nodded, squeezing her hand tight. "I know. She looks . . . Well, as June as ever."

Chloe burst out laughing.

True to form, June was dressed in the most outrageous wedding getup Kristine had ever seen. The dress was pure white, with a fitted corset that was perfectly molded to her upper body. Around the neck, a dramatic gathered neckline made out of red silk plunged down and across the bodice, where it was cinched into place with a dried white rose attached to a sparkling piece of jewelry.

"That's the flower from the bouquet," Chloe practically squealed. "Ben, look! Remember the bouquet?"

Thinking back to that day at the wedding, Kristine felt a profound sense of sadness. She and Kevin had veered off course and had no idea they had such a long journey in front of them.

As Kevin walked her mother down the aisle, Kristine watched him with a renewed heart. She couldn't imagine being separated from him for even a day, ever again. Opening her purse, she showed her daughter her collection of dried baby's breath from the bouquet at the wedding.

Chloe's eyes widened. "Hey! You told Grandma you threw that out."

Kristine grinned. "I was just torturing her." She clicked the latch on her purse shut. "Of course I kept it. I was carrying it with me last night."

Chloe smiled. "Nice one, Mom."

Ben leaned forward, squinting. "Wait a minute . . . My eyesight could be failing me but is June covered in flowers?"

Kristine pulled out her camera. "She sure is." Just below the sparkling jewel, a cacophony of blooming white roses moved with the delicate sway of the dress. The seamstresses had gone to work that very morning, to ensure the white roses were as fresh as possible.

"Now do you see why I had to drop out of this wedding?"

Chloe teased Ben. "It wasn't that I was secretly, madly in love with you. It was because it would have been impossible to outshine my grandmother. Who could compete with that?"

Kristine had to agree. The dress was spectacular. The wedding guests oohed and ahhed, several of them pulling out their phones to take pictures. As June swished by to join Charley up at the altar, the sweet waft of roses trailed behind her.

"It's perfect," Kristine sighed.

"And very symbolic," Chloe added, "considering they were brought together by roses."

Looking up at the altar, where Rose and Bernice fussed over June's dress, Kristine smiled. "In more ways than one."

She watched with pride as her husband kissed her mother on each cheek. As everyone in the church fell silent, Kevin gave June's hand to Charley. Then, he walked down the aisle toward Kristine. Sliding into the pew, he wrapped his arm around her. She placed her left hand in his.

"Dearly beloved," the priest began.

# Eighty-two

Walking through the entryway of the country club, Chloe stopped. "Wow," she breathed, grabbing Ben's arm. "This is beautiful."

An attendant swiftly took her coat, while another thrust a glass of champagne into her hand.

"June sure knows how to throw a party," Kevin said, clinking his glass against Kristine's.

Kristine smiled, adjusting the sleeves of her green satin dress. "You can say that again."

The entryway was perfectly decorated. The walls were draped with white flowing fabric while votive candles covered practically every surface. They were lined up in little vases along the floor, hanging from the ceiling in glass bubbles and glowing from holders on the side tables. The muted, flickering light gave the room a romantic, elegant feel.

Well-dressed guests were lined up to sign the guest book, and Chloe heard more than one person commenting on the floral arrangements. They were creations of decorative branches and roses woven through with strings of bright red cranberries and white pearls.

After a photographer shot a picture of the four of them, Ben holding Chloe tight, they walked toward the main room. Just before the entrance, they stopped to admire a five-tiered wedding cake with frosting as white as snow. It was accented with dark chocolate and topped with a crowning bouquet of lush red roses.

Kristine exchanged a confused look with Chloe. "Is that the cake we picked out?"

"Not even close," Chloe said. "Grandma must have had a backup plan."

Kevin grinned. "Or maybe she was just planning to surprise you." He nudged Kristine. "Like that time with the flowers?"

Kristine groaned. "Don't remind me."

"Come on," Chloe said, reaching for Ben's hand. "Grandma wouldn't do something like that."

Kristine gave Chloe an incredulous look. "Really?" They all burst out laughing, even Ben.

"Good," Kevin said, giving him a hearty pat on the back. "It sounds like you know exactly what you're getting into. Welcome to the family."

As they walked into the main room, Chloe squeezed Ben's hand. "It's so pretty!"

The ceiling was draped with white billowing fabric that gathered in the center and practically dripped with sparkling crystal chandeliers. Tables draped in deep reds were set with bone white china and elegant crystal goblets. In the center of each table, dramatic rose arrangements were topped with white tapered candles.

The room bustled with guests from all three generations and suddenly, Chloe felt self-conscious. Since Kristine and Kevin were so obviously together, there had been only minor confusion about the fact that they hadn't been up at the altar with June. But as for Chloe . . . Well, everyone knew she was supposed to get married that day. To someone very different than the man escorting her into the room.

For a split second, she considered dropping Ben's hand. Then, she came to her senses. It was hard to believe she'd come so close to spending the rest of her life married to someone other than her best friend. With that in mind, it really didn't matter what people thought. This was her life, her chance at happiness. She was not about to settle for anything less.

Reaching up, she gave Ben a kiss.

"What was that for?" he asked, his eyes sparkling with mischief.

Chloe grinned. "For that time I punched you in the face."

Taking her hand, Ben led her to the bridal table. June and Charley sat in the center, like a king and queen. June's cheeks glowed and Charley watched her with adoration.

"She looks so happy," Ben said. "And so do your parents."

Chloe looked down the table. They were talking and laughing with Charley's son and his wife. In the middle of a sentence, Kevin stopped talking to gaze at Kristine in adoration.

Even though Chloe still didn't know what had caused the rift in their marriage, it was obvious that something between them had changed. Gone was the tight-lipped, serious woman Kristine had been for the past few years. In her place was someone who looked younger and . . . Chloe studied her for a moment, trying to put her finger on it. Happy. Her mother finally looked happy.

After the guests had settled in at their tables, Chloe's father pushed back his chair and stood up. Clinking a fork against his crystal flute, he waited until the chaotic buzz of the room settled and the guests gave him their full attention. Then, in his booming voice, he said, "I would like to make the first toast of the evening." He gave June an impish smile. "This one's for you, Cupcake."

June's eyes widened. "Oh, no, no, no."

Kristine nodded. "Oh, yes, yes, yes."

Laughing, June buried her head in her hands.

Facing the room, Kevin said, "Over twenty-five years ago, I married my beautiful wife. Last night, we renewed our wedding vows. Thank you for helping us celebrate this happy occasion, along with the marriage of Charley and June." The guests burst into applause. "Twenty-five years ago . . ." He pointed at June. "This wonderful woman, my mother-in-law, made a speech at my wedding reception."

Chloe sat up straight, grabbing Ben's hand. The infamous speech!

"I was young and earnest," Kevin said. "And scared to death of her." Some people chuckled and nodded. "And the first words my mother-in-law said, in her brilliant, memorable, heart-warming speech were: *Kristine, if it doesn't work out, you'll always have your family.*"

"You didn't under—" June tried to say, but Charley silenced her with a kiss.

"At the time," Kevin said, "I was devastated. I thought, What am I doing? This marriage is not going to work out. My bride's very own mother doesn't think this marriage is going to work out. Not one person in this room thinks this marriage is going to work out. But as the years went on, I finally understood what her words meant."

Kevin looked at Kristine, who smiled.

"Marriage doesn't work out," he said, "a lot of the time. It takes hard work and determination and just when you get to that point where you think you can't do it anymore . . . you have your family to put you back on track."

June nodded, her eyes shining with tears. "Yes," she whispered. "That's exactly what I meant."

"So . . ." Kevin raised his glass. "June and Charley, I am here to say to you today, that if it doesn't work out, you'll always have your family. Because we love you. And we'll be there for you, no matter what."

The room was silent as snow. Then, it erupted into applause. Glasses clinked madly as June and Charley kissed, followed by Kevin and Kristine.

And of course, Chloe and Ben.

. . .

After the meal had been served and the cake had been cut, a DJ replaced the harp player and the cellist. Everyone crowded onto the dance floor. Ben performed not only the Chicken Dance and Macarena for Chloe, Sally and Dana, but the YMCA as well.

At the height of the reception excitement, June seized the microphone and took court in the middle of the dance floor. The music screeched to a halt as she cried, "Attention, attention." The DJ shined a spotlight on her and she blinked, smiling like a hostess on a cruise ship. "I think we all know what time it is." She thrust her hand up in the air. "The bouquet toss!"

Kevin and Kristine rushed to the edge of the dance floor, their cameras poised. Charley settled in next to them, smiling.

Sally sidled up and tucked a loose strand of hair behind Chloe's ear, while Dana whipped out a compact and quickly powdered Chloe's face.

"Hey," Chloe said, laughing. "What are you guys . . ."

Sally reached forward, pinching her cheeks. "There. You look great."

Ben nodded. "You do."

Chloe groaned. "Oh, crap. She's going to make me get out there, isn't she?"

Ben grinned. "Something like that."

Great. This whole thing was going to be nothing but awkward. Chloe smoothed her dress, which was slightly damp from their crazy dancing.

"Ladies and gentlemen," June cried. "It's time for the bouquet toss of all bouquet tosses! But just wait one minute." She pointed a finger at Bernice. The cute little old lady in her bright red shoes was already inching her way out to the dance floor. "This is not for *all* the single ladies. It's going to be for just one." June pointed and the DJ swung the light toward Chloe. "My granddaughter."

Chloe felt her face turn as red as Bernice's shoes. "Oh, geez."

Sally squeezed her arm in excitement.

"Today," June said, her voice appropriately somber, "Chloe almost married a young man we all love very much."

Chloe looked over at Ben, to see how he was handling this. To her dismay, he looked pale and uncomfortable. "I'm so sorry," she whispered.

Avoiding her eyes, he shrugged. A small trickle of sweat, either from the attention or dancing, trickled down the side of his face. He wiped at it with his left hand.

"However," June said, her voice bright, "after some soul searching, they both realized that they were in love with other people!"

A collective murmur swept across the crowd. Chloe noticed that June's friends were nodding. It was almost as though they, too, knew the match hadn't been quite right.

"So, with that in mind . . . Chloe," June called, shielding her eyes against the glare of the lights. "Will you come out here, please?"

Chloe covered her face in embarrassment. "Is it too late to run?"

Ben's face was bright red. "Kind of. Yeah."

June beckoned at her madly.

"Go, Chloe." Sally and Dana practically pushed her out of the crowd. "Get that bouquet!"

Straightening her spine, Chloe walked out onto the dance floor.

"My granddaughter," June cried, and the crowd went wild. Reaching for Chloe, June pulled her into a rose-scented hug. "Thank you," she murmured, "for humoring a sentimental old woman like me."

Turning, June took a few steps, her rose-covered dress swaying behind her. Suddenly, she stopped. Raising up the bouquet, she gave Chloe a mischievous smile. "Catch."

Before Chloe could even register what was happening, the bouquet was flying through the air toward her face. She put up her hands, more as an instinctive block than anything. A hard stem hit her palm and she felt her fingers wrap around it. Looking down, she stared at the pretty pink and white roses.

And blinked.

In the center of the bouquet, there was a pale pink rose that was dark around the edges. It was actually a dried rose, with a white ribbon dangling from the stem. And attached to that white ribbon was the most perfect, beautiful diamond ring she'd ever seen.

Chloe stared, willing herself to breathe. Was this happening? Was this *seriously happening*? Out of the corner of her eye, she saw Sally leaping up and down on the sidelines like a battery-operated cake topper.

As if in a dream, Ben walked through the crowd and got down on one knee. Slowly, he took the bouquet from her hands and unwound the ring from the ribbon.

"Chloe," he said, looking up at her with those bright blue eyes. "I love you more than anything in this world. I want to spend the rest of my life making you happy. But from this point forward, I don't want to be your friend. I want to be your forever."

Putting her hands to her mouth, Chloe realized she was laughing and crying. Reaching out, she pulled Ben to his feet. He cupped her face in his hand and kissed her gently. She kissed him back and the room seemed to spin around them in bright colors. Everything went quiet, as though they were the only two people in the world.

Until, of course, she opened her eyes. She was quick to see that she and Ben were not alone. They were surrounded by her entire family.

"Congratulations," June cried, yanking Chloe into her arms and kissing both cheeks.

"I'm so happy for you, son," Charley said, shaking Ben's hand.

Kristine beamed, squeezing Chloe tight. "I always knew you two would end up together."

Kevin clapped Ben on the back. "Welcome to the family, kid."

The group clustered around them, their faces beaming with excitement. Chloe shook her head, hiding a smile. "I tell you what, Ben." She indicated her family. "You have no idea what you're getting yourself into."

Taking her hand, Ben slid the ring on her finger and smiled. "Yes," he said. "I do."